ONCE A MARINE . . .

Can't we get an evac  Alexander Moore thought

Apparently not, Senat *Separatists are bringing* *Marine AIC says the best*

Did you explain to them them what would happen to us if the Separatists take us captive?

Yes.

All right, tell them we are coming to them and not to leave us.

Senator, the Marine AIC says that you should stay put.

Abbey, I don't take orders from the Marines and haven't for a long damned time. We are coming to them if they can't get to us!

Alexander glanced around the adventure store at the adrenaline junkie paraphernalia available. Then he thought of his wife and daughter being tortured to make him do and say things he shouldn't, which was exactly what the Separatists would do to him if they caught him here.

But there was no way to cover the tens of kilometers to the evac point in time. Flying was out. Any vehicle using that much power would set off all sorts of sensors. *Think, Major Moore! What would a good Marine do?*

He began eyeing the gliderchutes on the far wall of the store. *Abigail, is there a way to get to the outside top of the dome?*

Perhaps, Senator. I will see what I can find out.

"Reyes, my good man, have you ever done any base-gliding off the dome?" He grinned at the store manager while trying to ignore the look his wife was giving him.

Oorah! he thought.

BAEN BOOKS by Travis S. Taylor

ONE DAY ON MARS

BY TRAVIS S. TAYLOR

BAEN

ONE DAY ON MARS

Copyright © 2007 by Travis S. Taylor

A Baen Books Original

Baen Publishing Enterprises
P.O. Box 1403
Riverdale, NY 10471
www.baen.com

ISBN 10: 1-4165-9157-5
ISBN 13: 978-1-4165-9157-3

Cover art by Kurt Miller

First Baen paperback printing, March 2009

Distributed by Simon & Schuster
1230 Avenue of the Americas
New York, NY 10020

Library of Congress Cataloging-in-Publication Data:
2007028327

Printed in the United States of America

10 9 8 7 6 5 4 3

To all of Uncle Sam's
Misguided Children
past, present, and future. Oorah!

Chapter 1

Nancy peered through the viewport at the faint blue-green luminescent hue of the planetscape as it skittered beneath them at a few hundred kilometers per hour. To the north there were several geodesic domes giving off slight metallic glints each time Sol peeked through the smoky gray plumes being emitted from the exhaust portals atop each of the greenhouse gas factories. The smoke poured and rolled gracefully upward and mixed with the tropospheric breezes scattering the smoky plume's content across the planet's atmosphere.

Nancy took a brief moment and thought of how the little plutonium reactors within each dome slowly crept deeper into the Martian soil melting and vaporizing water ice, iron rich soil, oxygen, and various forms of soot smoke into the smoky gray steam plumes boiling upward into the sky above the metallic domes. Occasionally, one of the reactors would reach a water rich depth and the cloud would turn to mostly white steamy water vapor for a while. Those domes were very easy to distinguish from the others for weeks at a time.

Terraformer domes, Allison said directly into Nancy's mind.

"I know that." Nancy whispered softly, not wanting to disturb the calm moment but still reflexively using audible speech.

Yes, of course. The artificial intelligence counterpart or AIC replied.

Nancy watched the domes pass behind the ship as new ones appeared over the horizon both to the northeast and to the south. *There must be hundreds of them*, she thought.

Seventeen hundred forty one in this region. More in other regions. Allison responded.

Nobody likes a smartass, Allison. Nancy thought.
Indeed.

Each of the domes was at least the size of a large sports arena and perhaps taller. The exhaust stacks flooded the Martian atmosphere with greenhouse gasses and oxygen and had been doing so for nearly a century. The atmosphere on Mars was dense enough to support life but not yet warm enough or oxygen rich enough for humans to survive unprotected. In fact, there was bordering on enough oxygen to be similar to that of Earthly high altitudes like on Mount Everest, but there still remained far too much carbon dioxide in the atmosphere to safely breathe it. The Martian trees and grasses were slowly taking care of the carbon dioxide, but it would still be a century or more before Mars would be Earthlike enough to go outside without oxygen or scrubbers. Pressure suits had not been needed for decades, but heated environment suits and oxygen supplies or carbon dioxide scrubbers were still the common fashion of Martians, tourists, and of course the military.

Nancy, being from Virginia, had only studied about the Martian geology transformation industry. Being half Martian, on her mother's side, she had also heard stories first hand from her mother of Mars and how wonderful it would be someday. Her mother had been from the southern glacial region, which was a hemisphere away at the moment, where the water ice was being heated by large space based laser systems that were in non-Keplerian orbits about the planet's pole. Standard Keplerian orbits actually circumscribe a planet, but the nonstandard orbits of the space based lasers allowed them to hover over a single Martian location while not being at the Mars synchronous orbital altitudes.

The spectacle of the large glaciers being melted away into shining clear sublimating pools of water by invisible laser beams from space was a story her mother had often told her as a child. The wild rainbows created by the quickly dissipating moisture clouds cast a beautiful chiaroscuro of light on the surroundings.

But those days of Mars had been gone for more than thirty Earth years during Nancy's childhood. Once the Separatist movement started and one of the laser spaceships had been hijacked and in turn used to vaporize more than seventeen thousand American workers in the algae farms of the Elysium Planetia the space based Martian terraforming assets were removed. United States Naval Fleet warships had long since replaced them.

The only thing left of the terraforming efforts was the algae farms, trees, and the atmosphere production domes. Mother Nature had begun to help out. As more and more influence from Earth appeared on Mars; other Earthly contaminations such as robust desert vegetation, cacti, and shrubbery had been popping up across most of the populated Martian regions. Earth tundra wildflowers spread across the wetter regions in the north, scattering red, yellow, and purple colors amidst the blue-green algae and brown sage. Undoubtedly, some Martian thought it would be a good idea to plant Earth vegetation on the former red planet—in many cases the Earth vegetation adapted to its new environment quite readily. In a few cases, Earth conifer trees—not the genetic Martian hybrids—had been planted and survived.

But there was little vegetation visible from the altitude and speed of the supercarrier. The domes presently skittered by underneath while Nancy gathered as much of the Martian imagery in her mind as she could. There was some awe and nostalgia, of course, but she had a mission to do and a bird's eye reconnaissance was always useful before an operation.

Nancy shifted the helmet of her suit subconsciously in her lap and fingered the carbon dioxide scrubber intake hole. She hated waiting. To the far south she could see the first dome that was not producing an exhaust cloud. It seemed out of place.

"Nancy, this is Jack. Uncle Timmy says seven minutes!" a voice over the intercom said. "I'll meet you in the hangar."

Uncle Timmy, actually Lieutenant Commander

Timmy Uniform November Kilo Lima Three Seven Seven or UNKL377, the AIC officer of the *U.S.S. Sienna Madira*, had already relayed that information to Allison through the quantum membrane wireless, but Allison had been hesitant to notify her human counterpart that it was time to go to work at the moment. She seemed to be in the midst of a serene, halcyon moment and appeared to be contemplating life, her life—Allison had been monitoring her vital signs and had worked with Nancy long enough to judge her moods. Nancy was amazingly tranquil considering their current situation. But Allison and Nancy had been through a lot in the last seven years since they had left the "Farm" in Virginia. The "Farm" as it was affectionately known by its alumni was better described as an advanced training camp for super spies being trained as special operatives for the Central Intelligence Agency. On the "Farm" Nancy and Allison had been trained in the fundamentals and some advanced tactics for handling the stressful situations of being an undercover agent. All training aside, after that ordeal in New Africa, there was very little in terms of danger and stress that seemed to shake either of them. Allison remained quiet for another moment.

Nancy stood and took one last look through the portal as more domes without the serene smoky gray plumes passed by underneath the supercarrier—more sign of the disruption of the Martian terraforming plan, a disruption of peace, a disruption of the American way of life. The steady gray smoke had seemed to have a power over her as if they could calm the stormy winds of the planet beneath her and bring peace to her . . . to humanity. But it was a false tranquility because war had been an on again off again fact of humanity throughout history. There were several of the domes ahead and southeast with smoke clouds rolling wildly from them, but these clouds were black and violent looking—foreboding of even worse times to come. Then the ship rocked to port and then tossed to starboard. Then it lurched and dropped over a hundred meters as warning klaxons and lights began to ring throughout the ship.

Ma'am, better hurry.

Right, Allison. Nancy pulled her helmet over her head and attached the life support seal ring with a twist, the faceshield still in the open position as she made her way to the elevator system. The upper deck hallway of the supercarrier was dimly lit and the metallic features of a naval vessel were accentuated dramatically by the red and yellow flashing incident lights.

"Down ladder. Make a hole!" Nancy said as she slid down a small stairwell to the main hall that led to the ship's elevator on the forward port side. Two young female ensigns and an older male chief stood backs against the wall as she bolted down the stairs by them. Their reaction more surprise than respect.

"General quarters. General quarters! All hands, all hands man your battle stations immediately! Radar shows multiple ground targets with incoming surface-to-air defenses. Prepare for evasive!" Uncle Timmy announced over the 1MC intercom as well as directly to all AIC implants.

"Hold the elevator please," Nancy nodded to the Army lieutenant colonel in full tank mecha commander's armor that was holding the elevator open as she approached.

"Deck zero please, lieutenant colonel." He reacted instinctively and defensively to Nancy's appearance at first. Then he must have recognized her or at least saw the American Flag over her left breast pocket. No doubt the lieutenant colonel's AIC for sure had been briefed of a possible interaction with an oddly dressed civilian on board. No doubt they had all been briefed with "you never saw her."

The colonel was part of the ground contingent that would soon be dropped on the Separatist Army after the Navy Aviators had softened them up from the air. His nameplate on his armor read "Warboys" and he was wearing a Martian algae field camo environment suit with tank mecha armor hardpoints and there was the typical mecha neural interface jack on his helmet. His visor was in the up position, putting off a slight glare from the yellow warning lights blinking in the elevator, but Nancy could read "Warlord One" painted on his helmet's forehead through the visor. His environment suit, not accounting for the mecha hardpoints, was standard issue and state-of-the-art. The difference between the Army environment suit and the Separatist suit Nancy was wearing was never more obvious—like night and day.

Her suit was more worn, ragged, and just old looking. Or at least that is how Nancy thought of it because it just *felt* that way to her. If any members of her family even knew she were still alive and by the off chance could see her in the suit, they might remark how much like her mother she looked at the moment. But they didn't know she was alive, never would see her in this suit, and perhaps never see *her* again.

"Certainly." Warboys pressed the elevator button and caught himself as the ship lurched hard to port again. "Jesus H. F'n Christ! We must be getting goddamned hammered if the inertial controls are having this hard a time compensating." The *Sienna Madira* jerked hard upward again. "Shit."

"Probably," Nancy replied. *Shit*, she thought while trying to balance herself with a handhold on the elevator safety rail.

"Well, I just hope the bay plating SIFs holds. Last run we lost forty-nine percent of the drops before the tanks ever got out of the bay!" he said.

"High casualty rates, sir. Hope you fare better today." She nodded emotionlessly as the elevator door opened on deck two and the lieutenant colonel hurried out.

"Thanks. Good luck!" he grunted and told himself that he had "never seen her".

"You too, sir." Nancy held her balance as the ship rocked again and the elevator door closed. The eleven seconds that passed before the elevator doors opened again on the hangar deck seemed like an eternity—a very bumpy eternity.

"Well, this is what we're here for." Nancy stepped through the elevator door, let out a long slow sobering sigh, and made her way toward the end of the hangar bay.

Yes, ma'am it is. Allison added.

The Ares class aerospace fighters filled the hangar from one end to the other and the technicians, flight deck officers, and pilots were scurrying all about in t-shirts or coveralls of solid reds, greens, blacks, yellows, or oranges, depending on their particular jobs. The scene was reminiscent of a fireant mound that had been kicked over. Nancy allowed her mind to rest on that image for a split second. *How likely would it be that she'd ever see a fireant mound again? Hmm, had fireants made it to Mars and did they survive there?*

Where are you, Penzington? Navy Lieutenant Commander Jack Boland called on a wireless AIC-to-AIC connection.

Just got off the elevator. Be there in a sec.

Nancy picked up her pace to the end of the large fighter plane hangar. The room was approximately four hundred meters long and at least a hundred meters wide. There were rows and rows of Ares fighters lined up on each side of the hangar and there were more of them hanging from the ceiling. Techs and pilots were scurrying furiously about them preparing for the pending attack deep into the Separatist Reservation.

Stop, Nancy! Look out! Allison warned her by shouting in her mind. Nancy stopped to let an automated equipment lift full of munitions and power-packs hover past in front of her. Had she not stopped the pristine black and yellow caution stripe painted two ton lift would have flattened her and never looked back. Her mission would have ended before it had even started!

Thanks for the head's up. Fortunately for Nancy, AI's communicate with each other and the lift's AI had warned Allison. She finally reached fighter bay one thirty-three none the worse for wear.

"About time, Penzington. You ready?" Jack smiled down at her with the confidence of an ace naval aviator who had seen and lived through his share of bad scrapes.

"Been ready for about two years now. Let's get on with it." Nancy stepped up the rearward ladder into the backseat of the Ares. The little fighter was a sleek swept wing craft with directed energy guns (DEGs) mounted on canards in the front just behind its blunt nose. The snub wings of the vehicle were only a few meters long and at the swept forward blue-gray wingtips were seven millimeter railgun cannons that fired a hundred rounds per second. On top and below each wing were rows of mecha-to-mecha missiles each of them only a few centimeters in diameter and perhaps a meter long. The little plane had to have at least a hundred missiles on its wings. And underneath the belly of the fighter plane was a single larger missile with red and black radiation warnings painted on it. It, Nancy knew since it was her idea, had a purpose.

Nancy glanced at the rows of skulls mimicking the Separatist banner insignia across the empennage of the fighter and reassured herself that Lieutenant Commander Jack Boland was the right man for the job. There were three rows with ten skulls each. The fourth row began with two little geodesic domes and nothing else.

"Jack, I understand that the skulls are Separatist fighters, but what are these two domes?" Nancy eased herself into the backseat of the snub nosed fighter as two crewmen began strapping her in.

"Don't ask. Freakin' politics!" he spat. "That is why I *used* to be the CAG," the fighter squad leader smiled. "One day, goddamned politics is gonna kill us all. You mark my words, Penzington. Mark my words."

Nancy guessed that he meant he used to be the commander of the air group and for some reason got demoted from the position. Obviously, there must have been some political backlash to whatever he had done. Were it important Nancy could get the files on the incident fairly easily, but it had no bearing on her present mission and therefore she didn't concern herself with it.

"Ma'am, you'll need to give me your ship and flag patches and any other tags, codes, and I.D." a young Chief in an orange jumpsuit and Mars red helmet standing on a scaffold beside the Ares fighter told her as he continued attaching her safety harness to her ejection system. The *Sienna Madira* continued to rock wildly from the surface-to-air defenses bumping Nancy around inside the cockpit of the fighter a bit. She showed no emotion other than slightly chewing the right side of her lower lip and rubbing at a bruise here and there.

"Thanks, Chief. Here, I'll not be needing them any longer," she replied and held out her right arm for the tag neutralization scanner the chief passed over her. There was no pain, tingle, or even the slightest tickle, but Nancy's identification as a U.S. citizen had just been wiped away from existence. Only a DNA sample analysis back at Langley could change that.

"Roger that. Good luck, Ma'am."

Nancy just nodded and closed her faceplate. The scrubber kicked in and her oxygen supply read full and not being used—the scrubber was getting plenty of good air from the hangar bay.

"Good hunting, DeathRay!" The chief snapped a salute.

"Roger that!" Jack saluted back.

Jack settled into the front seat, pulling the hardwire

connection from the universal docking port (UDP) of his Ares fighter and plugged it into the thin little rugged composite box on the left side of his helmet that made a direct electrical connection to his AIC implant via skin contact sensors in his helmet. The direct connection wasn't necessary, but functioned as a backup system in the case of enemy jamming of the wireless connection between the AIC and the fighter. The wireless connection was spread spectrum encrypted and almost unspoofable.

"Hardwire UDP is connected and operational. Lieutenant Candis Three Zero Seven Two Four Niner Niner Niner Six ready for duty," Jack's AIC announced over the open com channel. Then directly to Jack, *Let's go get'em Commander!*

Roger that, Candis!

Jack saluted the flight deck officer and brought the canopy down. The harness holding the fighter lowered and detached, dropping it the last twenty centimeters to the deck with a slight squish feel from the landing gear suspension. Jack followed the flight deck sequence and moved in line for take-off.

"Ladies and gentlemen, this is your captain speaking. Please make sure all trays are in their upright and locked position and all carry-on luggage is stowed away for take-off. We'll be taxiing out to the catapult field and soon after will be flung into a hellacious shit storm of anti-aircraft fire and enemy Gomers. Please sit back and enjoy the ride. If you intend to fly in the near future may we suggest you don't fly in the midst of a fucking war next time!" Jack laughed and looked in the rear view to see how his cargo was doing. He couldn't be certain, but other than chewing on her bottom lip she almost looked as if she were taking a nap. *Okay, humor wasn't the way to go*, he thought.

Probably not, sir. Candis replied.

The fighter two up in front of him was "at bat" and eased into the catapult field and almost immediately disappeared out the open end of the bay. The one directly ahead "on deck" began to follow suit. Jack was "in the hole."

"Fighter one-three-three call sign DeathRay, you are cleared for egress. Good hunting, Lieutenant Commander Boland!" the control tower officer radioed.

"Roger that, tower. Y'all just keep the beer cold and DeathRay will be back soon enough." Jack eased into the "on deck" spot as the fighter "at bat" vanished in front of them.

"Here we go, ma'am. Y'all hang on." Jack told his precious cargo.

"Roger that" Lieutenant Commander Boland. I'm hanging on." Nancy swallowed hard and gripped her harness a little tighter until her knuckles turned pink and white.

"Fighter one-three-three you are at bat and go for cat! Good hunting, DeathRay!" the catapult field AI announced.

"Roger that. One three three has the cat! WHOOOO! HOOOOOOO!" Jack screamed and was thrust hard into his seat.

The catapult field took about one thousandth of a second to grasp that there was a matter field inside it. Following the physics of repulsor fields and the Meissner effect that matter was not there when the original magnetic field lines were put in place and according to the superconductor laws those magnetic field lines would do just about anything to stay the way they were originally. So the catapult field did the only thing it could do. It expelled the little snub nosed Ares fighter craft out the aft end of the field at over three hundred kilometers per hour. Without the inertial dampening controls of the fighter the occupants of said craft would have been accelerated against their seats and restraints so harshly that they would have been turned to a bloody mush. From zero to three hundred kilometers per hour in one tenth of a second is considerable acceleration, indeed— eighty-five Earth gravities! Even with the inertial dampening controls the occupants of the fighter felt more than nine gravities for a few seconds.

"What a rush!" Jack shook his head and squeezed his thighs and abdominal muscles as tight as he could. "Aaaarrrrrrrrr uunnnnnnnnk mmm!" he grunted as the overwhelming g-forces subsided and there was no longer anything to worry about but the sky full of anti-aircraft fire and enemy fighter planes. He forced the throttle full forward, pushing the fighter to over two thousand kilometers per hour. It took about seven seconds to reach top velocity while conducting evasive maneuvers, and again there were massive g-forces to deal with as well as a hellstorm of anti-aircraft cannon fire. His thigh harnesses squeezed tighter around his legs, forcing blood from them. He flexed his stomach muscles as hard as he could and yanked the fighter hard left as an anti-aircraft missile zipped past them to the right.

Candis! He screamed in his mind.

Got it, Jack! The AIC replied and almost as immediately the DEGs pulsed with a bright green flash of high intensity light focused on the missile. The missile ablated and flew apart, pounding the Ares fighter with shrapnel at a delta velocity between missile and fighter of over seven hundred kilometers per hour. The shield microplating did its job as multiple *spitwangs* rang through the fighter.

Seppy Gomer, Jack! On our six at angels twelve!

"DeathRay! DeathRay, this is EvilDead . . . you've got a Gomer on your six, copy!"

"Aaaaaarrrrhhhh! Got it, unnnhhhh, EvilDead!"

Jack pulled the fighter up and fired the pitch spin-drive, bringing the nose of the fighter one hundred and eighty degrees, flying backwards and upside down but still maintaining the fighter's current trajectory.

"Copy that . . . unnhhhhh . . . .wooooooh . . . arrrrrrr . . . Gomer on six!" Jack grunted over the net. Holding down the railgun trigger he tracked back across his pursuer's flight path with sudden death. The railgun bolts ripped through the blue-gray Separatist Gnat fighter, spinning it wildly out of control just before the g-forces tore it apart into a cloud of shrapnel. The enemy fighter pilot was smashed and flung asunder by the massive g-forces as the plane's inertial dampeners failed.

Thirty-one. He thought

"Great shooting DeathRay! Now get off your ass and get the fuck out of here! EvilDead out!" The CAG officer and number one pilot ordered him.

"Roger that Lieutenant Commander." Jack replied and switched to the internal comm.. "Hold on back there!" Jack yelled and yawed the fighter to the left, firing at other targets of opportunity as Candis pointed them out in his mind's eye.

Nancy held on.

Chapter 2

"Approval ratings for President Alberts today are the highest in the history of the United States." Walt Mortimer one of the so-called expert panel members for the Round Table of News and lead White House columnist for the *Washington Post* commented on the news of the latest polling data from the nation's capitol. Mortimer had long been considered one of the "gray beards" of reporters on Washington D.C. and system wide politics. Actually, he was just another of the millions of Beltway Bandits making a living by feeding shit to the American public. But, it was a good living.

"His policies are following a whirlwind of approval from pollsters," Mortimer continued. "System wide economic growth and a strong defense against inter-system competition of market goods and commerce due to cheaper products from the Colonies seems to be a big successful hot button for the American voters." Mortimer leaned back in his chair and scribbled some notes on a pad in front of him.

"That seems to be how the American people feel about

it, anyway," Britt Howard, the show's host and anchor for the Earth News Network (ENN) at the New York City anchor desk replied, "It would appear that a 'Buy American' policy has been the unofficial cry of the Alberts administration and indeed the President has lobbied extremely hard to increase the tariffs on all imports from the four extra-solar colonies. There has also been a push from the White House to tax the goods and services coming from the Separatist Laborers Guild on the Martian Reservation. This policy has also seemed to not only be accepted widespread by the American public, but the latest polls show that the public is overwhelmingly for higher taxation on the Reservation Workers' incomes and businesses," Britt Howard responded and then nodded across the round table at the only female on the panel.

"Well, I have to say that I think this will cause the wedge to be driven even deeper between the actual states here in Sol's System and the Separatists on the Reservation at Mars and the colonists at Proxima Centauri, Ross One Twenty-Eight, Lalande Two One One Eight Five, and Tau Ceti." Alice St. John of the *System Review* interrupted the panelists. As the youngest member and with her shoulder length black hair and more modern dress and demeanor she was often used for the radical dissenting voice on the panel. After all, Alice never minded showing the tiniest hint of her cleavage or any restraint when calling one of the "elder reporters" on something that she thought was utter bullshit. Fortunately for Alice, she was smart and pretty and therefore what little bit of radical viewership the Earth News Network had liked her and so she was able to keep her job secure.

"The Colonies have shown little interest in supporting these new White House policies since, on the surface at least, they appear to be nothing more than the statement that the citizens on the Reservation and in the Colonies are second class citizens with little voice," she continued.

"I agree, Alice. That does seem to be the present view of the radical Republicans and the Independents. They are complaining and campaigning that the Reservation should become a state and so should the Colonies. But since there is no longer an electoral college making those territories states will do little to overturn any major population majority votes. The people of those regions already get to vote. Calling them members of a new state wouldn't really matter, would it? Most feel that this is just a ploy of the GOP to usurp power from the other two parties again. Again, the radical Republicans claim it would enable Americans to 'take back' their country," Mortimer debated.

"Careful, Walt. That sounds a little revolutionary." Britt laughed. Of course neither he nor Walt would ever think that any members of the United States of America could *ever* consider such an archaic concept any longer. Civil Wars and Revolutions were things of the past. Oh there were terrorist skirmishes but not all out war.

"Well in that case, Walt," Alice replied. "Wouldn't you have to agree with the Separatists and the Colonists that they have no voice and that their votes really do mean very little? With no electoral votes the measly few percent of the popular vote they have is easily swayed by say, the New African votes, or the Mexican votes or the Chinese votes or the Indian Nationalist votes or the Luna City votes and there are strings of other special interest groups that are much larger than the few million Separatists votes or the few million Colonists votes. A few percent voting block is no longer a large enough piece to really sway the elections of anything one way or the other."

"Ha, ha. Alice, I most definitely wouldn't go that far. This is still a democracy and the majority status rules." The elder reporter Walt Mortimer laughed. "The guidance of our forefathers tell us that 'majority rule' is best. And in the end every vote counts."

"Come now, Walt. Every vote counts? Oh sure every vote gets counted. But there is a large difference in the nuances of the two statements," Alice corrected her colleague. She held her composure well but she grew a bit red in the face with anger at the seasoned reporter's judicious use of incorrect statements as facts. "And 'majority rule' isn't history at all. In fact, the United States was actually designed as a Republic and the Electoral College was created to prevent an uneducated majority rule. Our forefathers actually feared the thought of majority rule once the majority grew complacent and learned how to vote themselves power, hence the Electoral College."

"This isn't a history debate, but I recall there also being an issue of voting technology as a factor in driving the need for an Electoral College. People walked or rode horseback to vote on a piece of paper in their general elections. The states counted the votes and then the representative from the Electoral College would travel to Washington to cast his distribution of Electoral votes based on the general vote."

"Ok, I have to comment on that." Steam nearly escaped

from Alice's ears as she approached the boiling point. She kept her composure, almost, and that is what her radical fans liked about her, emotions. "Walt, that is just not true historically. Oh, the geographical representation was considered, but not for that reason. The forefathers that are now known as the 'Framers of the Constitution' didn't doubt public intelligence of the time, although they feared it could happen in the future and that the Electoral College could help prevent it in from happening it was not the issue of the day; but instead they feared the problem of the 'favorite son' scenario." Alice paused for a second to see if there was recognition of the scenario from her colleagues' faces. She saw nonplussed poker faces, which meant they were probably having their AIs download backup information for them and summarize it to them as quickly as possible. So she sighed and continued.

"The 'favorite son' scenario is that without sufficient information about the candidates running for President from outside their state, locals have no reason to vote for an outsider and would most likely cast their votes for the "favorite son" from their own hometown region. The local boy would always win the local election over a stranger from out of town; that was the fear. The worst fear was that no president would *ever* be elected with a popular majority of the votes to govern the whole country without bitterness from other regions. Another fear was that the popular majority choice of president would always be from the largest and/or most densely populated states which would pretty much render the votes of the smaller states superfluous and irrelevant. Does this sound familiar to anyone here? Déjà vu anyone?" Alice threw up her hands.

"Well, be that as it may, and it may be a topic for a full show sometime," Britt interjected himself into the debate with an attempt to stall Alice's soliloquy. "The main issue for today is that the Separatist and the citizens in the four colonies do seem to have little desire to support this administration or its policies. In fact the governors of Tau Ceti and from Lalande Two One One Eight Five have issued statements that their lawyers believe that President Alberts' new tariffs proposal to the Congress is in violation of the Inter-System Free Trade Agreement and that they are indeed seeking appeals of the policies through the Supreme Court."

"Well I think that is the right course of action, or perhaps, the only real course of action that could be taken from a colonial standpoint." Mortimer replied. "If they don't like the law either challenge its constitutionality or rally Congress to change it or the President to veto it. The Supreme Court is their best shot."

"Walt, again, is that really true? From a colonial perspective what did the original colonists of the thirteen colonies of the United States do when faced with similar impositions from England?" Alice explained history to the elder reporter who had long been accused of being a mouthpiece for the DNC and biased, but only the GOP extremists would ever say such a thing.

"Goddamned rightwing nut!" President of the United States of America William Alberts sat in his West Wing office of the White House watching the news. He always enjoyed the Round Table on ENN. Mortimer and Howard were so stately and wise, but that damned broad on there was a hot headed radical, almost comical she was so radical. She came across that way and so nobody ever really took her seriously; otherwise, the president would not be supporting the ninety-six percent approval rating across the entire country. The country loved him. There was a present economic flourish of upward activity, there hadn't been a terrorist uprising since a year ago way out at Triton and that crazy Kuiper Station affair from his first year in office in his first term, which was all but forgotten by the general populace. The only bit of trouble was the Separatist Extremist terrorists on the edge of the Reservation and the armed forces had been able to keep that at bay and the news was playing it fairly low key. The overwhelming might of the U.S. Fleet prevented any terrorists from truly revolting and besides that, the media loved him.

Things were looking good for the administration and the legacy of President Alberts. With only a year to go until the election his successor, Vice President Michelle Swope, could ride his high approval rating wave right into the White House and give the democrats four more years.

Mr. President. Paula, his AI staffer interrupted his train of thought.

Yes, Paula? He leaned back in his desk chair and propped his feet up on the desk. It was his office, it was his country, why not? Was it disrespectful? Will didn't think so.

The Secretary of Defense, the National Security Advisor, and the Director of National Intelligence is here for the Daily Intelligence Brief. The AI said into Alberts' mind.

Shit. Didn't I do that yesterday? The President asked.

No sir.

Well, when was the last time I read that thing? It couldn't be that long ago.

It was thirteen months and four days ago, Mr. President. The AI paused. *Sir, your wife is also requesting you meet with her and the Reservation Historical Fund Society this morning.*

Shit again. Tell her I have an important meeting with the Sec Def, the NSA, and the DNI that I can't get out of today. He replied.

Very well. And the Sec Def, NSA, and DNI sir?

Oh hell, send them in.

"Ok Conner," Alberts held up his left hand and looked up at the Secretary of Defense. "All this secret stuff just isn't any good for the country. The polls show that these clandestine operations makes the public distrust the government. You know who the government is, Conner? Me, that's who. Did you see my approval rating today? We don't need to be doing a bunch of this clandestine stuff that is gonna screw that up in my last year in office."

"Uh, yes, Mr. President we thought of that. But the DNI's office has intelligence that there has been a lot of technology being transferred from somewhere into the Reservation," The Sec Def replied.

"Is this true, Mike? Where did we get this intelligence from? I thought none of your forays into the Reservation had ever delivered anything other than a hefty bill." Alberts said smugly.

"Well, yes, Mr. President. In the last raid at the edge of

the South Elysium border of the Reservation near the crater line of Nepenthes Mensae we met heavy armored resistance. The imagery data from the telescopes on the *U.S.S. Nelson Mandela* got shots of what looked like mecha deep within the territory. The imagery is a bit limited as there was heavy SAM and cannon fire but analysts believe there was a mecha division moving into the Elysium region," The Director of National Intelligence Mike Netteny explained.

"Yes, they have mecha. They've had Orcus drop tank mecha for years but that is obsolete technology compared to our M3A17-Ts and our FM-12s as you have explained to me before." Alberts was growing impatient with this Daily Brief. He had never had much use for it. The end result was that the DNI would always suggest that they needed more money to conduct some harebrained cheap spy novel heroics that would never pay off and the Secretary of Defense would tell him that the Joint Chiefs need more money for more weapons systems and the National Security Advisor would always say that there was an imminent threat from the terrorist movement from within the Reservation.

"Mr. President, from this picture it is quite clear that this is not a Seppy drop tank," The DNI replied.

"Mike, that is a racist word and you know I don't like it." Alberts said.

"Sorry, Mr. President. But this is not a drop tank," The DNI repeated.

"Now how the hell could you tell that. Look at it. The damned thing is so small it is just one damned pixel. Hell, it might even be a Martian conifer tree as far as I can tell."

Alberts shook his head and ran his fingers through his light brown and gray hair. Once his term in office was over he'd have that damned gray removed, but for now the people seemed to like it. It made him seem more presidential.

"Well, Mr. President, if you will notice here." Netteny pointed his pen at the point in the picture that was supposed to be the mecha. "Then notice this dark spot here. This is the mecha's shadow. And note that the two aren't touching at the bottom."

"Yeah so?"

"That means it is in the air, sir. And knowing the details of the optical system and its pointing angles at the time and from the angle of the sun and the length of this shadow we can tell how big this mecha is and how high off the ground it is."

"Cut to the chase, Mike."

"The mecha is larger and much higher in the air than the standard drop tank. This is something new, Mr. President." The DNI didn't grin triumphantly but he wasn't still frowning at Alberts either.

"Ok, so the Separatists have a new experimental mecha. Good for them." The president sat up straight and started to close the brief.

"Wait, Mr. President. Look at the image on the next page." The DNI pointed at the briefing. With a sigh the President flipped the page and began to study it for a moment.

"What the . . ." he replied. The image showed a squadron of the mecha in nearly the same level of resolution. "How many is this?"

"Maybe as many as thirty, sir. It was hard to tell from this data. But, turn to the next page," The DNI offered.

"Ok, I've seen this before right? These three big ships are full sized Separatist cargo haulers on the ground. What are these dark lines here?" Alberts said as he pondered the imagery data. This picture was much better. The tag on the bottom right hand corner of it showed the source of the image was from an orbital spy platform over the Reservation. The lines leading into, or out of, the large haulers ran for a kilometer or so into the side of a small mountain and then vanished. But there was no mecha in any of the pictures.

"Right sir. Those are haulers. And the dark lines in the Martian grass are tracks from vehicles. Heavy vehicles. Analysts suggest three haulers full of vehicles, Mr. President," The DNI explained. "But the next image shows more."

"Are these, footprints?" Alberts asked.

"Yes sir. Mecha footprints. Thousands of them."

"Well, Mike, if they have that many of these new mecha that sure raises a couple of questions that sort of foul up the logic." Alberts ticked off on his fingers. "One is how did they march all those out of that mountain hanger and into these haulers without the CIA and the NRO and the entire space reconnaissance wing of the United States getting a single picture of one of them? Two, why didn't they just land right up next to the mountain and do it under cover anyway. And three, where in the hell could they have gotten that many mecha without us knowing it?"

"It doesn't add up Mike. I agree with the President." The Sec Def added.

"Mr. President, in order. Let me see: One, they are invisible, at least to our sensors or they managed to cover the road between the mountain and the haulers with camo netting. Two, they parked the haulers far enough away that they had to walk over to be loaded in the open on purpose so we would know they were invisible. After all, the Separatists know we have our eyes and ears in the sky above the Reservation." Mike had to pause from the President's reaction.

"What? Invisible? That doesn't seem likely. We've been working cloaking technology for centuries right? And you're telling me the Separatists developed it first? No, don't go spread that nonsense around. I think the netting idea makes more sense."

"I'm just describing the data, sir. We know that they are at least invisible to our sensor platforms or as you say were camouflaged very well. And finally, the answer to your third question is that they didn't get the mecha from anywhere in the Sol System. That must mean, the Colonies."

"It takes a year or more to get to or from the Colonies and you think they've developed those things that long ago. The FM-12s just went into operation six or so months ago and they had the might of the entire military-industrial complex working on them. The Colonies have a few tens of millions of people with limited resources. What do you think, Lake?" The President turned to the NSA Lake Rostow.

"I think we should check it out, sir. Could prove to be something here. This is either too fantastic to be true or not good for us. Either way I agree with Mike that we should check it out," The National Security Advisor Lake Rostow replied.

"All right then. Draw up the mission plans and go do something and let me know how it goes. But, in no circumstances are we to engage further than the current truce lines. The fighting stays in the gray zone," he replied.

"Uh. Sir. We are planning to engage deeper than that today for operation Bachelor Party."

"Who authorized this?"

"Uh. Sir. It has been in the brief for more than six months now." The Sec Def back pedaled a little. "You told us to get better intel on where the Reservation was getting its resupply and that you would authorize it."

"That's right, sorry, Conner. I do recall this well. If they are buying supplies from somebody in system or out they aren't paying taxes on it." Alberts recalled the brief from the Chairman of the House Permanent Select Committee on Intelligence. One of the manufacturers in his district was certain the Separatists were buying arms, or at the absolute least resources, and not from legal vendors in the United States, which was bad for the economy. So the political action committee for the arms firm had their Representative check into it. Nearly the entire state of Bolivia worked for that firm and reelection was coming up. "Ok. I remember that. What is happening with this Bachelor Party?"

"We are pushing the lines and attacking the sub mountains of Phlegra and are dropping intelligence gathering sources there, sir. Deniable sources, sir."

"Right. And let me know what you find out so we can put a stop to this illegal arms trade and get Congressman Aldridge off my back."

Chapter 3

"The haulers are loaded and away, ma'am!" the Commander of the Air Wing informed Elle of their status. The large space cargo haulers lifted lazily off the Umbra Spaceport in the northern most region of the Reservation where the Umbra region and the Boreosyrtis region met. General Elle Ahmi stood and tugged at the ski mask she always wore to hide her face. In her position, which for decades had been one of attacking and hiding like many of the great freedom fighters throughout history, keeping your true identity closely held was not only a good idea, but pretty much a requirement for survival. There was nobody within the Separatists—Americans as they liked to call themselves—that would betray the great general. But occasionally there had been attempts on her life by the CIA that kept her always on the alert and vigilant of the constant threat.

"Good, commander." Elle looked up from the computer display in front of her at the control tower and checked the locations of the haulers on the radar. "The cloaking countermeasures are working, I assume." She looked out the window of the tower at the spaceships that were now drifting into the Martian night sky and slowly out of sight.

"As far as we can tell ma'am, but until they engage the enemy we can't know for certain," he explained.

"Yes, I realize that. Any word from the carrier group?" the general asked.

"Yes. They are poised for hyperspace on your command, ma'am."

"The Exodus?" Today was a day of days. This day would be long remembered in the history books of the human race—that is, if all went according to plan.

"All is moving according to plan, general."

"Excellent." The general pulled at the long dark hair hanging unruly out of the back of her ski mask and tied it into a pony tail, pulling it up through the hole in the back of the ski mask that she had made in it. She often wore her hair in a ponytail if there were possibilities that she would be seeing any action. The red, white, and blue mask contrasted against the black hair and pale Martian skin and her tall slender athletic frame misleadingly portrayed her as late twenties or early thirties and an average Martian female, not a great general that held off the Invasion of the Martian Desert with an extremely inferior force in numbers and technology more that thirty years prior.

The general's deep brown eyes shined with deep intent and purpose such that nobody would dare second guess her timing or her resolve. Her plan had been in the working for decades—four or five decades. Oh sure it was a dynamic plan and some aspects of it had changed over the years, but the general purpose of the plan had always been the same. Only recently had there been hope of foregoing the plan when the President of the United States offered to send an ambassador to meet with the Separatists Laborers Guild to discuss tariff relief. But once the administration chose an ambassador the level of seriousness that the White House was taking the Separatists became quite clear.

The President of the United States gave the task to a low end second term senator simply to appease pressure from the opposition parties in the Senate. It had become quite clear to the Separatists now just how serious the United States was about the disconnect between the Separatists and themselves—not very. And this day, this one day on the red planet the United States would regret their decision.

President Alberts had chosen an unknown upstart senator from Mississippi from the GOP to act as the arbiter and ambassador to the Martian laborers of the Separatist movement. Senator Alexander Moore was a competent man, but had little power within the U.S. government as only a second term senator in supernumery positions of unimportant committees. The general not only knew this Senator Moore, she knew him well, very well. She had done some background checking to make certain, but it was the same Alexander Moore that she owned for several years following the Martian Desert Campaigns. The arrogant Americans had sent in the entire Luna City Brigades to push the Separatists out of the Syrtis Major Planum and back into Elysium, but they had not expected an organized military force like the one that General Ahmi had amassed.

Ahmi had implemented terrorist, resistance, and guerilla tactics from the great asymmetric battles of history and literally laid the American military forces to waste.

The Separatist Army quickly decimated the American infantry and Marines much the way the so-called "Task Force Smith" had been decimated at the onset of the American-Korean War centuries before. Stupid complacent American policy makers never learned from their own history. Many of the Marines were captured and kept in Separatist POW camps. They were tortured and were fed propaganda on a daily basis, but most of the Marines died before the American government accepted peace terms allowing for the release of the POWs. During that time Ahmi had the young Marine Major Alexander Moore in her camp. He was unbreakable, an excellent soldier, and even in the last of his days with her remained a true patriot to his country.

No matter how wonderful of a soldier Moore might have been, now he was a second rate politician. He was a small fish in a very large ocean filled with sharks, barracudas, and killer whales. Their past relationship would probably be of little use to her, but Ahmi was smart and calculating and patient. She never underestimated her opponents nor did she ever overlook a potential relationship that could be exploited for the benefit of her plan. She hoped the brave bullheaded senator didn't get all caught up in the coming day's events. There was a soft place in her heart for all her POWs and she remembered Moore most fondly. Most. Fondly.

"Are there any issues that I need to address right now?" Ahmi asked the commander.

"No ma'am. All is moving smoothly," he replied,

"Very well. Give me a few moments alone, please." She wanted to look across her beloved red, blue, and green planet and at the late night sky one last time. After the day ahead of her, it would likely be a very long time before she would have Martian soil under her feet and the Martian sky over her head. She decided to take a quick bounce across the compound. There was little that she needed to do just yet anyway since the plan was taking care of itself for the moment. She looked up at Phobos and Deimos through the window at the edge of the spaceport hangar bay. Elle picked up her e-suit helmet and slipped it on over her ponytail and mask and gave it a twist to seal it on. A gust of cool oxygen rushed over her face as the scrubbers kicked online. The general walked to the edge of the airseam in the hangar bay door and stepped through the force field into the Martian atmosphere. She had time to take a short stroll in her new armored transfigurable fighter mecha.

Her Stinger, as the Freedom Fighters were calling them, was as close a copy of the U.S. Marine fighting mecha known as the FM-12 Strike Mecha as it could be from the intelligence that the Separatist spies were able to gather. The mecha was transfigurable like the Orcus Drop Tank Mecha that the Separatists had been using for decades, but the design added a third configuration that mimicked the FM-12's eagle mode. The Stinger could fight upright as a giant humanoid looking metal beast in bot mode. It could fight as an aerospace fighter plane in fighter mode. Or it could fight as a hybrid fighter with arms and feet much like a metal eagle with hands in the new eagle mode.

The Stingers had taken the Separatist agents, engineers, laborers, and aerospace scientists more than a year to design even with the stolen data on the FM-12. Once the design was settled upon, it took another year to find suitable manufacturing capabilities to build more than just a prototype. Then the fighter went into production outside the Sol System. That had been the most difficult aspect of the effort—the long range communications and transportation over the multiple light years gulf between the stars.

Elle bounced up to her private Stinger and thought through her AIC implant to open the cockpit. The Stinger sat like a bird perched on the end of the taxiway in eagle mode. Elle gave a quick tap on the ground with her jump-boots and bounded upward and into the pilot's couch of the new fighting mecha. Elle was proud of her Revolution and what they had accomplished and what they could accomplish. Her Stinger was the culmination of all that. The code that she had helped develop—her original occupation more than a three quarters of a century before had been as a software engineer and wireless technician—would render the mecha invisible to the targeting systems of the enemy and therefore make it a veritable harbinger of death and destruction upon the U.S. military forces. Of course, Elle realized that the sensor systems, structural integrity field generators, armor plating, and the weapons targeting systems were not as advanced as the bird's American counterpart, but the little software surprise would help even the playing field.

The general and leader of the Separatist Revolution strapped herself into the seat of the mecha and cycled the cockpit canopy down. Then she addressed her AIC to preflight the bird.

Copernicus? She thought with her mindvoice.

Yes ma'am?

Run up the cloaking software and let's go for a spin while we still have time.

Yes ma'am. Software engaged and power plant coming online for main propulsion systems. You are ready to go, the AIC said as the humming sound of the engines coming online grew louder as they spun up.

The Separatist mecha shook slightly as it lifted from the ground throwing whirlwinds from underneath each of the wings as the vertical take-off engines pushed it upward from the ground effect. Elle gripped the throttle and pushed it full force forward with her left hand while controlling the flight path with the stick in her right. The standard hands on throttle and stick controls mimicked most fighter control systems that had been developed for centuries. The exception, of course, was the direct-to-mind control links between the plane and the pilot and the AIC. The DTM connections enabled modern fighters to do things that no others in history could have.

Ahmi toggled the mode control to bot mode, which in turn rolled her through a series of twists and rolls that in the end left her in the cockpit in the torso of the fighter mecha as it flew upward head first as a giant metal armored robot. The general cut the throttle back and performed a "head over" into a dive toward the ground rolling all the way over in a forward flip so as to land on the mecha's feet on the Martian ground with a big *kathunk!*

This thing is an absolute dream, Copernicus. She

thought to her AIC while she maneuvered the mecha into a full speed run across the northern Martian planes bouncing and flipping the vehicle over dunes and rocks and crevasses.

Lets hope so, general.

Don't be such a pessimist, Copernicus, she thought and then was forced to grunt gutturally and squeeze her leg muscles tight as the flipping maneuver imposed a lot of g-forces on her body.

Yes ma'am.

The general known as the most wanted terrorist in the human race flew the high tech fighter mecha with the giddy and joy of a school girl playing hopscotch at recess. She bounced and zigged and zagged the mecha and even attempted a few martial arts style rolls, which she flubbed pretty badly. The rolls shook her up momentarily, forcing her to catch her breath cautiously and almost painfully from the air bladders of the pressure suit squeezing on her. Elle wasn't the trained fighter pilot that her soldiers were and she only had a few hundred hours in the machine. Although she didn't intend on flying one into battle unless all things really went to hell, she extremely enjoyed the rush from piloting one for fun. In another life, one without politics and revolutions and insurgency and unfair taxation without representation and second class citizens, Elle might would enjoy being a test pilot or even a fighter pilot. But that was just a fleeting fantasy.

Ma'am it is approaching seven thirty a.m. in Tharsis, her AIC told her.

Right then. I guess I should order the attack to start, she replied.

Chapter 4

Senator Alexander Moore held his six-year-old daughter's left hand with his right. His wife, Sehera, held their daughter's other hand, occasionally little Deanna would pick up her feet and swing from her parent's hold. The swing was a slow pendulous arc in the low Martian gravity that thrilled the precocious six year old child. Deanna was cute in all aspects that a six-year-old could be and had been fortunate enough to acquire the best traits of each parent. Her mother's long full bodied dark curly hair and milky white smooth Martian skin gave her a baby doll cute appeal while her father's Mississippi State University starting fullback frame made her appear as a physical force to be reckoned with, even at only six Earth years old.

The three of them were thoroughly enjoying their low gravity stroll through the shopping and mall district of the largest environment dome at the Mons City Resort. The unearthly architecture, dim lighting from Sol mixed with city lights, and light gravity of the Martian city was a pleasant and welcome change from Capitol Hill, which is normally where the family spent all their few and far between together moments.

"Look Mommy!" Deanna pointed to a large holo projection at the doorway of a shop called *Mons Adventures* at a man hang gliding down the side of Olympus Mons. The image shifted a moment later to a group of carefree adrenaline junkie tourist adventurers rappelling down the side of a Martian canyon and then again switching to tourist hiking across the open desert in jumper boots, taking twenty meter leaps at a time across the Martian desert scrub brush. "Neat! Can we do that, Mommy?"

"That looks like fun doesn't it!" Alexander smiled. The senator missed real life action packed fun. His days on Capitol Hill seldom required him to work up a sweat and the only place he managed to do that was in the gym. He missed his more athletic days in college and the military—though he did not miss the pain and daily threat of death from the latter.

"Bah!" Sehera replied. "That is insanely dangerous and I'd better not ever catch either of you doing it."

"Mommy, you're a fraidy cat." Deanna laughed and repeated "fraidy cat, fraidy cat."

"Fraidy cats live long lives dear. Nine of them," her mother said.

The three continued along looking as nothing more than tourists. Alexander had not been away from the Beltway in a long time and this trip to the Martian Summit was proving to be something other than the political career booster he had originally intended it to be. It was more of a much-needed family vacation.

They continued through the shops along the sidewalks and into an open court area filled with local cuisine and hot dog stands. There were a few trees both of Earth and Martian variety casting shade over the blue-green grass covered area. The sound of various Earth birds could be heard over the bustle of the tourists and locals with the occasional hovercar screeching by in the background noise.

The dome had a large transparent ceiling and a spectacular view of the south side of the Mons City Skyline in the shadow of the great mountain itself. Olympus Mons covered an area nearly the size of the state of Arizona and the mountain was over twenty-five kilometers tall at the peak. Mons City's main dome was built on the escarpment over two hundred kilometers from the peak on the southwest side of the ancient volcano. Summit City was built atop the mountain along the edge of the volcano's ridges and surrounding the caldera of the ancient volcano. The caldera or pit of the giant volcano was over eighty kilometers across and more than two and a half kilometers deep. Summit City had sprung up around many different tourist activities that ranged from base-gliding off the caldera, to climbing and rappelling on it, to even the five kilometer luge that snaked down the north side of the caldera ridge. The southern ridge of the caldera was peppered by several observatories and naval outposts that were adjuncts of the base further down the mountain.

The caldera floor was covered with dwelling domes of the locals and a major shopping center dome that was nearly twenty kilometers in diameter. Interstate transport tubes covered the floor like a spider's web and turned up the ridge to Summit City at about every forty degrees around the pit's circumference. Smaller street tubes and tunnels cut in and out of the mountain walls. If the peak of the giant Martian shield volcano sounded like it had become a metropolis it was because that is exactly what it was. But, it was more like Las Vegas back on Earth than it was like New York City. Mons City on the other hand rivaled any of the megalopolises on Earth and spiraled and grew out over most of the southwestern face of Olympus Mons from the escarpment to the summit.

The peak of the mountain was littered with hundreds of minor domes and highway tubules, but there were five major domes that were considered boroughs by the locals. The main dome was over thirty kilometers in diameter with four ten kilometer domes spread out equally around it. The four secondary domes of Mons City were spread out across the face of the southern side of the giant state sized mountain at the three, six, nine, and twelve o'clock positions about the main dome. The domes were really cities within themselves. But the entire complex was the largest construct in mankind's history.

A little further east and up the mountain one could see the naval base. There was continuous air and space traffic in and out of the base, a sign that there was more going on than day-to-day travel—like, a war. A war that had been waging on and off for more than three or four decades. A war that most of the American population wouldn't admit was even a war.

"What's that, daddy?" Deanna asked and pointed toward the large supercarrier hovering over the outskirts of the naval base.

Abigail? Senator Moore asked his staffer AI.

Yes Senator. That is the U.S.S. Supercarrier Winston Churchill.

"That, my dear," Senator Moore paused for dramatic effect, a trick he'd often used on the senate floor, "That is the *U.S.S. Supercarrier Winston Churchill* from the great state of South England."

"What's a supercarrier, daddy?"

Alexander smiled at his daughter. She was smart and beautiful—it pleased him, a lot, that she was inquisitive. But, the Senator had other things on his mind. The summit meeting at the Olympus Mons Resort had been dragging on for weeks now with no end in sight. The second term senator from Mississippi had come to Mars with the hopes of making a name for himself in political history by bringing the war that was raging at that very moment on the other side of the planet, just a few thousand kilometers away in Elysium, and elsewhere in the Sol System to a halt.

But he had had no luck. He had known for some time that he needed to be there at Mons City for the summit. But he was beginning to wonder why. He was a minor member of the Senate Appropriations Committee; he simply wasn't powerful enough to make the deals needed to sway the Separatist Traders and Laborers Guild to cease hostilities and get back to work—the "great" work of the United States of America. And somehow, the Separatist had become seriously armed with mecha and aircraft and other weapons. There were even rumors in the press that the extremist of the Separatist movement had acquired weapons of mass destruction such as a gluonium warhead. If that were true, then the Separatists could take out an entire mega city with one bomb—if they could deliver it without it being detected.

There was more going on with the Separatist than people generally wanted to admit. The Separatists were getting materials from outside the U.S.A.—in other words, outside of the Sol System. But where? There were only four extra-solar colonies known to man: Proxima Centauri Planet Two, Ross One Twenty-Eight Planet Three Moon Beta, Lalande Two One One Eight Five Planet Three, and Tau Ceti Planet Four Moon Alpha. Alexander had a very good idea of what was going on, but he had desired and needed to know more about how the U.S. could handle the situation. He needed access to more information—to classified information.

So, Senator Moore had tried to finesse his way onto the Senate Select Committee on Intelligence or the SSCI, pronounced "sissy" as he had learned, for all of his latest term. Without being exposed to the intelligence and what was really going on in the Local Bubble, it was hard to be effective in negotiations with the Separatist delegation at the summit. The Appropriations Committee members just do not get the access to Top Secret and special access information that the SSCI does.

The fact that the current administration had chosen to send such a low echelon, only second term, politician as *the* representative for the U.S. government at the summit meeting hinted as to America's sincerity with the Separatists. In other words, the current administration could care less about the Separatists' and their plight. It was only a political "grass roots" hot button that had forced the President to take action and force the SSCI to

brief Senator Moore into the pertinent information. After
all, the young senator was the mouth of the "grass roots"
folks. He had always wondered why him, a senator from
Mississippi, and not one from a Martian region. The GOP
supporters would spin that they suspected the President
was subconsciously a bigot toward Martians, or at the least
he was a class elitest.

More information on how the country was planning on
winning the war and with what new technologies, gave
Alexander a better hold on the summit talks, even if the
general population could care less about the war between
the U.S. and the Separatist movement. The "grass roots"
groups simply wanted their tax dollars on Earth to quit
going to a war on a planet that most of them had never
been to. And the skirmishes in the outer part of the solar
system were deemed an even bigger waste of tax dollars.

At times it seemed that only the Separatists cared. The
latest news polls showed that most Earth and Luna citizens
were so far removed from the actual war that the loss of
life was being dismissed and Americans in general were
sticking to their guns about "not dealing with terrorists."
That battlecry, at least for now, would outweigh the cost
of the war—but eventually the cost of the war would
completely drive the politics.

By and large, the general population of inner Sol
System thought of the Separatists as terrorists. *Terrorists
don't have armies, mecha, and air support*. The Gnat
aerospace fighter and the Orcus Tank Mecha were
expensive pieces of equipment and the Seppies had been
using them for decades. There had long been rumors that
the U.S. didn't really care about the aged combat systems

because some of the spin-off companies in the Belt, or the Kuiper Belt, or maybe even at the Colonies, were manufacturing them at huge profits that were being used to grease certain politicians within the U.S. government. Most of the systems of the vehicles were manufactured on Earth, Luna, and Mars and then they were assembled somewhere else. So as long as the flow of money for the components and subsystems continued to keep millions in jobs across multiple Congressional districts throughout the system the purchase and therefore the assembly of the Separatist mecha and fighters was likely to continue.

Terrorists historically had not been known to have the type of economic and political power required to enable the continued support of what for all intents and purposes could be called an army. Of course, most terrorists throughout history hadn't had a region nearly the size of Africa cordoned off and given to them as their own place to live and protect. The Reservation was in essence its own country separate of the United States, much like the American Indian Reservations of the past.

Why would the government continue to allow them to arm themselves the way they had, for decades? The fact that the Separatists had mecha had come as surprise during the initiation of the Desert Campaigns, but for thirty years after they still had mecha pop up here and there in skirmishes and nothing had really been done about it. Alexander was quite certain that the Separatists were much more than just terrorists. The ones he had fought against in the Martian desert thirty years earlier most certainly were soldiers, not terrorists. Again he thought, *terrorists don't have armies, mecha, and air support.*

Unless he could somehow get the Separatist representatives to guarantee no further actions and to begin talks of getting back to work, this trip had been nothing more than a Martian vacation for his wife and daughter. If most people only saw the devastation on Triton, the bodies from Kuiper Station, and the fighting near the western edge of Elysium they would realize this was a war—a serious war and not just terrorists. Now if the President would have come instead, as the Martian delegation had begged of him . . .

"What's a supercarrier, daddy?" Deanna tugged at Senator Moore's sports coat, impatiently snapping him out of his mind-racing train of thought.

"Huh, oh. It is a very large spaceship that carries a whole bunch of smaller spaceships and thousands of people and tanks and is an awesome display of America's great strength and power. And Marines! You can't win any real war without a bunch of U.S. Marines!" He smiled and gestured flamboyantly with his hands open wide and his chest out. He then subconsciously turned his U.S. Marine Corp ring a few times. His wife grunted at his answer.

"Don't encourage her, Alexander." Sehera glanced at him. "It is a *carrier,* honey, because it *carries* other ships and people inside it. It is a *supercarrier* because it is superdy-duperdy big."

"I understand, Mommy." Deanna smiled and went back to swinging between her parents.

The supercarrier was indeed an awesome display of American military might as its sleek structure of over a kilometer and a half long, two-thirds of a kilometer wide, and a quarter kilometer tall hovered over the largest mountain feature on the Martian landscape. The large vehicle turned on a slow arc and looked as if it would pass right over head in a few moments, casting a giant shadow over the city domes. But the large brilliant orange, yellow, and red fireball erupting from the port side of the spacecraft caused it to list starboard rapidly. Then the *Churchill* appeared to have lost all gravity modification control and the supercarrier started losing altitude.

"Look!" Deanna let go of her parent's handhold and pointed.

"What the hell?" Senator Moore stopped dead in his tracks as the supercarrier lost propulsion and started on a downward trajectory.

"Oh my God!" Sehera instinctively picked up her daughter and held her tight to her, not sure what to do but certain she would protect her child at all costs. The Martian childhood in her triggered years of instinct and hazardous environment training that someone could only get from living there and being forced to survive in that harsh environment. Alexander Moore on the other hand, having grown up in the southeastern North American continent, knew not to stand in fireants, play with copperheads and water moccasins, and always steer clear of skunks and polecats. His youth couldn't help with the hazards of Mars. But the seventeen years he had spent in the Luna City Brigade Special Forces might.

"That thing is gonna hit one of the domes! We have got to get out of here!" Alexander grabbed his daughter from his wife and turned down and alleyway that led to the stairwell toward the main exit. Fortunately, they were not far from the exterior hall that led around the main dome's circumference where the circumference interstate circled the city. There was a greenway that ran between the interstate and the dome that had leak shelters placed along it every few kilometers. "Come on! If that thing hits us we're going to lose atmosphere."

Abigail!

There is a leak shelter on the northwest wall greenway very near us. The AI staffer anticipated her counterpart's question.

"Run," Alexander told his wife.

I have requested a Secret Service detail to pick you up, Senator. But, unfortunately, there are none available. There is a contingent of Martian Marine Reserve that has dispatched a squad of troops to us. They have all rallied to the governor's request for help.

Thanks.

"Stop Alexander, wait!" Sehera grabbed at his shoulder.

"We'd better hurry and get to the shelter, Sehera." Alexander warned.

"No! Alexander, the shelter is on the other side of the greenway at the northwest most wall of this dome. That is over three kilometers away. It could take us a long time to get there and by then the crowds of tourist and locals will have filled it beyond capacity." Sehera was running survival plans over and over in her head. *Any good Martian would tell you that the first thing to do is put on your suit and grab your air scrubber!*

The supercarrier continued to fall on a ballistic trajectory until it clipped the bottom southwest side of the ancient

Martian volcano mound. The large rugged ship ricocheted off the side of the mountain and fell right on top of the southern most secondary dome of Mons City—the six o'clock borough. The rupture of the side dome flowed precious atmosphere out into the Martian wind. With the air went the life of hundreds of thousands of citizens in a matter of tens of minutes. Rescue crews were scrambled and several naval fleet ships were dispatched to the mountain but it would be tens of minutes before the fleet could arrive.

Over one hundred and seventy thousand survivors from the attack had been lucky enough to make it to the main Mons City shelters and more had taken shelter in the northern, eastern, and western secondary city domes—though the travel tubes to the western, eastern, and main domes had taken some damage from what appeared to be secondary impacts and explosions. It is likely that casualties could reach into the millions by the end of the day.

Fortunate for the Moore family, they had been in the main dome of Mons City, which had not been damaged by the crashing supercarrier or the secondary effects. Senator Moore and his family however, *were* too far from the shelters to risk the long hike. If the main dome gave while trekking to the shelter they would die in minutes or less of exposure or suffocation.

"Reyez, those goddamned stray cats got into the storeroom again," one of the adventure store assistant managers, Rod Taylor, called from the doorway leading into the back stockroom.

"Well, just chase 'em out if they're still in there." Reyez replied.

"Put the power pack there honey," Sehera demonstrated for her daughter how to snap the vacuum energy power supply into the suit pack. She kissed her daughter on the cheek then slid the environment suit over her head, twisting the seal ring tight.

"Don't close the faceshield down unless you need it. No need to waste our power and air if the dome doesn't crack." The *Mons Adventures* store manager, a young man in his early twenties, twisted his bright red helmet on and continued to instruct the few tourists and passersby that had the presence of mind to find a place that sold or rented environment suits.

"Makes sense," Alexander smiled reassuringly at his daughter and motioned to her how to release the faceshield hinge if she needed to. Sehera on the other hand needed no instruction. She had been in and out of environment suits most of her life as a native.

"Anybody know what is going on?" one of the tourist asked. Obviously he was from Earth and had never been in a suit. The short fat man was having trouble sealing the life support ring.

"Yeah, the supercarrier blew up and crashed into the dome, duh." Deanna frowned. Rod looked up from helping one of the others with their e-suit functions and burst out with laughter at her response.

"Ask a stupid question . . . " the other young man that worked there, Vincent, added.

"Be nice, dear," Her mother scolded her. Deanna stuck her tongue out at the man.

Abigail, any info available? Senator Moore thought to his staffer.

The best source of news seems to be, well, the news, sir. The long range wireless is being jammed. I do have a connection to the Marines that were dispatched to get us, the AI replied.

Well?

Their transport was shot down over the south dome and they are taking heavy casualties. And even worse, sir, they are cut off from us.

Casualties! From what?

This appears to be an attack, senator. There is a ground force overrunning the city and parts of the naval base. It is only a matter of time before they enter the main dome, Abigail informed her counterpart and boss.

"Hey, listen," Senator Moore got the young shop manager, Reyez's, attention. "Can you put the holo or a screen on MNN?"

"Of course. I don't know why I didn't think of that." The *Mons Adventures* manager looked up from adjustments to one of the environment suits and the wall monitors flipped to the Mars News Network, MNN. Then Reyez and the other two employees of the shop, Rod and Vince, went back to adjusting the suits of the few tourists that had at least been smart enough to find a place that had suits. There was just no telling how many tourists had gotten lost in the main dome and never found the leak shelter or a place with suits. No telling how many casualties there would be if the big dome cracked a seal.

Alexander held his wife and daughter's hands and pulled them closer to the video monitors. The MNN

correspondent was on the north side of the dome near the
shelter. The scene was of an overcrowded room with too
few seats. The occasional local with an environment suit
would be noticeable in the crowd of tourists.

" . . . the main dome is still holding as far as we can tell.
A few minutes ago the U.S.S *Winston Churchill*, a Navy
supercarrier, exploded in mid air and then crashed
through the skyline of southern portions of Olympus
Mons City destroying parts of the lower and smaller
domes. We have no idea of the massive damage that must
have been caused and are not certain of the casualties.
The scene here is currently of shock and survival. We can
only hope the leak shelters hold since the majority of the
people here do not have environment suits. Shennan, is
there any word as to what is going on?" The image shifted
back to the MNN anchor desk and Shennan Haggarty.

"Right now, Amanda, we know very little. However, we
do have some footage of the attack. That's right, attack.
Mons City is under a full-scale attack from ground troops
with aerial support. The data we have right now is still
very sketchy, but it appears as if a cargo and waste disposal
transport ship appeared out of hyperspace in orbit above
Mons and dropped a full contingent of mechanized drop
tanks, infantry, and fighter support and then completed a
suicide run at the naval blockade in orbit. The ship was
engaged by the fleet but it appears to have self-destructed
destroying several ships along with it and damaging many
others. These events seem to have coincided with the
explosion of the *Churchill*. Right now we can only assume
sabotage is what caused *it* to explode. Just a moment . . .

I'm told we have audio from Gail Fehrer in the south dome . . . can we go to that?"

"This is Gail Fehrer. I'm in the south dome of the Olympus Mons Skyline. The dome has a massive hole in it the size of several skyscrapers. There are giant girders from the geodesic ribs hanging from the gaping hole. Oh my God, there are skyscrapers collapsing along the path of the crashed ship and explosions going off in the distance. There must be thousands killed or wounded. Once again, just a few moments ago the supercarrier *U.S.S Winston Churchill* crashed here destroying most of the southern borough of the city. Almost immediately following that several what appears to be Separatist mechanized troop carriers dropped from the sky and then a squadron of enemy fighter-bombers plowed through leaving behind death and destruction. It looks as if the bombers may also have taken out portions of the eastern skyline as well, before they met any resistance from the Navy."

"Gail, can you see any of our troops anywhere?" Shennan asked.

"Shennan, I just saw a group of Martian Marines pass through toward the fairgrounds. One of the soldiers told us that they were heavily outnumbered and hoped their superior training and firepower would allow them to hold off the attack until the Martian 34th Mecha Unit arrived."

"Gail can you give us a description of the scene and mood there?" the anchorman asked.

"Yes, Shennan. There is an extreme amount of dust clouds and smoke in the vicinity all around us and there is rubble everywhere. There is the distinct crack of railgun fire and missile detonations in the background. The

Marines just went towards what appears to be the most devastated part of the city and where there are still flames and explosions from secondary effects of the crash sounding in the distance. My guess is that *there* is where the first conflicts are..."

After more than an hour of waiting in the adventure store and feeling the large vibrations of exterior explosions outside the main dome the survivors were more than just panicked. Many of the two-dozen survivors that gathered and waited in the adventure store had AICs that were connected to the Internet, but what they found in terms of news was not very reassuring. MNN and local wireless seemed to be the only functioning communications. And the footage on MNN had been looped through so many times that it was getting old hearing the news analysts trying to think of new things to say about it. All other longer-range transmission systems were being actively jammed. This bothered Senator Moore immensely. Nobody, to his knowledge, realized that the Separatist had that type of advanced jamming technology. Sure they had tanks and fighters and armored e-suits, but they were old technology and they were years behind the QM transceiver communications technologies used throughout the systems.

Abigail, what is going on? How are they jamming the long range QMs?

Well, senator, it appears to have been a full-scale attack on Mons City. A fleet of Navy ships was dispatched but apparently the Separatists were ready for them with surface-to-air missiles and a fleet of ships appeared in orbit out of hyperspace just now. MNN will start running that soon. Don't know about the communications jamming. I'll work on that.

How do you know all the other stuff?

I've tied in directly to the MNN anchor desk's producer AIC. I had to promise you would give them an exclusive later.

Good girl!

I try senator.

The ships that appeared in orbit . . . ours?

Apparently not, senator. It would appear as if Mons City is surrounded and under siege, sir. And now there is sufficient orbital support. My guess is that it is only a matter of time before the main dome begins filling with Separatist ground forces.

What about those Marines? The 34th Mecha and the rest of the Army? Hell, I'd even settle for the Martian Air Force.

The Marines are cut off on the other side of the southern dome, Senator. They continue to take heavy casualties. The Marine tactical AIC I'm in contact with has received no contact from the 34th but they do expect an evac lift to be available in one three hours. Since the transport tubes between the south dome and the main dome have also been destroyed they had to turn back. The evac is on the south escarpment of the mountain just outside the south dome. The Marines also expect the entire city to be overrun soon. They are fighting them as best they can but with little luck. The attack is a full fighting force, sir. There is a serious numbers advantage in favor of the invaders right now.

Could we get to them, to the evac lift? Alexander held onto his wife's hand as he thought of possibilities. He knew that if the Separatistss found a U.S. Senator and family that they would be killed as spectacle and shown on a system wide broadcast. Alexander was not about to allow that. He had spent seventeen years—seventeen hard years—in the Luna City Brigade during the first Martian Desert Campaign and he knew how to fight if he had to.

He had fought in units that had started out with hundreds and ended with two or three and then ended up captured and in a POW camp for years. The Separatists, on the other hand, had fared a little better than he. After years of hard fighting the U.S. with dated weapons and terrorist tactics the Separatists made the war too expensive for the U.S. to desire to continue with it. So the Americans sued for peace, leaving the desert of Syrtis Major to them. Most of the Separatists went back to within the "Reservation" borders near Phlegra and continued on with working on the terraforming of Mars. But others, the leaders of the Separatist armies under the direction of Elle Ahmi, had maintained a continuously growing military structure within the Separatist community. There were weapons stockpile efforts and occasional terrorist activities. After seventeen years of the desert war between 2336 and 2352, an uncomfortable peace had lasted a decade or two—depending on which history book you read—and then Elle Ahmi the general of the Desert Campaigns finally rose to absolute power within the Separatist Union. It was unclear how exactly that had happened. Peace had been unraveling for several years and skirmishes were popping up throughout the system. And so once again Alexander was called back to Mars, but this time as a diplomat and not as an armored e-suit Marine.

Alexander had fought politically to aid in the peace process and that was why he was on Mars again, he thought. But there was always the nagging thought in the back of his mind that he was just a bone thrown by President Alberts and the dems of the House to appease the snapping dog of the GOP and the Independent Party. The last time he had been on Mars he was wearing jumper boots and a USMC armored e-suit, but that had been over thirty years before. It didn't matter. *There is no such thing as a former Marine,* he thought to himself. He would *not* let his family be killed as a spectacle for terrorists.

There's no way to get out to the evac?

Perhaps, but the Marines are cut-off from us, sir. The MNN reporter Gail Fehrer reports enemy mecha positioned along the remains of southern travel tubes and on the periphery of the dome. We would either need to go way around them on the outside or over or under them, Abigail explained.

Can't we get an evac to the main dome?

Apparently not, senator. Without fighter support the Separatist mecha is bringing down most air transport.

Shit! We can't just sit here and wait to be captured. Been there and done that, got the freaking t-shirt. I'm not spending time in a Separatist prison or getting us tortured to death. Moore rubbed his nose and eyes with a thumb and forefinger as he let out a short sigh. There had to be something he could do besides sitting around with his thumbs up his ass.

The Marine AIC says the best bet for civilians is to hold tight.

Did you explain to them who I am? Did you explain to

them what would happen to us if the Separatists take us captive?

Yes.

Shit.

Yes, sir. Shit.

All right, tell them we are coming to them and not to leave us. Moore had made up his mind. Sitting around couldn't be the safest thing to do. *Download me as detailed a set of maps of Mons City as you can get. I mean down to the architectural and engineering drawings if you can get them. Street maps, tunnels, sewers, power conduits, everything. And get me the coordinates for the evac ship.*

Yes, senator. But with the global down, I'm not too optimistic on the maps.

Just do what you can. Try the local library.

Senator, the Marine AIC says that you should stay put.

Abbey, I don't take orders from the Marines and haven't for a long damned time. You tell them that we are not going to sit around here to be taken hostage. We are coming to them if they can't get to us!

Yes senator.

Alexander glanced around the adventure store at the adrenaline junkie paraphernalia available. Then he thought of his wife and daughter being tortured to make him do and say things he shouldn't, which is exactly what the grunt Separatists would do to him if they caught him here. Who knows, they might just torture and kill them all three for show like they did poor Congresswoman Zander on Kuiper Station. The gruesome video of them chopping her hands, then arms, and then legs off with a laser welder flashed in his mind for a split second. The welder cauterized her wounds so she didn't bleed to death and the Seppy doctor administered adrenaline to her to keep her conscious. Then finally, Elle Ahmi appeared on video, in that descript long brown hair trailing out from under her red white and blue ski mask, and doused the poor congresswoman in alcohol. Ahmi then calmly and nonchalantly set her on fire.

No sir, he was not going to let that happen to his wife and daughter! Though he didn't expect Elle Ahmi would be a problem. Nobody had heard from her since the assault on the Belt three years ago. There were rumors that Ahmi was dead or left the system. But whoever was leading this faction of the Separatists would be just as nasty for certain. Alexander knew they had to escape.

But there was no way to cover the tens of kilometers to the evac point in time. The roads were likely destroyed, blocked, or any traffic on them being shot. Stealing a hovercar was probably not a good idea. Flying was out. Any vehicle using that much power would set off all sorts of sensors. *Think Major Moore! What would a good Marine do?*

Alexander picked up a pair of jumper hiking boots, and began eyeing the gliderchutes on the far wall of the store. *Abigail, is there a way to get to the outside top of the dome?*

Perhaps, senator. I will see what I can find out.

"Reyez, my good man, have you ever done any base-gliding off the dome?" He grinned at the store manager while trying to ignore the look his wife was giving him.

Oorah! He thought.

Chapter 5

"Oorah!!! Take that you goddamned Seppy motherfuckers!" Sergeant Clay Jackson shouted as he brought down three support troops for a drop tank about seven hundred meters down Lowell Street, the last rounds from his railgun punching through the Separatist armored environment suits with little effort. Jackson could see one of the enemy soldier's mid section splatter red against the brick behind him and then fall forward dead. The return fire that had been chewing up the street and building behind him finally ceased. He looked down the side at the garbage truck he was perched on and saw several railgun pellet entry holes. The wall of the building behind the truck was blown to pieces. Fortunately, the drop tank hadn't taken him seriously, yet. He had only had to deal with the ground troops.

"Sergeant Jackson!" the Marine Second Lieutenant Thomas Washington called out over the deafening crunching and whirling sounds of the collapsing sky rise building down the street. Dust plumes and a rolling cloud of debris washed down the main street of the southern borough of Mons City. He looked over the body of Private Allfrey as he knelt by him.

Shit! Shit! Shit! He thought to himself as he gathered the private's ammo and ordinance, snapping the containers on the pack belt of his armored e-suit. The dust filling the air from the crashing buildings blocked out most of the sunlight and the small white light diode lamps of the suit helmet cast a cold still deathly hue on the dead private's face and the red blood oozing from the corners of his mouth.

Sir, the VIP thinks he is going to come to us. The young officer's AIC, Second Lieutenant Tammie One Niner Seven Oscar Hotel Three Three alerted him.

Shit, what does the idiot think he is doing? Tell him I said to stay put.

I did, sir. He says he doesn't take orders from the Marines.

Goddamnit all to hell! Where is it he thinks he's going?

To the evac point, sir. The AIC replied.

Evac point. Shit again! That is ten or fifteen clicks from us! Has to be forty or fifty or more for them.

He says they will be there, sir.

Goddamnit.

Yes sir. Goddamnit. The AIC agreed with her counterpart.

"Sir!" Sergeant Clay Jackson squawked back over the net without letting up on the trigger of the hypervelocity automatic railgun (HVAR). The lieutenant could hear the *spitap spitap spitap* of the railgun fire over the net. The standard issue firearm tracked small three millimeter diameter maximum density packed pellets of carbon and aluminum atoms at near one percent the speed of light across the street, leaving whirlwinds and pockets of inflow in the rolling smoke that filled the street along with a faintly glowing ionization trail acting as a tracer.

The pellets impacted and cut through the building four hundred meters north. Larger debris was flung wildly from the pellet impacts while near the actual impact point the building materials were vaporized in a green fluorescent flash, leaving a hole the size of an e-suit helmet. On the other side of the building is where his sensors were predicting one of the Seppy drop tank's trajectories would end. Jackson's hope was to put such a shit storm where that Seppy tank wanted to be that it would either get killed or fly away. Jackson preferred the former, but as long as it left him the fuck alone he didn't really give a rat's ass.

The noise of the Separatist drop mecha force had been drowned out momentarily by the collapsing buildings to the east and the cutting away of the building to the north by Jackson's HVAR. The smoke and debris from the battle, the crash of the *Winston Churchill*, and the collapsed buildings were heavy, but the gaping hole in the dome about ten kilometers to the south of them was pulling the gas and debris clouds due to the differential pressures and the airflow channels through the city buildings and then out into the Martian atmosphere. War was not necessarily bad for terraforming but it sucked royal for whoever had been in that dome when the supercarrier hit. Second Lieutenant Washington didn't think too highly of it at the moment either. The city was a deathtrap with Seppy bastards scurrying everywhere like termites or angry bees.

"Jackson, that building is creating so much dust we can't see a damned thing. Nothing on IR either. Can you see anything from your vantage point?" Second Lieutenant Washington asked over the direct link he was keeping open with the sergeant. Once Captain Fasim bought it at the insertion point where the transport was shot down the second lieutenant had assumed command. But he kept the link to the NCO open at all times in case Jackson had any "advice."

Unfortunately, Master Sergeant Sarah Nathan had bought it when the Captain did, so the squad's new NCO was an E5 and was almost as new as its lieutenant. The two of them had seen action, serious action, on Triton together, but they weren't the seasoned Marines that the captain and the master sergeant had been.

"No sir, I can't see a goddamned fucking iota. We are sitting goddamned ducks here, sir. If I were a Seppy bastard, I'd be coming in on the other side of that shit with guns blazing ready to cut us to fuckin' hamburger." Jackson scanned the area again with all his passive systems afraid to go active as "homers" might lock onto him. *What a goddamned mess!*

I agree, sarge! Jackson's AIC Corporal Susan Seven Seven Seven Niner Mike Bravo One replied.

"I agree with the sergeant, sir." Tammie, the second lieutenant's AIC voiced over the net so both could hear. "Still no word from CMTOC. Only the local QM coms are working. Nothing longer range than about sixty kilometers is working. I've daisy-chained a com patch through various local hubs to the Marines on the north side of the dome and one to an Army unit on the west side, but they are taking heavier losses than us. No word at all from the 34th." Somehow the Seppies had managed to jam every communications system except for local quantum membrane (QM) transceivers. The smaller QMs were limited somewhat in range.

"Yeah, without any support or word from HQ we keep pushing on with the mission at hand. There is nothing more we can do for the VIP other than hope he makes it to the evac himself. So, we need to see if we can't slow down the Seppy advance through this city and somehow get to that evac point in time to get ourselves out and give the VIP some cover if he gets there. Ideas?" Washington asked.

"We need better cover sir," the sergeant responded.

Yeah, and a fucking miracle, Washington thought to himself. His AIC didn't respond.

Sergeant Jackson thought up a different display on his visor that showed his fellow "misguided children" as blue dots on the overlay map of the city. An explosion dropped another building about two clicks north of him and two of the blue dots blinked out. Corporal Gomez and Private Sauro had bought it the hard way—death by falling skyscraper. *Fuck!* No doubt a black and blue dot showed up back at the Casualty Management and Tactical Operations Center or CMTOC (pronounced "simtoc")—wherever the hell that was.

They were getting picked off little by little. What had started out as a rescue mission of twelve lightly armored troops was now down to Sergeant Jackson, Privates Packer and Kufad, Corporal Shelly, and the second lieutenant—more than fifty percent casualties so far. But, their mission changed from rescuing some fat-assed VIP to holding the city after they had been deployed. To start with, they were not equipped for the mission and they were *way* outnumbered. Then things went to hell in a hand basket once the squad started taking on heavy casualties. Surprise attacks were that way, but by God, the United States Marine Corp, a.k.a. Uncle Sam's Misguided Children, didn't train for whining about their situation. It trained Marines to make the best out of a really shitty situation and to kill as many of the rat-bastard enemy motherfuckers as possible before they kill you! *Semper Fi!*

"Shit! Sir?" Jackson commented to the loss of the two troops. The sergeant's AIC began running an inventory list of available equipment from the remaining troops. At the same time, the lieutenant's AIC, Tammie, began recalculating battle plans and running force-on-force simulations. There were way too many red forces compared to blue for the AIC's taste and none of the simulations turned out . . . well.

"I saw it, Sarge. I'm tired of this sitting around and waiting shit. We can't hold this position and I'm with you. As soon as that dust plume gets to us we are done for. Our reinforcements may not ever be coming either. And the backup evac is still four hours off." The second lieutenant scanned through his maps of the southern borough again.

"What do you want to do, sir?"

"Those buildings are falling because the Seppies are there. Sergeant, I say we take some of this fuckin' mess to them for a change."

"Oorah! Sir!" Jackson was tired of waiting too. Like any good Marine he didn't like sitting around with his thumbs up his ass and waiting to get smashed to hell and gone, especially over some fat-assed politician, which was the reason they had been deployed into this shit storm in the first place.

"Goddamned Seppies are turning the south borough into a killing field of raining skyscrapers. I wonder just who the hell they are trying to kill?" The second lieutenant said matter-of-factly.

"Probably survivors of the *Churchill*, if there were any. Orders, sir?" The sergeant buzzed back over the net.

"Okay." The lieutenant thought a few commands bringing the remaining members of the squad online and putting a map on their displays. "We are going to take cover in the smoke all the way out of the dome. Tammie is modeling and updating the fluid flow dynamics of this shit through the city. We follow the predicted flow path down these side streets." Streets on the map started highlighting in green to show the path. "If it changes she'll update the map. And we stay quiet and check fire until we are on top of the mecha. Once there we'll drop some shit on their Seppy asses and then run like hell out of the dome. Got it?"

"Oorah!" resounded from Jackson, Packer, Kufad, and Shelly.

"You heard the Lieutenant," Sergeant Jackson said. "Kufad, you and Shelly are too far north of us to take this side of the plume. Make way down Tharsis View Drive and rendezvous with us at Dome Circle. Follow the streets Tammie maps for you. From there we'll make through the debris at Aureole Road if there ain't too many Seppies in the way. Looks like Aureole will take us right to the edge of the dome. If there ain't a hole there we'll make one. Keep your goddamned heads down! And move."

"Oorah."

Sergeant Jackson slithered backwards to the edge of the garbage truck he had been using for a vantage point. The truck had been such an unusual sight at first that he had to check it out. Every other vehicle and building along the street had been toppled or otherwise rendered useless and damaged by the blast of the supercarrier crash. But the oversized heavy garbage truck was sitting amongst the debris untouched. It had made a decent cover and vantage point but it was time to go.

He sprang himself over the side of the tall vehicle and landed with a *kathunk* on the fractured and debris strewn sidewalk. The jumpers in his armored boots softened the landing and he used the gained energy to launch himself more than thirty meters down the alleyway towards the lieutenant's position. The long arc he made in the low Martian gravity brought him high enough to see over some of the debris and smoke down various alleyways and streets. Enough sunlight filtered through and refracted off the dust pouring a faint red hue over the cityscape. Being above the heavy smoke made Jackson feel nervous; since he was above the cover of the cloud he felt naked and visible—vulnerable to Seppy sensors. He decided to shorten the height of his leaps and lengthen the breadth of them instead from then on.

Each step with the jumper boots added to his own strength allowing him to cover a half of a kilometer block in about thirty seconds, Jackson carefully picked each step so that each time he landed it was in a shadow-covered section of the alleyway—a trick he had learned the hard way in the Triton campaigns the year before. He also made certain to stay either below debris and building level or below the dust cloud height.

"Packer, where the hell are you?" Jackson could see the blue dot overlaid on the map in his visor. The private's blue dot was practically overlaid upon his own, but Jackson could not see the private anywhere.

"Oorah!" Private Jessica Packer bounded a few meters to the sergeant's right and then back upward out of sight.

"Goddamnit Packer, I nearly shot your ass! Next time I might not be so restrained." The motion startled the sergeant for a microsecond. Then he had his AIC reset the resolution of his maps to show altitude detail. The map quickly jumped from his visor to his mind. Three-dimensional active maps were better displayed directly to the brain. They were easier to understand that way. Jackson tracked the private now that he had figured out what she was doing. She was using the buildings as springboards and jumping from a building wall on one side of the street to one on the other rather than ever landing on the street, another tactic learned from having been shot at before. The unit had seen its share of action over the last year.

Sergeant Jackson, on the other hand, liked having ground underneath his feet. Call him old fashioned or afraid of heights, but he thought walking, running, and jumping was best done from the ground. Besides, after he fell through that building on Triton and into the midst of a Seppy shit storm he didn't care to bounce on them anymore unless he had to, absolutely had to. The two Marines continued down the alleyway, covering each other as best they could while making toward the smoke plume. A couple of times they had to cover and freeze as Seppy mecha flew overhead. This slowed them down a bit.

Lieutenant Washington was still somewhere a quarter of a click or so ahead of them and from the map in the sergeant's mind he could tell that the lieutenant was using the building tactic the same as Private Packer. The sergeant could hear the enemy tanks and troops from time to time and could occasionally see dust plumes from their movement, but the passive sensors of his armored e-suit were picking up nothing. Nothing! They were being jammed by some fancy equipment. Either that or the Seppies had developed a new stealth encryption that rendered the QM sensors useless. Jackson didn't like it. He may have only been an E5 but he knew a rat when he smelled one. Even on Triton the QM sensors worked. *How could the Seppies have that kind of technology?*

Jackson and Packer continued carefully bouncing through the city toward Dome Circle, the map in their heads showing five blue dots converging. Dome Circle was the largest driving circle in the Solar System. Fourteen different roads converged on the ten-lane circle that was about seventy meters in diameter. Several lanes formed from overpasses above it and two from underground. The lanes twisted and turned until they smoothly dumped out onto the circle. In the middle of the driving circle was a twenty-meter tall monument to Sienna Madira, the one hundred and eleventh President of the United States and the first from Mars. The great lady was also the leader of the Martian Marauders who stopped the first wave of civil war in the Tharsis Montes region of the planet.

Sergeant Jackson and Private Packer held their position on the edge of the driving circle's eight o'clock position, taking shelter under the pillars of one of the overpasses. Jackson had spotted the second lieutenant about thirty meters to their right in the mouth of one of the tunnels just south of the six o'clock spot. According to the map in his head, Corporal Shelly and Private Kudaf were on the far side of the circle approaching the two o'clock position. Unfortunately, the smoke clouds were being pulled through the circle with cyclonic force and whirled such a mass of debris and dust that there was no seeing past the statue in the middle. Using radar was out of the question.

"Lieutenant, Packer and Jackson are in position."

"Roger that, sarge," the lieutenant replied.

"Incoming!" Shelly called over the net. "Goddamnit Kootie, get the fuck down!"

"Corporal Shelly! What's going on?" the lieutenant called back over the rapid HVAR fire sounds coming through the net. "Everybody converge on Shelly and Kudaf! Move!"

"Mecha, sir! We've got mecha everywhere!"

Chapter 6

"Holy shit! There's mecha all over the place! Where did they get that much mecha? Jesus, the Seppies have been busy." Lieutenant Commander Boland dropped his bombing run load over the mass of Seppy drop tanks that were wreaking havoc on the Fleet's ground assault forces. The attack on the far side dome farms of Elysium was going as planned although the resistance was considerably higher than the Fleet had expected.

Although the sun had long set, the mecha was easily detected with the IR and QM sensors. The curious thing to Jack was how did the Seppies build or acquire so much mecha without the orbiting reconnaissance platforms detecting them? Even if the factories were underground there would be tale-tale signs that the orbiting sensor stations would have uncovered over the years.

"You still hanging in back there, ma'am?" He pulled the Ares fighter into a roll-out to avoid surface-to-air fire from one of the tanks. Flak *spitanged* off the shield

73

plating and shook the fighter harshly, giving Jack and Nancy wild jerks and shudders even after on-board systems implemented the inertial compensation field.

"How much further to the drop site?" Nancy asked through gritted teeth. Her knuckles were white from gripping the safety restraints on the back seat of the little fighter-bomber. Of course, her AIC knew exactly how far it was to the drop site, but she had to show some sign of coherence or the lieutenant commander might think she was unconscious or dead and not carry through with the mission.

She had to make it past Elysium, the edge of the Martian Separatist region that Sienna Madira had forced the civil disobedient citizens to retreat and live in into Phlegra or perhaps Propontis, two of the major untouched Separatist stronghold cities deeper within the Reservation. And her mission was to figure out just where the hell the Separatists had been getting all of their recent military build-up from and who was supporting them under the covers—and how.

Thirty years ago, an inspection team would have just flown into the region to see what the hell was going on. But that was before Elle Ahmi in her descript red, white, and blue ski mask, long brown hair, Martian desert camouflage, and black fingernails had appeared as if from nowhere as the new terrorist leader and set a fire in the bellies of all the Separatists of the Sol System and perhaps even in the other colonies as well. Nobody was quite certain what Ahmi looked like without the mask, but the various intelligence agencies had been working the problem for three decades.

Once Ahmi became the undisputed leader of the Separatist Union she gave any non-Separatist two Earth days to leave the north region of Mars from Elysium all the way up to Propontis, and then the Seppies began a cleansing effort the likes of which mankind had never seen. The cleansing wasn't genetic; it was philosophical. The Seppy troops used special AICs allegedly developed by Ahmi herself to determine the thought patterns of the Separatist citizens. If they were sympathetic to the U.S. they were fried on the spot—literally fried, doused in oil and set aflame. Fire seemed to be a preferred ritual execution method with the Seppies.

Mankind had often imagined a "thought police," but the day had finally come when over four hundred thousand people were murdered because of the thoughts in their heads. What it had left in the Reservation was a core million or so of pure Separatist zealot U.S. haters. And after thirty or so years of polygamous procreation the projected population of the Reservation was around eleven million fighting age adults and twenty million children. Of course, the Seppies considered an adult to be fourteen Earth years old. All thirty one million of them were most certainly pure Separatist brainwashed zealots. Allison, Nancy's AIC, had been training almost all of her life to overcome and fool the "thought police". Hopefully, the AI CIA agent was up to the challenge.

The administration at the time thirty years prior was too spineless and public poll driven to send the full military might in and stop the Separatist cleansing. Instead, the damned politicians had an insufficient number of troop divisions dropped into the Reservation borders expecting the Separatists to turn and run or bow down to the military might of the United States military. It was a massacre instead.

There were only a few Marines from the Luna City Brigade that even survived the conflict. Entire Army mecha platoons were lost and the artillery was completely overrun and destroyed. Due to political reasons air support wasn't used. Had the campaign been run from space instead, history might have turned out a lot different. But as history had unfolded, the last thirty years had been a mess of war, uncomfortable peace, and "skirmishes" that from any sane frame of reference were battles of a continuous war effort.

The handfuls of Marines that did survive the original Desert Campaigns had been captured and had spent years in prisoner of war camps before they were released back to the U.S. government officials at the Elysium Embassy. Since then, the Separatists had fiercely guarded their borders. They conducted business negotiations at the Elysium Embassy or in Mons City but never within the Reservation. Outsiders were simply not allowed within the borders of the Separatists' country—ever. And, they had been receiving support from somewhere, but from where?

"We are still another three hundred kilometers west of the drop zone ma'am. We'll be there lickety-split." *If we don't get killed first*, he thought.

SAM Commander! The lieutenant Commander's AIC warned of the approaching surface-to-air missile.

Got it, Candis!

"Hold on! Uuuunnnnnnggggghhhh . . . aaaaaarrrrrrr . . .

hhhhuuuoooooooowww!" Jack squeezed every muscle in his body to force blood to his brain as the fighter took evasive maneuvers from the surface-to-air missile rapidly encroaching on their personal space. Candis automatically released countermeasures, but they were too late. The countermeasures triggered the missile detonation too close to the fighter, rocking it hard yaw to the right. The shield plating held but the fighter, was tossed into a flat spin.

"Unnnnnnnhhhhhh . . . aaaaaaarrrrr . . . wwooooooohh!" Jack screamed another grunt and pulled the HOTAS (hands-on throttle and stick) controls full back, which didn't help at all.

"Aaaaaaaaarrrrrrr . . . wwwoooooohhhh . . . hhhhuuuu-uuoooooooowww!" he continued to grunt as the fighter whirled helplessly out of control spinning its occupants at mind bending g-force levels.

"Yaaaaaaaaaaaaaa!" Nancy let out a panicked cry as the world around her began to tunnel in. She could see a dim light at the end of the tunnel way off in the distant.

Nancy! Nancy Penzington! Breathe, two, three, grunt! Allison screamed in the CIA operative's mind.

"HOTAS full forward, Jack!" Candis said over the speakers and into his mind at the same time. *"Full Forward on the HOTAS!"*

"Warning unsafe g-loading . . ." the fighter's "Bitching Betty" voice blasted over the cockpit speakers.

"No shiiittt!" Jack grunted.

The Ares fighter was built tougher than any fighter craft mankind had ever managed, but even it could only take so many gees before the wings ripped off. As the fighter rolled within its now tumbling spin Jack could see lights high in the horizon that must be the Phlegra Montes in the distance. He sure as hell didn't want to see them any closer. Ares fighters had been flown into mountains before—the mountains always won.

"Ggggooodddammnittt . . . unnnnnhhhh . . . aaaalllll toooo helll!" Jack forced the HOTAS as hard forward as his g-loaded arms would allow. His AIC began automated recovery controls and between the two of them the tumbling spin began to dampen out. Jack eased back on the stick and grunted again to force more blood back into his brain.

"Shit that was close!" he said. The fighter righted itself and he pushed it full throttle forward to put more distance between themselves and the SAMs.

"If I'm going to get killed, Jack, I'd prefer it be after I'd actually started my mission." Nancy grunted and panted for breath. She was slowly regaining her sight back from the momentary tunnel that had been closing in on her, caused by the massive g-forces the evasive maneuvers and the tumbling spin had imposed on them. *Nancy had to complete her mission.*

One would wonder why not just drop in from space on the Reservation rather than taking such a circuitous and extremely dangerous route. That *had* been tried by at least seven agents over the last decade. A few had tried just walking in and several had tried going in through transports from Kuiper Station. None had ever reported back.

Nancy worked with analysts for more than four years to determine the best plan of action for getting into the

Separatists' trust, and there really wasn't a good solution. The brightest boys back at CIA headquarters deep underground in McLean, Virginia, were still baffled why they lost contact with the other operatives. But this mission plan was different. Nancy had confidence in it. If the plan worked right she would appear to be a survivor from the first deep attack within Separatist borders in decades. The missile silos and factories along the western side of the Phlegra Mountains were about to be toast. Hopefully, so would most records of the people from that region. Nancy then could join the survivors fleeing the attacks and moving further inward over the mountains and into Phlegra City on the eastern side of the mountains. It would succeed. *But isn't that what all the other agents had thought before their missions?*

Everything had to look real, had to be real, and there was nothing more real than a sortie in the middle of a war. As the battle raged, pushing into the periphery of the Separatist Reservation, the hopes were that some misplaced Separatists could be replaced, joined, or infiltrated. And Jack had a "special surprise" under the belly of his little snub-nosed Ares swept wing fighter that would add to the confusion. A small twenty-kiloton tactical nuke should render enough confusion for most, and then some. Once the missile base was "softened" then a second wave of fighters would follow behind Jack by exactly twenty-seven minutes. The time wasn't an arbitrary choice; four years of simulations suggested it to be the best delay for mission success. Nancy would have very little time to get to ground, cover her tracks, and join up with survivors moving eastward through the mountain chain.

Jack held the HOTAS gently and continued to push the fighter to full speed. The g-forces weighed heavy on Nancy and she was more than ready to get her feet back on the ground. Jack, on the other hand, was in his element. In a dark and testosterone filled sort of way, he had even enjoyed the tumbling spin and recovery, but only in as much as it hadn't killed them.

Nancy scanned the area through the QM sensors as they passed over the Phlegra plains. The giant conifer trees of the plains could just barely be discerned with QM sensors after dark and at that altitude and velocity it took a trained analyst or a computer with special sensors and algorithms to find them. The trees were there and as they approached the mountains were increasing in number.

Jack, we are approaching the target zone, Candis said.

Roger, that. Prepare arming sequence, authorization Boland, one, one, three, one, four, alpha.

Arming sequence verified and target has been acquired, sir.

"Ok, Penzington, we are about to lower the boom. Prepare yourself for deployment," Jack said, smiling at her in the rearview.

"Thanks, Jack. Let's get the show on the road, hey?" Nancy returned the smile.

Nancy, you should take your injection now. Allison reminded her.

Right.

Nancy pulled the radiation dose treatment from her breast pocket and unsheathed one of the one-centimeter long needles. She pulled back an armor plate on her left thigh and slid the needle through the puncture seal layer into her leg muscle. The needle quickly made a hissing noise and then clicked. Nancy pulled the needle from her leg and watched as the puncture seal filled the tiny hole in her suit leg. She replaced the armor and then squinted her eyes and gritted her teeth as the serum began working its way through her body, causing her ears to ring and her eyes to sting. The ringing in her ears got louder, the stinging in her eyes worsened, and her head began to pound like a repulsorhammer.

"We've got a good target lock and are ready to go on Hellstorm missile," Jack said into the coms.

"Roger that one three three. You are authorized to go Hellstorm," replied a voice over the net.

Jack depressed the fire button and the little missile zipped out from under the starboard swept wing of the fighter. The missile cleared the fighter and then accelerated toward a moderate Separatist city outpost a few tens of kilometers from Phlegra. Nancy watched as the missile contrail traced its trajectory downward into the periphery of the Separatist Reservation as deep as any U.S. vessel had ever made it before. The propellantless propulsion system of the missile whizzed it through the Martian atmosphere, creating a faint blue ion trail that tracked behind the missile all the way to the target.

Multiple SAMs and heavy AA fire, Jack!

Evasives, Candis! He yanked and banked at the HOTAS.

"Nancy, this is as far as I go! Time to make your exit. Good luck," Jack yelled as he banked the fighter left then right. Then he pulled straight up to gain as much altitude for Nancy's deployment as he could manage in the anti-aircraft fire.

"Roger that, Boland. Thanks for the lift. You take care of yourself. Retracting rear ejection portal!" Nancy said as the canopy above her slid backwards into the aircraft's fuselage, leaving an open circle above her head. The airflow was dampened some by the inertial dampening field but the noise and pounding from the Martian air was debilitating.

"See ya, Jack! Eject, eject, eject!" Nancy hit the ejection switch and then depressed the handle.

The miniature catapult field system ejected her upward and out of the Ares fighter at over four hundred kilometers per hour into the cold Martian night sky. The inertial dampening field and the e-suit protected her from the harsh g-forces and the Martian environment—the flack and anti-aircraft fire was another matter all together. Nancy spun wildly for a couple of microseconds and then the seat released itself from her and the inertial dampening was no longer available to her. For a brief instant she felt as if she would be torn asunder but the atmosphere quickly dampened her motion to critical velocity, which was much more tolerable. Just as she began to gain her wits a brilliant flash filled the sky about thirty kilometers to her north.

The mushroom cloud rose to a perfect round peak with a bright red and yellow fireball filling it. Rings of dust and smoke encircled the stem of the mushroom cloud and rose upward until they collided with the head of it at the forming and rising fireball. Nancy could see the shock wave spread out surrounding the blast area. She continued to fall toward the surface and stabilized her skydiving position. *Focus*, she thought.

Nancy, shockwave in three, two, one! Allison warned.

The shockwave hit with high velocity but with low pressure at that altitude. Low pressure or not, it was plenty of force to send Nancy tumbling in a wildly chaotic uncontrolled fall. She fought the g-forces of the spin by spreading her body out as flat as she could to slow the neck-jarring tumble. With a few adjustments of leg and arm positions and the arch of her back, she managed to right herself into a flat spin and then into a skydiver's prone falling position.

Engage the gliderchute! Nancy thought to her AIC.

Gliderchute engaged. Allison replied and the harness around her waist and shoulders yanked her tight and Nancy's diving descent rapidly averted from a downward plunge to a slow sauntering enjoyable glide. Nancy shook her head and squinted her eyes until she regained her senses.

IR and QM, she thought to the suit's sensor array. The night vision system kicked in with a big white saturated bright spot over the target zone. The nuclear blast over the outpost was still too hot to view directly. *Allison, adjust the contrast nonlinearly on the hot spot please,* she thought to the AIC.

Right away. Tree detection system is active and will be marked in the view, the AIC replied.

Good. Overlay latest map on the view, also.

Roger that.

Any pedestrian or vehicle motion? Nancy asked. The AIC ran motion detection and change detection algorithms searching for any flickers of motion within the view of their sensors that might appear something other than random motion. There were no telltale signs of motion with a purpose.

None.

Nancy guided the gliderchute through the now chaotic winds of the aftermath of the explosion. There were occasional whirlwinds and updrafts that would alter her course and cause problems with the gliderchute harness cords, but she managed to stay on course and avoid the chute being ripped away. As the gliderchute fell through the Martian night and closer to the now devastated mountain basal city, Nancy caught a glimpse of Phobos to her south and just above the faded and scattering mushroom shaped dust cloud. There must have been a high altitude jet stream moving southward she surmised from the southward stretching misshapen mushroom cloud. She spiraled her flight path southward around the edge of the total destruction zone and closed in on her landing target zone.

Radiation dose is growing rapidly but still within the parameters of the injection, Nancy, Allison informed her.

Mm hmm, Nancy thought as she checked the altimeter readout on her visor. She was at five kilometers above the westernmost part of the total destruct zone, flying southward and counterclockwise around the periphery of the aftermath of the nuclear explosion. The sight was anything but tranquil or serene. The fires raged across the outpost city and secondary explosions triggered from gas mains or escaping oxygen from domes every few seconds. To the north in the distance Nancy could see occasional AA fire and missile contrails. The fighting was getting closer. Time was getting short.

Her plan was to bleed off altitude and drop into the eastern edge of the moderate destruct zone at the three o'clock position. She put the gliderchute in a slip and checked her tree detection system. The Martian conifer trees could reach as high as three hundred meters tall so they could cause problems when gliderchuting at night. But her detection system was functioning perfectly. There were just no trees or buildings of much concern. The blast had taken care of that. It had taken care of other things too.

There was very little activity beneath her, the AA fire that had tracked the Ares fighter that brought her had stopped once the nuke detonated, and she could see nothing in the local vicinity flying. The electromagnetic pulse and just general mayhem due to the devastating tactical nuclear device had done their job and disabled the local perimeter sensors of the Reservation periphery mountain city defenses. This allowed Nancy to slip in undetected— the plan had been carefully calculated for years. It was all working well, so far. Detonating a small nuke just to infiltrate the Reservation might have seemed like overkill, but all the recent intelligence suggested that bad things were on the horizon from within the Seppy homeland and the CIA needed to know just what those bad things were. After all, the president had approved the plan, including the tactical nuke.

Nancy kept a close eye on the altimeter reading—one thousand meters and dropping. The moderate destruct region of the city surrounding the Separatist missile base looked anything but moderate. The shockwave from the blast had strewn debris to and fro and fires raged in almost every direction. She looked for a dark spot with no fires but they were few and far between. Altimeter reading— six hundred meters and dropping.

There! She thought as she spotted a dark spot in the flames. *Allison, zoom in there.* She pointed.

Got it. The AIC zoomed in on the dark region and increased the sensitivity levels of the QM sensor suite of her e-suit helmet. Then the spike detector went off.

"What the . . . " Nancy muttered to herself.

Trees. Allison responded matter-of-factly.

Why aren't they burning then?

Who knows? Blast dynamics are weird that way. Allison explained.

Well, whatever. It looks like a park. Those buildings there to the west must have shielded them. Trees around the periphery and a flat field in the middle, looks like a jumperball field, I think. This should do nicely, Nancy thought and brought the gliderchute into a tight spiral over the field, careful of the trees as her altitude was now dropping to treetop height. She spiraled inside the circumference of the circular field and increased the illumination of the IR and QM sensors, her night vision visor, at full intensity. The ground was coming up fast. Altimeter reading was at one hundred meters . . . fifty . . . twenty . . .

Nancy hit her IR diode helmet lights and the ground lit up beneath her just in time for her to flare the gliderchute and stop her descent about one meter from the surface. The gliderchute caught some last minute ground effect turbulence and jostled her around, causing her to lose balance. The left wing of the chute dipped and then jerked upward again. Nancy was tossed forward and slammed into the Martian ground, very, very hard.

Shrub-grass, she thought as she saw it dragging under her helmet visor a couple of centimeters from her nose. The chords of the gliderchute twisting and turning in the wind and dragging her through the clearing while the chute continued to billow in the eastward and chaotic winds overpowered her senses for a brief moment. Nancy's speed picked up across the small circular plane's floor as she was dragged face down. She managed to pop the harness from her left shoulder strap allowing her to roll over onto her back. The harness still held her from the right shoulder and the waist and the chute pulled hard on her rotator cuff straining her shoulder muscles to keep her arm in place.

Nancy fought against the wild jumbling ride with her free hand, managing to stay on her back, but having little luck releasing the right side harness fasteners. She could feel painful impacts against her back but the e-suit's armor protected her from anything serious. Then she saw a tree several meters in diameter streak by her head only a meter or so away. She fought panic because she knew that if she hit a tree trunk at the speeds she was being dragged it could be fatal, especially, if her head hit the tree first.

Knife, Nancy! Your knife! Allison screamed in her mind.

Nancy quickly squelched her panic and set about the business at hand. Another tree, near miss. Then another. But Nancy had unsheathed her knife from the left shoulder scabbard and was slicing away at the harness on her right. It gave way, leaving only the attachment at her hip. She sliced at it with one quick motion and then the gliderchute pulled free of her and whisked away with the wind out of sight into the dark Martian night. Nancy rolled over onto her stomach and slammed the knife blade, her free hand, and toes into the grass to slow her to a stop.

Completely still, Nancy did a quick assessment of her body and decided nothing was permanently damaged. *Minor bruises*, she thought as she rolled over. There were no stars above her. Between her and the sky was a canopy of conifer trees and beyond that was smoke, dust, and radioactive fallout all glowing in the eerie orange and red tint of the burning city. Nancy stood and dusted herself off and then sheathed her knife. About fifty meters away she could see the remains of her gliderchute tangled high in a conifer tree.

Now that's a pain in the ass, she thought. *How the hell am I going to get up there?*

Too high for jumper boots, Allison said.

Chapter 7

"Well, it is too damned high for jumper boots. How do you expect to get up there?" Sehera shrugged her shoulders and pointed at the dome ceiling nearly a half of a kilometer high above them.

"The maintenance shaft will take you to the exhaust system about two-thirds the way up the dome," Reyez Jones, the adventure store manager said. "I've jumped from there before. But I've never jumped from the absolute top of the dome before. Not sure how to get up there. There is a twenty-meter high electric fence that surrounds the peak of the dome. I've tried to figure out how to get over it, but had no luck. The dome is too slick to use jumper boots to get over it. I'm not sure why the fence is there either."

Abigail? How far will two-thirds of the way get us? Senator Alexander Moore asked his AI staffer.

It will put you a good ten kilometers short, senator. But with jumpers that is not such a bad run, the AI thought.

"It'll have to do. Who is with us? You can either stay here and be captured when this city is overrun, or you can go with my wife, daughter, and myself," he asked the cadre of tourists taking refuge in the shop. The only takers were Reyez and a woman from Triton, Joanie Hassed, who had seen first hand what the Separatist soldiers were like. The remaining tourists couldn't believe that Mons City would fall for even the briefest moment. The two assistant managers of the shop, Rod and Vince, had raided a package store next door for food and beverages and were well on their way to being completely inebriated. They were going nowhere. The others were debating on finding the nearest shelter or just staying put in the adventure store.

"The U.S. Navy will take care of us," the little fat man that Deanna had stuck her tongue out at earlier replied. He stuffed chips in his mouth through the open visor and then sipped at a *Mons Light*.

"Hear, hear! To the Navy!" Rod and Vince held their beer bottles up in toast to the Navy.

"Though I prefer the Air Force," Rod replied as he tilted his bottle again and took a swig.

"Yeah, you were in for what, six weeks?" his coworker goaded him.

"Hey, it was a medical." Rod sneered and tried to think of a better comeback, but taking another swig from his beer was the best he could manage.

"Suit yourselves." Senator Moore didn't really care for the extra baggage of tourists and drunks anyway. "We're going."

Reyez, Alexander, and Sehera packed the gliderchutes

under Reyez's instruction. Alexander had made hundreds of jumps decades ago, but these were new civilian systems and he was smart enough to listen to an expert when he had one. Reyez carefully inspected the four packs and harnesses and ran through a quick explanation how to guide them. Then there was a brief uncomfortable moment where Reyez was afraid to ask who was tandem flying the child. In Reyez's mind, there was no question that he was the only person in the group qualified to do that. Alexander caught on to the apprehension and squelched it immediately.

"Deanna rides with me," he said.

"Sir, are you sure you can handle that? I've jumped with thousands of kids in tandem before." Reyez protested.

"Listen to the man, Alexander," Sehera warned. She didn't talk that often but when she did it was always with the authority of a woman who wouldn't take no for an answer.

"No. I've got hundreds of jumps into a helluva lot worse situations. I'll take her. She's my daughter, I'll be responsible for her," he said in a tone that clearly stated the topic was no longer up for discussion. Deanna looked back and forth at her parents and never said a word. Alexander wasn't certain his daughter really grasped the magnitude of the predicament they were in, and of that he was glad.

"Okay. Let me go through the tandem harness with you, at least?"

"Absolutely." Alexander smiled a diplomatic grin. "Then let's get on with it and get the hell out of here."

★ ★ ★

"Kootie, lay down cover fire on that tank!" Sergeant Jackson shouted. The Seppy drop tanks were moving into flanking positions on the north and east sides of the driving circle. They had been staying to the smoke cloud that was being sucked from the city as cover but for some reason several tanks were hovering through the interstate system southward out of the smoke. Some were in bot mode running; the tanks were more vulnerable that way, but much more maneuverable. Occasionally, one of the tanks would fire defilading fire backwards into the cloud. Every now and then one of them would fire a mecha-to-mecha missile back into the smoke as well. It was obvious that this handful of Seppy drop mecha were running from something, and they had not expected to run into a team of U.S. Marines.

"Got it, sarge!"

"Sergeant Jackson?" the second lieutenant called over the QM wireless.

"LT?" Jackson turned the aiming and trajectory sighting computer on the Seppy drop mecha in bot mode running behind several city buildings, trying to get a flanking shot at the Marines. Sergeant Jackson's sighting system chimed and turned red on his visor screen as he depressed the trigger of the HVAR. Hypervelocity railgun rounds chewed the buildings up as they tracked across the mecha's path, intercepting it at the joint where the legs met the tank canopy. The left leg of the mecha gave way with a white hot plasma spewing explosion that in turn caused the mecha to tumble forward canopy first.

"Sarge, I can see more than a dozen or so drop tanks between our north and east flanks. We are *so* outnumbered

here. I think we're gonna have to make a run for it."
Second Lieutenant Washington said.

"Sir, let's go over 'em!" Private Packer offered. She
jumped twice and then bounced up the side of a building
and then across a side street to the top of a building to the
left, all the while tracking an enemy tank with her HVAR.
The arm of the mecha flew off in a shower of sparks and
began spewing hydraulics as the railgun fire tracked
through the now weakened armor of the canopy and
punched through the pilot.

"Packer, goddamnit, get your narrow ass back down
here!" Corporal Shelly ordered her.

Packer flipped backwards off the building onto a lower
one and then zig-zagged from one building to the next
until she bounced a few meters to the right of Kootie and
then slid prone into a cover firing position and continued
laying down cover with Kootie. The sergeant smiled and
just shook his head left and right.

"LT, that ain't necessarily a bad idea. What if we go
through 'em? They appear to be running from something." Jackson offered.

"Well, we can't stay here for long." The rubble pile that
the lieutenant was using for cover unexpectedly exploded
throwing debris and shrapnel around him at deadly
velocities. A metallic shard about a half-meter long with
concrete still attached at one end penetrated his left leg
midway between the knee and hip. The leak seal layer of
the e-suit closed off around it before his air could leak out
and before he lost too much blood.

"Jesus, fucking, goddamned, shit!" The lieutenant was
flung backwards onto the center lane of the driving circle

in the open and was overcome by the hot searing pain in his leg. He screamed madly and flailed wildly like a fish out of water, flopping on the ground for a second or two longer.

Thomas! Second Lieutenant Thomas Washington! Return fire! Second Lieutenant Thomas Washington return fire! his AIC screamed in his mind. Studies had shown that an authoritative voice using the full name and rank tended to snap soldiers out of panicked behavior. Theories were that it was conditioning learned in basic training, listening to the barking orders from drill sergeants. Whatever the reason, it worked.

"You motherfucker!" The second lieutenant pulled his HVAR up and depressed the trigger, releasing a full auto spread. The wound nearly throwing him into shock had affected his aim and he wasn't hitting any critical points of the tank, but it was enough to force the mecha to take evasive action.

"Lieutenant!" Packer leapt from her cover position forward and somersaulted in mid air above the mecha, firing the HVAR directly downward at near point blank range into the tank. The tank stopped moving and grew quiet before Packer ever bounced to ground on the other side of it. Just as her jump boots hit the ground she was cut in half by a forty millimeter cannon round from the mecha's wingman. The cannon round passed through her stomach taking out most of the vital organs of her abdomen. The malfunctioning e-suit tried to seal the wound but the gaping hole was just too large. Private Jessica Packer bled to death in seconds.

"Oh God . . . " she whispered through blood soaked

lips. Her life signs went dead and her blue force tracking signal converted to a fatal casualty location and her AIC set up a downed soldier beacon transmission to the CMTOC.

"Goddamnit!" Sergeant Jackson bounced in serpentine trajectory to the second lieutenant and swept him up as he landed beside him. With a continuing bounce he managed to dodge cannon fire and roll the two of them behind the iron statue of Sienna Madira in the middle of the driving circle. Jackson struggled to hold the lieutenant down while he grabbed the pain injection from the lieutenant's right breastpack. He unsheathed the needle, slid back the armor plate on the lieutenant's neck and jabbed the needle in. With a hiss and a click the pain medication rushed over the lieutenant's body. The sergeant tossed the needle aside, slapped the neck armor back down, and rolled his back to the statue preparing to fire.

"Shit." The second lieutenant shook his head as the pain in his leg went away. He managed to force himself to look down at the large piece of metal protruding from his armored leg. He had expected to see blood, but the seal layer closed quickly enough that none escaped out the front of his e-suit. He wasn't sure about the back side of his leg.

"Kudaf and Shelly disperse, immediately! Get out of harm's way and make for evac as best you can!" he ordered and tried to catch his breath, the pain meds and adrenaline now washing away the aftereffects of trauma and shock. Then he raised his rifle to ready.

"Well, this is just like Triton, hey, lieutenant?" Jackson said and nodded at the second lieutenant.

"I don't see how, Clay. As I recall, it was you that was

wounded and at least there the other guys had a fighting chance!" he said and rolled around to the side of the statue, careful not to bang the metal sticking out of his leg, disseminated cover fire, ducked and covered quickly, and then repeated as needed.

Tammie, is there no contact with anybody close enough to help?

None that I have been able to contact, lieutenant.

Drop mecha had them flanked and were overrunning their position quickly. The sergeant checked his visor for Corporal Shelly and Private Kudaf. From the three-dimensional map in his head he could see that they had taken to the underground tunnels on the west of the driving circle and would come up ahead of them to the northeast a few clicks well into the smoke cloud and closer to the crash site of the *Churchill*. That would put them further from the evac point.

What the hell were they thinking? Jackson crouched behind the fountain wall of the statue and eased counter-clockwise to view the north flank. He rose quickly and fired the HVAR, cutting away at another mecha. Without precise aiming, however, the railgun pellets spalled in showers of ionization on the thicker tank armor, doing little damage. The mecha on the other hand were cutting away at the iron statue and the concrete fountain with the forty-millimeter cannons fairly rapidly. The second lieutenant and the sergeant were sitting ducks waiting to be cut up and fried for dinner.

"There is the main elevator to the maintenance floor." Reyez pointed at an elevator tube more than a kilometer across the middle of the shopping district open court. The shaft was a shiny metal rectangular tube that extended upward more than thirty floors. The city opened up and spread out around it like the inside of a hotel, where the shops and offices were on the outer wall of the Open Court Mall with balconies and overhanging restaurants and shops teetering on the edge of walkways over the fishponds and greenery below. The Open Court was on the periphery of a very large Central Park.

"The maintenance floor is on the top, floor thirty-seven. There we switch to the other elevator for seven floors and then we climb a service ladder about ten meters to the dome exhaust catwalk." Reyez explained.

"Okay. Sounds good to me." Senator Moore peeked around the edge of the alleyway and looked as far down each open avenue as he could. There was no sign of any activity other than the occasional looter breaking a window of a shop and running off with an armful of something. "We stay together and as close to the building walls as we can."

"Alexander," Sehera took her daughter's hand, "I'll watch her. You should take the lead." She nodded her helmet.

"Good. Reyez, you take the rear, all right?"

"Sure, man."

"You keep a watch behind us for anything," Moore ordered him.

Abigail?

Yes sir?

Can you patch into any of the local street and security cams and track around our position for activity?

Already on it, sir. We are clear right now. Just like back in Elysium, huh?

Shit, I hope not. The senator thought. *What about the communications? Ever get anywhere with what is jamming us?*

Only one thing. There is a sporadic blip in the data rates between all of the other AIs locally and myself, but the blip seems to be causing an increase in data rate rather than an increased error rate as usually occurs with jamming.

Like that time at Tholus Summit? Moore recalled a battle from decades passed.

Exactly like it, senator. Abigail emphasized the word "exactly."

That . . . can't be. Can it? He thought about how General Ahmi had spoofed the mecha coms in the battle of the Summit by inserting a virus into the system that simply told the communications algorithms that there was no data and to shut down. The virus had been simple and ingenious. But Ahmi here? Now? That *was* unexpected.

The frequency shift is the same region of the spectrum, but I don't know where to start in order to find the frequency hopping sequence. I've got several of the casino AICs from the north dome gambling district working on cracking it. I'll keep you posted. The AIC understood that the problem was multifaceted. The spectrum hopping transmission was broadcast at a large range of different frequencies and only one or two of those frequencies would be transmitting at a time and for just a few bits of data. Then the frequency would hop to another set. In order to crack the transmission Abigail would need to determine what range of frequencies the transmission was using and in what order the transmission would hop from frequency to frequency and how often.

Good girl! I'll think on it too. Maybe she has said something in her various public rants over the years that will give us a clue to the spectrum sequence. The sequence could be generated by any random string of numbers or it could be a string of numbers that meant something. Sometimes the sequence was randomly generated by a computer but in many cases it was based on some type of code scheme so that other members of your team or cell or squad could decode it.

Alexander thought of all the latest video footage of Ahmi that had stopped about three years prior. He thought of the years in the Separatist POW camp where he and the other prisoners were tortured and had heard her rants over the intercom daily and nightly. He tried to think of everything she had ever said. Maybe something in there would help to uncover the frequency hopping sequence code.

I'll do the same. And in the meantime run a dictionary hack on it. Abigail paused for a brief moment and then continued. *Senator, there is a convoy of mecha and Separatist troops entering through an airseam on the southwest wall. It appears as if they will be on a direct coincident path with us if we don't hurry. Also, the troops to the north have been overrun and we will probably soon see more Separatist soldiers coming in from that direction . . . very soon. The gambling district AIs tell me that the north dome is basically an occupied territory.*

Got it. Time is short.

"Let's move fast, people. No telling when the Seppies

will show up." Moore nodded knowingly to his wife. She got the message and did what she could do to hurry her daughter and the Triton woman Joanie along. Alexander had begged Sehera to get an AIC in the past, which would have been beneficial at moments like this, but the Martian in her led her to have bad feelings toward AICs. After all, it was "tainted" AICs that allowed General Ahmi and her thought police to mass murder American sympathizers and Sehera had seen that as a girl. Some things from the past were hard to shake. So, visual cues, gestures, and communications over the e-suit's QM would have to do.

Alexander bounced them cautiously from one street intersection to the next and then would cross together in one jump each time. Abigail kept close monitor on the approaching troops and their little fleeing refugee pack's progress to see when and if they would converge. Unfortunately, her simulations never had them making it to the elevator before the troops got there.

Too late, senator. We just are not going to make it.

Shit. We need a new plan or route. Ideas?

Not really.

"Okay, listen up. We are too late. The Seppies are already at the open court." He said over the QM com. "Reyez, is there another way up the dome?"

"Daddy," Deanna interrupted.

"Just a minute baby, daddy is trying to think." Alexander replied and continued to scan the area for a new approach.

"I don't know of any other ways." Reyez Jones just shrugged. In the e-suit it was a gesture that was hard to do and just as hard to notice.

"But, daddy," Deanna pulled away from her mother's handhold.

"What, Deanna?" the senator tried not to show his temper.

"Can't we just go down a floor and get on the elevator?" she asked.

I can't believe it. Of course we can, sir. There are seven floors beneath us containing infrastructure equipment. We would have to do some backtracking to get down there, though. Abigail illuminated a city tourist map showing the maintenance levels. *It just never dawned on me to go down. Sorry, senator.*

"You are something, you know that?" Alexander grabbed his daughter in a hug and tried to kiss her through the open faceshield. When that didn't work he just hugged her again and then patted her little helmeted head. "Follow me and we'd better hurry." He turned back the way they had come toward the nearest entrance to the maintenance and infrastructure levels.

We are running out of time, Nancy. We had better hurry. Allison warned of the impending second wave of the aerial assault on the mountain range.

I know, I know. I wasn't expecting this. Where are all the people? She asked. They had been bouncing for several kilometers from the landing site and yet to see a single body, screaming or walking wounded, or any sign of human life. *It's almost as if the city had been warned and had been evacuated before the bomb had hit.*

That is nearly impossible. Only you and I, a handful of operations analysts, the deputy director, the director, the

NSA, the Sec Def, and the President know of our mission. Unlikely, one of them is a mole, Allison responded.

Yeah, well, its just plain weird if you ask me. Where the hell is everybody?

Nancy continued bouncing eastward and directly radially outward from the center of the bomb blast. The map on her visor showed her position at about twenty-seven kilometers from the center of the blast zone. There was little sign of the explosion at this range other than the occasional strewn debris that could have been blown around by the Martian winds anyway. Oh, and there was the small matter of the radioactive fallout, though the injection she had taken beforehand was taking care of that.

The region was little more than a rural outpost of the city that had been littered with lightweight trash and debris from the lingering winds of the nuclear blast. The streets were Martian soil, mostly, and were more like paths that had been pounded out by jumper boots, buggies, and hovercraft. There were domes and rock dwellings and shops scattered about the mountain's side, but there was no sign of people.

Nancy bounced up on top of one of the geodesic domes that was probably a single family dwelling for a better vantage point. She scanned full-circle around her for motion and to get a better understanding of her path. The city behind her was still aflame and dying with occasional explosive bursts and pressurized environments explosively decompressing into the Martian atmosphere.

There is wireless activity ahead. Must be that we have found the evacuees, Alison alerted Nancy. *There is a lot of multi-path and I am having a bit of trouble locating the transmitters, but it looks like multiple transceivers. I'm training a neural net on it.*

Just keep me posted. Maybe some of the other sensors will work better.

Nancy looked up at the sky briefly and for the first time could see stars through the dust cloud. There was Jupiter shining brightly overhead and Saturn not far above it. The sky to the west was still covered with clouds of dust and smoke and every now and then a star would twinkle through the cracks between them.

Motion, Nancy! Coupling the motion sensors and the wireless multi-path I've trained the sensors to locate the motion. Looks like multiple bogies. The nearest is about four hundred meters away, Allison warned her biological counterpart.

The three dimensional view in Nancy's mind zoomed slightly northeast and down the street about four hundred meters. The starlight, IR, and QM sensor systems gave a data fusion image that was crystal clear in the pitch black Martian night.

A child? Nancy thought as she studied the image. She zoomed in on what appeared to be a child sized e-suit rummaging through a storage bin on the outside wall of a small dwelling dome. Then a second set of views highlighted and zoomed in her visor, and a third, and then the tracking algorithms learned how to spot the motion and hundreds of targets began to pop up on her map. They all appeared to be evacuating in generally the same direction some moving more slowly than others. *The plan was working.*

Nancy focused back on the child and the motion nearest

it. The algorithm generated tracking trajectories that suggested the two nearby regions of motion appeared to be tracking the child. One a few blocks south of the child and the other a few blocks east. Further zoom revealed that the two tracks were adult-sized e-suits.

They're looking for the child, Nancy thought.

Most likely, Allison agreed. *They had better get out of here within the next ten minutes because all hell is about to rain down on this city. Same goes for us by the way.*

Right. I've got an idea. Are these three suits broadcasting? Nancy highlighted the child and the two near it.

Yes, standard wireless with no encryption around twelve gigahertz, Allison replied.

Open the channel.

Open.

". . . Kira . . . Kira . . . where are you?" a female child voice repeated.

". . . Lelandra! WHERE ARE YOU? Come here to your mother right now!"

". . . Listen to your mother, sweetie! Come on, we have got to go!"

". . . But we can't leave Kira, daddy!" the little girl said.

Any idea what Kira might be, Allison?

I'm scanning . . . Allison ran the e-suit's sensors across the spectrum for any type of signature in the local area around the girl. There were several low level controller systems in household appliances and a few entertainment systems that the electromagnetic pulse from the nuke had not disrupted.

There! An AIK broadcasting spread spectrum center pulse at two three three six megahertz! Allison highlighted a region behind several large storage canisters stacked at the edge of a garage dome about ten meters from the little girl. *Has to be what she is looking for.*

Great work, Allison. Got it. Can you soothe the thing?

Already on it. Allison communicated code to the low level artificial intelligence that would put it in a calm state.

Nancy leapt from the top of the dome she had taken perch on in a high sweeping arch toward the "AI Kitty" or AIK. In four quick bounds she landed atop the storage canisters beside the little mechanical kitten and grabbed it before it had a chance to run off. Then she stroked it gently with her gloved hand and then bounced quietly about thirty meters to the west of the child.

"Hello? Helloooo," Nancy broadcast on the open channel in her trained Martian accent. From the abrupt motion changes of the three tracks she was calling to she was certain she had startled them. "Is anybody there?" Nancy stepped onto the street behind the little girl where there was just enough light for the child to see her and her artificial intelligence kitten. Nancy could feel the little AIK purring in her grip.

"Kira!" The little girl ran to Nancy, taking the AIK and hugging it to her.

This is gonna work. List the common Separatist last names for me.

Allison began scrolling a list of names in Nancy's mind until Nancy stopped her.

That one will do nicely, Allison. Open the backstory files, she ordered the AIC. A complex and detailed life story had been developed for the mission that had been kept classified even from her until it was time to implement the cover. It was an ideal way to maintain an undercover identity—the fewer who knew the cover, the fewer who could blow it. *There, that is a good one. I'll use it. Set the emotional tags in the story to stimulate my hypothalamus accordingly.*

"Is this your kitty?" Nancy knelt beside the little girl and looked into her face. "Where are your parents?"

"Kira! I thought you were gone. Don't run off like that again! You could have missed the train!" the little girl scolded her kitty. The little red mechanical kitten purred and nuzzled the little girl with her neck. From just looking and holding the cat there was no way to tell that it wasn't real.

"Hello, whoever you are, grab my daughter, please and tell me what street you are on," the mother's voice exclaimed.

"Hi, we are on . . . " Nancy ran through the map in her mind quickly. "Uh, looks like the corner of Tholus and Valley."

"Great! I'm almost there." The girl's father replied over the wireless.

"Me too!" Her mother said.

Nancy, reached over and patted the little girl on the top of her helmet and smiled at her.

"What's your name?" The child asked.

"Oh, I'm Kira Shavi. And you are?" Nancy began sinking herself into her cover persona. She emphasized the pronunciation of Shavi as "Shaaa-VEE" with similarities to Elle Ahmi apparent.

"My name is Lelandra but you can call me Lela and this is Kira. Wow, you have the same name as my kitty."

"Isn't that funny?" Nancy laughed with Lelandra. The two adults rounded different street corners from opposite directions and bounced toward them. The larger of the two who Nancy assumed was the father grabbed his daughter and held her to him.

"Don't ever run off from us like that again, you hear me! You scared us to death!"

Nancy, five minutes.

Right!

The parents continued to scold their daughter, paying little notice to Nancy. Nancy had Allison run the suit's scanners on the three. For the most part they were common low end e-suits that intel had suggested most of the Separatists on the Reservation wore.

"Excuse me," Nancy interrupted. "It hasn't been that long since the Americans bombed the mountain. I suspect they'll be back soon."

"You're right," the mother said nervously. "We still have at least a couple of minutes or so. But you *are* right. We should be getting underground to the evac train."

They are evacuating. Do they know of the coming second wave or is it just a good idea to evacuate after a nuclear attack? Allison asked. Nancy could barely perceive that a mole could get that deep into the United States of America to know of the details of this operation.

Unlikely they know? Most likely they are playing it smart, Nancy thought nervously.

Play it carefully.

Agreed. But we should hurry them along as best we can.

"Are you separated from your unit?" the man asked,

noting the more elaborate e-suit Nancy adorned. Her suit was of the type the resistance fighters wore.

The cover seems to be working...

So far it does. Allison replied.

So far! Be more optimistic.

"You could say that. My brothers and I were retooling the long range SAMs at the foothills when the attack started. They were all killed by American Mecha and their raining death from above . . . pah, cowards! I returned to the mountains to regroup with others but was delayed by the nuclear blast." Nancy recited from her cover story memories file as she read them in her head.

"How did you end up here?" the man asked.

"Enough, Fayad, we must go now. The train for the evac ships leaves in twenty minutes." Obviously his Prime wife, the small framed woman in the e-suit ordered. "Kira, you should come with us. If your unit is sacrificed there is little else you can do from here. Ahmi has been served. You can rejoin with your family at the rendezvous."

Evac ships? Ships to where? Nancy thought.

Now we are getting somewhere.

"Very well. But I am alone. My family was killed at Elysium a year ago."

"Then you can come with us," Lelandre said.

"I'd like that," Nancy agreed and nodded her helmet. "But we should hurry, I think."

The three adults, one child, and one robot cat bounced further northeast and away from the nuclear blast area. As they bounced further Nancy caught glimpses of many more evacuees' motion with her e-suit sensors. The QM and IR revealed pockets of e-suits bouncing through the small rural dome outcroppings and all of them were bouncing in generally the same direction. There were actually casualties and some minor wounded that they would stop and help from time to time, but there were no wounded on the order that would have been expected from a nuclear blast. No, the Separatists had left the blast region or were in the process of leaving *before* the nuke was dropped. Nancy hoped to find out why.

Allison?

Yes, Nancy?

I'm Nancy no more. For now on, I'm Kira Shavi, understood?

Yes, Kira.

Right.

Chapter 8

"We'd better fucking hurry, lieutenant colonel, sir!" Corporal Shelly downloaded the QM map from his visor to the Marine Strike Mecha through the optical line-of-sight port. They could communicate with each other on the QM wireless but Lieutenant Colonel John Masterson's AIC had warned him that the Seppies didn't know they were there, and since they were spoofing the QM communications and jamming the long range it might give away the fact that an entire squadron of U.S. Marine Strike Mecha survived the crash of the *Churchill*. The long range coms were still being jammed completely.

"Roger that, corporal. Looks like your second lieutenant and sergeant are in a heap of shit." Masterson adjusted his optical sensor net to update continuously from the QM data collected by the two armored e-suit Marines that had run into his strike squadron. That way only the presence of the two AEMs would be compromised. Of course, the fact that his squadron had wiped out several handfuls of

111

Seppy mecha since the crash may have exposed them anyway. But until he knew for certain he was going to use every advantage and take every precaution.

"Okay, Cardiff's Killers, let's get in there and pull these two Marines out of the fire before it's too late. Converge on Dome Circle and kill those bloody Seppy bastards."

"Die, you Seppy bastards!" Sergeant Clay Jackson ducked back behind the steel and concrete fountain wall surrounding the giant metallic statue of Sienna Madira for cover. The Seppy ground support troops and the Mecha were literally only tens of meters from them and had only halted their progression due to the horrendous return of hypervelocity automatic railgun fire that the sergeant and second lieutenant had managed to maintain. But the two of them were running out of ammo and had to take more precise shots with very little defilading fire. Both of the Marines had exhausted their complement of grenades and it was unlikely that hand-to-mecha combat would turn out in their favor. They were outgunned, flanked, and seriously outnumbered. Not to mention that the second lieutenant had a big fucking hunk of metal sticking through his leg.

"It's been an honor, Clay!" Second Lieutenant Thomas Washington rose to a knee and took four aimed shots at a drop tank in bot mode lumbering cautiously toward them. The shots hit the right ankle joint, toppling the mecha forward onto the ground between them and a small group of approaching Seppy ground troops. The flailing mecha formed a nice barricade between them. Washington dropped back below the fountain wall.

"Right back at you, sir!" Clay took his turn taking shots.

Forty millimeter cannon fire from the enemy mecha *splunged* against the statue, flinging hot metal against the sergeant's armored shoulder. A piece of shrapnel penetrated the armor and seared its way through the seal layer and into the flesh of his shoulder. "Shit!" he grunted in agony as he fired fifty or so rounds off by accident into the smoke and dust and approaching enemy troops.

"You all right, sarge?"

"Just a flesh wound, I hope. Burns like goddamned hell." He rubbed at the hole in his armored shoulder and looked at the seal layer as it healed itself over the hole in his arm.

"Any ideas, sarge?"

"Well, lieutenant, other than dying I'm fresh out." The sergeant leaned back against the wall of the fountain and panted for breathe a few times.

"I was afraid of that. I wonder if they'd let us surrender?" The second lieutenant cracked a somber grimacing smile and rose to fire a few more rounds until his HVAR weapon clicked and displayed the out of ammo warning on his visor. "Shit, I'm out!"

Sergeant Jackson held his railgun barrel up over the fountain wall and peered at the visor display for a target. There were plenty. The QM tracking and sighting system showed forty-three known targets while his ammo depository displayed one hundred and seven rounds left. He aimed as best he could from behind the wall at the nearest mass of ground troops that were hammering away at them with railgun fire and depressed the trigger. The Seppy troops were moving too fast for an over the head shot to be useful as a pinpoint shot, but as cover fire it slowed the ground troop advance some—if a second or two could be counted as *some*.

A whining screech and then an explosion a few tens of meters on the enemy side of the fountain sent shrapnel flinging into the already black smoke filled part of the city. Brilliant flashes of mecha cannon fire and directed energy weapons lit up the smoky battlescape of the largest driving circle in the solar system. The whirling winds caused by the gaping hole in the dome continued to whip the smoke and debris into small dust devils and gustnados across the highways that converged on the driving circle and were illuminated by bright orange and red flashes from mecha exploding. Then several more whining screeches followed with explosions and then forty millimeter cannon fire picked up continuously. The *spitanging* of HVAR rounds on the fountain and statue ceased but the *spitap spitap spitap* of HVAR rounds being fired only increased, flinging shrapnel buzzing around the other side of the fountain like many angry bees.

Lieutenant Colonel "Burner" Masterson ran his configurable FM-12 Strike Mecha at full trot in bot mode onto the north side of Dome Circle and pierced through the whirling smoke clouds into the opening, firing anti-mecha missiles into three Seppy drop tanks and then fired his jump thrusters, launching the sleek Mars red humanoid formed fighter mecha into a full forward flip while multiple beams pulsed from the main directed energy gun in the left hand of the FM-12. The mecha looked like a giant robot with an armored cockpit in its upper mid torso through where a head should be flanked on either shoulder with swiveling forty millimeter HVAR cannons.

"Fox three!" Multiple mecha-to-mecha missile tubes stacked along the torso of the lethal vehicle left faint blue and purple ionization trails as the missiles scattered from the FM-12 seeking Seppy targets to kill.

"Aaaaaarrrrrrrr . . . uunnnnhhhhh . . . ssshhhhh-haaaaaaawwwoooo!" Masterson grunted to offset the g-loading on his lower extremities. The heads-up display (HUD) on the canopy was lit up with multiple targets having locked onto him and his warning klaxons and the "Bitching Betty" were ringing loud in his ears. "Now come get me! Guns 1, Guns 2!" He let out a howl and released multiple bursts from the shoulder mounted cannons and several DEG bursts.

As the Seppy Orcus drop tanks focused on the lieutenant colonel the remaining twenty-three FM-12s of Cardiff's Killers brought death from the sky, behind buildings, within the whirling smoke debris clouds, and one even tore upward through an overpass. The surprise of two dozen American Marine strike fighting mechas threw the more numerous Separatist drop tanks into a state of confusion.

At first they scattered aimlessly, like mice skittering for cover with no clear plan or forethought into where that cover might be. After the initial shock of the surprise attack dulled, the veteran Seppy mecha pilots began to fight back with some effectiveness. But their numbers had been dwindled to even or less with the Americans'. And the Americans were moving swiftly and deadly. Cardiff's Killers were doing what they did best—kill.

★ ★ ★

"LT? Sarge?! Can you make a run south?" Corporal Shelly announced over the QM. "The mechaheads are covering the north and me and Kootie are bouncing to ya!"

"Oorah! Shelly!" Sergeant Jackson called back as he brought his city view back to the forefront of his visor. There were the blue dots for Shelly and Kudaf but not a sign of the FM-12s or the Seppy Orcus drop tanks he could see with his own eyes. *No time to think about that*, he thought. *We ain't gonna die today damnit!*

Oorah! His AIC Susan replied.

"Shelly, we got you. Sarge and I are bouncing south for better cover. We're out of ammo. You gotta give us some cover." Second Lieutenant Washington tried to bear crawl away from the fountain as best he could with a half meter long hunk of steel sticking out of his left leg. The pain resurfacing from each movement forced him to grit his teeth and focus. He knew he had to focus on surviving and getting the hell out of there.

Tammie! Where do we need to go? We need a retreat route now! Thomas asked his AIC.

Here, sir! The southbound interstate overpass gives you the best cover! she replied and highlighted the escape path on the map in his head. She then transferred the same data to the sergeant's AIC.

"Shelly, Kudaf, here is our rendezvous point!" he relayed the data to them through the QM. "Let's bounce, sergeant!" He stood quickly and released the jumper field on his boots, flinging him twenty meters southward. The jarring motion of the jumping rushed up through his bum leg and sent sharp needles of pain piercing through him. The pain medication was beginning to wear down. He needed medical attention. The second lieutenant gritted his teeth and dreaded the next landing and bounce. He adjusted his stride so that most of the impact would be taken by his right leg instead.

"LT, hang on to my shoulder." Sergeant Jackson saw the second lieutenant shudder on his first bounce and thought he was going to collapse, but the tough young officer pushed through the pain. Jackson caught him by the second bounce and grabbed his left arm. The two men bounced as fast and far south as they could manage. Fortunately, the Seppies were otherwise preoccupied.

It had taken nearly thirty minutes for Alexander and his band of misfit refugees to backtrack through the main dome without being spotted by the Separatists that had overrun Mons City to the nearest downward accessing elevator. There they had taken the elevator down three levels to a maintenance travel shaft, where they took a small electric buggy through all the way to the main elevator shaft of the city. The Separatist troops had not bothered to make it as far below the city yet. Hopefully they would keep it that way.

For a brief moment, Senator Moore and his AIC had considered walking out of the dome through the lower levels, but that would place them at the edge of the dome more than seventy kilometers from the evac point south of the dome—too far to run to in time. On the other hand, if they traveled up the elevator to the maintenance shaft and then up again to the top of the dome they could base jump with the gliderchutes and cover the territory in ten or twenty minutes, depending on the prevailing winds. Jumping still seemed like the best option. The other alternative might be to hide out in the city bowels until the city was liberated by the American forces, but that seemed dangerous. The fact that it seemed more dangerous than jumping off the top of the city dome might have been debatable but Alexander preferred action and escaping rather than evading and hiding in occupied territory. He had been captured before in his life and it was no fun then. He didn't care to repeat the experience, especially with his wife and six year old daughter, an adrenaline junkie, and an older woman from Triton.

"Okay, we get in the elevator and go up through the hatch on top of it. We'll ride up there in case it opens on the occupied floors. And everybody keeps quiet. Got it?" he said.

"Got it," was the answer he got back with resounding nods. The group had learned in the process of their trek just who was in charge and making decisions. None of them cared to oppose the decision either, as Alexander seemed to know what he was doing. Nearly two decades as a Marine had that effect on people.

"Good. Let's do it." He pressed the elevator button. "Everybody hide. If nobody is on the elevator then we get on it." The little band of unlikely refugees backed down the hallway to a crossway in the halls and turned around the corner out of sight. Alexander stood to the side of the elevator door with his back against the wall.

The elevator seemed to be taking its time as if it were making multiple stops along the way. He had been afraid of that. If the Seppies were guarding the elevator then it should be obvious that it would not descend to the lower levels unless somebody had pressed a button. The elevator stopped at the ground level in the open court according to the display above the elevator door. Then it started up again pinging with each floor level it passed. *Ping*, basement level one, *Ping*, basement level two, *Ping*, basement level three . . .

Good luck, major! Abigail shouted in his mind. *Oorah!*

Oorah! he replied. His fight or flight reflex was on full alert and adrenaline coursed through his body. *It's been a long time.*

The elevator opened with a *woosh* and then there was a *click* as somebody hit the stop button inside it. Alexander pushed himself back against the wall as tight as he could as the flood of elevator music washed over the quiet hallway. Had he pressed back any harder he might have crushed the drywall. The dull gray barrel of an HVAR rifle poked out the edge of the elevator door on the opposite side pointing in a direction that was just in front of him by a few centimeters. A second barrel pointed out from his side of the elevator in a similar fashion.

Move, major!

Alexander grabbed the rifle barrel closest to him with both hands and yanked it back against the elevator door, using the leverage of the door facing to force it free of its owner. As the rifle flung free he adjusted his grip on the barrel and forced it butt first against the barrel of the rifle across the elevator door, pinning it against the door facing. He rushed the elevator door, and stepped inside the firing path of the pinned down HVAR, then recoiled the HVAR in his hands, and then hit the man holding that weapon square in the nose through his open faceplate with the butt of the rifle, cracking the bone in his nose and tearing a bloody gash, stunning the man. Alexander then used his body to wedge the man's rifle against the wall of the elevator.

In a single spinning motion, Alexander spun clockwise jamming the barrel of the HVAR he had commandeered completely through the open faceplate of the other Seppy bastard in the elevator, poking the man squarely in the forehead. By this time the Seppy soldier who had taken the rifle butt to the face had regained his composure and was fighting for control of the rifle Alexander held. Inadvertently, one of them, and Alexander wasn't sure which one he or the Seppy soldier, managed to pull the trigger just as the barrel began to recede from the face-plate of the other soldier's helmet. The hypervelocity round removed a major portion of the back side of the man's head and punched a hole through the elevator wall, splattering red foamy gray matter and skull across the wall of the elevator's plush green and yellow decorative wall paper.

Alexander struggled with the soldier on his back for several seconds trying to get an upper hand or elbow or headbutt, with little luck or effectiveness. Neither of them could seem to get advantage on the other or maintain a grasp on either weapon long enough to do any damage to the other one. Several times the HVAR in Alexander's hands was triggered *spitaping* hypervelocity rounds down the hallway and through the walls.

Jumpboots, major! Abigail barked at him in drill sergeant fashion.

Alexander dropped below the Separatist soldier, allowing the man the high ground. He took the bait and bear hugged Alexander from behind and wrapped up on his e-suit helmeted head. Once Alexander was certain that the man's head was above his he squatted lower, tucked his own head in as best he could, and bounced his jump-boots. The boots accelerated the two of them upward through the elevator ceiling snapping the Separatist soldier's neck, killing him instantly.

Stunned and uncertain of his attacker's condition, Alexander continued to fling wildly at the body behind him but both were stuck in the hole they had made.

At EASE, major! Abigail calmed him. *Sir! Senator, he's dead.*

It took a few seconds for Alexander to regain his focus, but the jumpboots had worked. Now he was stuck in the elevator's ceiling with a dead man on his back. He squirmed and tugged for a few minutes until he managed to work his right hand free. A few more minutes and he managed to pull himself up through the hole in the elevator ceiling and turn himself over onto his bottom, sitting with his legs hanging through the hole. He dropped the dead Separatist soldier back through the hole and began checking himself for damage. None that he could see. Good.

That could have gone better, he thought.

How do we plan to get past them now? No doubt they will stop the elevator if it starts to move again. Abigail noted.

Shit, this isn't going well. We'll have to climb. I should have had a better plan. Too late now. He thought.

Alexander had been a slow thinking politician for the last decade or so and had been a long time away from combat strategy and tactics. He was angry with himself for now having given their position away and for endangering his wife and daughter. He had to think. But first things were first.

Alexander dropped back through the hole in the elevator ceiling, landing astraddle of one dead Separatist soldier. A second lifeless bloody mess lay against the back left corner of the elevator. The stop button was still depressed and the doors of the elevator open wide.

"Wait out there for a moment, girls," he warned his wife, holding out his left hand palm forward. Sehera was peeking around the hall corner at the elevator to see if the coast was clear. "Reyez, come here a minute."

Reyez peeked his head around the corner to see if it was safe, then he straightened himself up and walked tall to the senator. Seeing the red bloody mess in the elevator the adrenaline junkie had to turn his head and vomit.

"Aw shit!" Alexander moaned. He grabbed the body closest to the elevator door and dragged it out by the feet. "Get out of my way if you can't help." He told Reyez.

"No, I can help. I just never . . . uuuhhhhh!" Reyez began to heave again. Alexander just pushed him away from the elevator door with a swift kick in the ass and then set about moving the other body.

"Soft kids these days," Joanie Hassed, the little Triton woman, stepped in over the first dead body and gave Alexander a hand. "Saw a lot more than this on Triton during the raids."

Alexander understood what she meant. The raids on

Triton were some of the bloodiest battles in the past decade—hell in human history, for that matter. Even the civilians ended up fighting for their lives. The Great American Plan to bring peace throughout Sol and the four colonies was still a long way from being successful. Many of the kids from this generation and one prior who lived on Earth or the Moon and a few places on Mars—like Mons City—had no idea of the utter horror humanity was still inflicting upon itself elsewhere.

"Thanks. We need to . . . " Alexander was about to explain that they needed to strip the two men of their e-suits and take all their weapons and gear, but the little Triton native was half way through the process on the first body.

"Uh huh." Joanie nodded.

"Right then." Alexander smiled. A good Marine had to smile when he saw a real survivor. Reyez gave him no smiles because he was soft, a product of his irresponsible generation. But, Joanie Hassed was a product of war, a time tested method for putting one's character through the crucible and smashing it up and pouring out a hardened metal composure or a pile of useless goop. Joanie must have been the former.

" . . . Manuel . . . Charlie . . . are you there? Report!" Alexander heard faintly out of one of the e-suit helmets.

These suits, are still keyed into the Seppy coms! The Seppies had older and less state-of-the-art suits that did not go encrypted when the occupant was incapacitated like the American e-suits did. That technology had to be fifty years old.

ON IT! Abigail immediately started handshaking with the suits' low level AI functions.

Can you spoof it?

Just a second. There. You can eavesdrop on this channel. I'll keep the audio open for you, Abigail replied.

Great work. Are they connected to the jamming signal at all? Alexander asked the AIC.

No. Not as I can tell.

Damn.

Yes, sir. Damn.

Well, keep on it. That jamming signal was the key to this whole mess, Alexander just *knew* it was.

Senator? The AIC added.

Yes Abigail?

These suits are keyed into the Seppie IFF. The AIC said into Alexander's mind with what felt to him like excitement. The IFF or Identify Friend and Foe system in the Separatist e-suit helmets were keyed to understand the encrypted wireless signals and signatures of the Seppie troops and enabled their locations to be followed and mapped in HUDs or direct-to-mind maps. The U.S. troops used similar systems but ones that were more state-of-the-art. DTM had been the way of the warrior for many generations—it went as far back as the first Martian War in Sienna Madira's day.

Can you transfer the code to me? Senator Moore thought.

I think so, sir. But it will take a minute or two. And I'm not sure we have a minute or two. We'll have company soon.

Can we take his helmet?

No, sir, we'd need his AIC. The average Seppie didn't carry an AIC, but years of intelligence on the troops showed that *they* apparently did. Or perhaps, Elle Ahmi required it so she could keep tabs on all of them. General Ahmi was either brilliant at understanding and managing massive amounts of data or was a stone cold paranoid whack job or maybe a little of both.

Where is it?

Here. The image of the Seppie appeared in Alexander's mind with a spot on the back of the dead man's head highlighted in red.

"Uh huh." Moore grunted and unsheathed the knife he'd liberated from the adventure shop and then twisted the man's e-suit helmet off. "This is gonna be gross." He nodded to Joanie to look away but instead she took the blade from him. Reyez looked as if he'd vomit again.

"Wait. I've done that before." The little woman from Triton hefted the dull gray two decimeter long monomolecular blade in her hand and studied its point for a second. "This'll do."

Joanie slid the point of the blade just behind the man's ear and pounded the base of the grip with the palm of her hand hard enough to crack through the skull bones. She twisted the knife and then pulled it out slowly. Dark red blood oozed out around the blade. She then repeated the process, this time slightly to the right of the previous bloody stab wound. Then she yanked the blade upward fairly hard and with a twist, causing bloody gray matter and pale white and pink skull bone fragments to crack free and spring upward, being held together only by hair and skin. Joanie slid her finger into the man's brainpan just behind his left ear and fished around for a second.

"There it is." She pulled out a small orange and bloody

red plastic device about the size and shape of a sunflower seed in its shell, maybe a little smaller.

She did it, senator. We have to go, now. They are coming down alternative elevators and stairwells. Here and here. Abigail showed him in his mind. *I'll let you know when I get the IFF transfer.*

"Great work, Joanie." He took the implant from her.

"Well, you know you have to smash that thing or they can track us?"

"I'm counting on that . . . and a few other things. We have to get out of here now," he said as he listened to the Seppy open channel. The Seppies were missing their two buddies and were sending someone else to look for them. The dead Seppie's AICs could have alerted others of their presence as Abigail couldn't be sure if her jamming attempts had worked or not. At least now they had two rifles, a handful of ordinance, and the enemy communications channel. And soon, hopefully very soon, they would have the enemy IFF.

"Look, Daddy," Deanna tugged at her father's arm pointing to a line of small holes in the drywall down the hallway.

"What is it, baby?" Moore knelt beside his daughter.

"Mommy and I were right here." Deanna pulled her father around the corner at the hallway crossing and crawled down onto the floor on all fours as best she could in the child-sized e-suit. "See?"

Alexander did see. Not only was his daughter smart, but she was lucky. The HVAR rounds that had gone off in a random spray during his scuffle with the Seppy soldiers had penetrated the wall in the main hallway and continued right on through the crossing hallway just above where

Deanna and Sehera had been hiding. Reyez and Joanie had been on the other side of the hallway, but Moore's family had been right in the line of fire and very lucky and he had been very stupid.

"Jesus!" Alexander and Sehera both grabbed their daughter and began running their hands over her suit looking for puncture wounds. There were none. "Are you okay, sweetheart? You're okay, right?" Alexander gulped hard. "Sehera, you sure you're not hit?"

They are unharmed Senator. Abigail ran a quick vitals sweep with her QM sensors.

Shit, that was so stupid of me. We have got to get them out of here, he told his AI.

"Alexander." Sehera looked at her husband sternly. "We can not do that again."

"I know. I'm so sorry, dear. We have to get out of here."

"Look, I hate to break this up and all," Joanie interrupted. "But we should keep moving. Everybody is all right here, yes?" She nodded knowingly at the former Marine turned politician.

"Right, let's get moving."

Lieutenant Commander Jack Boland wiped the sweat off of his face and set his helmet on the seat of his Ares fighter. For some reason the fighter squadron had been recalled and were zipping in through the braking field and slamming into the landing deck as fast as they could ingress.

"What the hell, Chief? I thought we were doing a second wave deep into the mountains past Elysium," he said as he returned the salute to the maintenance chief climbing the ladder on the other side of the fighter and then stepped down another rung of his own ladder. Jack pulled the seal ring on his gloves and removed them with a *pop swoosh*. He tossed them beside his helmet as an afterthought.

"Yes, sir. It appears that the *Madira* and most of the fleet has been called to the Tharsis Mons region. Mons City has been overrun by a large invasion force and we are pulling out to there."

"No shit?" Jack couldn't believe what he was hearing. *Mons City under attack, those Seppy bastards have got some kind of balls.*

I agree, sir, his AIC Candis replied.

"Well, pull that back seat hardware out of my fighter and reload it with standard gear. I suspect I'll be going back into the mix when we get there along with the rest of the Gods of War." Jack nodded to the chief. "Meantime, I'm gonna get some chow."

"Yes, sir! I'd avoid the meatloaf, sir. The stuff gave Hull Technician Third Class Joe Buckley the worst case of the shits I ever saw. He literally almost shit himself to death. Doc says he's gonna make it though." He laughed but his warning was serious. After all, it was the chief's job to make sure his pilots and their gear was always running top notch and ship shape. He had to do his part in taking care of the men. Sure the CAG would say the pilots were his men, and the Captain of the *Madira* would say they were his, but the Chief knew different. He looked out for *his* men.

"Thanks, chief. Has double zero reported in yet?" Boland asked.

"You haven't heard?" The chief turned three shades of pale.

"Heard what?" Jack stood deathly still. He'd seen that look on the chief's face before. Even through the smut, oil, and other grime covering the chief's orange coveralls from head to toe he could tell the chief was hurting inside.

"Lieutenant Commander Tyler was shot down south of Elysium about fifteen minutes ago. Both her and her AIC were lost." The chief looked at his boots for a brief moment.

"Shit!"

"Yes, sir. Seppy motherfuckers! Some of the pilots were saying there was a new Seppy mecha out there that got her. Did you see any new vehicles sir?"

"No. But I didn't engage them as long. I did see a whole shit load of mecha on the ground though."

"Remember, sir, don't eat the meatloaf."

"See ya later, chief. Shit, I can't believe it. And get that back seat shit out of my plane."

Jack couldn't believe it. Sarah Tyler, call sign EvilDead, good ol' double zero, the CAG, was shot down. Jack had known Sarah for years. They went through flight school together. *Shit!*

Yes sir. Shit! Candis agreed. *Jack, the XO's AIC has ordered us to see him ASAP.*

Tell him we're on our way. I guess the meatloaf can wait anyway.

"Lieutenant Commander Boland, Sir!" Jack snapped a quick salute as he stepped into the XO's office. The chief executive officer looked up from his coffee cup and glanced to his right at his office couch. Captain Wallace Jefferson nodded to them both as well as to a man whom

Boland had seen only one other time—the briefing where he met Nancy Penzington.

"At ease, gentlemen," the captain said. The man with no name wearing a Lieutenant's insignia just nodded. Jack doubted that the man was in any branch of the military, since the last time he saw the man he was wearing an army colonel's uniform.

"Sir." Jack stood at ease with his hands behind his back.

"Have a seat, son," the XO said waiving to an office chair. Jack just nodded and took a seat.

"First things first," the captain started. "Was the package delivered?"

"The package was delivered coincident with the ordinance, sir." Jack said in a low quiet tone. All the cloak and dagger stuff tended to make one lower his voice subconsciously.

"Good enough?" Captain Jefferson nodded to the "lieutenant" and shrugged.

"Excellent. Thank you, Captain, Colonel Chekov, and thank you, Lieutenant Commander Boland. Your country owes you a bit of gratitude. There will be a sealed classified commendation added to your personal records," the man said, offering to shake Jack's hand. Jack rose and shook the man's hand.

"Thank you, uh, lieutenant." Jack smirked.

"Captain." The man nodded and made his exit from the XO's office.

"Is that all, sir?" Lieutenant Commander Boland asked.

"One more thing, Jack. Your new flight number is double zero again. Try not to blow up any civilian domes this time," the captain said.

"Yes, sir."

"We'll expect you to say a few things at the service," Colonel Chekov added. "Sarah will be sorely missed."

"Yes, sir. She will. She has a daughter but she is grown. Still, she'll miss her mother," Jack said and then straightened himself up. "Other orders, sir? What about this Mons City thing?"

"Well, Jack, it appears as though you'll be going to work in a couple hours or so. No rest for the CAG. Mons City has been completely overrun and the *Churchill* has been completely destroyed by sabotage as far as we can tell. Also, our long range communications into the area has been completely jammed. We are getting data out from daisy chained QM coms and from the Mars News Network AIC feeds. Even the hardlines have been cut."

"Jesus," Jack muttered.

"My sentiments exactly, son." The captain paused for second.

"How did they sabotage the *Churchill*, sir?"

"We have zero intel or BDA at this point. We have no idea how they managed to get onto the ship and with ordinance. Maybe they used some ordinance already on the ship, but then how did they get to it? We could go nuts trying to figure that out without any data. So don't, that's an order," the CO explained.

"Yes, sir."

"Just know that we are upping the security on all the ships in the fleet as we speak."

"Makes sense, sir. What do we do about Tharsis?" Jack was certain there was a big fight coming. *Seppy bastards can't just blow up a U.S. Navy Supercarrier and attack a city and expect to get away with it,* he thought.

Absolutely not! Candis agreed.

"The air and space over the entire Tharsis region has been secured by the Seppies," the CO continued. "Initial drop tanks came in a large cargo freighter and dropped on the city at the same time the *Churchill* was destroyed. Then the freighter evaded the rest of the fleet over Tharsis just long enough to lure them in and detonate itself. The thing went off with the energy of a gluonium bomb and took out most of the local fleet."

"Holy shit, sir. Gluonium? Where did they get that?"

"Good question. There's more. Only minutes after the freighter's detonation, six carriers dropped out of hyperspace from somewhere out past Kuiper Station. Drop tanks and other Seppy mecha have been scattered across the region. The bastards can only hold the space for a few more hours with just six ships. We are going to bring all eighteen supercarriers and more than ten lesser sized vehicles of the fleet in and crush them if the president gives the go ahead. Unfortunately, there are over five million hostages in the Olympus Mons area, and more than twenty-five million spread out in the other Tharsis mountain cities, all assumed captured, with many thousands dead. We've received no terms from the Seppies so who knows what they are planning."

"Where did they get six carriers from, sir?"

"Your guess is as good as any right now. And Jack, there is one more glitch here."

"Sir?"

"We just got a courier from Earth in a small ship capable

of hyperspace. The courier brought us this data straight from the Pentagon. Since the long range coms are jammed we are sending messages back and forth the old fashioned way." The CO continued, "Read this intel. It is quite alarming. The Seppies have a new fighter mecha that appears to be a poor man's copy of the FM-12. Analysts' details are in there, but if you haven't heard yet, we encountered a squadron of them after you had gone past the engagement zone. They are formidable and there are eyewitness accounts and computer analyses of them in there as well. All I can suggest is that you read this intel and plan accordingly."

"Aye, sir."

"The main thing is to prepare air support for an attack on six carriers with the *Sienna Madira* running point and minimizing damage to the civilian population and hostages and at the same time allow for a VIP extraction at the ground coordinates in the file. I want you to have the air group ready in ninety minutes. We attack in two hours and thirty minutes. Understood, Lieutenant Commander?" The captain stared at him tight lipped.

"Sir! I'm on it."

"And . . . DeathRay . . . "

"Sir?"

"Good hunting."

"Yes sir!"

Chapter 9

". . . This is Gail Fehrer with MNN on the ground in the central dome of Mons City. My crew and I were able to escape the war zone in the southern borough domes and sneak into the main dome with the moving Separatist troops. That was quite a harrowing experience, Shennon." The reporter whispered into the video as she scanned over her shoulders for activity.

"How long did it take to get from one borough to the next, Gail? We've been told that the tunnels from one dome to the next have been cut off," the anchorman said deadpan, as if reading from a teleprompter or, more likely, repeating from his AIC.

"It wasn't an easy trek, Shennan. The Seppies have an exterior route set up where they are trucking troops and equipment from dome to dome and from drop ships that have landed between them. We hitched a ride on the back of one of the equipment loads. We were almost discovered two or three different times. We just uploaded some video to you that shows some of this as well as the enemy movement through the airseam on the South wall of the main dome just north of the central city recycling plant. The airseam down there is large enough for lightly armored vehicles to get through. The main dome of Mons City is overrun by the Separatist forces and as far as I can tell any civilians from the city have either been taken to the shelters where there are Separatist guards and tactical operations centers or they are hiding out somewhere. We have seen some sign that the Separatist troops are rounding up the civilians and moving them inward toward the center of the city. We don't know where to at this point."

"Well, as far as we can tell here at the MNN building, the entire city including the boroughs are being held captive by this invasion force. There has been no word from any of the Separatist leaders at all and we are really uncertain why MNN is still being unjammed and allowed to broadcast. Any idea of what the Separatist forces have in mind? I mean, they can't really believe they can hold off the United States Fleet do they?" Shennan asked with a little more animation than before.

"Throughout history General Ahmi has proven to be wiser than this and has tried not to create an all-out engagement with the U.S. on what is considered mainland U.S. soil. There haven't been skirmishes on Earth in more than a century and few on Mars since the Martian Desert Campaign. Since that skirmish more than thirty years ago she has shown no signs of desiring a full-scale war. But, Shennan, I'd have to say something appears to have changed that policy. The forces we saw outside the domes and moving into the domes are well organized, equipped, and appear to me to be ready for war. The death toll already must be hundreds of thousands if not more. This is war, no doubt. And the question still remains as to where they got so much support and . . . " Fehrer nodded as if her cameraman had said something to her and then she turned to look over her right shoulder.

"Gail, what is it?"

"Shennan, I'm sorry, but we have to go now. We'll contact you when we can. This is Gail Fehrer for MNN reporting." Then the video feed went blank.

"Wow, amazing report from MNN correspondent Gail Fehrer. God speed and be safe, Gail. Let's go now to . . . "

"Alexander, we can't fight these soldiers. Deanna is too . . . "

"Yeah, dear, I know. I should never have faced off with the men in the elevator. This was a bad, very bad plan." Senator Moore carried his daughter as his band of refugees fled through the bowels of the Mons City infrastructure. Using security feeds and other sensors such as automatic door activations and elevator operations and eavesdropping on the enemy communications channels his AIC staffer was helping them evade capture. The AIC continued to hack away at the security protocols of the commandeered Separatist soldier's AIC, with marginal luck. For now Alexander kept the small implant in his pocket, but if Abigail couldn't hack into it within the next five minutes he was going to smash the thing.

"Mr. Moore." Reyez Jones who was taking up the rear position a hallway behind them called to him on the e-suit to e-suit wireless.

"Reyez?"

"I was down here once about a year ago and I think there is a garbage incinerator a few hundred meters from here," Reyez said.

"And?" Moore held up and waited for his wife and Joanie Hassed to cross the intersecting hallway, to be followed closely by Reyez. Moore motioned to Reyez to hold the conversation until he was in audible distance. "Let's stay off the radio if we don't have to use it. So, what about the garbage incinerator?"

Abigail, DTM the blueprints for this floor showing this incinerator if you can get them, he thought to his staffer.

Already working on it, senator. All I've got are the same engineering blueprints we've had for these lower levels of the city. The highlighted pathways are the route to the garbage collection and destruction system.

Thanks.

"Well, if I remember right," Reyez rolled his eyes to the ceiling in thought or recollection and was distracted momentarily by the brown mold stains scattered about by the leaky plumbing system of the city's engineering infrastructure. "I seem to recall a service lift for reclaimable resources that could be transported to one of the manufacturing domes. I think it goes to a highbay and an airseam at the Southeast side of the dome."

"Alexander, I'd rather take my chances outside than inside," Sehera added.

"We could hide out there easier. There are sensors and electronic gates everywhere here," Joanie Hassed agreed. Her life on Triton during the terrorist insurgency there had taught her the valuable lesson of lying low and staying out of sight. She would have rather kept Senator Moore from engaging the Seppies all together, but it was too late for that now. And the big man seemed to know what he was doing.

"Ok. We go to that elevator and then out of the dome. We'll see about transportation to an evac once we get that far." One thing a former Marine could do was to adapt and improvise. He continued to think in the Major Moore mode rather than as Senator Moore. He hoped that would keep them uncaptured and alive.

Abigail, how is the IFF hack coming?

It is harder than I thought it would be. The Separatist AIC technology is better than I had expected. A few more minutes. The AIC seemed uncertain of itself.

We don't need to risk a few more minutes right now, unless you are certain you are jamming it. Are you?

No, sir.

Thought so. Keep thinking about it and maybe we'll get another sample later. But for now, I don't want them tracking us directly with it. Moore fished into his breast pocket and dug out the little sunflower seed shaped implant and then dropped it on the ground in front of him. He twisted it into the floor with the ball of his jump-boot, causing a barely audible *crunch*.

Understood, sir.

How are you coming with the cloaking hack counter-measure?

I know the signal is there because there is more energy over all the bandwidth than should be there. But without the encryption sequence I can't find it. The dictionary code breaking search is still running but could take years. Any suggestions? Abigail asked.

Yeah, keep at it. Moore was ready for something to go their way, but so far his plans had been falling apart on him. Perhaps he should have listened to those two idiots at the adventure shop and just stayed put there.

"You want another beer?" Rod Taylor finished off his Mons Light and then crushed the can against his forehead. "Reckon those idiots made it to the top of the dome?"

"I'll take one." Vincent Peterson belched and then took out a pack of cigarettes and started to light it up. "Who knows. Hate he had to take that little girl along with them. They're liable to get her killed. Idiots."

"Hey man, this ain't a smoking section of the dome." Rod smiled and handed his young friend another light beer. "Yeah, poor kid."

"Uh, Rod. Look outside that freakin' window."

"Yeah? What about it?" Rod shrugged his shoulders and reached into the red and white cooler they had liberated from the beverage store down the street for another beer himself.

"I don't think with all those Seppie bastards out there anybody's gonna give a flying shit if I have a smoke." Vince pointed at the armored trucks convoying down the street and shook his head.

"Well, it just ain't considerate is all . . . " Rod started but was interrupted by a group of Separatist troops in e-suits that had begun to unass outside the door of the shop. Two of the men were coming through the door with two behind them in standard two on two coverage formation.

"What's up?" Vincent looked up at the Seppie railgun barrel lowered at him and lit his cigarette. "We're closed."

Lieutenant Commander Jack Boland sat in the middle of a row of ten simulation consoles in the Battle Operations and Scenario Simulation Room or the BOSS, as it was known. The low level lighting of the room was accentuated only by the flickering of changing scenes on flat panel computer displays and cast a dim blue hue over the overcrowded computer battle lab. The display screens were mostly for secondary data acquisition and list display, as most of the simulation was done through DTM link.

Jack's AIC was connected hardwire for maximum data rate to the BOSS wargaming, logistics, tactics, and strategy computer system. The BOSS main computer ran trillions of calculations per second to help squadron commanders plan and simulate upcoming operations. The BOSS implemented state-of-the-art AI software and genetic algorithms to predict the outcome of multiple coupled dynamical systems and perform calculations that consisted of thousands of differential equations all tangled up and connected in some form or fashion to each other.

The prediction requirements were orders of magnitude more complicated than those of the Navier-Stokes equations defining the chaotic realm of weather prediction. In fact, weather prediction and even chaotic phenomena injection was a subroutine implanted within the BOSS architecture and a small one at that, compared to the detailed wargame models and logistics support simulations. It had been taught at war college for centuries that wars were lost and won due to the military handling of logistics implementation. The BOSS was designed to ensure a win.

The BOSS was the culmination of four hundred years of mathematically modeling warfare, and it indeed *was* the boss when it came to wargaming, and mathematical game theory and understanding the minutia of every piece of hardware, software, order, plan, tactic, strategy, and logistics effort was within its capability. The simulation was downloaded through the AIC link DTM simply because there was more information to be transferred between the BOSS and the user than *could* be displayed via any other means known to man. To be a certified BOSS user actually took several months of training and to understand the system and truly implement that as a battle planning tool took years of experience or a natural knack for the complex DTM modeling and simulation environment. Fortunately, Lieutenant Commander Jack Boland had both.

The Mons City recapture battle plan was nonstandard in that there was a problem with the collateral damage. In previous battles over the Separatist Reservation or guerilla training camps they were always over target zones with little infrastructure that was important to America. Well, that is, except for those two civilian terraformer domes Jack had so efficiently disposed of a few months back. But Jack had decided then that the domes were worth giving up if the U.S. Navy forces were able to take out the entire insurgent cell that was using them for cover. There were some politicians who hadn't agreed and when the images of the two domes pouring fire and black smoke into the Martian atmosphere hit MNN Jack was busted from CAG and the talks of getting a full third pip on his collar had ceased almost immediately following the incident.

Imagine what they'd do if we took out a major dome at Mons City, he thought to Candis.

At that point, if you didn't go to prison, I would recommend retirement, Candis chuckled.

Funny.

Jack straightened himself in his chair and reached out into the virtual dogfighting and bombing runs swarming his head. Through the DTM interface, of course, he was the only person that could see the simulation around him. The other battle planners and logistics experts sitting at the row of consoles had similar simulations or perhaps were merely moving equipment from point A to point B, but the effect was the same. The BOSS Room was filled with men and women in Navy uniform swatting about their heads at non-existent pests. The simulation room had long been coined as the "Looney Bin".

Jack reached out with his right hand toward his virtual squadron of Ares fighters that were strafing virtual Seppy drop mecha around the Mons City domes. Long wavelength infrared laser imaging detection and ranging (LIDAR) equipment located above his console detected the movement of his hand and the exact positioning of it to within a millionth of a meter was determined and fed back into the simulation computer system. In turn, his AIC detected that Jack intended to move the objects in front of him by hand and fed this information to the same computer. The simulation environment calculated new positions and then fed this into the wargaming models and moved the little virtual Martian red camo fighter planes around the virtual Marsscape accordingly.

The DTM interconnect downloaded and updated the simulation changes into Jack's head continuously and real-time faster than human reflex lag, so the interface was immediate as far as Jack could tell. Of course, Jack had planned hundreds, maybe thousands, of operations before and it had been since Navy Officer Battle Ops Simulation Training Course that he had even thought about how the BOSS system worked, so all of this was transparent to him. He just moved an object, and it moved. In the very old days of Naval warfare the Flag officers would use real models and marker boards. They would push model airplanes around on a two dimensional mockup of the battle decks called a "Ouija Board". The Looney Bin with the DTM technology had made the Ouija Board a thing of ancient history.

The simulation was looking good and he was planning on using the Gods of War to lead the insertion into the occupied territory for the VIP extraction. The simulations showed heavy casualties in his squadron and a serious amount of collateral damage to the local city infrastructure. It couldn't be helped. And this simulation was based on the sketchy intelligence data of the Mons City insurgency and occupation forces. Jack knew that a simulation was only as good as the model and the data it was based on, and there was no way of knowing just how accurate the data on the Seppy forces was.

CO is never gonna go for this, he thought.

Maybe, Candis replied. *But, it may be the only choice*

we have if we plan to take back the city and take out the
Seppies.

Shit.

"Shit, that has got to fucking hurt, Second Lieutenant!"
Kootie commented on the bloody piece of metal rebar
hanging out of Washington's leg.

"Hell, private, I didn't even realize it was there."
Second Lieutenant Washington forced a grin that was
almost lost on the private, as the faint amber city street
lighting was just barely bright enough to see through the
tinting on the faceplate of the lieutenant's e-suit helmet.
The atmosphere being sucked through the large gaping
hole in the dome and the continuous addition of dust,
debris, and smoke from the ongoing fighting had created
a low lying dense and very dark gray cloud system within
the dome. Violent twirls, down drafts, updrafts, and low
lying cloud scud fell just above the tops of the tall city
buildings, blocking out all but the amber and neon artificial
lighting of the burning city itself. Dust particles and water
vapor fell in a low gravity drizzle like a strange hybrid of
rain, snow, and volcanic ash.

"Check it out, sir," Corporal Shelly nodded down the
street and up above at the top of a skyscraper where a
large metallic humanoid figure stood scanning the region
with a DEG weapon held at the hip ready for action. The
bot mode Martian red camo mecha stood motionless like
a stalwart metal statue with swiveling forty millimeter
cannons on each shoulder protecting the Marines below
and seeking out potential prey. Unseen to the AEMs taking
shelter in the alley street thirty stories below were the

optical LIDAR scans and acoustic sensor sweeps the mecha's pilot ran continuously to monitor any Seppy activity. Passive sensor systems ran full sweeps as well.

"FM-12s," Sergeant Jackson added.

"Good. We could use as much support as we can get. We still need to get to the evac and support our VIP's evac. If he makes it there." The second lieutenant relaxed slightly.

Another FM-12 Strike Mecha in bot mode dropped off a building just to the south of the one standing guard and transfigured itself as it dropped to the street level. Just as it reached street level the vehicle that had looked like a ten meter tall metal robot transfigured itself and looked like a space fighter with two metal feet reminiscent of a bird of prey's talons and underneath the wings were arms with humanlike hands at the ready, like those of a boxer or a martial artist with the main DEG held in the left hand. The main forty millimeter cannons swiveled from a mounted position one under the belly of the bird and one on top just aft of the cockpit. If the armored bird and its cannons and DEG weren't enough fire power the row of missile launchers spread out across the bottom of each wing would make for a good backup.

The empennage of the sleek red camo killing machine was lined with Seppy flags and just under the cockpit read Lieutenant Colonel John "Burner" Masterson. Burner was the leader of Cardiff's Killers, the Marine piloted FM-12 Strike Mecha Squadron assigned to the now destroyed *U.S.S. Winston Churchill Supercarrier*.

The mecha lit softly with a slight metallic *chunk kachunk* onto the street as its talons grabbed the pavement a few meters from the survivors of the AEM squad. The armored bubble canopy of the bird slid back and the pilot in a Martian camo flight armored e-suit catapulted upward from the pilot couch and then bounced carefully beside the AEMs. Cardiff's Killers had just pulled the squad leader and their NCO out of the frying pan. It had only taken the Killers a brief sweep through the Dome Circle district to wipe up the inferior Seppie drop tanks. Burner had taken out three of them himself. The local region was secured, for the moment.

Washington, Jackson, Kudaf, and Shelly took relaxed positions underneath the wing of the mecha that was presently in eagle mode, resting on two landing pads with wings folded like a bird of prey sitting on a perch ready to attack. The aircraft offered them some shelter from the drizzle, though in the AEM suits the drizzle was only a nuisance to the faceplate view. QM and IR sensors could overcome the blurring by the water droplets on the face-plate quickly, but the human habit of getting out of the rain was a million years old or more and some instincts are hard to overcome. Burner nodded at the AEMs to remain at ease and picked out their leader as he joined him under his plane.

"Looks like that hurts, Marine." Burner noted the metal bar sticking out of Washington's left leg.

"Yes, sir. Like fucking hell, sir!" Second Lieutenant Thomas Washington replied. "But not near as bad as it would've if you guys hadn't showed up when you did. Thanks, sir."

"Yes, sir. It is a damned good thing Shelly and Kootie stumbled into you," Sergeant Jackson added with a thin lipped smile. "We had them right where they wanted us."

"Right, you don't look the best in the world either, sergeant. We have a medic as one of our drivers. Maybe he can get you two fixed up." Colonel Masterson smiled and thought a command to his AIC. *Angel, get Boulder over here.*

Yes sir, right away, his AIC responded and sent a call to First Lieutenant Jason "Boulder" Cordova.

"Just relax. We'll get you fixed up," Masterson said. "Now just what in the hell were you two doing at Dome Circle anyway? We were pushing an entire squad of Seppy drop tanks right into you."

"Well, that explains why they were running toward us but shooting backwards, uh, sir," Sergeant Jackson added. The mecha pilot just grunted and grinned thinly.

"We were deployed just after the *Churchill* went down, sir. There is a Senator Alexander Moore in the main dome that we were sent to extract. Unfortunately, we got hit hard before we ever got started and ended up crashed in the south boroughs. Then shit started getting worse . . . sir. My AIC has kept on top of him, but . . . " Thomas looked up and down the street at the noise he heard in the distance, uneasily fingering the safety on his HVAR, *his empty HVAR,* until he realized it was another FM-12 configuring itself into Eagle mode beside the colonel's bird. The canopy of the fighter slid opened with a low volume *swish* and a Marine holding a medic pouch leaped from the cockpit in a long slow arc and bounced off the side of a building across the street and then to the ground by Burner.

"I got a call that somebody was having a baby over here. Thought I'd pop in and see if I could help." Marine First Lieutenant Jason "Boulder" Cordova kneeled down beside Washington and looked at the piece of bloody iron rebar protruding out of his left leg.

"Yeah, and I'm having serious labor pains, doc." Washington grimaced and relaxed his grip on his HVAR completely.

"Call me Boulder and just hold on a sec." Cordova pulled an injector gun from his kit and plugged it into the seal layer on Washington's e-suit under the armor access port on the neck of the suit. "I'm gonna give you some more pain meds and I'm giving you a shot of immuno-booster so your immune system can eat that metal out of your leg." Boulder pulled out a directed energy cutting tool and zipped through the protruding piece of metal like hot butter. The little pistol shaped cutting tool sprayed out a focused green beam of light that cut the metal bar so quickly that it didn't have time to get hot. The metal rod exterior to Washington's leg fell slowly to the street pavement with an extended *claaaaang*. The seal layer of Washington's e-suit quickly covered the end of the metal bar and sealed off. Clean red armor plating hardened over the new readi-seal material as his suit began to heal itself.

"Is that it?" the second lieutenant asked.

"That's it. Oh, you'll run a high fever for a few hours until your immune system dissolves that bar in your leg, but the pain meds will keep that from being a problem. That side might be a little weak for another half hour or so, too, and you probably won't need any mineral supplements for a few days. Sometimes that much iron in your system will make you constipated for a day or two, but I'd say it beats the shit out having a metal bar sticking out of your leg. Otherwise, you are a killing machine Marine." Cordova grinned.

"Oorah," Washington replied.

"Right. Now sarge, let's look at that shoulder of yours." Cordova went to work on Jackson, giving him a slightly lower dose of the immunobooster. Without a foreign object in the sergeant's shoulder, his boosted immune system would literally heal the wound within a matter of minutes.

"Ok, Thomas, now back to what you were up to." Masterson helped the young lieutenant up to his feet. "Senator Moore's extraction, I believe is what you were saying."

"Yes, sir. That mission went south badly. We are the only ones left of our deployment. We lost our commander and NCO in the first few seconds and several others not long after that. I didn't see how we could get to the senator and we were cutoff. About that time this senator QMed my AIC and said that he would meet us at the extraction coordinates. I told him to stay his ass put, sir, but he said he didn't take orders from the Marines. So our plan was to make a nuisance of ourselves and make way to cover the VIP's evac." Washington turned his head slightly in his helmet and bit down on the water tube, taking a long slow drink. His heightened immune system was using up body fluids and was making him thirsty.

"When and where is your evac?"

"Tammie, send the coordinates to the colonel," Thomas vocalized. A second later Masterson nodded in understanding. "In about two hours, sir."

"Is there any hope that the evac will still happen? We've been able to contact nobody outside the city for a good while now," Sergeant Jackson added.

"I doubt it. But we have had even less contact than you have because all of our QM systems are disabled," the lieutenant colonel explained.

"Why sir? I mean, why are you only using laser coms?" Corporal Shelly asked.

"One of my killers—an engineer—found too much energy in the QM coms spectrum and he thought it was a virus. So we shut 'em down and therefore we were cloaked off of any QM nets." Masterson thought about that for a moment and then added, "It is probably how the damned Seppy drop tanks are cloaked off our systems. So we are fighting all optical right now."

"That explains a lot, sir." Sergeant Jackson worked his shoulder around and around a few times to work out the kinks. "We could see the bastards right there in front of us but they weren't on our screens at all, sir."

"Yeah. I had two of the drop tanks trying to snake me in the tailpipe before we bumped into these two," Cordova said, nodding at Shelly and Kootie. "Fortunately, the LIDAR is working and the passive multi-static radar systems are too or I'd be a messy spot a few kilometers northwest of here. Well, and Burner got one of 'em off my ass, too. Probably a lucky shot."

"Luck counts. Boulder and you should be damned proud of it." Burner said, taking the zing out of Boulder's lighthearted comment.

"Oorah, sir."

"What if this senator gets to the evac point and there

is nobody there to cover him or to evac him?" Masterson thought out loud and more pointedly to the second lieutenant.

"Good point, sir, but we could sure use some reinforcements if we are going to get to him anytime soon." Washington was quite skeptical that his squad could manage it, but Marines did what they had to in order to get the job done. Improvise. Adapt. Now if the lieutenant colonel wanted to offer up some support on the other hand . . .

"He's a senator. We'd better get him out of here. If those Seppy bastards catch him he will be toast, literally." Masterson thought for a minute then decided on a plan of action. *Angel, optically link through Washington's AIC and QM to this senator. Figure out where the hell he is and what the hell he is doing. And ask him if Rose Bowl of '35 means anything to him.*

On it, sir. His AIC replied. *Rose Bowl, sir?*

Just a hunch, Angel.

"We'll get him out," Burner said to himself more so than to the AEMs.

"Sir, what about the *Churchill*? Any survivors there?" Jackson asked. "And, do you have any spare ammo for standard seven millimeter HVARs? We're flat out, sir."

"As far as we could tell the *Churchill* was completely destroyed with no survivors. Captain Samuels was a good leader and she led a great crew. We found no one. No. One. We did notice that some Army hovertanks were missing. Maybe some of the tank pukes got out in time. But the area was too hot to stick around to do a lot of recon." Burner paused for a brief silent second and then turned to Cordova. "Boulder, get these Marines whatever we can and let's get rallied to that evac point. From there we'll try to get in touch with somebody who knows what the fuck is going on."

"I'm on it, Burner."

Chapter 10

The garbage incinerator room was larger than a basketball arena and had a piercingly pungent odor. The odor was so thick it could practically be cut with a laser welder or could even be seen hovering like a foul smelling fog. The air was heavy and damp and just plain rank.

The city being under attack hadn't stopped the reclamation and redistribution drones from their work. Large AI controlled robot systems plowed through the mountainous refuse piles and separated them into various types of recyclable materials. Piles of multicolored plastics that ranged from translucent green soda bottles to the bright reds and yellows of children's toys made from previously recycled plastics rose like mountains from the cavernous room, some of them reaching peaks of more than a hundred and fifty meters high.

Nearest the far exterior wall of the room were plumes of smoke and steam rising from organically composting piles or scrap foodstuffs and bodily waste products that would be worked until the soil composting process was complete and then trucked to agricultural areas and beautification sites within the city. With millions of humans and animals in the Mons City complex there was plenty of organic waste of the smelly variety to be found. If the agricultural needs were met while there was a surplus of good soil, the surplus would be shipped out to other domes or agricultural projects via AI driven robotic transports. Not only were the materials recycled or destroyed there, they were also redistributed.

Slightly south of the organic piles were the non-reclaimable materials that went into the incinerator. The reclamation robots worked the piles diligently, placing load after load of combustible stuff into the cavernous inferno. Some of the heat from the inferno was pumped throughout the city while the rest was used to melt soil and ices and the exhaust gasses released into the atmosphere. There were similar incinerator systems in every dome city across the planet. Every little bit of terraforming gasses released into the atmosphere helped. And the materials reclamation had proven to be a thriving industry for the Martian economy. Luna City, Triton, and Kuiper Station were almost completely dependent on the Martian reclaimed materials for construction resources.

"Over by the organics," Reyez Jones pointed out the large lift across the way and below their vantage point on the entry catwalk and control tower used to oversee the reclamation operation. Of course, it was all automated, but the control tower was put in so that several union jobs could be established to "oversee" the AI workers. "There, see it?" Reyez leaned over the catwalk rail and fantasized for a brief second that the two hundred meter drop to the cavernous room's floor would make for a fun base jump.

"Got it. Look, the methane levels over there will have to be horrendous. By the time we get halfway there we should close our visors and go to scrubbers as long as we can. I bet we'll have to go to O2 to go through that mess." Alexander Moore had been thinking about the city dump for several minutes and was concerned that in the closed system there would be noxious volatiles and vapors that might pose a threat. Hopefully, the Seppies would know this as well and would have steered clear.

"Seems like a dangerous walk across that mess, Alexander." Sehera didn't like the thought of traipsing her little girl through mountains of unstable pointy objects with no telling what types of infectious bacteria, molds, and fungi growing in them.

"Daddy, it stinks too bad in here. I'm gonna throw up." Deanna heaved dramatically over the catwalk rail and then froze in her tracks as a big multi-armed and multi-legged metallic spider-thing, sauntered up to the top of the first debris pile just beneath their position by ten meters or so on the opposite side of the catwalk that Reyez had been salivating over. Deanna's fake heave quickly turned into a frightened gasp as the spider-thing raised upward and spewed a black oozing mud from its rearward chamber with the thrust of flatulence that only a Martian garbage eating monster could. The pungent odor in the local vicinity did not improve, any.

Perhaps I can help, sir, Abigail thought to her counterpart. *I've shaken hands with this one and it has agreed to give us a lift.*

Good work, Abigail, the senator thought.

Yes sir. Meet Reclamation AI Bravo India Lima Seven One One Six. He has auditory comms as well as AIC wireless.

"Don't worry, baby. That is our friend. He is gonna take us for a ride is all."

"That thing is gonna eat us, Daddy!" Deanna said with her eyes wide.

"Deanna, listen to Mommy." Sehera knelt beside her daughter and put her hand on her shoulders to calm her. "That is just a robot that carries garbage around from one place to another. It is not going to eat anybody. And, who knows, you might like him once you get to know him." Sehera smiled at her daughter and looked her in the eye.

"Ok, Mommy. But I bet he stinks . . . bad."

"Awww, don't worry little one I will not harm you. My name is BIL Seventy One Sixteen. What is yours?" The odd looking garbage robot asked.

"This fucking stinks, Vince." Rod stumbled as the line of Mons City refugees crowded forward into the central open court area. The Separatist troops had rounded up any of the stragglers that hadn't made it to the shelters and were moving them into the large open court. Rod couldn't figure out why, but he didn't like it.

"You're telling me, bud. I don't like this. I'm beginning to think we should've gone with that senator guy and Reyez." Vincent's cigarette end hung out the open face of his e-suit helmet and the white smoke twirled upward around his head, whirling with each new drag he took. Occasionally, he would puff out a smoke ring.

"Why are they gathering us up like this, I wonder?" a woman to Rod's right and one step in front of them asked of nobody in particular.

"It is quite obvious ain't it?" the fat mealy-mouthed man from the adventure shop said.

"If it is so fuckin' obvious, then why don't you tell us then," the woman replied in a panic.

"They need to keep track of us so they know where we are. This way we are all in one place and they don't have to worry about us sneaking up behind them," the fat man said knowingly.

"What do you think, Vince? He right?" Rod turned and looked at his friend hoping that was the only reason, but at the same time was pretty certain that it wasn't.

"Hmm. Could be, but I don't think so," Vince said and pulled the cigarette down to the filter with a deep inhale the end glowing red with the embers.

"Then what?" the panicky woman looked back at him.

"Am I wearing a Seppy e-suit? Can I read freakin' minds? No, I can't. I don't know what they are doing." Vince shook his head and then slowly scanned around the open court at the thousands of people that were being crowded in. "But I've got a bad feeling that somebody is wanting to make a point with us." He spit the cigarette filter onto the ground in front of him and twisted his e-suit jumpboot heel on it.

"Hell, if they want to make a point they have tens of thousands of people in the shelters they can use," Rod disagreed.

"And I'm sure they will, bud. I'm sure they will." Vincent felt through the breast pocket for his pack of cigarettes.

★ ★ ★

"Shavi, Kira Shavi. Anti-aircraft Defense Unit Technician, Elysium." Kira told the guard at the underground train station entrance and held up her arms as if in a stick up. The guard only slightly raised an eyebrow at the mention of the Elysium unit, a sign that he had to know how hard the Americans had hit the place. Kira kept her arms raised so the guard could hose her down. "How hot am I?" she asked the man.

"You took a pretty good dose, Sergeant Shavi." The man obviously understood the rank markings on Kira's Separatist Military e-suit. "Were you able to take anti-rad meds in time?" The guard whistled at the readings on his radiation monitor. The woman had been very close to the explosion at some point and took a serious radiation dose. Her suit was covered with fallout and was reading off the scale.

"Yes. We all did. Unfortunately for my brothers the meds do nothing for the shockwave or the fireball." She maintained the idle conversation with the train portal guard.

"I didn't realize there were still any troops that far out in the city. How did you manage to survive? Turn around." He asked and then motioned her to turn so he could hose down the back of her e-suit. He whistled again at the sight of all the scratches and dings in the rear of her armor. "You took quite a beating, too."

"I was down in the silo venting launch coolant when the bomb went off. My youngest brother kicked the silo door shut and triggered the coolant flood. I was trapped inside the silo, submerged in cryogel for more than twenty minutes before the outside environment cooled off enough for the silo auto drain switch to throw. I had to crawl out through the coolant drains. A few times I had to set off demo charges to blow out the drain grates or to widen an opening large enough to get through. A couple of times I used a little, uh, too much," Kira explained. "I was lucky, I guess. But my brothers were not."

"Ahmi was served. You were very resourceful and the Free People are fortunate to have brave ones like you." The man nodded and looked at his monitor again. "You're green." He switched off the hose and the white foam stream dribbled to a stop.

"Thanks. Ahmi was served," she replied. White anti-radiation foam dissipated and drained from her suit slowly in the low Martian gravity.

"Blower vents are around the corner just before the air locks."

"Got it."

"Next!" the train portal guard shouted.

The wait and then the loading process for the train hadn't been that bad. Kira and her new found friends kept each other company to pass the time. Kira was beginning to connect with the little girl if not her parents as well. As the fifteen car subway train floated to a stop at the loading ramp it bobbled up and down with a swish, and then the doors opened. There were only a handful of people getting off the train. In fact, it was mostly empty, all of the cars were. There were hundreds, maybe thousands, on the other hand waiting to get on. Some of them seemed calm, others panicky, and many at all ranges of moods and hysteria in between.

"Come on, Kira. You can sit with me and kitty." Lelandra took Kira's hand in hers and tugged her onto the train.

"Uh huh. That would be nice." Kira smiled shifting the weight of her e-suit backpack over onto her shoulder. Fortunately, the short wait, and the fact that they were now indoors had meant that everyone could shed their e-suits. Kira was glad to get out of hers and into normal clothes, Although all she had with her were Separatist Army issue battle dress fatigues and skins.

Kira Shavi sat with her backpack container resting in her lap and watched as the tunnel walls zipped by. The temperature on the train was cool but not unbearably so. The second skin she was wearing under the Seppy issue battle dress uniform that had been packed in her e-suit was more than enough to keep her comfortable. She pulled an energy bar from her pack and tore the wrapper clear. The bar heated itself almost instantly and the aroma of warm cinnamon, chocolate, and oatmeal filled her nostrils and made her mouth water. It had been a long day.

An occasional dim tunnel light would streak by and cast a faint glare on the train windows. Lela and her robot kitty nuzzled against her left arm. Kira would have offered her some of the food bar but the little Martian was fast asleep.

Out of the e-suit the little girl was obviously very cute and the spitting image of her mother. Her tall and slender frame with milky white skin and long black hair, typical of Martians, made her look older than she was, but Kira was used to looking at Earth and Luna children that didn't grow as quickly due to the heavier gravity fields—natural gravity on Earth and artificial on Luna. The little girl and her AI kitty snored lightly as they rested against the pack in Kira's lap. Kira had definitely made a new friend in the young Martian. The little Separatist girl's mother and father, Elise and Fayad, sat across the aisle from them speaking very little. Kira held the energy bar up in offering but they had waived it away.

"So, where are we going?" Kira asked.

Careful. Allison warned her. *Shouldn't you know?*

I don't know, but I'll qualify it. Kira thought about how to do that for brief moment. *I'll play it like an uninformed soldier.*

Good idea. That should work. More than ninety percent of these people appear to be civilians, if there is such a thing when it comes to Seppies. And have you noticed that they all seem to be leaving? They are not taking shelter from an attack, rather, they are leaving to somewhere.

I know. This all seems to have been planned whether or not we nuked one of the Reservation's cities. And, I never heard a second explosion or attack, so what happened there? There were some missing pieces that Kira couldn't put her fingers on, but there was more going on here than just a reaction to an attack. This scurrying around and evacuation of Separatists seemed to be part of some larger plan. The CIA's plan might have been implemented just in the knick of time and luckily at precisely the right moment. Kira was beginning to feel lucky.

"I mean, which route are *you* scheduled to take?" Kira pointed to the couple and their fast asleep little girl.

"Ah. You never were on a relocation list were you?"

Fayad said as matter of fact more than as a question. "One of the sacrificed," he said in an elitist fashion. Kira was surprised by the tone and didn't realize such castes existed in the Reservation culture. She had thought they were socialists but was beginning to rethink that.

"Uh . . . " Kira hesitated slightly not sure how to respond.

"Fayad, you are such a callous and unthinking brute!" Elise elbowed her Prime Husband. "She lost her entire unit. Is that not enough? Ahmi was served and she needn't sacrifice more, even if I have to sponsor her. She has more than earned a spot on our transport as far as I am concerned."

"I just meant that she was originally slated to stay behind." The man said sheepishly. It was obvious that his Prime Wife had just scolded him, and in public. Kira wasn't quite sure what the cultural protocols were for such a display but guessed that it would hold further ramifications for Fayad later when the couple were behind closed doors. Kira's training and cover personality development had drilled one thing deeply into her mind and that was that the Prime Wives ruled the Reservation.

"I knew that is what you meant. Pay no attention to him, Kira. Many of those with slots to go will not make it. My AIC has assured me of that. And besides, many with slots that will go I would gladly swap for some of our younger and braver heroes like yourself," Elise said. The fact that she had an AIC implant surprised Kira. "You are welcome to join my family if you wish. You found Lelandra for us and have helped with the wounded all the long trek to the train station. All of that above and beyond your sacrifice at Elysium."

"I'm honored." Kira wasn't sure what to say. Standard policy in espionage is if you aren't sure what to say, say little or nothing at all.

She has an AIC? Kira thought.

We knew our intel on the Separatists was missing a few things. Maybe Prime Wives carry them since they run all the business of the family. I could see how it would come in handy bookkeeping wise. Maybe she was in the Seppy military. That would explain it too, Allison replied. *But I haven't found a wireless signal from it or any other AICs from them. I'll have to broaden my spectrum. Pay attention to more of them for DTM facial expressions. AICs may be more prevalent in the Separatists than we originally thought.*

Probably right, Allison. Try expanding the QM spectrum around that of the AI Kitty spectrum. Maybe they like that frequency domain better for some reason. Next Internet hub we go by I'll do a quick search on AIKs.

Good idea.

This all seems too easy. Why would she just right off let me in her family? Kira was more than a little uneasy.

You found their daughter and helped with wounded. Maybe that was genuine enough. Maybe she is just the trusting sort.

I don't believe that for a minute. A naive Seppy Prime Wife? Not likely. There will be more to come I'm sure. Kira ran the scenario of her brothers' death through her mind again. The implanted emotional tags made the story feel so real that she came to tears for her dead brothers. A few tears streamed slowly down her cheeks and in the pale lighting of the train Elise had noticed that she was crying.

Kira dried her eyes with her fingers and her sleeves and then sniffled once while clearing her throat. She turned and looked out the window embarrassed.

"It is all right, Kira. You have sacrificed enough." Elise said softly to her. "We have all lost family in this crazy struggle for freedom. But we will prevail," she said more sternly.

"Sorry." Kira turned her head back around and looked at Elise. "So. Where are we going?"

"We're leaving on the *TCA Barge Tangier I* from Umbra Lake to rendezvous at Oort Seven Three Nine Nine Zero One with the rest of the Exodus. From there we will QMT to New Tharsis," Elise offered very matter-of-factly.

"I see. How many can we squeeze in the belly of the *Tangier I*?" Kira asked as if she knew what she were talking about.

Exodus? QMT? New Tharsis? Oort Seven Three Nine Nine Zero One? Any ideas Allison?

Exodus is from the Bible when Moses led the Jews from Egypt. Perhaps the Separatists are planning to leave the system. QMT, never heard of it, but perhaps it has something to do with quantum membranes as standard QM sensors do. New Tharsis, wherever we are going is named after Tharsis on Mars. Oort Seven Three Nine Nine Zero One must be a Separatist designation of some object in the Oort Cloud. I don't know any more than that, the AIC replied.

We do know one thing, now.

What is that?

We are going to Tau Ceti.

Of course! TCA Barge Tangier I. Tau Ceti Alliance Barge Tangier I. New Tharsis must be there. I hope it is a lot more inviting than the old Tharsis, and we are in for a long ride. I don't see how they think the millions of the Reservation can escape the system without major resistance, Allison replied with an inquisitive tone added to her mindvoice.

"Oh, I guess I keep forgetting that the troops in the field really haven't been fully briefed on everything have they? But why worry them with the details of moving nearly thirty million people from the planet all at the same time when they have to be focused on the diversion?" Elise nodded and squinted as the train passed a service center and the lighting brightened for a brief moment. "The *Tangier I* can hold about a million if you really pack them in, but for a point eight five light year trip we can only accommodate about six hundred thousand or so very friendly people. It'll be difficult and trying, but New Tharsis is well worth it and the QMT is a very easy trip. I've seen New Tharsis probably fifty times. It is indeed as beautiful as it is rumored to be."

"Most certainly worth the sacrifice then?" Kira added.

"Yes, the three month trip to Oort rendezvous will be . . . trying for most. But our estate rooms will be less so," Fayad said almost egotistically, again.

"Do not boast, Fayad. We will share our fortunate life with those less so." Elise scolded her Prime Husband. It was clear to Kira who wore the pants in that family, but again the intel briefings back at her CIA training had shown her that the Separatists were matriarchal. She was really beginning to understand *how* matriarchal the culture actually was.

"Estate room?" Kira asked and reshuffled her weight slowly, trying not to wake the child lying against her. Lela grunted and moved only slightly. The lazy AI kitty raised its head and looked at Kira as if to complain about the movement and then went right back to sleep.

"Yes. My aunt owns *Tangier I*. It is a nice ship as far as barges go," Elise said nonchalantly and then looked as if she would add something more but decided against it.

Kira?

Yes Allison?

How could she have seen Tau Ceti fifty times? At best military speeds we are limited to about a light year per month. Tau Ceti is nearly twelve light years away. A round trip would take two years. I doubt Elise is over a hundred years old. She looks too full blooded Martian to be that old yet. Oh, and add the trips to this Oort Cloud destination makes another twenty-five or more years. That puts her to at least one hundred and twenty-five if she started traveling when she was an infant. It doesn't add up. The oldest human is only three hundred and seventeen and an Earthling, The AIC commented.

I was doing the math in my head and reached the same conclusion. But Elise doesn't seem the type to lie or exaggerate. This is odd. Maybe we're not going to Tau Ceti?

I don't know. Tau Ceti seems like the solution Occam's Razor would suggest.

Then that means the Separatists are far more technologically advanced than the rest of the human race . . . following Occam's Razor of course.

Yes it does. Allison was as confused as her human counterpart but logic was logic and the answers that were logical didn't make any sense. Allison realized that that little fact alone was creating a paradox in her logic process. They needed more data.

Kira sat motionless and remembered she needed to respond to Elise verbally.

"I've only been as far as Luna City once and to the raids in Triton. Both times in asteroid mining haulers hidden away inside ore containers. I've never even seen an interstellar barge before." Ignorance was always a good cover tactic. The sudden urge to yawn overcame her and Kira squinted and shook her head. "Forgive me. The day has been longer than I had realized." Long indeed. The radiation meds were wearing on her like the flu. Also, she had been flung at high speeds from a supercarrier in the midst of a major air battle, flown through high g-force maneuvers in a harrowing dogfight, nearly shot down on several occasions by both SAMs and Seppy aircraft—Gomers as Lieutenant Commander Boland had called them—and ejected from an Ares fighter at high velocity at about the same time a nuclear bomb was detonated only a few tens of kilometers from her. And that was just the start of her day. Her gliderchute ride, the radiation, the long bounce across the foothills until she found any survivors of the nuclear attack, and then the radiation shower all made for a long day. Kira was pretty sure that her day was just a sign of harder days to come.

"Yes. Close your eyes for now. We have at least thirty minutes to Umbra. We will have plenty of time to talk further." Elise bowed her head slowly and then turned back to Fayad, who had already dozed off. His head was against the window and his mouth open as he snored and drooled down his chin. Elise shook her head in disdain at her Prime Husband but then looked back at her child in reverence once again and decided to close her eyes as well.

Kira had uncovered way more than she had expected to so quickly. She understood some vague concepts of the Separatist culture and their plans. But she only had a few solid pieces of information. It was too early to attempt a contact back to Langley. Her mission was going as planned—actually it was far exceeding any expectations already. For now, there was little to do but to close her eyes and rest for a while. It *had* been a long day so far.

Chapter 11

"So BIL, have you seen any other people wander through here lately?" Sehera asked and tried to hold on to a hand hold in the wall of the belly of the mechanical beast in an attempt to maintain her balance. The several ton robotic spider-thing sprang with tremendous agility from one mound of garbage to the next and made its way toward the large elevator, making it a bumpy ride.

"No ma'am. You are the first humans I've seen in more than four years. The Union strike that started the pull out of the Separatist workers in 2379 caused the government to cancel the contract for the human workers here. It has been . . . lonely since then." The AI garbage hauler vehicle sounded almost sad. "I am very happy to greet you. It has been a long time since my auditory systems have been put to use."

"That's sad, BIL." Deanna pouted and stuck her bottom lip out for effect but it was lost on the garbage drone as there were no optical sensors in its belly.

"Yes, I guess it is," he replied.

"So BIL, do you have any communication with the outside world at all? I mean, how do you know what to do?" Joanie asked the AI. The bouncing of the garbage hauler launched the little Triton woman nearly a meter into the air with each stride. It grew tiresome, but Joanie and Sehera had managed to make it a game with Deanna. Alexander was only paying them partial attention.

"Oh, it is simple. This pile of plastics over here must be moved to there and that pile of metals there needs to be loaded into the smelting system. The piles are always there and so I always have plenty to do." BIL replied.

"But what about the outside world?" Senator Moore asked.

"Sure, I am connected to all the local and wide area network systems including the infrastructure QM. I have to schedule with the other domes on how much of what materials they need or are sending here. That way I can be certain which pile to work on first. And many times we get orders from elsewhere for particular materials," BIL continued to explain his mundane daily routine.

"I'm not sure I follow, BIL," Reyez laughed. Reyez displayed an expression on his face that plainly stated that he couldn't believe that he was talking to a garbage bug, much less inside one hanging on for dear life as the thing skittered up and down the mountains of garbage in the reclamation and redistribution center. When this adventure was over and the war calmed down, Alexander was certain that the adrenaline junkie would work an adventure store angle on riding in, or maybe on, a giant robotic garbage hauler. After all, the ride was invigorating and exciting, if not smelly. But adrenaline junkies would endure serious discomfort for a new thrill. What was a little stench?

"Yes, let me see. The naval vessels often need to drop waste here and I schedule that—a really good source for methane distillation and soil composting that. Hold on," BIL warned his passengers just before he made a quick squatting bend and then bounced high across a crevasse in the mountain of refuse.

"Weeee!" Deanna screamed and touched her toes cheerleader style as she did the splits in the air. The ride was more like a parabolic flight trajectory to simulate weightlessness than it was a rollercoaster. A better description would be like putting a children's moonbounce in the back of a flatbed truck and then to drive it across seriously unleveled and rocky terrain. Add to that the extremely dim lighting in the belly of the robot spider-thing accentuated by the bouncing white lights of the e-suit helmets and the effect was a full up bouncing disco on steroids. The only thing missing was the dance music. At least it stunk.

"How much further?" Joanie asked. The bouncing was beginning to take a toll on her physical strength. She was sweating profusely in her suit, but the seal layer would absorb that and reclaim the water and salts.

"Almost there," BIL replied over the speaker system.

"So BIL," Alexander was making a point to minimize his physical effort as he might need his strength later, so he had tried to let the bouncing of the beast throw him around and then use his jumpboots to soften the landings. If the giant bug had been equipped with seats this ride would have been a snap. "Tell me more about your outside contacts. When was the last one you had?"

"Well, I get them pretty much continuously. It is a big system." It was obvious that the AI had longed to talk because he took twice as long to say what needed to be said. "This morning I received an alert that there were no loads of frozen algae coming in from Elysium and a few seconds ago I was given instruction that there was a need in Luna City for aluminum, iron, and titanium. I've called the shipping companies trying to schedule a barge but for some reason they are all grounded today." BIL's voice sounded as if he had shrugged when he made the last statement.

"Wait a minute, BIL. You just a few seconds ago talked to Luna City?" Senator Moore asked.

"Yes."

Abigail!

Yes sir, I heard it. I'll talk directly with him to get access to his communications protocols. Perhaps we could get some communications outside this jamming phenomena. Moore had confidence that his AIC understood what she needed to do. She just had to convince the AI garbage hauler to cooperate. The way the poor AI was longing for attention it probably would agree to anything within the law and maybe even then some. And if he was communicating outside the jamming field then that meant that the Separatists techs had missed the infrastructure layer of communications. Unless they had missed it on purpose.

Hull Technician Third Class Joe Buckley was reading over his current set of orders that were continuously being updated by the brains up in the Looney Bin. Typically, his orders were always the same whether or not the *Madira* was going to battle or not. But then again, the *Sienna Madira* was always going into battle or at least it had been ever since he had been onboard her. His duties were actually quite simple. He was to make sure the reclamation systems were not overflowing and that there were no deficiencies in the materials bins. In other words, make sure the sewer didn't get too full of shit and that the officers had plenty of toilet paper. He also was in charge of keeping the ship's coolant flow systems operational. Being in charge of sewer duties meant that he often had to put up with a lot of shit—in more ways than one.

Joe prayed for the days where his spot in the flight deck cleaning rotation was due. On those lovely days he would get to walk back and forth on the upper flight catapults picking up trash, removing bird shit—those hybrid Martian vultures were nasty critters—and checking for exterior hull plates that were outgassing that weren't *supposed* to be outgassing. Yes, those days were bliss compared to his weeks at a time in the "shithole". Otherwise he never saw the outside of the ship.

Looks like another shitty day. His AIC said the same old, very old, joke that she had told him every day for the entire sixteen months of Buckley's tour on the *Madira*.

Yeah. Into the never ending fray for God and Country we go. Forever protecting our best and brightest's wonderful shithole! He recited. *Mija, it looks like we are about to get really into the thick of some bad stuff so we better start running the combat readiness flush and purge sequences.*

Buckley scrolled through the daily task orders in his planner. The battle drill was simple. Batten down all the toilet lids, which was a euphemism for turning valves to certain plumbing systems. And to close up the shitter so that when the ship started listing left, right, and up, and down that smelly stuff didn't burst out of the miles of plumbing throughout the massive ship or to rupture the Olympic swimming pool sized septic bladder.

Roger that, Joe, Petty Officer Third Class Mike India Juliet Alpha Kilo One Tango Edgar, "Mija Kitty", replied.

Buckley and Mija had been through hours of training classes explaining how any excess human waste in the plumbing system during high g-force compensation maneuvers could stress the structural integrity of the plumbing system and therefore create a smelly safety hazard during a combat situation. On more than several occasions they had been in the wrong corridor at the wrong time when the plumbing failed because some Deck Petty Officer on a different shift neglected to flush the system, purge it with compressed dry air, and then lock it down before a maneuver. Buckley was often jeered for having a "shitty job," and needless to say, he kept his immuno-booster shot current and gave it a good workout. And as the Captain had exclaimed on several occasions in all hands briefings, "There is no job on my boat that is less important than any other. Remember, this is the flagship of the United States Space Naval Fleet." Buckley repeated that to himself every night before he could manage to go to sleep. But he managed to maintain a level of pride about the job he did. Hell, it was an important job. What if a flow system went out near some important electronics system? There were toilets, sinks, and disposals on every deck and getting the refuse moved around safely without damaging other complex technical systems onboard the supercarrier was indeed an important job. Perhaps it wasn't a glamorous job like being a fighter jock, but his life expectancy was a hell of a lot higher.

Buckley was just finishing up the organization of his battle plan task list when the order of his tasks reshuffled and slipped each order down a notch on the screen in front of him.

"Aww shit. I just got those straightened out and prioritized. Now what?" He rolled his eyes, leaned back in his chair and sighed with a few more expletives to follow.

Looks like we have a new order request, Joe. It appears to be from the Mons City Rec and Redist AI, Mija replied. She was just as surprised as Buckley was.

As order number one an information packet from the Mons City reclamation and redistribution tracking AI, of all places, marked "Deliver to Captain *Sienna Madira* Immediately," popped up in the schedule on the screen.

Mija can you open this? This isn't some kinda joke is it? The Hull Technician Petty Officer Third Class had seen his share of tasteless jokes.

Ok, Joe. Here. Mija Kitty paused for a second. *I don't think this is a joke!*

"What the hell," Buckley muttered to himself.

"That is un-fucking-believable, sir! And out-god-damned-standing if you don't mind my saying it." Sergeant Jackson couldn't believe what he was hearing. This Senator Moore, as it turns out U.S.M.C. Major Moore retired, had somehow managed to find a crack in

the local Seppy jamming field and was in direct contact
with the *Sienna Madira's* Captain.

"You got that right, Sergeant. Tammie has Burner's AIC
continuously linked with the *Madira* now. We do have an
extraction plan. And we have a means to coordinate the
other troops across the region back to the main fleet. I
might have to move to Mississippi so I can vote for
this Marine," Second Lieutenant Thomas Washington
replied.

"Semper Fi, sir." Kootie added.

Washington sat on the left shoulder of Burner's FM-12
Strike Mecha and Sergeant Jackson sat on the right. Each
of them straddling the forty millimeter cannons mounted
there, the barrels extending out between the armored
e-suits' legs like a giant and deadly robotic phallus. Kootie
and Shelly rode similarly on Boulder's transfigurable fighting mecha. The ten meter tall armored vehicles trotted
and jumped from block to block in bot mode looking like
giant gladiators hiding behind the city skyscrapers. A
handful of the fighting mecha skittered about the streets
around them in eagle mode with their DEGs at ready in
their left armored hands. Every now and then the AEMs
could catch a glimpse of one or two of the fighting mecha
in fighter mode just above the city building tops.

"So what is the game plan, Lieutenant?" Corporal
Shelly asked.

"We stick with the Killers all the way. They can cover the
ground a lot better than we can. And, they are better armed
and sensored up." Washington was a lot more hopeful of
their chances of surviving this mission and actually being
successful at it now that they had a complete squadron of

Marine fighting mecha with them. Two dozen FM-12s and four AEMs were a significant fighting force.

"Second Lieutenant Washington," Burner interrupted the chatter.

"Sir?"

"I just got a map of the evac area downloaded and I overlaid it with our tactical plan." Burner started explaining the plan as the topographical three dimensional map was DTMed to all of the AEMs and the mecha pilots as well. "You can see here that just to the south of the extraction zone is a sheer cliff wall over a thousand meters of drop-off." The image of the cliff wall highlighted in the DTM image.

"Roger that." Washington instinctively nodded in his e-suit helmet.

"Worst case, if things go to hell, you AEMs hang on to one of us and we'll drop off the edge there for cover. Best case, we'll go to eagle mode and hold on to you and just fly out to the supercarrier." Burner ordered.

"Sounds like a plan, sir!" the second lieutenant replied.

Simply flying out of the region to another city or base wasn't an option, at least not without cover from space or larger vessels. The intelligence from the *Madira* showed that there were at least six Separatist carriers in the region. The anti-aircraft systems and fighter squads of a carrier would be hell on his fighters out in the open without any cover. Fighters were better adapted to close in agile maneuvering along the surface of a city or even a carrier, but given that there could be six carriers worth of Seppy aircraft in the area a fly-out operation might prove suicidal. Burner knew it would be best for them to lay low until they had some cover from the Madira and a few dozen Navy Ares fighters.

As they neared the wall of the dome just south of the gaping hole made by the crash of the *Churchill* the slope of the dome changed dramatically and so the buildings were not as tall in this part of the city. From the view of the almost now vertical dome wall it was apparent that the four AEMs and the two dozen FM-12s from Cardiff's Killers would soon be at the edge of the city where they would escape out into the Martian mountainside and then make their way towards the evac—fighting all the way if need be. The clouds overhead grew darker, thicker, and swirled more violently as they approached the massive leak in the dome.

"This is where we go up, Deanna," BIL told the little girl bouncing tirelessly and joyously in the belly of the AI garbage hauler. The AI had enjoyed talking to actual humans, especially the child. He had also especially enjoyed being able to speak, but mostly listen and pass through data, with all the AICs and humans now using his data link for communications. BIL was a reclamation and scheduling AI and had paid little attention to politics or the war but he could tell that his companions seemed to think all of this was extremely important and that their lives depended on it.

"Thank you, BIL. Have you ever been out of the garbage room before? It sure does stink in there," the little girl asked.

"Only to the top hangar floor to take in or deliver a load of materials. The smell doesn't bother me as I don't have a nose," he replied, adding a tone of humor to his artificial voice.

"That's silly. No nose." Deanna laughed and made a funny face at her mother and the Triton woman.

"The big metal spider has no nose." Joannie laughed with the little girl.

"I'm quite looking forward to traveling out into the actual Martian atmosphere with you. I've never been out of the dome before," BIL replied. He really liked the little girl and didn't want to see any harm come to her. He was deciding that presently the garbage could wait and that his current cargo was more precious. BIL was also fairly certain from his wireless interaction with the senator's AI staffer that his keeping the little precocious first grader's curiosity entertained was much appreciated. BIL didn't really know a lot about humans, but he was pretty sure that these were tired and very frightened of something.

The big robot spider-thing scampered its four ton body onto the giant lift. BIL shifted his weight onto seven legs and pushed some debris out of the way so he could completely work his body onto the front right corner of the platform. He wirelessly activated it, triggering the actuator field to spring to life. The elevator, surprisingly, moved rather rapidly upward for its size and BIL had to adjust his weight on his eight legs to adjust for the added g-forces of the lift acceleration. The large platform passed through the first subsurface floor and then to the surface in about twenty seconds and came to a stop in the loading end of a very large hangar that at one end had the largest airseam on Mars. Through the dome could be seen a very large landing port and there were several barge cars and smaller cargo vessels sitting on the landing field. There were a few privately owned aircraft and space faring vehicles located on the periphery of the hangar and outside on the airfield. Some of the vehicles were white and silvery and shiny and obviously very expensive while others were dinged up, oily black, and grimy from use and continuous repair and obviously held together on a shoestring budget. The scene was reminiscent of practically any airfield and spaceport across the system.

The landing field and the hangar were buzzing with activity that, on the other hand, was not reminiscent of any civilian airfield. There were hovertrucks and Separatist drop mecha running here and there that were carting armored Separatist soldiers in and out to their various assigned defensive or offensive positions. Every few seconds an Orcus drop tank would either land or take off across the Martian landscape to some unseen designation. Armed and armored e-suit Separatists were bouncing outside by the dozens, loading and unloading materials and even wounded. At the far end on the northeast side of the airfield was a hospital tent that had been inflated just outside the far edge of the airseam. Medivac aircraft landed almost nonstop on several of the pads and even on the taxiways of the northeast side of the spaceport. Ambulances came and went from the front of the tent then through the airseam, probably headed into Mons City to make use of some of the better hospital facilities in the city. As far as the garbage hauler AI was concerned, the sight was magnificent. There were people everywhere—including other AIs.

"BIL, we cannot be captured by those people," Senator Moore told the AI. There were no windows or screens in the belly of the garbage hauler but the hauler did have cameras and sensors on the outside to aid it in its daily reclamation job. BIL had worked directly with Abigail, the senator's AIC, to develop a mosaic algorithm for the sensor images and linked them DTM to the senator.

"I understand, senator. What would you have me do?" BIL asked.

"Why don't we just walk out like we are on a standard garbage dump or something?" Sehera offered. The bouncy ride through the garbage cavern had tired them all and the two women and the little girl were sitting down and leaning against one of the sticky smelly walls of the garbage hauler's interior. The smell inside the vehicle would have been more than the humans could withstand were it not for their e-suits. With the helmets sealed off the scrubber filters would remove any of the unwanted pathogens, allergens, and chemicals.

"Well, ma'am, there are no dumps into the local Martian region. All the garden zones are further south a bit." BIL explained.

"Mommy, who would know that?" Deanna asked her mother.

"What do you mean, dear?"

"Yes, of course." Moore was continually amazed by his daughter's ability to see the obvious. "BIL, these Seppy troops will have no idea what your job is. Just tell them that you are on a scheduled job to go south to reclaim an abandoned dwelling dome. Can you do that?"

"Certainly, if it will help you secure your safety. I can

even change the schedule in the infrastructure system to show that I am supposed to be doing just that." BIL liked his companions and didn't want to see anything happen to them and a little freedom with the scheduling system wouldn't hurt. BIL was wondering why he had never thought of doing that before. Unbeknownst to him, Abigail had taken some liberties with the AI's regulations and ethics protocol software. Of course, Abigail could not alter his being; after all AIs were living entities. But she could rewrite the rules that he was told to follow. As far as BIL was concerned, he had just never thought of going for a walk outside.

"Thank you, BIL," Sehera said in a maternal tone. "Be careful."

"Very well. To the airseam then. Hold on please." The spider's legs again started quickly shifting back and forth one over the other like the giant hybrid Granddaddy Longlegs spiders of the Elysium Planitia algae fields.

Once Gail and her cameraman had made their way into the main dome of Mons City they had been forced to take refuge in a convenience store at the edge of the hangar deck of the air field. There had been so much Separatist troop movement coming and going that they had decided to lay low for a few moments and take a much needed break in the action. They had been through several close calls as it were, one of them actually while they had been broadcasting live to MNN. They had had to cut their report short and take cover. It had never occurred to her that the Seppies had to have the technology to track the video link transmissions back to the main MNN router system. Apparently, the Separatists were not interested in stopping the news, but Gail didn't think of that. She was more concerned with hiding and not being captured—she had seen what happened to reporters captured by the Seppies on Triton. Not good.

And, Gail and her cameraman were getting hungry. The convenience store made perfect sense. Once they had sneaked by the troop movement and into the back door of the little store they had relaxed a bit and helped themselves to the junk food and sodas stocked on the shelves and in the coolers. They were even able to reload the e-suit reservoirs with water. Having been outside and before that in the damaged borough of the southern domes the two of them had been sealed up in their e-suits for hours and used up a lot of their water. There was another aspect of being sealed up in an e-suit that required patience or regular breaks and that was the claustrophobia aspect. Being in the main dome that was not yet breached was literally a breath of fresh air to them and a chance to take off their helmets and stretch their necks, scratch their heads, and run their fingers through their hair for a bit. And it made eating and drinking stolen junk food a whole lot easier.

"Hold on, Calvin. What the hell is that?" Gail Fehrer had paid little attention to the lift platform at first. In her mind it was just a very large cargo elevator. But then she realized that something was out of place that was riding on the lift platform. At first all she could make out of the scene was that the lift rose and was littered with recyclable materials and general trash, but then a very large section of the trash started to move on its own, which startled her.

Then she had realized that it was a giant metallic gray mechanical spider, which was completely unexpected and a little bit unsettling.

"That thing is odd looking. What is that?" the MNN cameraman asked and choked down the last of a candy bar since he knew that break time was over. He had been with Gail long enough to know that she would want to take a closer look at anything out of the ordinary. And a giant mechanical spider traipsing around in the midst of a bunch of Separatist troops could at the least be described as "out of the ordinary."

"I don't know. But whatever it is, get it on video," the seasoned field reporter exclaimed. It was news, Gail was certain of it. "We've got to figure out how to get closer and get a better look at that thing."

"Preferably, without getting caught, Gail," Calvin added. "Gail, are you listening to me?" Obviously, she was not so Calvin just sighed and continued to gather himself up to follow her off into some foolish and quite dangerous journalistic endeavor, as he always did.

The metal beast began to gingerly scamper across the large lift platform toward the airseam field, its eight long legs moving back and forth almost too quickly for the eyes to make sense of. To their surprise, so far, the Separatist troops were paying it little or no attention. Gail wasn't sure what to make of the sight, but her seasoned journalist's insight understood when something was news worthy.

"Come on. Let's follow it and see what it is up to," she told Calvin while twisting her e-suit helmet seal ring tight. "I smell a story."

"Somehow Gail, I knew you were going to say that."

The camera and communications tech grabbed the gear, which consisted of a small repulsor field stabilized camera platform and QM wireless transceiver all no larger than a softball, and swigged one last swallow of the Dr. Deimos in his hand. Calvin dropped the silver lettered maroon can on the floor then squished it under his right jumpboot heal. "Ready when you are," he replied and twisted his helmet into place.

The small storefront was typical of the industrial end of the city and was sandwiched between an aviation mechanical shop and a plumbing store. The stores faced the street that made up the east face of the hangar entrance that was on the city side of the hangar. There were large windows on the front of the marscrete and plastic construction buildings, all of which had multi-colored logos and advertisements painted on them.

The store owners had apparently left for the shelters in such a hurry that they had neglected to bring in the newsstands and potato chip racks from outside the front door. Originally, Calvin had to cut through the lock on the back door—camera techs had to be resourceful in the network news industry. Then the two of them made themselves at home in the small store, helping themselves to junk food and soft drinks. The videoscreens and the lights were on so the store looked as if the owners left in haste without giving it a proper shut down, which was understandable considering that there had been the threat of terrorist attack and the dome giving way.

Their search for useful tools in the store uncovered a set of keys that allowed them to unlock the front door. This made it easier on them to follow the mechanical robot and keep it in sight. Had they been forced to take the back door the spider might have been gone before they could make it down the back building alleyway to the next street-crossing nearest the hangar entrance.

"Let's go and keep the camera running." Gail eased out the front door of the little convenience shop and stayed as close to the walls of the buildings on their side of the street as she could. Calvin followed her lead and made every attempt at staying in the shadows while at the same time keeping the giant metal bug in the camera viewer.

They slipped silently down the street until there were no more buildings to stick close to. The street turned ninety degrees southward and followed the outer wall of the hangar bay until it met the taxiway for the space traffic. There were loading docks and cargo movers parked along the hangar bay wall. There was also the occasional privately owned aircraft parked in a small paved parking lot at the dome wall side of the taxiway. Gail and Calvin ducked behind parked forklifts and private planes leapfrogging each other from one to the next until they reached the edge of the dome near the airseam field generator just to the right of the adit.

The spider-thing had made its way to the edge of the airseam field with little if any attention being paid to it. Then the airseam light went green and the giant bug scampered out into the Martian atmosphere. As it passed through the seam's force field an iridescent hue of violet and blue rippled across the large plane of the opening.

"Come on." Gail grabbed Calvin by the wrist and bounced three times along the dome wall and then through the airseam field right behind the metal beast again generating the iridescent ripples in the field. Once outside the dome wall they took cover underneath a parked tugship's landing skids about fifty meters from the spider. "Your getting it, right?"

"You have to ask? After all these years?" Calvin smiled at his partner but kept the video centered on the bug.

"Sorry. Why do you suppose nobody is paying that thing any attention at all?" It didn't make sense to Gail. If a giant metal spider came traipsing along in front of her she'd damned well pay it some attention—especially during the middle of an all out attack.

"Who knows? Maybe it's supposed to be there?"

"Well, we need to stay with it. Let's stow away on it." Gail crawled out from under the tugship's landing gear and bounced to the nearest ship that could be used for cover. For a brief second she was in the open and viewable and vulnerable but nobody saw her. Calvin, likewise, followed right behind her unnoticed as well.

The reporter and cameraman continued to press their luck, bouncing from cover point to cover point until they were ahead of the spider's path. Finally, in a mad dash, Gail and Calvin bounced three times across a taxiway, on top of a parked cruiser, and then came to a *clanking* landing on top of the mechanical spider.

Gail landed on her jumpboots but the swaying jerking motion of the spider's walking made her lose her balance, causing her to fall face first into the dingy metal surface of the garbage hauler. Calvin landed with a little better finesse but then fell immediately onto his posterior and then backwards onto his head. Gail reached out and grabbed the ankle of his jumpboot in order to keep him from sliding headfirst and upside down off the spider.

As they gained their composure they did their level best at staying out of sight of the troops scurrying about the spaceport below them. But, holding onto any crease or bulge in the surface of the beast proved to be harder than they had expected since the exterior of the garbage hauler was basically smooth and metallic with no bumps or hand-holds. The two reporters pressed their stomachs to the surface of the thing as best they could, keeping their arms and feet spread wide.

The spider's body consisted of two sections. A smaller rounded head section that most likely carried the sensors and control systems and looked as if it could carry a couple of passengers had a forward looking windscreen and two side windows. This head compartment looked empty. The rearward section was more boxy in shape and had no windows. There were mechanisms that ran beneath the spider's rear compartment that suggested that it could dump that compartment over like a dump truck. There was also a door on the rear of it. But they had seen this only as they rushed to jump on the spider. They were much more *intimate* with the top of it now.

The top of the spider was much more flat than rounded as a biological spider looks and as they inched their way along on their bellies and toward the center of the thing's back they realized that it caved slightly inward to a seam that ran down the middle of its back. The seam ran parallel with the direction the spider walked.

Once they managed to slide to the bottom of the v-shape where the seam ran front to back of the rear compartment and largest section of the spider Gail and Calvin were able to maintain their position because gravity was assisting them and they were at the bottom of a small gravity well. In other words, the garbage trailer of the beast had two doors that met in the middle of the beast's back like two sliding garage doors. The two sliding doors met running down the middle of the hauler's back, creating a seam that Gail and Calvin could wedge themselves into.

"So, what do we do now?" Calvin asked, hanging on for dear life. It was a seriously bumpy ride.

"I don't know," Gail answered with a shrug and shifted her weight from left to right and then forward and aft as the spider's odd eight legged motion jerked her about. "Be patient."

"Uh oh, do you feel that?" Calvin felt along the seam where the garage doors met. The doors felt as if they were vibrating and pulling away from each other.

"Feel, whaaaaaaaaaaaa!"

Chapter 12

12:32 PM Mars Tharsis Standard Time

The opening in the top of the garbage hauler cracked just wide enough for a bright and blinding splinter of white light to seep through. Just as quickly and silently as the doors atop the empty garbage container more than ten meters above them had opened they began to close. Just as the doors were closing Alexander Moore could see two human figures flailing helplessly, silhouetting in the splinter of light as they fell slowly in the Martian gravity to the floor of the garbage hauler.

"Yes, I see them BIL, thanks." Alexander brought his Separatist HVAR off the sling on his back and lowered it to his hip, pointing in the general direction of the two *thuds* that he heard about seven meters to his left and dead center of the empty garbage hauler.

Abigail, any ID on them? The senator thought to his AIC.

Yes, senator. They are emitting press badge signatures, Abigail replied.

No shit. The press? No matter where we go, the press is gonna find us, hey? He chuckled and at the same time muttered it under his breath. *Goddamned press.*

"Nobody moves a muscle," Moore said over the speaker of his e-suit and broadcast on the suit-to-suit QMs. He swept the suit lights over their two unlikely stowaways and could tell they weren't hurt, just stunned by falling and landing off balance inside an empty garbage hauling mechanical spider. Perhaps what stunned them the most was that they found people inside it, armed people?

"Who are you?" Gail Fehrer asked holding her hands up in front of her face to block out the bright light from Moore's e-suit helmet.

"I said don't move or I'll shoot you, damnit!" Moore said with more venom and tilted the light away from them just enough for them to notice that not only was he pointing an automatic rifle at her but so was Joanie. "Now, I'll ask the questions. Who the hell are you?"

"Gail Fehrer, MNN," Gail stated sounding as if she were signing off of an on air report. "And this is my cameraman, uh, Calvin Dean."

"Ok. What are you doing here?" Moore kept the rifle centered on the two reporters.

"We were in the South Borough when the supercarrier crashed and have been following the Seppies ever since. We stowed away on one of their convoy tankers here from the south to see what was happening in the main dome. Then we saw the damnedest thing marching across the airport." Fehrer nervously rushed her explanation. Moore could tell that she didn't like staring down the barrel of an automatic weapon known for firing seven millimeter rounds at ten percent the speed of light with the ability to bring down fighting mecha. In fact, Moore sympathized with her. He didn't like staring down an HVAR either and it was something he had never gotten used to no matter how many times he had been forced to do it.

"Ok, then you are in the wrong place. We are leaving the city, fast. As fast as BIL here can carry us. So I suggest the two of you hop the hell out right now." Moore said.

"Can we ask why you're leaving the city? And who you are?" Fehrer asked

"Are you transmitting with that thing? Reyez, take it." Moore nodded Jones to the video device that the cameraman was wielding.

Jones grabbed for the camera but Calvin yanked it back and started to put up a fight. Moore gave Calvin a rifle butt to the stomach and then swept his legs out from under him with a sweeping hook kick to the back of the knee. He spun around and placed a jump boot on Calvin's wrist, pinning the video camera to the floor of the garbage hauler and then placing the rifle barrel closer to the man's faceplate.

"You sit still, young lady." Joanie Hassed moved in closer to Gail, giving her a nice view of the wrong end of the other Seppy rifle.

"Wait!" Fehrer cried. "Stop, we can't hurt you because we're unarmed. Calvin, give them the damned camera."

Reluctantly, Calvin released his grip on the video device and rolled his head back, pounding the back of his helmet into the floor with disgust. Reyez grabbed the camera and made sure that the transmission and record were turned off. Abigail double checked it with her QM sensors also, just to make sure that Reyez hadn't missed anything.

"Hold on!" Fehrer continued. "We are just following a news story. We've seen the troop movement from here to the far south dome. We can help you. It's obvious that you're not Seppy troops or you wouldn't be hiding in here. Relax. We're on your side."

"Alexander, I think she is telling the truth," Sehera told her husband. Her daughter stood behind her hugging onto her left leg, hiding her face.

"Yes. We are telling the truth." Calvin Dean rose slowly and pulled himself to his feet grunting and coughing from the residual pain the rifle butt to the gut had created.

"All right. No sudden moves. And neither of you so much as sneezes without asking me first," the senator warned them. He had never trusted the press as far back as his days at Mississippi State. He had seen them generate news at the expense of his teammates' futures with very little thought. And the way the press handled the Desert Campaigns on Mars was nothing short of treason, but they had gotten away with it. As a politician, granted he was a public person to be scrutinized by the public, but in general, the press had never done anything but cause heartache and hardship as far as he was concerned. There were occasions for the exception though and of course he believed in free speech, but he also believed in ethics and honor. Moore had found that most of the mainstream press had neither ethics nor honor, just a thirst for the power of being a public figure. Moore had seen one or two out of the hundreds of reporters he had met that may have been worth killing, but only one or two. The rest weren't worth the railgun round it would take to blast them. The jury was out on these two at the moment. And Moore wasn't in the mood to put up with much at the moment.

"Ok. Could you lower your lights a bit, though? They're giving me a headache," the cameraman asked.

Abigail, dim the lights.

Yes senator.

"BIL, how much longer?" Moore asked out loud.

"We have currently accelerated to top speed of one hundred and eighty kilometers per hour and are about forty-seven minutes from the evacuation coordinates, Senator Moore," BIL quickly responded. Moore cringed when BIL used his title and name. Now he'd have to answer a bunch of damned questions. "I would suggest that you all sit on the floor and make yourselves as comfortable as you can. I will try to reduce the bumpiness of the ride as best I can."

"Thank you, BIL. Just get us there in time," Moore said and motioned for everyone to have a seat. Once they were all seated facing each other in a circle in the middle of the garbage hauler's floor he sat down too.

"Senator Moore? Alexander Moore from Mississippi?" Fehrer asked. "You're part of the Arbitration Summit right?"

"Yes."

"That's it? Yes? You're the first politician I've ever seen not in a hurry to wax poetic for the press." Gail laughed, wishing she could get her camera back and record this conversation.

"Well, if you haven't noticed, Miss Fehrer, we are under attack and under siege by a Separatist military force the likes of which hasn't been seen for decades. And my wife, daughter, and I are caught up in the midst of it all. So pardon me if I'm more concerned with the safety and evacuation of my family and these two citizens at the moment than being on the news."

"Sorry, Senator. I understand. Listen. Let Calvin have his camera back. We'll record only and wait to transmit until we are safely away from the Seppies. I wouldn't mind getting out of here either. I promise not to broadcast," Fehrer begged the rifle wielding statesman.

"All right. But my staffer is QMing you. If you so much as emit one iota from that thing I'll bust some rounds off through it and then squish it with my jumpboots, understand?" Moore eyed the two of them and raised the rifle barrel upward for emphasis, but he could tell they understood.

"Promise, Senator."

"All right then. Reyez, give the man back his camera." Moore nodded to the adventure shop manager and then turned back to the reporter. "I guess you've got questions?"

"Well, my first one is why aren't the troops interested in this . . . thing?" she motioned her arms around meaning the garbage hauler. "I guess you couldn't see it from inside here, but you just walked by hundreds of Separatists troop vehicles, all of which were loaded with troops. And not a single one of them paid you any mind at all. Why?"

"Because BIL told them not to?" the senator's daughter giggled.

"I'm sorry, BIL?" Gail asked.

"Yes. BIL, the garbage spider." Deanna replied again.

"BIL is the AI controlling this hauler," Moore started explaining. "He also controls the garbage hauler schedule for the Mons City Reclamation and Redistribution Center. He put on the schedule that this was a routine run out into the desert to pick up a downed vehicle for reclamation. Who pays attention to garbage haulers?"

"I see. Clever. How did you convince him to do this?" Gail asked in her reporter voice.

"We just asked him." Moore smiled at the seasoned reporter, half heartedly wishing that Deanna would stick her tongue out at the woman and say, *duh.*

"Hmm. So you were in the city for the Summit meetings with the Separatist Laborers when the attack started?"

"That's right," Moore said.

Laborers' Union, now that is a real joke. Laborers' unions don't have heavy drop mecha and thousands and thousands of soldiers. This is a Separatist army and the press is going to have to admit that. Hell, the country is going to have to admit that or we'll never stop this war. And that is what this is . . . war, Moore thought.

Maybe this is your opportunity to tell them, Senator Moore, Abigail suggested.

Maybe, Moore paused a moment and agreed with his AIC. *Abigail, you're right. This is a golden opportunity. Maybe we can make some lemonade out of this situation after all.*

"Larry, you looked over DeathRay's plans. What'd you think?" Captain Wallace Jefferson had asked his executive officer to go over the final battle plans that the Looney Bin experts had come up with. The two men had been DTMed the final battle plan simulations and were addressing details in the CO's office.

The fleet had been assembled and readied at the northern most Naval Base in the Hellas Basin and were poised to jaunt into a hyperspace orbit that would pop them out into normal space in firing range of the Separatist armada that had amassed over the Tharsis Mons region on the other side of the planet.

The Separatist Armada consisted of six supercarriers—vintage as they were—and many smaller vessels including commercial and industrial vehicles. The entire lower regions of Olympus Mons and most of the Tharsis territory was now under siege by the Separatists and was covered from above at near-space hovering altitudes all the way up to Mars synchronous by the makeshift Seppy armada.

"Well, Captain, reminds me a bit of that mess we made out of the civilian quarter in the Cydonian Mountains. Lot of collateral damage can't be helped, maybe tens even hundreds of thousands. But I got to say, if we don't drop in and kick these Seppy bastards out of Tharsis then they're likely to kill millions," the XO, Marine Colonel Larry Chekov, replied.

"Another fine Navy day, hey Larry?" the CO frowned. The *Sienna Madira* had seen her share of tough scrapes and battles but never one with so many potential civilian lives at risk. And just how many civilian, citizen, lives were acceptable losses? The CO would have to wait for authorization from the Joint Chiefs before an action this size could be ordered. All he could do was to prepare his fleet for battle, offer the Pentagon potential battle plans, and wait for the order to attack.

"Aye, sir." The XO nodded in understanding of the Navy sarcasm.

"Well, this is one of those situations that we are damned if we do and damned if we don't. And the political fallout is going to be hell." Captain Jefferson rubbed his neck and leaned back in his desk chair. "I guess we have no choice. Uncle Timmy?" The CO said out loud to the *Madira's* AIC.

"Yes Captain Jefferson? The AIC of the flagship responded over the speaker on the CO's desk.

"Upload the battle plan to the Pentagon and request authorization."

"Aye aye, sir."

"Well, let's see how big the President's balls are, Larry."

Chapter 13

The President of the United States of America sat at the head of the table in the Situation Room located in the basement of the West Wing of the White House. He focused intently on the opinion poll data being DTMed into his head. Following the outcome of rapid poll data had served the President well for all of his first term and most of the present one.

The present question being put to a rapid online poll, he hoped, would give him the public's desire for the present situation at Tharsis. Should he or shouldn't he move forward with aggressive action against the Separatist incursion of the Tharsis region of Mars and risk the lives of thousands, maybe hundreds of thousands, of voters in the Martian central mountain territory? There were actually over seventeen million inhabitants in the Tharsis territory and more than thirty percent of them were registered voters. If he took action that killed thousands, tens of thousands, maybe more of the registered voters' family, members it would have serious repercussions on the political outlook of the nation. Currently, the political outlook was one that the president and his party enjoyed. He didn't want to do something that would screw that up. His chief advisors and staff were giving him a moment to think while conducting similar analyses and simulations of their own.

Why did this have to happen now? he thought. To this point his administration had taken the Democratic National Party through nearly seven years with approval ratings near sixty-five percent. In the three strong parties of the American political system those were the best numbers any president—other than Sienna Madira, of course—had had for more than a century. It was likely that his vice president would be able to ride his wake into a whole next era of DNC control. The House and the Senate had benefited from the President's popularity and the DNC had grown to majority status and maintained majority control of both houses for longer than any other party since before the Sienna Madira years. All of the senior positions of the important congressional committees were held by the DNC.

"What do you think about all this, Conner?" President Alberts asked his Secretary of Defense Conner Pallatin. The poll data was split in three ways almost evenly over the three possibilities: 1) to do nothing and ride it out, 2) attack the Separatist forces, or 3) to surround the forces and ask for diplomatic discussions. There was a fourth possibility, but it was still sensitive and not released on the poll. The fourth possibility involved nothing more than a political "cover your ass" maneuver to rescue a member of the opposition party that had managed to get himself into a pickle. But, President Alberts didn't want to take the chance that the internal White House Staff polls would get leaked to the press and therefore the Separatists that there was an American Senator stranded somewhere in Mons City.

"I'm not so certain that the Separatists are going to just go away, sir. Somehow they have managed to amass quite an armada and have complete control of the Tharsis territory. The citizens there are trapped and are really at the mercy of the Separatists, Mr. President." The Sec Def had seen the polling data as well and wasn't sure of a good way out of this mess either. "We aren't even certain what the Seppies want, sir."

"Conner, you know I don't like that derogatory slang." President Alberts scolded his Secretary of Defense. "If the press got wind of somebody in my administration using it our approval rating could slide terribly."

"Sorry, Mr. President. As I meant to say, the Separatists have not even given us any demands, sir. We don't know if this is an act of war or if they plan to hold the region hostage as some bargaining aspect at the Summit talks," Conner replied. The reasoning behind the attacks was baffling to everyone in the system. There was no rhyme or reason for it that anybody could see. What advantage did the Separatist leadership think that an all-out attack against the much greater force of the United States would gain? There were some at the Pentagon suggesting that the Separatists had way overestimated their capabilities much in the same way that Hitler had near the end of World War II. There was no way the Separatists could hope to maintain such a massive war fighting machine.

William Alberts stood from his chair and stepped away from the long mahogany conference table that had been basically the same décor since President John Fitzgerald Kennedy had created the Situation Room back in the mid twentieth century after the Bay of Pigs incident. President Alberts walked slowly around the room where more than ninety-five other presidents had stood and pondered the heavy decisions of their time. The weight of the office bearing fully on his shoulders, he looked to history for insight. Was there some approach that his predecessors had used or some profound thought that had kept them on the right path that he could emulate?

How Nixon must have paced the room during the bombings of Hanoi? What did President Carter do as he analyzed the peace talks between Begin and Sadat? What of President Reagan during the many Cold War incidents, what of the father and son Bushes during their respective wars in the middle east? How had William Jefferson Clinton handled the fighting in Old Africa. What of the several presidents to follow and the Global War of Muslim Extremism? And how had the many presidents to follow the "Great Expansion" of humanity handle their various "situations" of slow economies, overpopulation, civil unrest between colonies throughout the Sol system, and political infighting for territorial control? How had President Charlotte Ames dealt with the creation of the New World Government Consolidation Act and the assimilation of all the world governments under one constitution, an America and United Nations based constitution? How had President

Victor Kolmogorov handled the news of the first interstellar spaceflight and the subsequent missions out of the solar system to other stars? How had the great President Sienna Madira handled the Separatist Secession and the creation of the Reservation in the desert of the red planet?

More importantly, Alberts thought, how would he handle this situation now in such a way that history would recall him as one of the great presidents of history? How could he salvage this incident for the good of the DNC? He searched the faces of his most trusted military and intelligence and political advisors around the room, but was certain that they waited for his direction. Politics was always that way—few were willing to be the first to stick their necks out onto the political public chopping block.

President Alberts had only made a few other such tough decisions and had used the Situation Room briefly in the past, but they were nowhere near the drastic scale of the decision before him. The Triton invasion was a much smaller mess and was so far away from mainstream America that most voters had paid it little attention. The Kuiper Station Raid was even smaller and further away. Otherwise, the economy had been cruising along steadily— the war didn't hurt that—and most Americans had gone on obliviously about their daily routines. His administration had been a good one. He sure didn't need this damned Separatist uprising so near the end of his term.

"Well, we're damned if we do and damned if we don't." The president paused for a brief moment and added more. "Popularity, I have always thought, may aptly be compared to a coquette—the more you woo her, the more apt is she to elude your embrace."

"Mr. President?" Secretary Conner raised an eyebrow in question of the comment.

"John Tyler, the tenth President of the United States of America said that. So true in eighteen forty-one and perfectly meaningful in twenty-three eighty-three. Just when we've got the approval from the public that we need, something like this comes along and inevitably will destroy all we've worked for. Possibly overnight, and maybe even in a few short minutes."

"Yes sir." Conner nodded agreement. "I understand sir."

"Damn it." Alberts paused for a second as if he were going to change his mind but then thought better of it. "We don't attack. At least not all-out."

"Sir? The longer we let them dig in the harder it will be to dig them out," the Chairman of the Joint Chiefs replied from the other side of the table.

"I realize that, Sandy. But we really need to know what they are up to. My Director of National Intelligence seems to be a little short on data in that regards, huh Mike?" the President scolded his DNI. The DNI only grunted in acknowledgement.

"We support the withdrawal of Senator Moore and that is all we do on the ground. The press would have a field day if I let a Republican senator get killed and do nothing to try and get him out. Beyond that, we take out the Separatist armada of ships above Tharsis. We do not go to ground with full mecha divisions. One division of tanks and one squadron of fighter support. Understood?"

"What about our troops still left on the ground in the region, sir?" The Chairman of the Joint Chiefs grunted. "We're not leaving them behind to die, are we?"

"They'll just have to hold out a little while longer while we look for a diplomatic solution." Alberts scanned the room for further insights but there were none. Again, the political chopping block was a lonely place to stick one's neck. It was obvious that the Joint Chiefs did not like his decision. But that was ok, they didn't have to like the order. They just had to follow it. "Let us move on it, people."

"Yes, sir," Conner replied and immediately began passing along strings of orders to the senior advisors in the room and across the system via AIC QM.

Alberts decided to take a stroll around the West Wing and wait for further developments. The end of his era was going to come soon and he feared now with much less praise than he had hoped for. His legacy was changing dramatically by the second.

"CAG on deck!"

"At ease." Lieutenant Commander Jack Boland stepped up to the podium in the front of the briefing room. The large gray nondescript military décor conference room was more than thirty meters wide and twice that deep and could hold an audience of more than a thousand people in the stadium seating. The room was crowded and standing room only at present.

"All right, here is our game plan fresh from the Looney Bin, up the food chain, and White House blessed," Jack started sarcastically. "Before I go into that I want to make certain that everybody has been briefed on the new Seppie Stinger Mecha that is comparable in capabilities to the Marine FM-12s. Everybody has been briefed at this point right?" Jack paused and counted silent nods and grunts and saw no hands go up.

"Good. Ok, here is how it will work. We are going to have two fronts of attack. The first is a support and cover mission for the fleet's frontal assault on the Seppy armada in space hover over the Tharsis territory. The electronic warfare and recon air wings will be deployed immediately following exit from hyperspace. Then Lieutenant Commander Chavez, you will take the Demon Dawgs in your Ares fighters and cover the *Madira* and, Rabies, keep the CO free of any Gomer Gnats and Stingers that might decide to pester him while he is giving what for to those damned Seppy rust tubs out there. You are to fly protection for the fleet, not to engage the Seppy boats, as the main fleet will be firing their supercannons, missiles, and DEG batteries full bore. Maintain full IFF squawk and stay out of the firing solutions." Boland paused for a moment and moistened his lips.

The sims he had completed in the Looney Bin had suggested as much as fifteen percent casualties for this mission. Out of the fifteen hundred or so pilots in the room about one thousand of them were combat pilots—the others were support, rescue, reconnaissance, electronic warfare, and rearming/supply vehicle pilots. The casualties within that group of pilots was usually fairly low. For this mission two hundred of the combat wing would be held in reserve. Out of the eight hundred combat pilots that would be deployed for the mission more than one hundred and twenty of them might not make it back. Jack never liked thinking about that part of the mission planning.

"Second layer cover for the *Madira* will be provided by

Captain Cameron's Utopian Saviors and their FM-12s."
Jack nodded at Captain Janice "Bigguns" Cameron. There
were those with less pure minds that often thought that
Janice had gotten her callsign because of two fairly large
assets that she sported proudly, but her nickname had
originally been "Big Guns" because she was a very large
caliber gun nut. Her other assets simply acted as a catalyst
to the evolution of her callsign, which eventually became
officially "Bigguns". Jack had had nothing to do with her
callsign.

"Lieutenant Cameron, tag up with Rabies after the
briefing. Any questions on the first attack wing?" Jack
paused and waited for questions. He scanned the room
and saw nothing but professional acknowledgement there.
The *Madira* had the best pilots in the system.

"The second group will be air and ground support for
the extraction of a small force of lost armored e-suit
gyrenes and a handful of civilians. Note that one of these
civilians is a United States senator and is to be protected
and extracted at all costs. Gods of War will fly cover and
Lieutenant Colonel Warboys and Warboys' Warlords will
drop the Army M3A17 Transfigurable Tanks for ground
and heavy fire support. At this point the SH-102 Starhawk
rescue vehicles will be dropped to extract the evacuees
and any wounded. Gods of War, make certain to support
the Colonel's extraction once the targets have been
evaced. Also, we have intel that there is heavy Seppy drop
tank activity in the area and there are some reported SAM
mobile sites as well. Watch for that. Your AICs have the
particulars."

"Another note here is that we expect to have the full

contingent of Cardiff's Killers gyrene FM-12 Strike Mecha from the *Churchill* along for the ride planetside. Keep in mind that the Killers, the AEMs, and the civilians have been fighting their way to this evac for several hours now and they are battered and tired and probably running low on ammo. We have to cover their backs and get them out. Let's step in and do the fighting so they can retreat, ladies and gentlemen. Finally, as soon as the civilians are gathered, immediately evac them to the Madira or the nearest orbital platform taking the least amount of heat at that time. Once all the civilians and the Killers are evacuated the Starlifters will drop in and load the tanks pulling out the Warboys. The Gods of War are last out flying cover."

"Are there any questions?"

There was dead calm and silence in the large conference auditorium. The pilots knew their jobs and didn't have to ask about the odds for survival. They had all seen enough combat to understand when things were going to get bad and they knew that some things were best left unasked.

"Very good. We hit hyperspace in twenty-six minutes."

"Hey, jarhead, wait up a sec." Navy Lieutenant Armando "Rabies" Chavez pushed a Navy ensign and an Army Lieutenant out of his way down the stairs as he was "going below" and trying to tag up with Bigguns. The stairwell, or ladder in Navy speak, was just big enough for him to squeeze by the junior officers. Rabies always enjoyed being paired up with Bigguns and not necessarily because she was a female. Hell, Bigguns was more than just "boat cute" a term applying to female sailors that weren't cute in a skimpy red bikini on a sunny day at the beach, but *would be* after three months away from port. In fact, Bigguns *would be* something to see in a bikini simply due to her callsign bearing assets, but she wasn't a supermodel either. Bigguns sported her red hair in the typical spiky short cropped haircut of the Marine pilots. Her skin was milky and she was about one hundred and eighty centimeters tall, which was typical of Martian women. She wasn't hard to look at, but that was only part of why Chavez enjoyed her company. Rabies had been through several scrapes with her and her gyrenes and they all were good at their job and goddamned "Uncle Sam and apple pie" all the way. Besides that, the girl could shoot damned good and Chavez was a bit of a "mad dog" about guns himself.

"What's up, deck spotter?" Bigguns used the derogatory term for her Navy colleague, meaning that he was no good at making carrier landings because he was so stupid that he would be panic stricken and stare at the deck rather than watch the ball like he was supposed to when on approach. Of course, Rabies was an expert pilot and had seldom had to be "waved off," but a Marine pilot would never admit such about a squid pilot.

"Hey," Chavez almost made another petty comment, but time was short and they had too much business to take care of. "I've gone through the Looney Bin sims on our sorties and I have an idea."

"Make it quick, Rabies. Before I hit the hangar I need to send a Marine to sea." Bigguns meant she needed to stop at the head, but Rabies understood. He wouldn't mind a Combat Dump himself if time permitted.

"Ok. The Dawgs are going to protect the *Madira*. Wherever the Seppy fighters concentrate is where we will be. If we go standard second wave we will just fill in the weak spots of the ship's coverage." Rabies had to stop walking down the corridor because Bigguns stopped to turn left to go to the head.

"So you want to do what?" Bigguns wasn't annoyed, she just had to go, bad.

"Look, I'll get my AIC to send you my sim and you can study on the pot," Rabies laughed.

"Good idea. Thanks." Bigguns nodded to the Navy lieutenant and rushed into the head looking for an unoccupied stall. "Squeeze it off, Seaman, I need that stall."

Janice, I have the sim from Rabies, her AIC told her.

DTM it, she replied. The sim started unfolding in her mindview. *Hmm. You clever little squid,* she thought.

The battle plan was constrained with the fighter support to stay away from the enemy carriers in order for the supercarriers to target them with their big guns. So, the engagement zone really was flying cover for the *Madira* in close proximity of the large fleet flagship. Bigguns liked what she saw. Instead of taking to space and being constrained to fighting with three dimensions of possible direction from which enemy Gomers could target the FM-12s, Rabies had them staying close to or actually on the hull decks of the supercarrier. This did two things. The first was it cut out half of the enemy's targeting sphere. The other is that it allowed the FM-12s to set up a killing field. The Demon Dawgs would direct the Seppy Gomers with their Ares fighters and appear to be letting them break through the lines to strafe run on the *Madira*. And that is where the Saviors would be waiting in bot mode targeting with their DEGs, cannons, and missiles. Very. Clever.

I like it. Bigguns grinned and then flushed the toilet.

It could work quite well. Her AIC agreed. *Nineteen minutes, Janice.*

Right.

"Don't they realize that we are all gonna start getting hungry and thirsty after a while? They can't just leave us out here crowded together like this." Rod stood from the park bench seat he had been on to let a pregnant woman have his seat. The Mons City Central Park Open Court was filled almost to standing room only capacity with civilians that the Separatist soldiers had rounded up. The Open Court area made for a good holding area.

Once Rod and Vince had been marched into the area Rod had noticed that the Seppies were setting up a barrier field. In essence, Central Park had become a makeshift prison. On several occasions panicking men and women had tried to rush the troops only to be shot down by Seppy rifles or to be stunned by the barrier field. There were a few public bathrooms and water fountains scattered throughout the park and an occasional vending machine, but there were nowhere near enough supplies to support the tens of thousands that were crowded into the area.

"Hey bud, chill." Vincent was getting antsy from lack of nicotine. He had run out of cigarettes over an hour earlier and didn't have any neutralizer or immunoboost with him either. So the nicotine withdrawal was beginning to make him, well, edgy. "I don't think they give a rat's ass about feeding or watering us. I think this is the temporary solution for something more . . . permanent." Vince grunted.

"More permanent?"

"Well, didn't you read the papers any over the last few years?"

"What'd you mean, Vince?" Rod didn't like where this was going, but he was pretty sure he knew.

"Well, remember what they did to the civilians at Kuiper Station? Or what about on Triton?" Vincent said somberly and with a calm matter-of-fact tone that chilled Rod to his core.

"Yeah. I was afraid of that." Rod had read the papers and watched the television, but it was always hard to tell how much of the news was real and how much of it was sensationalized for ratings. Most Americans had quit believing the news many decades ago—maybe even centuries ago—and considered it more a form of entertainment, commercials, and for the most part a political mouth for whichever party made up its constituent viewers. The news told its readers and watchers and listeners what they wanted to hear. And any particular story could be heard in any particular way depending on the channel, website, or forum.

Fortunately for humanity, though, word of mouth still existed. There were a lot of people throughout the outer realm of the system that had lost family to the Triton Raids or on Kuiper Station at the hands of the Separatists. Something like that just couldn't be kept quiet for too long and the spin from the news could be filtered by the word of mouth news.

"Well, if we are dead anyway, Vince, why are we just sitting around here?" Rod asked his long time friend and drinking buddy.

"I'm working on it Rod. I'm working on it."

"Wow. That is some story, Senator," Gail Fehrer said into the camera. "So have you figured out what this extra signal is yet?"

"No, but I'm working on it," Senator Moore replied. The clock on his visor showed that they were about ten minutes away from the rendezvous. He was ready to have this little adventure behind him and have his family safe and far out of harms way.

"How are you working on it?" the reporter asked.

"Well, my AIC has several AIs from the gambling district working the numbers on it and she has passed the data through BIL along to the *Sienna Madira* main AIC as well. I understand that the super AIs of the nation's flagship are cranking away at cracking the encryption. It is only a matter of time now." Moore was nervous about giving too much information away, but then again, there was no transmission taking place. Abigail was watching the reporters like a hawk and BIL promised to keep a sensor on them too. So for now, the senator was taking in all the free press he could. After all, his day job was as a politician.

Senator?

Yes?

The AEMs want us to update them on our position, Abigail informed him.

We tell nobody our position from here on to the evac point. We don't know how long it will be before the Seppy techs figure out that we are using low level infrastructure comms for data relay.

Understood, senator. I'll relay the message.

Just tell them that we will be there. And then we go radio silent until further notice.

"Boulder."

"Yes sir, Burner?" Lieutenant Jason Cordova replied to his boss over the optical net.

"I want you, Ace in the Hole, One Night, Bama, Epoxy, and BullNutz on the ground eagle mode and covering the AEMs." Burner trotted across the Martian soil in bot mode presently beside Boulder, two Marines each riding on their shoulders. The bot mode mecha could hold a pace of over eighty kilometers per hour on solid ground in one full Earth gravity. On Mars they could better that by about twenty percent. Of course in fighter mode the FM-12s could reach escape velocity of most of the planets in the system and they were equipped for space combat but not long range. Each mission had its own speed requirements. This particular mission required finesse not speed. Burner checked his passive sensors systems and the active LIDAR and saw no signs of Seppy Gomers. They had been lucky since they left the dome and had been pretty much alone as they crossed the lower desert drop of the southern foothills of Olympus Mons. The AICs that had linked together across the city had warned that the majority of Seppy activity was located between the domes and moving mostly toward the Main Dome. This far south seemed to be of little interest to them. However, one thing that bothered Burner was that the Seppies had been jamming their sensors all day. There could be drop tanks just over the hills and they would never know it until they were on top of them. Burner didn't like running blind, but it beat sitting around with thumbs up your ass and blind.

"Got it, Burner."

"Washington, I want your AEMs on the ground bouncing underneath Boulder and company, got it?"

"Yes, sir." Washington responded, eager to get on with this mission.

"Lieutenant, you keep pinging away with your QMs for any activity. Jammed or not, we might get that encryption downloaded from the fleet at any second and I want to know if our sensors start working," Burner ordered the AEM leader.

"Affirmative, colonel." Washington switched over on his NCO channel and touched base with Clay. "Sergeant, you stick with Kootie. Keep the private out of trouble. However the VIP shows up, let's get to them quick and move out quick. And keep your QMs pinging."

"Yes sir, Lieutenant." Sergeant Clay Jackson was ready to get this mission over with as well. It had been a losing battle since the start and he was ready to make something positive out of it.

"Ok AEMs," the second lieutenant QMed his personnel. "I know it's a lot of fun joyriding on this here fine Marine mecha but we need to quit gold bricking and start earning our pay." Washington pulled his HVAR up in front of his visor and checked the weapon. He was ready to go. "Sergeant, you and Shelly take the left flank. Kootie, you're on me. We stay low and under the Killers."

"Oorah, sir!"

Washington pushed himself up to his feet, balancing on the barrel turret of the shoulder mounted forty millimeter cannon of the striding bot mode FM-12. Before the running mecha's bouncing could throw him off balance Washington did a back flip off the giant robot and bounced to his feet on the Martian soil, bringing his left knee down as he impacted the red soil. The immuno-booster and the pain meds must have worked well, because other than feeling a little clammy on the fore-head, Washington was a new man. He was a heartbreaker and a goddamned life taker. He was an armored e-suit Marine!

Oorah, lieutenant, Tammie, his AIC, added. The second lieutenant was running on all adrenaline.

Sergeant Jackson, Corporal Shelly, and Private Kudaf followed the second lieutenant's lead. The four Marines bounced at more than seventy kilometers per hour in the open desert. Running downhill helped too. The Martian soil of the mountain side consisted of pebbles no larger than a marble that were embedded in red granular dust. There were occasional outcroppings of millennia old lava boulders, but they were few and far between. The AEMs and mecha bounced faster downhill, kicking up a rooster tail and dust trail of gray-red Martian regolith.

The rendezvous with the VIP and evac was on the south side of the mountain, a good piece downhill from the south borough dome. It had to be more than fifty or sixty kilometers south and east of the main dome where the senator was coming from. Unless they could fly or had commandeered some sort of transport it was difficult to see how they would make it to the rendezvous in time.

But the AICs had contacted each other and assured the Marines that the rendezvous was on schedule and going to happen.

The AEMs Shelly and Kudaf leaped from Boulder's mecha in long separating arcs, Shelly's arc landing just left of the second lieutenant and Kudaf's slightly behind the sergeant. As the AEMs hit the ground bouncing Boulder's FM-12 transfigured itself from a full sprint running robot to an eagle mode mecha that looked more like a bird of prey with human hands than anything else. The g-forces from the mecha transfiguration process had to be one hell of a ride for the mecha pilot. Five other of the sleek killing transfigurable fighting machines pulled into close formation overhead only a few tens of meters above the bouncing AEMs. The wings of the mecha were only a few meters apart from each other.

Lieutenant Colonel John "Burner" Masterson's mecha stayed in bot mode and was flanked by two on his left in bot mode and three on his right. The bot mode mechas serpentined down the mountainside and took giant leaps from side to side over each other in a concert of confusing patterns designed to disrupt mecha-to-mecha radar guided missiles. Behind and in front of them were six of the FM-12s in fighter mode.

In fighter mode the stealthy profile of the Mars red camo painted fighter plane resembled many of the iterations of the old joint strike fighter concepts crossed with a more modern, turned up wingtips and dual tail fins design. Above and below the empennage of the fighter were the forty millimeter cannon turrets and below the nose cone was attached the DEG. Just above the DEG and below the forward sitting canopy of the fighter were small canards that resembled meat cleavers.

The Marines were coming to the rendezvous at a full run and with guns blazing. So far they had encountered no resistance on the southern side of the mountain. The Marines hoped it stayed that way. But if it didn't, like any good squadron of Marines, they were ready to bring hell.

Chapter 14

"Well, Fireman's Apprentice King, just what the flyin' fuck were you thinking? If we were to pop out of hyperspace into a high-g situation, which by the goddamned way we are likely to with there being six, count them, six, mother-fuckin' Seppy rust buckets just waiting out there for a fight, with the coolant fluid bladder structural integrity field on nominal, what do you think would happen?" Hull Technician Third Class Joe Buckley routed the young enlisted man. HT3 Buckley had given the young ignorant fool the task of making battle ready the coolant flow systems, but fortunately the Hull Technician had taken the time to double check the Apprentice's work.

"Well, uh," Fireman's Apprentice King started but was cut off quickly by Buckley.

"Shit, Jimmy, I don't won't you to answer me," Buckley explained to the kid, not certain how he'd ever got accepted for supercarrier duty.

"Sorry, HT3."

"That was a rhetorical question. You've got to learn this drill or it could get this entire deck killed. That SIF," he paused because Jimmy obviously didn't know what the SIF was. "The *structural integrity field* reinforces the bladder for the catapult field generator coolant tanks. The bladder can handle most tough jerks. But if we pop out of hyperspace into a shit storm we could be in for it if those SIFs ain't at the fuckin' max. The inertial dampening system for the entire boat takes a few seconds to kick in between hyperspace mode to normal space mode."

"Not sure what that means ST?" the Fireman's Apprentice said more in the way of a question.

"What it means, Jimmy, is that for the first few seconds we appear into normal space that bladder will get all the force of every move and bounce the *Madira* makes. And it was not designed to take any sort of pounding. The SIF protects it during the short transition period from hyperspace to normal space. Got it?" Buckley was pretty sure the kid didn't get it.

"Ok HT3, SIF at max when going to hyperspace. Got it." The young tech wannabe grinned at Buckley.

"Apprentice, I don't think you do get it. That is liquid metal in that bladder, you know how hot metal has to be until it becomes a liquid?" Buckley had to admit to himself that he didn't either, but at least he knew it was pretty goddamned hot. Too hot to let loose in the deck is what Buckley did know. It was hot enough to eat through the deck plating, which was way stronger than flesh and bone. That, Buckley did know.

"Sorry, HT3. Had no training on liquid metal," the Fireman's Apprentice answered.

"Well, the shit will burn you alive instantly and destroy this deck and the one below it. Now do you get it!"

"Uh." The look on Fireman's Apprentice King's face suggested to Buckley that he did finally get it or at least that this was some dangerous shit and that it had better be handled properly. "What do I need to do, HT3?" he said eagerly and a little frightened.

"Its ok, Jimmy. I already took care of it. But you know about it now." Buckley smiled at the Apprentice approvingly. "We are about to get fuckin' hammered so why don't you strap in and start running the system flush diagnostics. We keep them running continuously during the conflict. You see anything that looks too cold, too hot, flowing too fast or too slow or not moving at all, or just out of place, you let me know."

Everything looks right, right Mija?

Looks spot on, Joe. Uncle Timmy's countdown for the hyperdrive system shows about two minutes.

All right. Good girl. You keep me posted on anything. Joe shifted his weight around in his seat. There were several flatscreens in front of him and multiple layers of information coming at him DTM. The direct-to-mind interface was just the only way the brain could handle that much data so quickly. Multi-tasking the DTM with multiple flatscreens took all of Joe's mental capabilities and took the added intelligence of the AIC to help maintain control of all the tasks in the fluids and structures control deck of the supercarrier.

Of course.

"What, do you mean we have to divert the coolant throughout the ship ourselves? During combat?"

Fireman's Apprentice King was a *very raw* Apprentice. Buckley wondered if he had ever been so raw himself.

"No," Buckley laughed. "The AIs do most of that. We just have to help them keep an eye on things. Sometimes, we humans see things the AICs don't. The AIs would catch the SIFs not being turned up also, unless there were some other software protocol overriding it. You see, that is the thing with AIs. They are still software and their code gets conflicting rules sometimes. Only the older more wise ones or the really really smart ones are good at dealing with those types of conflicts," Buckley said knowingly. Hell, he had seen firsthand what happened when an AI didn't toggle some safety protocols because of conflicting code.

He remembered his roommate from tech school who used to have his original two arms and legs, but no longer did because of some damned Seamen not double checking the low level AIs. Buckley hated to admit it, but hey, the truth was what it was and that truth was that he was an enlisted tech because he was not command and fighter pilot smart and didn't have the will power to stay in school long enough to get into OCS. The parallels between the human troops and the AICs were one to one. The smarter AIs got the cool jobs like the one Uncle Timmy had or those that were fighter pilot AICs. The dumber ones, well, they worked in the bowels of the ships. Buckley had long accepted the fact that he was the biological analog of the shit detail AIC. But even those were pretty damned smart, most of the time. And at least his shit detail was on the flagship of the most powerful fleet in the history of mankind.

"HT3. Refuse and Reclamation systems show purged and clear for lock down. Hope nobody has to take a shit."

"Well if they do, Jimmy, I think they'll be too busy getting shot at to worry about it."

"COB, any hiccups from the Army or the Marines?"

"They're good to go, sir." The Chief of the Boat Command Master Chief Doug Kurts replied as he sipped at his coffee. "Reminds me of that one time over the Belt when there wasn't any problems with them. You remember how that went, sir."

"Just make sure they're good, Command Master Chief."

"Aye sir. Good to go."

"Navigator, are hyperspace coordinates integrated through the fleet and ready for go?" Captain Jefferson sat in the command chair in the back of the bridge and buckled his safety restraints. Uncle Timmy DTMed the fleet status into his mind. He could see the full Martian contingent of the U.S. Navy in three dimensional formation behind the *Madira* ready to roar through a brief thirty second leap of hyperspace into action.

"Aye, sir." Navigator Penny Swain replied without looking up from her screens. She had the same DTM show as the CO did but with vectors, trajectory optimization calculations, and multi-dimensional plots of each vessel in the fleet overlaid over it. The trajectories were continuously realigning themselves. "We are go."

"All right, XO, are we go on your end?"

"Aye sir!" the Marine colonel replied.

"Uncle Timmy, sound the all hands."

★ ★ ★

General quarters. General quarters! All hands, all hands, man your battle stations immediately! Prepare for short hyperspace jaunt in fifteen seconds. Expect multiple ground targets with incoming surface-to-air defenses and multiple carrier class airborne targets. Prepare for evasive! Nine, eight, seven, six, five, four, three, two, one. Hyperspace. Uncle Timmy announced over the 1MC intercom as well as directly to all AIC implants onboard.

The *Sienna Madira* along with the rest of the fleet lurched then phased out of normal space with a reversed cascading shower of violet flashes of light, and then they were gone. The Navigator continued to follow the hyperspace field lines and the trajectories of the fleet vessels. They were following along their respective multi-dimensional vector spaces accordingly and as far as she could tell would emerge into normal space just as the battle plan required.

"Everything looks right, captain. Emerging from hyperspace in thirty seconds."

"Prepare for incoming. Air Boss is go for sorties," the CO ordered. The violet swirls of hyperspace spiraled rapidly around the fleet and the CO took a brief moment to stare out the stern viewscreen at the twirling, blinking, and flashing light show.

"DeathRay, sir!" Lieutenant Junior Grade Karen "Fish" Howser ran over to the CAG who had just stepped out of the elevator into the hangar bay. Fish gave a quick salute to her squadron commander.

"What's up, Fish?" Jack paused from running over and over the battle plans and scenarios in his head just long enough to size up his new pilot. About one and three quarters meters tall, short pilot regulation cut locks of black hair, attractive in an athletic sort of way and young. Jack knew that she was a *real* young lady, not a resurfaced and rejuvenated woman, but a true twenty six year old right out of training and fresh into the mix. And, as her CAG he also knew it was her first combat duty.

"Sir. Just wanted to thank you for pulling me as your wingman," the lieutenant jg said.

"Just do your job and everything will be good." Jack repeated the words his first wingman told him so many years ago. "Fish. Just keep your eyes open."

"Yes, sir. You can count on me." It was obvious to Jack that the young junior officer was nervous as hell.

"You sure you up for this duty, Fish?"

"Yes, sir. Damn, sir, don't go getting all touchy feely cat on me." Fish puffed out her chest and raised an eyebrow showing her bravado.

"Good, you watch my back out there, all right?"

"You got it, sir. Let's go get 'em!"

General quarters. General quarters! All hands, all hands, man your battle stations immediately! Expect multiple space targets. Prepare for evasive! Emerging from hyperspace in nine, eight, seven . . . Uncle Timmy called over the 1MC intercom and again directly to all AIC implants.

The CO gripped his chair a little tighter.

★ ★ ★

"Good hunting, DeathRay!" the chief snapped a salute.

"Roger that!" Jack saluted back. The chief backed down the ladder pulling several hardwire connectors and hoses from the fuselage of the plane.

Jack squirmed a bit into the front seat pulling the hardwire connection from the universal docking port of his Ares fighter and plugging it into the thin little rugged composite box on the left side of his helmet that made a direct electrical connection to his AIC implant via skin contact sensors in his helmet. Jack's training and years of experience assured him that the odds of needing the direct connection were slim. The direct connection wasn't necessary, but functioned as a backup system in the case of enemy jamming of the wireless connection between the AIC and the fighter. Every now and then, though, the damned Seppy tech bastards got lucky with some electronic warfare algorithms or gadgets and could shut out the AIC-to-fighter wireless, but that was rare. The wireless connection was spread spectrum encrypted and almost unspoofable, almost. The hardwire on the other hand required a physical intervention so it made a perfect backup. Jack had never needed it in the twelve years he'd been a Navy aviator.

"Hardwire UDP is connected and operational. Lieutenant Candis Three Zero Seven Two Four Niner Niner Niner Six ready for duty," the AIC announced over the open com channel. Then directly to Jack, *Let's go get'em DeathRay!*

Roger that, Candis!

Jack saluted the flight deck officer and brought the canopy down. The harness holding the fighter lowered and detached, dropping it the last twenty centimeters to the deck with a slight *squishing* feel from the landing gear suspension that Jack had felt so many times before, screaming out the ass end of the supercarrier into a storm of raining and streaking hell flying from all directions. Jack followed the flight deck sequence and moved out first in line for take-off.

"This is double zero, DeathRay," Jack called over the tac-net. "This is gonna get hairy, folks, and I want everyone covering their wings and following the plan. Good hunting and good luck."

"Fighter zero-zero call sign DeathRay, you are cleared for egress. Good hunting, Lieutenant Commander Boland!" the control tower officer radioed. "Handing off to cat control."

"Roger that, tower." Jack went through his ritual. "Y'all just keep the beer cold and DeathRay will be back soon enough." Jack taxied to the "at bat" slot and braced himself.

"Fighter double zero, you are at bat and go for cat! Good hunting DeathRay!" the catapult field AI announced. Jack throttled forward and switched to hover as the landing gear cycled and extracted. He bit down hard on his temporomandibular joint mouthpiece and eased the throttle just a little more forward so that the fighter slipped into the catapult field. He strained against his TMJ mouthpiece bite block and breathed shallow breathes through his gritting teeth.

"Roger that. Double zero has the cat! WHOOOO! HOOOOOOO!" Jack screamed through the mouthpiece as the support tube for the bite block started pumping oxygen in his face and mouth. The catapult field flung him out of the rear lower launch deck and Jack was thrust hard into his seat at over nine Earth gravities, accelerating the little snub nosed fighter to over three hundred kilometers per hour.

Without the inertial dampening controls of the fighter DeathRay would have been accelerated against his pilot's couch so harshly that he would have been crushed and probably had his brain sloshed around inside his head to the point of fatal trauma. From zero to three hundred kilometers per hour in one tenth of a second is about eighty-five Earth gravities! The inertial dampening controls of the Ares fighter craft reduced the effect by generating a dampening field around the aircraft. This field served two purposes: 1) add structural integrity to the fighter plane and 2) reduce the effect of the g-forces to something that human pilots could withstand.

"Hot Damn, what a rush!" Jack shook his head and squeezed his thighs and abdominal muscles as tight as he could, following the lessons he had learned from the years of training and actual high-g maneuver combat experience. He breathed rapidly like a woman giving birth and spat out obscenities almost as proficiently.

"Aaaarrrrrrrrr uunnnnnnnnk mmm!" he grunted as the overwhelming g-forces from the catapult acceleration subsided. Jack slowed his breathing a bit and scanned the sky, turning his head left and right slightly and looking at the viewscreens displaying under and behind him. At the same time his AIC DTMed a full-scale three dimensional and immersive spherical view of the space around him. Jack could look in any direction and see space outside rather than the interior of the fighter. The view was partially transparent so that he could still monitor other instruments and controls inside the cockpit that were not virtual.

The sky was littered with explosions and flashes of light above and behind him and beneath him was the red planet. In his virtual mindview Jack could see the other planes from his squadron being flung from the below and aft launch bay of the *Sienna Madira* supercarrier. His young wingman, Lieutenant Junior Grade Karen "Fish" Howser, pulled in beside the squadron leader on his right. Jack could see the inexperienced pilot scanning around her cockpit virtual view for bogies.

He could also see the main gun batteries of the *Madira* firing in rapid succession. Missile contrails spilled away from the mammoth warship through the upper thin Martian atmosphere, some of them impacting the Seppy rust buckets' shield plating and boiling off large chunks of the armor in brilliant orange and white flashes of debris clouds.

The DTM view showed that both the Demon Dawgs and the Utopian Saviors were dishing out a good bit of hell to the mix of Separatist Gnats and Stingers that were buzzing the fleet. The flagship, the *U.S.S. George Washington*, the *U.S.S. Margaret Thatcher*, the *U.S.S. Boris Yeltsin*, and the *U.S.S. Nelson Mandela* were pouring missiles and directed energy beams into the Separatist fleet. The Seppy rust buckets were maneuvering slowly but returning fire. They were attempting to use the cross-fire as cover and trying to mix into the Martian contingent of the American fleet to force the fleet ships to cease fire with their main guns in fear of friendly fire casualties.

The tactic was working fairly well for the Seppies. The

strategy, on the other hand, at the moment seemed all on the side of the Americans because the original five ships that came out of hyperspace first were bait. The ten or so Seppy ships, which included the six carriers, had not counted on the eight supercarriers from Earth, three from Luna, and two from the outer planets as well as ten smaller yet still powerful support vehicles to drop out of hyperspace nearby. The Martian contingent of U.S. ships had taken the first beating but were now making a run for it to get out of the way of the larger number of fleet vehicles to mop up. The Seppy rust buckets were outnumbered and going to take a serious beating!

Jack. We're clear of the engagement zone. Watching for SAMs and drop mecha. Lieutenant Colonel Warboys has already got his tanks on the ground, Candis alerted him. *Also, all the Gods of War cleared the engagement zone safely and are forming up, as you can see.* Jack scanned the DTM and eyeballed outside the cockpit for his squad. All was going according to plan.

Great, Candis. Give me the evac cover trajectory, Jack thought. A trajectory vector traced across the virtual view in his mind and led to four blue dots on the surface. The dots were moving rapidly to the escarpment edge that had been designated as the pickup point.

"DeathRay, DeathRay, this is Vulcan. Angels squad, search and rescue, is on the drop and clear of the engagement zone. We are on your six and ready to take to ground on your call," Lieutenant Junior Grade Seri "Vulcan" Cobbs, leader of the SH-102 Starhawk rescue vehicle squadron, announced on the tac-net frequency that the mission two teams were using.

"Roger, that Vulcan. DeathRay copies you. Give us two shakes to reach cover and recon the evac. Warboys is closing in on the drop zone from the surface now. I've got a lock on the gyrenes afoot but have no track on the Killers. I repeat no track on the Killers."

"Copy that DeathRay. Angels will hold back until green light. Good luck. Out."

Candis, where are the Killers?

IFF is turned off but they are covering the AEMs. I'm adding optical sensor data to the virtual. You should be able to see them from this range. Closing in on the drop point, the AIC answered.

Chapter 15

Lieutenant Colonel Mason Warboys had never needed a nickname or a callsign. Warboys was cool enough. The colonel's massive M3A17 Transfigurable Tank slammed across the Martian mountainside terrain on the hoverfield at over two hundred kilometers per hour, the big DEG turret swinging from left to right seeking targets. There were none to be found. His IFF sensor systems had four blue dots just seconds away near the evac point over the next ridge, but there was no sign of trouble. The Warlords tank squadron followed in behind their commander in formation, scattering dust and debris in a tailwind behind them.

Warboys throttled back his tank as he crested the ridge and saw nothing but about a half click of Martian dirt and ancient lava stones, but his DTM virtual world had the four blue dots dispersed near the edge of the bluff. And then the goddamnedest sight he'd ever seen skittered oddly up over the horizon to the northwest.

"Colonel, this is Warlord Three. Am I seeing things?"

"I don't know, captain. Could be. But if you're seeing a giant mechanical spider headed right for us then either we both are seeing things or it is really there." Warboys checked his multi-static passive radar and the sensor system used the background radio noise coming from sources all across the planet and in orbit to generate a three dimensional image of the spider thing. "Radar shows it is metal. And, it shows that there is nothing else in the area. My AIC tells me it's a garbage truck and that it's our VIP. Let's get him some cover," Warboys ordered.

The hovering M3A17 Transfigurable Tanks converged on the spider's location quickly. As the tank squadron closed the gap down to a few tens of meters the garbage hauler stopped. Warboys pulled to a stop and popped the hatch on his tank. He hit the repulsor ejector and shot himself out of the tank into a forward roll onto the ground just in front of the spider.

Several meters to the lieutenant colonel's left the dust kicked up and an AEM rose up from the ground. The blue dot on Warboys' DTM virtual view showed it to be Second Lieutenant Thomas Washington. Three other blue spots got dusty almost simultaneously and the rest of the AEM squad rose from their covered locations.

"Greetings, Lieutenant. You Marines look like you could use a lift." Warboys chuckled. "Haven't seen any FM-12s hanging around anywhere, have you?" He announced over the QM.

"Go to all optical and no QMs, colonel and I'll explain, sir," Washington said. Warboys sent an AIC command to the squad to go all optical comms.

"All right, how's that?" the lieutenant colonel asked.

"Well, I'll be goddamned if it ain't that Army puke, Warboys and his armored nimrods." Burner laughed over the optical net.

"Burner? Is that you? Where the hell are you? What the fuck is going on here?"

"We're under covers. They are tracking our QMs, Mason. They already had a fix on these AEMs so we thought we'd set a trap for them." Burner's answer made Warboys nervous. "I suspect you ought to be getting back in your tank, lieutenant colonel. We're expecting company in about three or four minutes."

"That can't be, John. We just dropped in and pinged the entire southern region. Even updated optical scans and saw nothing headed this way. It's all clear," Warboys informed his old jarhead buddy.

"Did you go eyeball, Mason? Or did you use sensors?"

"Burner, I was in a drop tank reentry shroud. How the hell was I gonna go eyeball?"

"That's what I thought. One of my boys found a spread spectrum signal down in the oddest damned part of the spectrum that is uploading a virus or some such thing somehow into the sensors that changes the code to tell the sensors that there are no Seppy mecha in the view." Burner's voice was deadpan serious.

"Shit Burner, are you telling me this is a trap?"

"Yep. But we hope to turn it over on the bastards," Burner answered.

"Hold one, John," Lieutenant Colonel Warboys said and keyed in the tac-net to DeathRay.

"DeathRay. Warboys. Do an immediate roll over and

eyeball the region for me. I mean eyeball, no sensors and tell me what you've got."

"Hold on, colonel." Jack rolled the fighter over upside down and searched the mountainside. The squadron was closing in at about ten kilometers altitude and twenty out, giving a slant range of about twenty-two. The resolution of the human eye at that range is about two meters. In other words Jack should have been able to make out a vehicle as a dot from that range. The dots were hard to see, but the dust trails from hundreds of vehicles only about ten kilometers out were not hard to see at all. There were mecha, trucks, and fighters—lots of them.

"Holy shit!" Jack tapped some keys and went all channels. "All hands, all pilots, be aware that the Seppies have us jammed on all sensors. Eyeballs only. We've got a Seppy convoy only minutes from the evac and probably more in the sky. Go eyeballs. I repeat go eyeballs! Holy shit!" A SAM zipped right past his Ares fighter, between him and Fish, taking out a fighter just behind his wingman. Several more missiles streaked by almost simultaneously, all of which hit home on one of the Gods of War before they could take action. "Evasives, goddamnit!"

"CO, did you catch that last transmission from DeathRay?" The XO of the *Sienna Madira* stood at the viewport of the bridge looking out at the swarming craft around them while trying to compare what he saw with his eyes to what he was seeing in his mind. The continuous audibles of the hundreds and hundreds of pilots filled the bridge in a concert of guttural grunts, missile and gun firing commands, and horrendous screams. The command level audibles were amplified and the various bridge officers had their AICs create audio filters to allow only certain communications to get through to their ears. Otherwise, the entire audio mix from the fighters and fleet ships would be overwhelming for any one individual.

"Play it back to me, XO."

"Aye sir!" The ship rocked to port sharply. Once the full fleet had gotten into the mix the Martian Contingent had pulled to the outer periphery of the engagement zone, but the Seppies had stayed with them, trying to keep the overwhelming numbers of vessels still hindered by friendly fire solutions on their main guns.

"Holy shit! All hands, all pilots, be aware that the Seppies have us jammed on all sensors. Eyeballs only. We've got a Seppy convoy only minutes from the evac and probably more in the sky. Go eyeballs. I repeat go eyeballs! Holy shit!" Played through the CO's audio filters.

"XO, check that!" Captain Jefferson ordered in response. *Uncle Timmy, spread the word around the fleet!*

Yes, captain.

"Quartermaster of the Watch!" the XO called.

"Aye sir!" Quartermaster Senior Chief Patea Vanu snapped away from his viewscreen and looked at the XO standing at the window.

"Captain, I'm hearing similar reports from the tankheads on the ground," the COB added. "This might be like that one time back in the Desert Campaigns where General Ahmi jammed the Luna City Marines, sir."

"Hmm, could be, COB."

"Senior Chief Vanu, get me about five lookouts on each deck of the ship that has a portal counting enemy ships with their eyeballs and comparing them to the virtuals. Make it fast," the XO ordered. He had to place his hands on the safety rail at the window in order to keep from losing his balance from the ship being thrown around by enemy missiles impacting the hull plating. "Jesus!"

"Aye."

"Where is that fire coming from?" The CO looked at four different virtual screens in front of him: one scrolling the *Madira's* health and stores, one scrolling a summarized version of the first for all of the Martian Contingent (the *Mandela* had a new wing added to it when one of the dying Seppy carriers had rammed it full throttle, both listed out of commission), one displaying battle damage assessments on the attacking Seppy fleet ships (two had already been completely destroyed and another one was heavily damaged), and one with continuous casualty reports. The virtual sphere around his head was a continuous update and display of the battle outside at a small enough scale to fit the battle in a one meter diameter sphere about him. The ship rocked hard to port again.

Concentrated fire from starboard, sir, Uncle Timmy alerted the captain.

"Sir, this is the CDC. We're taking a serious pounding on the starboard side lower decks. We've got a Seppy rust bucket rushing us head on! And it looks like they've figured out who's in charge because several ships are starting to concentrate on us," the officer of the Combat Direction Center two decks below announced over the comm.

"Ensign Marks, half speed to new coordinates: R equals three kilometers, Theta equals one eight zero

degrees, and Phi equals zero degrees. And give us ninety degrees yaw!" the CO ordered the helmsman.

"Aye sir!"

"Casualty reports don't look like we can't see the bad guys, sir!" the commander of the air wing added.

"I agree with the Air Boss, CO. I'm not seeing that," Colonel Chekov agreed but continued to view the battle outside the viewport just in case things started to change.

"Bridge. CDC."

"Go, CDC," the XO replied.

"We've got three hyperspace conduit signatures about fifteen kilometers in plane off the port bow! Sensors show no new target signatures!" the Officer of the CDC said.

"Senior Chief Vanu?" Captain Jefferson looked to his Quartermaster of the Watch.

"Aye sir! I've got eyeball reports of three cargo haulers dropping into normal space off the port bow coming in now, sir. Eyeballs show hundreds of mecha pouring out of them, sir." QMSC Vanu wiped sweat from his forehead and tapped some keys at his console to double check his reports.

"Yep, just like the Desert Campaigns." The COB nodded and took another sip of his coffee.

Uncle Timmy, 1MC and all channels to the fleet and transfer the coordinates of the enemy ships to the fleet.

Aye sir! the flagship's AIC replied.

"All hands, all ships, this is Captain Jefferson of the *Sienna Madira.* We have three large enemy ships at the coordinates being transferred now. These ships are somehow jammed from our sensors and invisible. Lookout reports show hundreds of mecha being deployed from these vessels. Pilots be aware that sensors are not detecting these enemy craft. I repeat eyeball detection is the only way to see these fighters for now. Good luck. That is all."

"Our fighters are sitting ducks out there!" the XO said.

"Larry, get the second wave off the deck!" The CO ordered.

"Dawgs! We've got serious problems here. Keep eyes out for Gomers not on the DTM or the screens. Let's pull in tighter and force our way into the middle of as many of the Seppy Gomers as we can following the coordinates being sent now!" Lieutenant Chavez ordered his Ares fighter squadron. He had hoped that staying in close to as many of the Seppy bastards as they could would limit the targeting from the ones that their sensors were blind to.

"Rabies! JavaBean. I've got visual on at least two full squads three clicks out on a vector for *the Madira!* Sensor show nothing there," Ensign Cory "JavaBean" Davis, Rabies' wingman, alerted the Demon Dawgs over the tac-net.

"Roger that, JavaBean! I see 'em too. Holy shit!" Lieutenant Junior Grade Wendy "Poser" Hill replied. Poser had been an Ares pilot with the Dawgs for more than a year and had seen her share of combat so her callsign often was a bit of a misnomer. Wendy was known as Poser because she had "posed" in an issue of a particular men's magazine entitled "Women of the Military". Originally it had been a bad thing and had almost caused her to lose her commission. But a marketing guru at the Navy recruiting office got wind of it and spun it around into a positive aspect for the service. What young man wouldn't want to be stationed onboard a supercarrier with a hot chick that flies fighter planes? It turned out that she had just been in a bikini anyway and the shot was a candid. The name Poser had stuck with her though. Wendy didn't care as long as she got to fly.

"Poser, I got 'em. You and BreakNeck pull in tight on JavaBean and lets see if we can't pull some of these guys in to the starboard flight deck to meet some of our friends and see if we can't get them into a good old fashioned knife fight," Rabies ordered. By now Bigguns should have the Utopian Saviors deployed across the starboard exterior flight deck in their Marine FM-12 Strike Mecha in bot mode and able to target their main DEGs with eyeball tracking and hip shooting.

"Roger that, Rabies."

"Boss, port of your three-nine line! Two Gomers. Shit!" JavaBean worked the HOTAS turning his fighter ninety degrees to the left and pitched at thirty while not changing his trajectory vector. "Guns, guns, guns!" he shouted, going to his DEG, which sprayed blue-green bolts of energy just above Rabies' cockpit and hitting home on one of the incoming Seppy Stinger fighter planes.

"Shit! Break right, JavaBean!" Rabies banked left and rolled his fighter as he did in order to get an eyeball shot at the incoming. "Aaaaaarrrrrrgggg . . . shhhhhiiiiiittt!" he grunted as his pressure suit squeezed his body to help him compensate for the g-loading on it.

"We're blind as fuckin' bats out here!" BreakNeck said. "Fox three!"

★ ★ ★

"We've got fire from the ground and we are flying blind as fuckin' bats!" Jack turned his fighter nose over and watched as the ground came up at him rapidly. "Gods of War, go for the deck and stay beneath the SAMs active trackers. Fish, stay on me girl! Goddamnit! Fuck!" Jack screamed as his hull plating was rattled with anti-aircraft rounds. The SIFs and the armor took a beating but he continued to force his fighter at maximum dive velocity for the deck.

Candis, say when!

Hold it . . . hold it! Candis screamed in his mind as she calculated the no return point of the dive where he would no longer be able to pull out of it. The objective was to pull out just microseconds before it was too late. Oh, the g-forces would suck, but it would put him rapidly through the AA fire and on top of the Seppy bastards that were shooting at him. If he survived the maneuver then he would unleash hell on them, if he survived.

"Caaanddiiiiissssss!" he screamed out loud and grunted, squeezing his abdominal muscles with all his might. He chewed down on his TMJ bite block and took rapid shallow breaths. The pressure system around his torso tightened hard and the bladders on his legs filled with air, squeezing his legs so tight they felt like they were being cut in two pieces.

Now, DeathRay! Now! Now! Now!

Jack pulled back on the HOTAS and rolled the fighter upside down, screaming and grunting and biting on his bite block the whole way. He pulled over fourteen gravities for a couple of seconds and Candis had to take over the controls for about four more.

Jack?!

"I've got it! Fox three, Fox three, guns guns guns!" he shouted, shook his head, blinked his eyes a few times, depressed the controls to fire the mecha-to-mecha homers, and then went full bore with the DEG blasting away at the drop tanks and missile launchers scattering across the Martian mountain beneath his fighter only a few tens of meters.

The mecha-to-mecha homing missiles used dumb sensors that were closed systems and not connected in anyway to the fighters other than the launch trigger. There were no AICs on the missile systems and therefore the jamming wasn't affecting the missiles accuracy at all. The DEGs on the other hand were having to be fired from the hip as the pupilary targeting system *was* being spoofed. Shooting from the hip along the violent flight path wasn't easy or very accurate. The ground effect and the flying debris trail buffeted the fighter harshly, or perhaps it was the AA fire and secondary explosions he was flying through. Hence, targeting the DEG wasn't easy.

"DeathRay! DeathRay, you got a Gomer Gnat trying to give you a rim job!" Fish grunted out just as she added, "Guns guns guns!" The Separatist fighter plane flew into pieces as Fish pulled her fighter into the same death defying roll that her wingman and squad leader had just done. "Aaaaaaaarrrrrrrrrrggggggg . . . uuuuuuuhhhhhuuuuuhhhh . . . wooooohooooo goddamn!" she grunted and screamed over the tac, "That's better than sex!"

"Then you're not doing it right!" came a response from an unnamed pilot over the net. "Oh shit! Guns, guns, guns. Take that you fuckin' Gomer!"

"Fish! Hit the front line to slow their advance some!" DeathRay rolled his fighter in a corkscrewing trajectory so that he was continuously seeing the ground then the sky, ground, sky, ground, sky. "Goddamn, this is gonna make me dizzy! Guns guns guns!" he grunted as the blue-green directed energy beam washed across the front of the Seppy convoy hitting home a couple of times, rewarding Jack with the red-orange fireball from a vehicle exploding.

"DeathRay! We're getting fucking hammered here," Fish screamed.

"I agree with Fish, sir!" Lieutenant Damien "Demonchild" Harris corkscrewed orthogonally across the Seppy convoy line of travel, firing several missiles. The fireball and dust plume thrown up from the missiles created a wall of zero visibility that the battered Gods of War zipped through in their mad twirling and sinewy trajectories, irrespective of the danger of flying blind. At least in the dust cloud the Seppy vehicles would be blind too. They hoped. "We could use a couple Hellstorms in here!" Demonchild wished for a couple nukes they didn't have.

"DeathRay, we got Stingers and Gnats out the ass over here!" came another one of the Gods of War over the net.

Jack had little time to go DTM and track his pilots to see how many were falling. It was all he could do to keep himself conscious and from being shot down and not necessarily in that order.

Jack we need to keep them off the AEMs.

Maybe we can steer them away. Hold one.

"Aaaaaaaaa uuunnnnnhhhhh, shhhhiiiiiiiittt! Guns guns guns! Fox three!" he shouted as another Seppy Stinger armored transfigurable fighter jumped from the deck in bot mode, unloading a salvo of mecha-to-mecha homers out of his torso batteries at him. Jack zigged left and then rolled over, winding in and out between the missile ion trails, almost sending him into an uncontrollable all-axis spin to avoid being blown to hell and gone. Going to DEG to burn the missiles swarming all around him, Jack grunted hard and rocked the HOTAS back and then sideways and the tough little Ares fighter shook violently from the nearby exploding missiles.

"Fox three!" he cried, letting loose a mecha-to-mecha missile that twisted through the fiery debris trails hitting the Stinger Mecha dead center of the pilot cabin. The enemy mecha exploded into a spinning orange and white fireball that Jack had to just grit his teeth and fly through.

"Where do you think you're going! Fox three!" Fish screamed. "That's another toasted Gomer."

"Yeah, well don't get cocky. There're plenty more where that one came from! Shit!" Jack flipped his bird a complete one hundred and eighty degrees without changing his flight path direction and grunted wildly at the pain from the massive g-loading. "Fox three!" He fired a missile, taking out the mecha that had taken position on Fish's six.

"Thanks, sir." Fish said sheepishly.

"Warboys, Warboys! DeathRay! Copy?"

"Warboys here! Go, DeathRay."

"We're gonna try to turn these bastards off of you if we can. But we're taking a pounding so you might want to hunker down in case it doesn't work," Jack told the Army tank driver.

"Negative DeathRay, that is a negative. If you can do anything to steer them, bring 'em on to us!"

"They have you waaaay outnumbered, colonel!" Jack warned Warboys.

"You let us worry about that. Besides, I got me some friends."

"Roger that." Jack's sensors only showed the AEMs, but four AEMs against a bunch of mecha couldn't be much advantage. Warboys was cooking something and the Killers were nearby, somewhere.

"XO! We're rapidly losing pilots!" Captain Jefferson's DTM lists of his crew were blinking out fast. Since the invisible Seppy ships had entered the mix the battle had turned in the wrong direction—seriously in the wrong direction.

"Aye sir! We need to pull the Ares fighters in, I think. They can't fight like this," Colonel Checkov replied.

"Can't pull them in now! Tell them to get out of the engagement zone at max velocity on any safe vector! And get me every gun with eyeball tracking capability we've got on the exterior decks," The CO ordered.

"Aye sir!"

Sir!

Yes Timmy?

The Yeltsin has taken heavy damage from one of the ghost ships. It is venting and on fire! The Thatcher has taken heavy damage and the Washington has lost its SIF generators! The Lincoln, Reagan, Kolmogorov, Ames, Crippen, and the Blair are completely out of commission and reporting no propulsion or weapons capabilities.

Shit. The CO thought and scrolled up the *Madira's* health monitor to the foreground in his mindview, the battle still raging in the mindview sphere around his head.

"CO! Word from Engineering is that the SIFs are holding but the coolant systems for the DEGs are battered to hell. We're going to lose the forward starboard DEGs soon!" the XO alerted the CO. Although the CO had health monitoring menus on the ship in front of him, it was the XO's job to get first hand reports from the sailors keeping the systems running.

"XO, the guns must fire! Structural integrity will do us no good if we are sitting ducks and not returning volleys," The CO ordered.

"Aye sir!"

"Helmsman Marks! R equal to four kilometers, Theta equal to ten degrees, and Phi set to one hundred degrees at maximum normal speed! Pitch, yaw, and roll to maximize port DEG targeting angles!" the CO ordered.

"Aye sir!"

"Fireman's Apprentice King! Lock that shit down right now!" Hull Technician Petty Officer Third Class Joe Buckley alerted the young enlisted man of the overheating flow valve on the starboard side main directed energy gun coolant system. The three dimensional DTM view of the ship's flow systems in both of their heads showed overheating systems in red and nominal ones in green. There was a look-up table ranging from green to red of different levels of status for the flow equipment. Some of the systems flowed liquid waste products while others flowed superheated liquid metals. The valve on the forward DEG coolant loop would have to be locked out and the flow rerouted or it could go critical and start a serious fire on the below deck of the weapon system.

"The software to the valve shows it locked HT3, but the flow meters are still reading seventeen megapascals on the flow pressure. The only flow valve down stream is from the SIF generator loop on the forward decks. Do I divert the flow?" Fireman's Apprentice Jimmy King had yet to see the *Madira* be hammered so hard. He had only been onboard for a few weeks and the previous day's mission had been his first combat. Oh, there had been pilots going and coming from the supercarrier going into battle, but this was the first time the *Madira* itself had been in the mix of a full-scale naval battle and taking on anything worse than a few SAMs.

"No! Jimmy, if the SIFs go out on that end we will have a standard coolant pipe with over seventeen megapascals of pressure in it. The instant that SIF went down the pipe would be a bomb of exploding superheated liquid toxic metals!" Buckley scratched his head in thought for a brief second. The *Madira* lurched downward suddenly and a little faster than the inertial control system could compensate for, leaving Buckley with the brief feeling that his stomach was somewhere on the deck above him.

"We've got to do something, boss. The pressure in that loop is rising and the main gun is just getting hotter!" the Fireman's Apprentice replied. "Shit!" He grabbed the sides of his station to keep his balance as the ship continued to jerk randomly.

"No, the cats on all ends are at minimal use now that

the fighters are out. Switch over the catapult coolant flow loops to the main gun coolant loops. Maybe that'll take some of the pressure off that stuck valve. The goddamned thing is probably seized open. That happened to us last year at Triton. That was ugly." Buckley grabbed at an icon for the cat coolant reservoir to read the internal temperature of the coolant bladder. Although the cats weren't going presently they had just taken a hell of a thermal load to launch more than four full squadrons of fighters, mecha, and drop tanks in the last few minutes. The reservoir was above midway on the look-up table, reading yellow and not that far from red. But yellow was better than red. "Fuck. It'll have to do."

"HT3!"

"What now!"

"Looks like the port side SIF generators are starting to overheat!" Jimmy said with a little panic in his voice.

"CO! Port SIF generators are overheating. Starboard DEGs are overheating. We can either take a pounding and not fire or fire and take a pounding!" the XO warned the captain of the *Sienna Madira*.

"Air Boss! I want all the mecha on the Starboard exterior decks now!" the CO ordered.

"Aye sir!"

"Senator, I think it is time you find a better hiding place," BIL announced over the speaker.

"I agree, BIL. Can you let us out of here?" Moore asked. Just as he did the rear door slid upward, letting the sunlight in. "Let's go! Everybody with me!" Moore grabbed his daughter from his wife and Joanie and dove out the ass end of the giant mechanical arachnid bouncing with fifteen meter steps at a full run. "BIL, go hide somewhere."

"Very well, senator. It was fun talking with you."

"You as well, BIL. Thanks for the lift."

"You are very welcome. 'Bye little one." The garbage hauler actually lifted one of its front legs and waved it at Deanna.

"'Bye BIL." Deanna waved over her father's shoulder back at the garbage hauler.

Reyez, Joanie, the reporter and her cameraman, and the senator's wife followed him, bouncing out of the garbage hauler onto the Martian soil. The cameraman, Calvin Dean, was videoing with every bounce and every breath. He paused for a second to get a shot of the two dozen American tanks hovering about the gorge's edge and the tank driver talking to a few armored soldiers. The mechanical spider had stopped and let them out very near the edge of the large drop off into the gorge marking the bottom of the giant volcano's outermost edge. The drop off must have been at least a half a kilometer deep or more in places.

"Ok, we're going to go to the edge of that set of lava stone outcroppings there and dig into the sand and hide until the evac gets here," the retired Marine ordered them.

Senator? his AIC said into his mind.

Yes, Abigail?

The FM-12 mecha pilots claim to have found the signal center frequency.

Yeah? Moore landed just behind the stone outcropping and set his daughter down against the largest rock. "Stay down and don't move."

"Yes, Daddy," Deanna said.

It has a center pulse at two three three six megahertz, sir.

Well, that narrows the search down to a bandwidth around that peak. Look for the hopping frequencies around that one. Alexander knew his AIC would have already thought of that.

I'm doing that, sir, but without more information that is still an excessive number of combinations. It might take a while.

Well, keep at it.

Of course, senator.

"Alexander, what now?" His wife Sehera bounced beside him, kneeling down to her daughter while panting for breath, the e-suit inner layer slowly absorbing and recycling the sweat rolling off her face.

"Dig!" He started digging a foxhole behind the rocks. "We dig a hole and hide until they can get us out of here. Where is our goddamned evac?" He looked around the horizon for an aircraft but saw none.

Abigail, where is the goddamned evac?

Hold on . . . the area is too hot right now, senator. There is a squad of Starhawks in orbit waiting for a green light.

Shit, get word to them that we have a child with us!

Yes, sir.

They all started digging. Alexander and Joanie used the butts of the Seppy HVARs for shovels. The Martian regolith pushed out of the way slowly, as it was cold and hard and filled with lava stones.

"Allow me," a voice said as a shadow loomed behind them.

"What the?" Moore spun around with the rifle but the large Marine standing there quickly blocked the barrel and held up the palm of his heavily armored hand at the senator.

"Easy, sir. We're the good guys," Sergeant Jackson said and pointed at the E5 markings on the shoulder of his e-suit. "I hear you should understand what that means, sir?"

"Your damned right I do, sergeant. Semper fuckin' Fi!" Alexander shook the AEM's hand. The armored hand engulfed the hand of the standard e-suit Moore was wearing. The sergeant motioned the senator out of the way, so he stepped back to let him through.

"Lieutenant, I've found them," the sergeant alerted the other AEMs, and then knelt to the rocks and started digging. The added strength of the armored e-suit enabled the Marine sergeant to dig faster and deeper than all of the civilians put together.

"Need a hand, sergeant?" Private Kootie and Corporal Shelly bounced into the beginnings of a nice foxhole and started digging.

"That was an interesting ride you folks had." One of the AEMs offered the senator his hand. "Second Lieutenant Washington, sir. I assume you are Senator Alexander Moore?"

"Lieutenant," Moore nodded. "That garbage hauler AI turned out to be pretty damned useful."

"Well if you ask me, senator," Corporal Shelly added, "spiders, mechanical or not, are just plain creepy. Why not make the thing look like a dog or a cat or something?"

"You got nothing better to do, corporal?" Sergeant Jackson looked over at the Marine, warning her to keep her mind on her job.

"Ha, I wouldn't have minded if it had been a pig. It got us here," Reyez said. "Smelled like a pig though."

Something the female corporal had said triggered a thought cascade in Abigail's neural network. There was something about animals that seemed to have a familiar pattern to it that she had trained herself to learn before. There was something just at the tip of her software mind but she couldn't quite place it. The AIC knew there was something important here. Something about animals . . .

Abigail! Cats! That's it! A cat! The senator was excited.

I know there is something about a cat, senator. But what? Abigail could just taste that she was near the answer to the jamming signal.

No! Don't you remember? Ahmi had that goddamned AI kitty every day in that fuckin' POW hell hole! A cat! What frequency do commercial AIKs use?

I don't know, senator. And, honestly, I'm not certain why I didn't remember that piece of information. But, BIL is still in range I'll have him look it up over the infrastructure communication line. Somebody on the Madira should know. I'll get started on it now.

"Does anybody here know anything about the spectrum of AI kitties?" Moore asked the AEMs as they spread out the fox hole and prepared it for battle.

"Sorry, senator. Look, we should get in the foxhole," The second lieutenant warned.

BIL, I need all the technical info on AI Kittys I can get as fast as I can get it. Can you help me? Abigail QMed to him on the infrastructure channel.

I'd love to help you, Abigail. You are such fun to talk with. Please stand by, BIL said.

Senator? BIL is searching.

Keep me posted. Alexander wished there was a way to just download the info DTM so that he would know it, but DTM just added another sensory approach and one still had to experience the data before they remembered it. Alexander had confidence in his AIC and she was good at summarizing the important parts of data from large amounts of information.

Yes, sir.

Chapter 16

"Everybody down! Now!" Second Lieutenant Washington ordered, pulling the civilians into the foxhole as several Ares fighters spiraled and corkscrewed overhead only a few tens of meters off the deck with a wake of noise and flying Martian dust trailing behind them. Two of them were being tracked by Seppy Gnats and there were several Seppy Stingers in bot mode bouncing and flying around in the mix.

The American tank squadron had gone to bot mode and were scattering fast along the ridgeline and had begun firing their cannons and main directed energy weapons. The DEGs were held in the hand of the bot mode tanks and were being fired from the hip.

A mass of Seppy Drop Tanks pounded over the hillside. There had to be more than two hundred of them and they were intermingled with ground vehicles and armored Seppy troops that were scattering the mountainside with automatic railgun fire.

"Marines! Hold off on cover fire and shut down the QMs. We are to keep the civilians out of harm's way! Understood," Washington ordered his AEMs.

"Lieutenant, those Army tanks are extremely outnumbered . . . shit!" Moore instinctively ducked his head as an Ares fighter screamed over his head, flying upside down and backwards while washing the sky with its blue-green directed energy pulses. A Seppy missile struck the fighter on the port wing, sending it reeling and slamming into the ground. Martian soil, fire, smoke, and debris flew upward in a slow arc across the edge of the escarpment.

"What would you have us do, senator?" the second lieutenant asked.

"Fight, Marine! Fight!" Major Moore said. "Fight and keep those Seppy motherfuckers off my family!" He rolled the Seppy HVAR off his shoulder and turned to Reyez Jones, who was cowering in the bottom of the foxhole. "Reyez Jones! If I give you the order you WILL pick up my daughter and jump over that escarpment with her. Do you hear me, Reyez Jones!"

"Uh, yes, senator! That is a hell of an idea. Why not do it now?" Jones perked up and peeked over the edge of the foxhole at the fifty meter run to the edge of the cliff.

"No!" Major Moore ordered. "You'll do it when I say so. That is a last effort, because we don't have any Marines or Army tanks down there to protect us. But, if I give the word you go! Go fast! And you protect my daughter with your life, understand!" The senator turned to his wife and held her hand for a brief second. "Sehera, you'll be right behind him, right?"

"I'll be right behind him, Alexander," Sehera replied

and nodded affectionately to her husband. If they hadn't been in e-suits she would have kissed him and her daughter.

"All right then, I'm gonna keep these motherfuckers off our ass!" Major Moore said and patted his daughter on the helmet. "I love you, baby." He smiled at the little girl and bounced about fifteen meters out of the foxhole and then four or five more times to another stone outcropping and took up a sniper position nearly seventy meters away.

"I love you, Daddy," the little girl cried. She wasn't sure what exactly was going on but she could tell by the reaction of the adults that something was serious and scary and the noise was terrible and she didn't like the tone of her daddy's voice.

"That's right, Marine, fight!" Joanie Hasad, the little Triton refugee followed right behind the senator. "I didn't want to go skydiving today anyway."

"Shit. Just what we need is a couple of loose cannon civilians," Washington said under his breath. "Clay, keep them covered! Kootie on me!"

"Yes, sir," Sergeant Jackson said. "They're covered, sir. Shelly, get those two down in the hole better and dig out the bottom a little deeper. We do not draw fire to this foxhole if it can be helped, understood!"

"Yes sergeant!" Shelly started digging the hole deeper.

Sergeant Jackson leveled his HVAR across the edge of the foxhole and kept a bead on the fight. His trigger finger itched.

The second lieutenant and the private leapfrogged each other up the mountain, taking up positions on either side of the senator and the HVAR toting woman. The four of them started picking targets and bringing them down. They focused on e-suit Seppies but every now and then a close shot at a Seppy drop tank's joints and other vulnerable spots were hard to pass up.

"Calvin, tell me you are getting all this!" Gail Fehrer patted her cameraman on the back and eased her head up to visor level with the top of the foxhole.

"Every Pulitzer winning bit of it, Gail. That senator is one balls-to-the-wall son-of-a-bitch!" Calvin held the camera ball over his head above the rocks and tracked the senator's activities through the view on his cameratech's e-suit visor display. Often he would be distracted by a hand-to-hand mecha encounter on the ground or by an Ares fighter screaming overhead in a spiral through swarms of enemy planes, missiles, and directed energy blasts firing helter skelter in return. Calvin was getting extreme close-ups of war from an inside-the-battle view. It would indeed be Pulitzer material.

"Watch what you say about my, daddy!" Deanna kicked at the cameraman's shin with her jumpboots. Sehera had to hold her zealous daughter down or she might have hurt the poor bastard.

"Like father like daughter." Sehera nodded to the big sergeant.

"I see." Sergeant Clay Jackson just thought this was the weirdest day he'd ever had as an armored e-suit Marine.

Lieutenant Colonel Mason Warboys and the Warlords were fighting blind without their sensors and the view from inside an M3A17-T was somewhat obstructed, so the tank squad commander had ordered his troops to all go to bot mode for better visuals since the cockpit of the tank was high on the torso and shoulders of the bot mode mecha. Warboys maintained a constant bombardment from his DEG into the Seppy drop tank's line and would go to the smaller but more rapidly aimable forty millimeter gun on top of the DEG turret for in close and rapidly maneuvering targets. The forty millimeter gun was usually running in anti-artillery and anti-missile mode, but with the sensors jammed they were not very effective on incoming ordinance. So Warboys had put the guns to use manually under his DTM control. While in bot mode the turret mounted railgun looked like a half dome head atop the bot's cockpit with the barrel sticking out for a nose.

"Shit! Guns, guns, guns!" He fired the main gun across the hillside at a rushing tank mode enemy vehicle. The bright blue-green pulse of energy separated the turret from the main body of the enemy tank. Running headlong at the exploding enemy mecha, Warboys jumped over the fireball and on top of the mecha's wingman, which was transfiguring to bot mode. Warboys rammed the fist of his heavily armored tank into the transfiguring enemy vehicle and punched through to the inner workings of the linkage between the torso and the right arm. The force of his fist broke through the linkage system, throwing sparks and spewing steaming black and red hydraulic fluids from within it. Warboys grabbed at the arm from the enemy tank, ripped it free, and then jammed it through the cockpit, running it through the pilot and mecha.

"Colonel, on your six!" Warlord Seven burned a

blue-green DEG bolt across the sky just behind Warboys, taking out a tank that had caught the lieutenant colonel unaware.

"Thanks, Seven. Damned Seppy jamming, we need our sensors!"

"You got that right, Warlord One."

"Warlord One, it looks like the Seppy bastards have figured out that their tanks are sitting ducks and are all going bot," Warlord Two noticed. "We gonna get that help anytime soon?"

"Just keep pounding at the fuckers relentlessly, Warlords! Whether we get help or not we kill as many of these Seppy motherfuckers as we can until there ain't a one of us left. Got it? The U.S. Army Tank Command Warboys' Warlords don't need no goddamned gyrenes to bring hell!" Warboys had to go to guns and fired blindly behind him as he ran and leapt towards an outcropping for cover.

"Oorah! Colonel!"

"One, you've got two on you trying to get you in a crossfire!" Warlord Six saw the two Seppy tanks trying to sandwich their leader and trap him at the edge of the gorge, leaving him with no place to go but Hell.

"Shit!" Warboys continued to fire the forty millimeter behind him blindly. Without sensors all he could do was shoot and hope for a hit. He scanned to his right and caught a glimpse of the mecha glinting in the Martian sunlight as it was slowly dropping behind the mountain. So Warlord One turned his gun toward the general direction of the glint and fired.

"Guns, guns, guns!"

Enemy cannon fire from his other side knocked him to the ground on his side. As Warboys tried to roll the mecha over onto all fours and then up he caught a quick glimpse of two armored e-suit Marines and two civilians with HVARs firing just over his head, and then they dove for cover as a bot with a missing leg at the knee tumbled over the colonel's tank and on top of them. The Seppy drop tank fell only a couple of meters on the other side of Warlord One. The lava rock gave the AEMs and civilians just enough cover to keep from being squished. One of the Marines, a private, rushed out from under the mecha and tossed a grenade into the cockpit and then dove for cover.

Warboys pushed himself up to his mechanized feet and strode back over the dead enemy bot and backed away from the gorge. With a quick shake of his head, a deep breath, and a fast prayer Warlord One turned back across the Martian battlefield to find more anti-American Separatist motherfuckers to send home to Jesus.

"Warlord One, Warlord One! Colonel Warboys, are you ok?" Warlord Two rushed to the side of his leader and turned his back to him, laying down more cover fire with his DEG, giving Warboys time to regain his composure.

"I'm all right, Two," Warboys replied. "We've got AEMs and civies back there. Let's push away from them! And see if we can't clear out an extraction LZ."

"Yes. sir."

The tank mecha squadron was holding their own but they were extremely outnumbered and would soon be overwhelmed. But Warboys had a plan. Actually, it was Burner's plan but it was working well so far. And, goddamnit all to hell, even a jarhead gyrene like Burner did have a good idea every now and then. As long as his tanks could last long enough to bait the Seppy mecha into the trap.

"Warlord Five, watch your six. There's two drop tanks about to crawl up your ass!" Warlord Four warned his wingman.

"Now, Warboys?" The commander of the Marine FM-12 squadron beckoned. His Marines were ready to go to work and their trigger fingers were *way* past itchy.

"Not yet, Burner! Not yet!" Warboys scanned across the Martian landscape and noted that the majority of the tanks hadn't engaged them just yet. They had thirty or forty continuously engaging them, but there were hundreds of them taking up position on the hill. Warboys, and his AIC, ran scenarios in his mind trying to figure out how to bring the enemy tank mecha closer in so the Killers could rise up and surprise the living shit out of them. He did have an idea. A dangerous idea. A courageous idea.

"Warlords, form up on me and we're going to rush the Seppy line!"

"Yes sir!"

"Oorah, sir!"

"Burner, get your gyrene ass ready!"

"DeathRay, I know it's hot. But we've got word that the senator's family including a little girl is in the LZ," Vulcan argued with the Ares pilot.

"It's too goddamned hot, Vulcan. I repeat. Too. Goddamned. Hot! No, and that is an order." DeathRay yanked the HOTAS left and rolled sideways to let a Gomer's missile flare by just beyond his cockpit.

That was fuckin' close.

Too close. If Jack went, Candis went with him and she didn't want to die any more than her human counterpart did.

"What's that, sir? I can't hear you. You're breaking up a bit! DeathRay, I'm sending in an evac now!" Vulcan replied.

"Shit!"

"Angels, anybody want to volunteer to rescue a little girl from a firefight?" Lieutenant Junior Grade Seri "Vulcan" Cobbs asked over the rescue-net.

"Vulcan. Yo-yo. Angel Seven will go if somebody'll take our wing!" Ensign Bobby "Yo-yo" Jones replied.

"Ok, Yo-yo. You're on my wing. Let's get on the deck and stay fast and stay low," Vulcan ordered. Vulcan turned to look back at her gunner Flight Gunner Petty Officer Third Class Sammy Jo Tapscott, "FG3, get ready to start laying down fire."

"Yes, ma'am!"

The two SH-102 Starhawks pulled away from the rest of the Angels orbit and went to maximum descent toward the red planet beneath them. Vulcan brought the search and rescue vehicle to the edge of its flight envelope and continued to push the throttle forward. The two ships slammed through the Martian atmosphere, heating up the nose of the boxy rescue vehicles from aerodynamic friction. Klaxons and the "Bitching Betty" started blaring through the cabin.

"Warning. Approaching maximum g-load limit. Warning. Enemy targeting systems detected. Warning.

Surface collision threat. Warning . . . " the "Bitching Betty" announced.

"The deck is coming up fast, Yo-yo. We'll flatten out and full throttle to the evac." Vulcan ordered.

"Right behind you, ma'am." Yo-yo gritted his teeth and hoped his gunner was strapped in. Otherwise, he was having a shitty day. And from the threat alarms sounding in the cabin, it was about to get worse.

"DeathRay, DeathRay, Vulcan."

"Go, Vulcan."

"If you can give us cover that would be nice. We're slamming air and about to make a run at the evac!"

"You sure about that, Vulcan?"

"Roger that, sir! You can court martial me if we survive."

"Good luck, we will plow the row a little for you." *Goddamn Vulcan*, he thought.

Senator! Fleet Angels Search and Rescue dropping in from orbit in thirty seconds! Abigail informed her counterpart.

About goddamned time!

"Second Lieutenant Washington!" Moore said over the QM almost at a scream to sound over the HVAR *spitap spitaps*, fighters careening overhead, and the mecha explosions and collisions.

"Yes, senator?"

"My AIC has confirmed two SARs vehicles incoming. Can you spread the word to the tanks to give them cover?"

"There!" Joanie Hasad pointed out the two dust trails streaking across the edge of the escarpment.

Senator! I've got the AI Kitty information from BIL.

And?

The AIK is a wireless AI that rides the Kitty robot and controls it through the wireless.

So?

Don't you see, sir . . .

At that moment a missile flared across the overhead and detonated not far from the other foxhole where his wife and daughter were. It was followed by enemy cannon fire and other missiles tracking onto the incoming evac ships. The SH-102 Starhawks yanked and banked as best they could and returned fire but it was too hot for them to attempt any type of landing. Cannon fire flared against the boxy Starhawks with splashes of metal sparks and fiery red plasma venting away as parts of the metal hull plates vaporized.

Over the side, Abigail! Tell the SARs to go over the side of the escarpment now!

Yes, sir! I understand, sir!

Warboys had pounded into the middle of the largest steady mass of Seppy drop mecha, leading his Warlords into the valley of death, and they were bringing more than they were receiving. Once they had fully engaged the enemy tanks in the full frontal attack it had thrown the Seppies off guard, briefly. The initial insertion through the line allowed them to do a lot of damage; but as the enemy regained their composure it was quite clear that the Warlords were outnumbered with odds they could not overcome.

"Warlord Three is gone! Warlord Three is gone!" Warlord Seven cried over the tac-net.

"I'm hit! I'm hit!" Warlord Four spun over backwards onto its back with a gaping hole in the right side of the mecha's torso. The cockpit vented atmosphere into the low pressure outside and the DTM interface inside the cockpit was blinking in and out. Viewscreens on the HUD went dark as electronics spewed sparks and began to smolder and then flame dully in the light Martian atmosphere. Warlord Four, Captain Salma Rodriguez, looked down at the gaping hole in her e-suit that ran from her abdomen to where her left leg and pelvis used to be as she bled out and coughed blood into her visor. "Oh Jesus . . . cough . . . oh fuck."

Vallery . . . self destruct authorization as the Seppy motherfuckers overrun us. Warlord Four ordered her AIC.

It was an honor, Captain. I'll maximize the damage to them.

You too, lieutenant. You were . . . a good friend.

Thank you, Salma. Are you sure you wish to self destruct, yes or no?

Yes.

"Oh Jesus!"

"Warlord Four bought the farm! Shit! Guns, guns, guns! Lay some cover back here!" Warlord Two shouted as an exploding missile tossed him forward nearly throwing him off balance. Warlord Two spun his mecha around just in time to go face-to-face with a bot mode drop tank. Warlord Two instinctively head butted the mecha and pushed it backwards with his right hand while at the same time sweeping its large mechanical legs with mechanized martial artistic brilliance. Warlord Two stomped through the Seppy drop tank's cockpit with a half ton mechanical foot before the poor enemy bastard had time to respond to being thrown.

"Retreat Warlords! Retreat to the escarpment and scatter. Lay rearward cannon fire as fast as you can." Warboys did a backwards flip, just escaping the grasp of an enemy mecha and rotated his cannon rearward, blasting it as he ran away. His DEG at the hip cleared a path for his squad. Warboys ran side-to-side and serpentined through the enemy mecha, firing his forty millimeter cannon and his DEG, and when that wasn't enough going hand-to-hand with the enemy mecha, ripping at them with the giant mechanized hands and feet of his vehicle.

"Fish, give those tankheads some cover on the north side! Demonchild, see if you and Hula and Stinky can't cover those Angels!" DeathRay dropped almost below ten meters from the deck, strafing the enemy drop tank lines, trying to draw some of the fire from the Warlords and to distract them from the evac ships. "Fox three!"

" . . . guns! Scratch four!" Fish exclaimed.

The problem with drawing fire was always that it meant you were trying to get more people to shoot at you. And at the moment there were plenty of Seppy Stingers and Gnats swarming and buzzing the sky trying to kill the Gods of War. That they didn't also need a bunch of surface dwellers pounding away at them too. But Warboys was in a fix! One of the downed M3A17s had just self detonated, taking out several of the surrounding Seppies with suicidal efficiency; that was just a sign that things were going to shit fast for the tankheads.

"Guns, guns, guns." Jack sprayed the DEG again, disrupting the tanks that were about to engulf Warboys. But the Warlords weren't giving up without some serious fighting. And the Gods of War were going to help out as best as they damned well could.

"Warlords, move!" Warboys fought fiercely and like a mad man to keep the tide of Seppy tanks off his Warlords, but he couldn't retreat and fight efficiently without his sensors.

"Sir, on your left!"

"Look out, Warlord Two!"

"Fuckin' Seppy motherfuckers!" Warlord Two screamed. "Fuck you! Fox three! Goddamnit all to hell. Guns, guns, guns!"

"There's just too goddamned many of them, One!"

"Well, Burner I guess now's a good a time as any!" Warboys finally called his gyrene pal for help and the trap was sprung in reverse. Warboys just hoped that the surprise and the superior fire power of the Marine FM-12s would be enough to overcome the extreme numbers game.

"Now, Reyez! Sehera! Go now! Go! Go! Go!" Major Moore stood up firing the Seppy HVAR full auto, laying down cover at any enemy motherfucker that looked cross-ways at his little girl. He bounced and zigged and zagged across the lava stones and was actually charging the oncoming rush of Separatist mecha. One unarmored retired Marine in a civilian e-suit with a commandeered Seppy HVAR that was running low on ammo charged an oncoming wall of enemy armored mecha. And for the moment he was a force to be reckoned with.

"Kootie, on your right!" Washington yelled over the QM. "Sergeant, give those civilians cover as hot as you can! Kootie, grenades!"

"Hold on, Dee! We're going for a ride!" Reyez Jones hugged the little girl to him and bounced out of the foxhole toward the edge of the cliff never looking back. Sehera bounced in right behind him.

"Go go!" Sehera screamed.

"Keep the video going!" Gail Fehrer yelled over the sounds of the battle at her cameraman. "This is incredible!"

"Yeah, if it don't get us fuckin' killed!" Calvin replied from behind the AEMs in the foxhole.

"Roger that, lieutenant!" Clay stood firing his railgun full auto and popping out the grenades from the under-barrel launcher as fast as he could action the slide. "You heard the lieutenant, Shelly!"

"Oorah, motherfuckers!" Shelly bounced up out from the foxhole over the ancient lava rock outcropping and rushed in to meet the senator. She was better armored and armed and could lay down more serious damage. The sergeant fell in behind, them pouring out grenade after grenade into the oncoming barrage of enemy tank mecha. The Warlords crested the ridgeline battered and bloodied and fighting hard as hell!

★ ★ ★

Reyez bounced one bounce away from the edge of the escarpment and tapped the ready switch on the glider-chute that he'd been packing since morning. He hoped that the little girl's mother remembered how to operate the chute system. With that thought he took a millisecond to look over his shoulder to check on Sehera. She bounced down beside him almost at the same instant running as hard as she could. Reyez might have been startled if he hadn't already been, literally, scared out of his mind.

"Come on!" she screamed at the man carrying her daughter and activated her gliderchute pack like a pro. Just as they crested the edge of the escarpment they bounced their jumpboots as hard as they could and the ground disappeared beneath them for at least a half a kilometer or more as they began to fall out of sight over the edge a swarm of FM-12 Strike Mecha rose up around them.

"Shit!" Reyez had to roll his body sideways to avoid hitting the wing of one of the fighter planes. Anybody other than a base jumping expert like Reyez would have probably hit the wing of the plane and been dead. As he rolled his body and arched his back he stared eye-to-eye with the mecha's pilot who seemed just as surprised. Reyez was so close he could read Lieutenant Jason "Boulder" Cordova underneath the fighter's cockpit. He pulled Deanna closer to him and it took him a second or two to stabilize his fall, but, he wasn't concerned at all, for this *was* what Reyez did for a living!

"Wait on the chute, Sehera!" Reyez was now in his element! "Wait!" He held onto the little girl with both hands as hard as he could, squeezing her to him. He reached down and grabbed his belt carabineer and snapped it onto the little girl's e-suit harness.

The floor of the cliff began to loom upward at them and they had fallen well below the edge of the escarpment by hundreds of meters and were picking up speed. Even though the Martian gravity was only thirty-eight percent of that on Earth, just under four meters per second per second of acceleration was pretty appreciable, and there was much less air friction to slow down their descent.

"Now!" Reyez shouted. He watched and waited for Sehera's chute to open so that she would be a second or two above them and then he pulled his cord. The chute opened and jerked them to a slow drifting fall. Deanna squeezed the adrenaline junky hard to her.

"This is fun!" she said. "Look!" Two SH-102 Starhawks pulled into hover formation behind them and followed the gliderchutes all the way to the bottom of the cliff.

Chapter 17

Senator! The AI wireless connection to the mecha and sensors! That is the key! Abigail said into the senator's mind. He had been distracted by his charge to protect his family long enough.

What! Moore fired the HVAR until it ran dry and then he dove behind a dead enemy drop tank for cover. "I'm out!" he announced over the QM.

"Shit!" Corporal Shelly bounced about ten meters to his right and her left arm was separated from her body at the shoulder by a cannon round. Before she had time to fall several more rounds chewed her to a red bloody mess into the Martian ground. Major Moore started to rush to her, but the armored Marine sergeant landing on top of him thought otherwise.

"Nothing you can do for her, sir." The sergeant said. The two men belly crawled under the downed enemy mecha as best they could.

The signal is continuous because it is a disruptive code

not a virus. The signal is controlling the sensors not, jamming them. Just like the AI controls the Kitty! Clever! Abigail had figured it out.

What do we do, Abigail?!

Hardwire!

Spread the word! There was still time to really turn the tide of this battle and minimize further losses for certain.

Yes, Senator Moore!

"Listen up! The jamming source is the wireless link between AIC and hardware! Go hardwire on sensors!" Moore shouted over the QM.

"What?" Washington replied. He and private Kootie were still rushing their position. "How the hell do you know that?"

"Hardwire between AIC and hardware is the key! Just do it!" Moore repeated.

Abigail!

I'm explaining it to all the AICs I can reach here sir. They're getting it done. the AIC staffer told her counterpart senator.

"Captain! We've got a solution to the sensor problem spreading throughout the fleet!" the XO said. The flagship was beginning to vent gasses from several decks and was getting a severe beating. Nine of the ships of the fleet had already been lost and the Seppies had the advantage due to their ghost ships. The *Madira* was holding its own better than others because it was the first to figure out the tactic of deploying its mecha along the hull to act as gun batteries. That tactic seemed to be buying them time and Captain Jefferson had issued orders that the rest of the surviving fleet should use similar tactics.

I have the solution, captain and I am resetting the ship's systems and shutting down any data critical wireless systems and transferring them via hardwire. Now, Uncle Timmy added.

Good, Timmy! the CO replied in his mindvoice. The DTM blinked off then on briefly in the captain's mind and when it came back up it was filled with enemy bogies and target alerts. "Air Boss, direct all the surviving fighters back into the engagement zone immediately!"

"Aye, sir!" the Air Boss nodded instinctively and reached out to several icons showing surviving pieces of squadrons and began pulling them together in the virtual battlescape around his head. His DTM now showed the Seppy bogies and they were seriously outnumbered. But the Air Boss knew the limits of the Seppy equipment and although there was an asymmetry in numbers the awesome capabilities of fully functional U.S. fighters and mecha more than made up for the deficit.

"All right, Demon Dawgs from Hell, y'all heard the Air Boss! We're to form up and insert into the engagement zone at maximum velocity with maximum ferocity!" Lieutenant Commander "Rabies" Chavez ordered his squadron.

"Rabies! I've got sensors and multiple targeting solutions! This is shit hot!"

"Roger that, I suggest we get in there and start giving some of those targeting solutions a go!"

★ ★ ★

"CO! CDC!"

"Go, CDC!" Captain Jefferson replied. The battle was coming fast at him now, with multiple splinter groups of large fleet ships and enemy ships fighting and evading and with swarms of enemy fighters that hadn't been visible before that now were literally . . . everywhere.

"Captain! Sensor nets have been reset and hardwired throughout the system and we're getting reports of large ship signatures in several different locations across the system that just shouldn't be there," the Combat Direction Center deck officer explained.

"What does that mean, CDC?" The CO had more to worry about right now than some lost ships in the system.

"Sir. They were cloaked like the others until the sensors were reset. That suggests they are Seppy ships, sir!" the CDC replied.

"Shit. How many and where, CDC?"

"Three large haulers and seven smaller passenger size vehicles at various locations all about two AUs away, sir."

"Time from engagement zone assuming maximum hyperdrive?" More ships into the mix would be bad. The fleet was getting pounded as it was. The CO didn't like this at all. Hopefully, the tide would start turning now that sensors were up.

"Assuming a quarter AU per minute sir that would put them eight minutes out . . . shit!"

"CDC?"

"Sir, reports from Triton station and Luna show hyperdrive conduit signatures and we just lost the ships off the sensor nets! Sir," the CDC officer said.

"Wire in a DTM alert to me of any new hyperspace

activity near us, CDC! I need to know the instant they show up." The CO scanned the virtual battlescape around his head and had Uncle Timmy run through a scenario or two, but never liked what he saw.

Timmy!

Aye?!

Alert the fleet that we've got three haulers and seven passenger sized enemy craft in hyperspace probably inbound for us. The CO looked up from his virtual world for a brief moment because the XO momentarily lost his balance due to the ship listing hard to port from an enemy fighter crashing into the exterior hull plating just below the command tower.

Aye, sir!

"Holy shit, Bigguns!" Second Lieutenant Timothy "Goat" Crow shouted in excitement. "I've got sensors and there are Gomers everywhere!"

"Roger that, Goat. Offspring has sensors too!"

"Well quit telling me about it, Marines, and shoot the fuckin' Gomers!" Bigguns ordered. Bigguns was running at a full trot, turning left and right, spraying at Seppy Stinger transfigurable mecha with her DEG and only occasionally going to missiles; at strafing range the guns worked better. Her FM-12 was now completely under her and her AIC's control and just became ten times more deadly.

"Shit!" she said, because the automatic avoidance system, which was more affectionately known as the ASS, launched her into a forward flip over a communications dish mounted on the hull of the supercarrier.

The Seppy Stinger strafing her forced its way through the surface-to-air fire from the *Madira* and was hell bent to go to surface and fight mecha-to-mecha. Bigguns tracked the incoming Stinger as it reconfigured itself to bot mode and slammed into the deck of the supercarrier a few tens of meters port of her.

"We've got enemy mecha on the hull!" Bigguns warned over the net. "Guns, guns, guns!" she tracked across the horizon at the thing, missing it as it ducked for cover behind an exhaust vent that jutted out of the deck. She cut the DEG off just in time to keep from blasting a hole in the ship herself.

This is gonna take some finesse.

Yes, ma'am! Her AIC started plotting possible trajectories for the enemy mecha.

"Bigguns! On your six!" Goat warned her.

"I got it Goat! Unnnnnnnnhhhhh . . . aaarrrrrggghhh-hh!" She leaped backwards through a full back flip over a second enemy bot mode mecha that had dropped through the lines on her and went to missiles for it and guns for his wingman. "Fox three! Guns, guns, guns. Take that, you Gomer motherfuckers!"

The first of the Stingers got off a round of mecha-to-mecha missiles that were tracking in on Bigguns' position fast at that short distance. The missiles arched upward from the mecha just as her guns took out the enemy fighter. As the missiles arched up and then back over they acquired a radar lock on Bigguns FM-12.

"Fuck!" She rolled onto her back, firing at the incoming missiles with her DEG and then up into a full run using ship structural features for cover. "Eagle mode!" she cried as the missiles twisted and turned around the structural outcroppings of the *Madira's* hull. The fighter rolled over into eagle mode with the forty millimeter cannons above and below the fuselage of the fighter and the DEG in the left hand. The main drive of the fighter now was capable of flying the vehicle at top speeds and to out maneuver the missiles.

"Unnnnnnhhhhhhh . . . .fucccckkkk!" the Marine captain grunted and bit down on her TMJ bite block hard as the fighter was thrown back and forth from incoming cannon fire. The armor and the SIFs held. Bigguns pulled the HOTAS back and pushed full throttle forward sending the FM-12 into a full speed high g-load climb away from the supercarrier and up into the enemy swarm of Gnats and Stingers. She pushed down on the right foot pedal and pulled up on the left one throwing a hard yaw into her flight path so she could target with her DEG as well as her cannons. Bigguns picked up several bogies along her flight path and started locking on targeting sensors.

I have a trajectory solution, captain! Her AIC alerted her and downloaded the vector to her DTM.

Got it!

Steady . . . steady . . . now!

"Fox three! Fox three!" Bigguns followed the trajectory and fired missiles at two different Gnats. As the Seppy Gnats exploded the fireballs confused the missiles that were tracking her and detonated into the shrapnel fields left from the exploding enemy ships.

We're clear, captain. Great flying!

Let's get back on the deck, shall we? Bigguns turned

the FM-12 back into an extreme dive toward the *Sienna Madira*. And rolled it up hard as the deck approached.

Bot mode! she thought, causing the fighter transfiguration software to cycle the linkage mechanisms in a whirling, rolling, and snapping action leaving her FM-12 standing upright on the deck of the *Sienna Madira* as a ten meter tall armored mechanical warrior.

Jack! I'm cutting the wireless radio off and going hard-wire UDP.

What?

Hold one . . . there!

The DTM virtual threat system lit up like a Christmas tree with Seppy Gomers painted all over the sky and ground. Lock-on warnings started blaring and the AIC-fighter connection began targeting multiple bogies.

"Holy shit, DeathRay! I've got sensors and targeting!" Fish announced over the net. Similar calls began coming in across the planet and the sky. "I've got multiple targeting solutions."

"Well, quit telling me about it and fucking fire, mister!" DeathRay replied while following his own advice. "Fox three, fox three, guns, guns, guns!"

"All right, Killers, let's show these Seppy motherfuckers what real mecha is!" Burner ordered the Marine squadron of FM-12 Strike Mecha into the fray. The FM-12 Strike Mecha was considered the most efficient high technology piece of armed lethal force in the known universe and the Marine pilots knew that it was even more lethal in the hands of a full-blooded heartbreaking and life-taking

United States Marine! Burner never even backed off the throttle or the guns as he rolled from fighter mode into bot mode at a full velocity run. Full velocity with maximum ferocity was the motto of the Marine FM-12 Strike Mecha drivers. Lieutenant Colonel John "Burner" Masterson dove headlong over the top of Lieutenant Colonel Warboys—an Army puke who had gotten himself into a goddamned pickle—tackling a Seppy drop tank that was in bot mode and chasing Warboys' ass.

"Guns, guns, guns!" Burner judo twirled and tossed the enemy mecha over a tank mode mecha thirty meters to his right and fired the jumper jets on the mecha's feet. As Burner rolled in the air over two oncoming enemy bot mode tanks he was forced to twist and maneuver the body of his FM-12 in order to maneuver through the onslaught of their missiles and cannon fire—a feat that couldn't have been accomplished without his AIC-to-fighter combination working properly. The missiles spiraled around trying to gain purchase on the Marine's mecha but Burner was too good for them.

"Guns, guns, guns!" He set the twin shoulder mounted forty millimeter cannons loose in full anti-missile tracking mode. The purple and blue ion trail from the cannon rounds tracked across the path of the first missile, detonating it into a nearly perfect round orange fireball. The shrapnel from the lead missile performed an act of fratricide by detonating the other missiles in turn.

"Fox three!" A missile flew off, taking out a Stinger on approach to strafe him just as Burner righted his mecha, standing behind the two enemy bot mode tanks. He reached out with the butt end of his DEG and slammed it through the cockpit of the mecha on his left while stomping through the back of the mecha on his right, all the while his AIC firing continuously at multiple targets, and hitting them.

"Sweet goddamn, it smells like victory!" Boulder screamed out triumphantly over the net. "Guns, guns, guns."

"Scratch three!" One Night replied.

"BullNutz! BullNutz, you got a Stinger dropping in on your six at cherubs two!" Ace in the Hole said.

"I got 'em!" Epoxy replied as his DEG targeting system locked on and burned the Seppy fighter plane with a blue-green energy bolt that nearly ripped the Stinger in two. The enemy mecha fell with a hard *thud* to the Martian ground with the enemy pilot inside lifeless.

"Oorah, Epoxy!" BullNutz thanked his wingman.

"Oorah!"

Chapter 18

"CDC. CO." Captain Jefferson was having trouble under-standing the warnings going off in his head. They were launch warnings of undesignated vehicles, but there were so many that it made no sense. The virtual sphere in his head changed scale to encompass Mars out past the Belt and all the way to Luna City. There were trajectories scat-tering the sphere that, at that scale, were merely blinking red dots. But there were so many red dots that the CO was having trouble comprehending what it was he saw.

"Aye, sir?"

"What the hell is going on? I'm seeing hundreds, maybe thousands of launch warnings. Several hundred from Mars space, the Belt, and, well hell, all over the damned system!"

"Yes, sir. It looks like every damned ship in the solar system just lifted off. We are also getting hyperspace signatures as soon as they clear the gravity wells, sir." The CDC sounded as confused as the CO did.

"Hyperspace! Here?"

"I don't think so, sir. Some of the ships going to hyperspace are leaving from Mars and have been in the conduits longer than it would take to get to you. No exits detected, sir?"

"What the . . . "

"Sir, we just lost the main DEGs on all forward decks!" the XO said. The overheating had been a problem since the Seppy ships had started focusing their attack on the flagship. The SIFs holding the hull plating together on one side would overheat while the DEG coolant systems were overheating on the other and there was no balance that seemed to be working. Were it not for the Marine mecha pilots on the hull of the ship and the Ares pilots in the mix, the supercarrier might have to abort the mission and attempt a run at hyperspace.

"Goddamnit, Larry, get me my main guns back on line!"

Kira Shavi and her AIC Allison had made an impression on the right Separatist First Wife and her daughter. Elise Tangier had turned out to be the niece of Gisele Tangier the true First Wife of the Tangier shipping dynasty of the Separatist Laborers and Shipping Guild. The Separatist's view of economics had often been considered socialistic by intelligence reports. But from all that Kira could discern, they were nothing less than purely capitalistic. True, the Separatists held a centric mindset to evolve and free the entire Reservation, and all resources seemed to be spent toward that goal. But the direction of any individual's resources appeared to be fully owned and controlled by that individual. It didn't appear to Kira or Allison that General Ahmi told Gisele Tangier what she could or could not do with her wealth. Although, for some reason, all of the wealth of the entire Separatist culture seemed to be focused toward something, some single goal. This Exodus that Elise had spoken of was the most likely candidate. And it was often noted that the Separatists would use the phrase "Ahmi was served!" enthusiastically and emotionally, but Kira was still uncertain of its true meaning.

Kira sat in the small, but very accommodating, state room that Elise had put her in once they boarded the *Tangier I* at Umbra Spaceport on the northernmost region of the Martian Reservation. Kira knelt on the bed with her hands resting in the sill of the large portal overlooking her small bed. Phobos and Deimos glimmered faintly in the foreground of the red, green, and blue planet.

What a view, Kira thought to Allison. Mars began to shrink below her rapidly as the large cargo ship accelerated beyond low Mars orbital altitudes and approached the hyperspace initiation distance.

Yes. Enjoy it now. No telling how long it will be before we see Sol System again, the AIC said.

True. What now? Kira thought and then yawned. Almost simultaneously her stomach growled. It had really been a long hard day.

Food, perhaps? Maybe a shower and then a nap? Kira's AIC had long taken care of her human counterpart since back during her training on the "Farm," and the AIC knew that she often would be too mission oriented to take care of the essentials. That is what AICs were for. That is what best friends were for. And Kira and Allison had been through a hell of a lot in the years they had worked together for the CIA.

Good idea. We'll take it slow. After all, it is a full long month, at least it sounds like, that we'll be in this ship. Plenty of time to snoop around. Kira looked around at the little room. It reminded her of the room her and a classmate in college had shared on a sea cruise that she had taken in the Caribbean on Earth. That cruise hadn't been the time she'd lost her virginity, but it had been the time she was most free and uninhibited in her life. There were some fun memories there and Kira couldn't help but smile and nod from the emotions that were triggered by them. College had been a lifetime ago it seemed.

The room was about three meters wide and about five deep. The bed stretched across the end of the room by the outer bulkhead where the large oval portal allowed for great views of space. Sitting on the bed and looking back across the room she saw there was a Martian oak changing table and a pine desk on the right side and a small couch opposite those, leaving just enough room to squeeze between them. There were three drawers in the changing table. Kira rummaged through the drawers and found basic female essentials including undergarments and socks. In the desk was a notescreen that had a schedule of meals, laundry pickups, and a list of virtual entertainment programming channels. There was also Elise's AIC email address scribbled on it, with a note to link to her for dinner plans.

Past the furniture was a closet on the right with a full length mirror for the door. Opposite that was a three quarter ornate, yet small, bathroom. The little bathroom was typical of state rooms. There was just enough room to squeeze in it and use it, but not enough to loiter around in it for a long period of time. The accommodations were far better than those that she had seen on the Navy supercarrier she had recently been on, but they were far from Earth's version of comfortable. On the other hand, they were quite luxurious for interstellar travel.

Kira stuck her head in the closet and noted that it was full of clothing that as far as she could tell was her size. Her e-suit pack was stored at the bottom of the closet as well as several pairs of shoes ranging from athletic gear to dress heels.

Allison, have you linked to Elise's AIC yet? Kira asked and pulled off her clothes. She had been through a hard day and wanted to get out of the worn Seppy BDUs.

Yes.

She requests that you meet her for breakfast in the morning to discuss realigning your talents to duties onboard the Tangier I.

Good. I'm glad she didn't want to meet tonight or I'd have to take some stims. Kira yawned again. She could go without sleep for several days without too much difficulty, but today had been unusual and had taken a lot of energy. She really need to shower, eat, and sleep. The radiation treatment had given her a pounding headache all day long and was wearing her down like a bad case of the flu.

Actually, she did request that. But I told her you were incoherently tired and grieving the loss of your brothers. She understood. The memory trigger brought tears to her eyes and she felt an overwhelming urge to cry. Kira sniffled lightly and dried her eyes. Her AIC was specifically designed to trigger her hypothalamus with appropriate emotional response to her cover sory. The emotions seemed as real to her as the ride in Lieutenant Commander Jack Boland's fighter plane did and more immediate to her than the memories of her carefree Caribbean cruise from her college days.

Ok. Then I'm taking a shower and why don't you order me some food? However it is that we do that. The BDUs hit the floor as she kicked the soiled and worn red Martian camouflage into the closet with her left foot.

Instructions for ordering are in the notescreen, but I can take care of it.

You know what I can't figure out? Kira opened the bathroom door and stepped through the very narrow opening.

What is that?

How in the hell do millions of Separatists just up and leave the system without any military action or at least some of them getting stopped? This diversion that Elise mentioned must be one hell of a diversion. The toothbrush on the sink was new and Kira had to remove the safety seal from the small plastic box. She placed the small one centimeter cube in her mouth and activated it with her tongue. The cube instantly expanded and filled the front of her mouth with tiny micro fiber bristles that crawled across her teeth, removing plaque, microbes, and stains as Kira chewed on it. With each chew a refreshing burst of spearmint flavors and germ killing fragrances filled her taste buds. She spat the toothbrush back into the box and paused to watch it curl the bristles back into a cube, a scene that had amused her since she was a little girl. Some memories would always be more real than others. Kira then drank a cup of water using the small clear plastic reusable cup from the dispenser on the edge of the sink.

We do have news channels and I've downloaded some summaries into your screen, but we are about to jaunt to hyperspace and will lose live feeds. I've been screening some of it. Take a shower and I'll catch you up, Allison said. Kira had pulled back the shower curtain and was about to step in. The warm water and steam filled the room and felt so inviting on her naked skin. Kira moaned slightly at the thought of how good a hot shower was going to feel.

We're about to jaunt? Kira reached over and slapped the water off.

Yes.

Shit, why didn't you say so? Do we still have an internet connection?

Yes.

Good. Send the following email to mom20505@ gomail.com.earth. Kira paused for a second to think of what to say exactly to her case agent back at the Directorate of Operations at CIA Headquarters in Langley, Virginia on Earth.

Hi Mom! The bachelor party was an absolute blast! It was tough to find at first but I ended up getting to it. I picked up a good looking guy and went home with him. He says he is from Tau Ceti. How about that? I hope it is more than just a one night stand. Don't worry about me, I'll find a ride home. By the way, I made lots of tips and will buy you a present real soon. Call you when I can. Love you, your daughter.

The message has been sent. About thirty seconds to jaunt now.

You know I like to watch! I can't believe you weren't going to tell me. Kira turned and carefully squeezed out of the narrow bathroom door.

Sorry, Kira. I thought you were so tired that you just wanted to shower and crash. Allison hoped her counterpart wasn't too sore at her. And she didn't want to ask Kira at this point if she didn't think sending the message to HQ was a bit premature. But Kira had always managed to pull them through every tough spot they had been in and there was no need to start second guessing her human counterpart—her friend—now.

Ask next time. Kira closed the bathroom door and made her way to the small cruise ship style bed, walking naked across the room, too tired to look for something to put on. Kira again knelt on the bed with her palms resting on the window sill. Mars only filled about a third of the sky from their present orbit and was slipping away fast. She made out several features that she had studied in school at Langley. There was the Planum Boreum ice cap lakes and the Korelev crater steam plant, the artificial ocean at Syrtis Major Planum; due south of that in the middle of the planet, there were the scarred Elysium Planitia green and red algae fields, and the Tholus and Phlegra mountain regions that were covered with forests of Martian conifers and oaks she had so recently seen up close and personal— too close and too personal for her tastes.

"All hands, all passengers, this is the captain speaking. Prepare for hyperspace," a woman's voice sounded over the intercom and was followed by three long blasts of the horn.

A violet and blue reverse cascading shower of sparkles suddenly appeared forward of the *Tangier I* and a whirling blue tunnel opened at the bottom of the converging iridescent light vortex. Kira leaned quietly in the window and watched Mars and the stars in the background converge into the distance at a single point and then vanish in the collapsing violet sparkles. The hyperspace tunnel swirled around the ship, spreading the whirling blue dim flashes of light over the ship and washed over Kira's naked body. The absolute beauty and strange magnificence of the interworkings of the other dimensional conveyance through the universe took her mind from her present predicament for a brief but enjoyable moment.

"Well, that's that," Kira said. Immediately, her mind went back to running scenarios for gaining access to more useful Separatist strategic planning information without getting herself killed. And how the hell was she going to get that information back to Earth? All of that could wait. For now, Kira's mission had been a success. The entire plan was to get somebody on the inside of the Seppy culture who could blend in and work up to a level of trusted status within the Separatist Resistance movement. Kira had planted the seeds for that with Elise. Her mission had indeed been successful so far. Now all she had to do was play along and wait a while. Access to more detailed information would come, but today was all about phase one of the plan. Phase one was complete. Now Kira could think about phase two, after she took a shower, and maybe after she had eaten something, and maybe after a long, very long, night of sleep.

★ ★ ★

"Mr. President! It's coming over every known frequency across the system and is playing on millions of websites simultaneously," the National Security Advisor informed President Alberts.

"What is it?"

"It is a repeating message saying that General Elle Ahmi is about to make a system wide statement in one minute." The NSA nodded to a technician who was adjusting the inputs for the flatscreens in the Situation Room in the basement of the West Wing of the White House. The technician nodded that the screens were ready.

"Well, don't keep us hanging here." Alberts leaned back in his chair and took a sip from his Ohio State coffee mug that the governor of the state had given to him.

"There," the NSA said as the image on the viewscreen went from blue to the Separatist Resistance Flag and a timer counting down. Five, four, three, . . .

"Check out the JumboHoloTron." The pregnant lady sitting next to Rod Taylor pointed towards the main elevator tube at the edge of Mons City Central Park. The giant JumboHoloTron was a three dimensional upside down cone that continuously surrounded the elevator shaft with advertisements, terror alert status, stock market data, and breaking news ticker tapes. There were also music videos, commercials, and mini-movies playing on the larger portions of it. The size of the screen was such that it could be seen from most of Central Park. The giant conical holoscreen stretched from the street level up to the thirty-third floor ceiling and made contact with the top of the dome.

The JumboHoloTron had a very large captive audience today—captive being the key word. The Seppies had rounded up and packed several hundred thousand citizens and tourists alike into the main field of the plush green Earthlike city park and then surrounded them with mobile force fields. There were only a few exits to the field and at each of these bottlenecks were several divisions of heavily armed Seppy troops.

"Well, maybe some of this damned waiting will be over with," Vincent Peterson replied with a bit of an edge to his voice. He sorely needed a cigarette or at least a beer to take the edge off his nicotine habit.

"Well, maybe the Seppies are finally giving up and going back home to the Reservation with their tails between their legs." Rod didn't use sarcasm normally, but there had been nothing normal about this long Martian day.

"Maybe so, bud." Vincent didn't care much for the sarcasm either. The Separatist flag being displayed on the giant holographic screen faded out and a familiar face of terror took its place.

". . . Citizens of Sol's System! I am General Elle Ahmi." The female most wanted terrorist of the system had been long thought to be dead, but apparently the intelligence of her death had been a bit premature. Ahmi stood in front of a large bot-mode Separatist Armored Stinger fighter craft, and beside that was an American flag. From the view angles of the video camera it appeared that there was a blue-gray Martian sky behind her, seen through an atmosphere dome. Elle Ahmi was somewhere on Mars!

She wore a Separatist armored pilot flight suit with the helmet off. She was in full battle rattle as if she actually were going into combat. Over her face was the long renowned red, white, and blue ski mask and her long straight black hair hung freely out the back of it. From the image there was little that could be said about her physical age or attributes other than she was female and about one hundred and ninety centimeters tall and had brown eyes. There was no doubt to anybody that had seen or heard her before that it was indeed her.

"This is a tumultuous time for the human race. Earlier today the Separatist Freedom Fighters dealt a great blow to the tyranny and oppression of the past century that the Great American Nation has thrust upon the Free People of the United States! Since your President Sienna Madira forced the free people of Mars across the planet, slaughtering tens of thousands of them in a tyrannical death march to what is now known as the Reservation more than fifty-eight years ago, WE, the Freedom Fighters of the United States of America, have opposed such tyranny and oppression with the blood, sweat, and tears of our sons and daughters, our mothers and fathers.

"Today as the great power of the United States Navy was forcing its way into the periphery of the so-called Separatist Reservation near the Elysium fields to slaughter yet more innocent mothers, fathers, sons, daughters, brothers, and sisters in the name of the once great country, WE, the Free People of America, have risen up and said NO! No more! It stops here and goes no further!" Elle Ahmi stood stalwart and stern, her brown eyes peering from beneath the red, white, and blue ski mask through the video camera and into the screens of people across the system. There was no doubt of the steel resolve behind those eyes.

"Today was obviously not the first time that American tanks, fighter planes, and mecha have rolled and marched over gallant men and women fighting to redeem the independence of their homeland. Nor is it by any means the final episode in the eternal struggle of liberty against tyranny, anywhere in this system, including Earth itself! It will happen again!" She pounded her right fist into her armored left hand. "But I say not from the people you would know as the Separatists!"

"My entire life I have dreamt of a truly socially just and truly free society and exactly for this reason I have always led the Free People of the United States of America to speak out against tyranny and to strike it down with all of the might that can be mustered only by a truly Free People. I believe America, the Great America of our revered forefathers, is lost to history. Then, in those great days of the Great America and only then, when justice and freedom existed, could human problems be solved in a peaceful and fruitful way. I have truly always felt in my heart of hearts that only through the solution of these problems could human values be realized and mankind reach its full and amazing potential. Mankind is meant to live in freedom! True freedom! Freedom from taxation without true representation! Freedom from being forced to accept the stagnation and quagmire of a species, because political gain is all that drives the will of those of what is left of the Great America. A truly free individual, a true American citizen who lives justly, is beaten down by

American law and can no longer offer all that he or she has to offer; all of the citizen's greatness and all of the citizen's human dignity is lost to the corruption and self-serving darkness that has become America!

"If the Great America still exists, then why do the average citizens of Earth read and perform math skills at levels that were far exceeded a century ago? If the Great America still exists, then why does the average citizen not understand the nature of government and the concept of law? If the Great America still exists, then why does only one in a thousand understand how even the simplest of technologies operate with no hopes of understanding the sciences that drive them? If this is the Great America, then why has humanity had the means for interstellar flight more than a century but there are only four extra-solar colonies? And why have there only been a handful of expeditionary missions? If this is the Great America why is it not safe to walk down the streets at night only a few blocks away from the White House and the Houses of Congress? If this is the Great America, why are the prisons overcrowded with animals who only desire personal gain from evil purposes? And why will those evil men and women never see the executioner for the deeds they have done? If this is the Great America, then why must the federal government be involved in the approval of most all aspects of free citizens' lives? It is this final aspect of what has happened to the Great America that triggered the American Civil War and indeed what originally drove our forefathers to revolt against England! Why have we let this happen again to the Great America?" Ahmi paused briefly and nodded to someone off camera.

"I will tell you why. This is not the Great America of
our forefathers and of history. America died centuries ago
with the taking and grabbing and giving away of the Great
Freedoms given to Americans by the Great Constitution,
simply because of a culture ridden with fear of offense to
special interests groups and the destruction of the moral
base from which the country's laws were governed.
Splinter factions of idiots and charlatans with nonsense
ideologies and lust for power for power's sake discovered
that it was easy to usurp power from the American citizens,
as they had grown docile and ignorant. The forefathers
were quite correct in their fear that once the lowest
common denominator of the American society learned
how to vote themselves into money and power the checks
and balances of the Great Nation would fall into an abyss
of devolving culture of greed and stagnation of welfare
and false racism. By the time General Madira was elected
as President of the United States of America our nation
had already folded into something far, far inferior to the
Great Nation it once was.

"But the Free People of the United States of America
understand this, and when it was clear to us that the
oppressive socialists of the Sol System government would
no longer listen to reason, would no longer understand
why we lash out in violent opposition, would no longer
even consider us worthy of sending a true ambassador to
the peace summit, we decided it was time for something
new. Something that would change mankind for the better.
Indeed, something that has been evolving for centuries.
That something is freedom. The Free People of the
United States of America are leaving Sol's System today!

In the greatest Exodus known to the history of mankind and in order for American law to prevail and the freedom of mankind to flourish, we are leaving and taking those dearly held philosophies that so many Americans have given their lives for and, to paraphrase a Great American President, that we here highly resolve that these dead shall not have died in vain—that this nation, under God, shall have a new birth of freedom about a new star—and that government of the people, by the people, for the people, shall not perish from the galaxy!

"But finally, I warn you people of Sol's System. Do not try to stop us! We would have left in peace but you would not have allowed such an Exodus. Your decomposed government and economic system would lose its middle class workers and lose its economic tax base. So instead, like our true Great American brothers that died so bravely in the pursuit and the defense of liberty, many of us will stay behind and fight you to the very last breath of the very last one of us so that others may escape this system's tyranny and the ideal of America shall live elsewhere in the universe! Why should fear, killing, destruction, displacement, orphaning, and widowing continue to be the fate of the Separatist People, of the Free People, while security, stability, and happiness at the expense of the hard working Free People remains the fate of the corrupt and dark government of this system? This is indeed unfair and the balance of nature must sway back in our favor. It is time that we help tilt that balance; it is time WE, the Free People, get revenge upon you for the slaughter of our loved ones and our true heritage. You will be killed just as you kill, and will be bombed just as you bomb. And expect

more that will further distress you and make certain that
you will not follow after us. The Free People are making
their last mark on the Sol System today as we leave. Do
not try to find us! Do not try to stop us! Do not try to bring
us back into your evil devolved fold!

"As one last conundrum I give you this. Do you make
attempts to stop humans who only wish to be free from
this system or do you try to stop the last of the Separatist
Military from destroying the millions of your people in the
Tharsis regions and great Mons City of Mars? You have
only moments to decide."

Chapter 19

1:59 PM Mars Tharsis Standard Time

"I am so glad that bitch finally shut the fuck up!" President Alberts pounded his fist against the Situation Room table. Wind from his fist flung papers scattering across the long mahogany table. The Joint Chiefs of Staff traded looks back and forth at each other in amusement.

"Sir, what are your orders? Mr. President?" the Chairman asked.

"What the hell are they planning for Mons City!?" President Alberts had to think quickly. There was no way to get opinion polls out in time to make a decision on what to do, so he was going to have to do something that no president had done in decades or more; Make a decision on his own. That thought literally terrified him.

"Mr. President, the extraction of Senator Moore was obviously a trap and reports have the entire fleet surrounded and in serious jeopardy from the engagement," the Secretary of Defense Conner Pallatin reiterated to the president. What had started out as a rescue mission for a senator and his family had gone really bad.

"Yes, Conner, I have heard the same reports as you." The Secretary of Defense was really a politician and not a soldier. What did he really know about dealing with such dire situations? The president and several of his predecessors had been fighting the war against the Separatists for decades based purely on political polling data. What could they do to stop this and was there still a way to salvage the next election for the DNC? The president was not very certain on either front.

"We need to show strength, Mr. President," the Chairman of the Joint Chiefs said. The Joint Chiefs unanimously agreed. The National Security Advisor nodded in agreement as well.

"What will the public think if we go into a full fledged war against the Separatists?" the President's Press Correspondent asked frantically.

"We need to think about how the public will react about us sending troops into war." Alberts sighed and pushed back in his chair.

"With all due respect sir, we've lost thousands today already. We are *in* a full fledged war," the Chairman replied. "The Navy, Army, and Marines have been in serious combat for decades, spread out across the system fighting these Separatists. We've been at war for a long time."

"I'm sure the president understands this, general," the weasel sec def responded.

"If it is war they want, then give it to them. Drop all the divisions we have on those fleet ships onto Mons City and shut down those Seppy bastards. And give the fleet authorization to go to full subnuclear arms to stop those ships!" President Alberts was proud of himself and scared out of his wits at the same time. No president had made such a decision without the knowledge that the public was behind him or her since . . . well, since Madira. This would be the end of his legacy. The DNC would excommunicate him from the next convention. He would be lucky even to get an invitation to view it from a long distance via satellite—a very long distance. In other words, politically, he was fucked . . . royally.

"Well, that is just fucking great! The goddamned White House waits until we are already engaged and blasted to shit to give us the go ahead on gluonium!" The XO was tired of being tossed around by enemy fire and, from his outburst, it was apparent to the CO that he was extremely tired of being jerked around by goddamned spineless, gutless, mindless fucking politicians.

"Check that, XO! Does us no good," Captain Jefferson told his trusted second in command. "The big bombs are a non factor as long as the Seppies have us wrapped up like this. We can't get away from them to go nuke and we are running out of options on tactics. We need a new strategy!"

"Orders, sir?" the XO asked.

"Keep taking it to them, XO. And where in the hell are my goddamned guns? Conventional missiles and mecha fire is not doing the job."

"Working the guns, sir. Hull Tech below says all the coolant reservoirs are overheated and it will take several minutes to get just one battery back on line. He is doubtful on getting more of them up." The XO maintained a handle on the ship's health monitoring systems and the outlook was getting grim.

"Quartermaster of the Watch!" the XO called.

"Aye sir!"

"Get fire teams down there to help out the Hull Techs on the coolant levels!" the XO ordered.

"Aye sir!"

"CO! CDC!" came over the net.

"Go, CDC!"

"You should be getting alarms now, sir!" Just as the CDC Officer of the Deck had said that klaxons and flashing red dots went off in three separate locations in the DTM virtual sphere in the CO's head.

"Roger that, CDC! Our vanished Seppy friends, I assume?"

"Most likely sir . . . aye, sir! We have signature verification coming in now. The autocorrelation software gives a correlation confidence of eight seven percent, sir," the CDC officer replied.

"Copy that, CDC." The CO studied the battlescape for a brief moment and watched as Uncle Timmy plotted possible trajectory solutions in his mind. The battle had been spread out from near-space of fifty kilometers or so to almost mars-synchronous orbit of about thirty-three thousand kilometers. The fleet had started with eighteen supercarriers and ten smaller warships; they were down to eight supercarriers with heavy damage and three smaller warships. All of the supercarriers listing helplessly in space still had mecha. Captain Jefferson would make use of that against the four carriers, five haulers, and four smaller passenger sized vessels the Seppies still had fighting.

"Fleet! CO *Sienna Madira*! All flight worthy and combat capable vessels are to deploy from all Fleet boats immediately! Deploy and engage the enemy!" Jefferson ordered. "Any drop tanks capable of deployment are to drop on Mons City immediately and take the city back!"

"CO! Air Boss!"

"Go, Air Boss!"

"We have three squads of M3A17-Ts winding up for the drop! One from the *Washington* and two from the *Thatcher* are starting the drop now. And the *Mother Teresa* has a mix of FM-12s and M3A17-Ts on the bounce. The *Thatcher* has also scrambled seventeen Ares fighters; they have a few dozen more but their cats are down."

"Roger that. Good. Tell the *Teresa* to drop the FM-12s below with the tanks. And tell the Air Boss of the *Thatcher* to blow a hole in the side of the fuckin' ship if they need to but get those goddamned fighters into space now!" Jefferson looked at the virtual space around him. The new Seppy ships had entered into normal space at high orbit and at maximum velocity but separated by thousands of kilometers. Several of the smaller Seppy ships already in theater had pulled from engaging and started retreating toward two of the ships that were closest together.

"CO *Madira*! CO *Franklin*!"

"Go, CO *Franklin*!"

"We're closest to the main group of Seppies, Wally. Give me the *Andy Jackson*, *Bryant*, and the *Patrick Henry* and we'll take it upstairs to them," the CO of the *Benjamin Franklin* requested.

"Roger that, Mike! Good hunting! *Madira* out!"

Captain Jefferson turned his attention back to the ships on the other side of the battlescape.

Captain?

Go, Timmy.

Thatcher has blown the lower deck plating from the aft hanger deck and Ares pilots are flying out from the gaping hole.

Son-of-a bitch. That Captain Walker is hardcore.

Aye, sir.

"Holy shit! Sir!" Helmsman Marks screamed following the brilliant flash about ten thousand kilometers above them.

"What the . . . " Jefferson had to squint his eyes from the virtual space flicker created in his mind that was in the general direction of the splinter fleet that the *Franklin* and three other fleet supercarriers had gone after. Subnuclear detonation proximity klaxons started blearing throughout the ship.

"CO! CDC!"

"Go, CDC!"

"We've got a gluonium detonation from the enemy ships at . . . "

"Roger that, CDC, we see it." The CO cut him off as the virtual sphere reset itself. There were two missing Separatist haulers, several smaller ships, and there were four missing U.S. supercarriers. "Fuck!" He slammed his fist against his chair. "It was a goddamned trap!"

"CO, do we want to get close to the other Seppy hauler?" the XO asked.

"Negative. Fleet. CO *Madira*! Engage Seppie hauler at

distance only. Repeat. Seppy hauler is to be engaged from distance only. Suspect WMD boobytraps!"

Captain?

Go, Timmy.

New plot of the hauler's trajectory suggests it is on a collision course for the Main Dome of Mons City!

Goddamnit, Timmy. We've got to stop it. The CO concentrated for a fleeting second, hoping for a spark of some tactic that might help. *Suicide bombers.*

Sir?

How do you stop suicide bombers?

Sir?

Fight fire with fire, Timmy! Can we clear the fighters in time to hit that thing with a subnuke?

We would suffer major losses but could possibly save the city.

Shit.

"Fleet! CO *Madira*! Steer clear of enemy vessel on trajectory for Planet's surface. Retreat to maximum safe distance now and prepare for subnuclear detonation." Captain Jefferson ordered and started drawing out new vectors in his virtual battle for the surving members of the fleet.

"Sir?!" the XO said. "A suicide mission?"

"Well goddamnit, Larry, if you'd get me my main guns back we might not have to go to such extremes!"

"Yes, XO! Aye sir! Aye sir!" Hull Technician Joe Buckley almost saluted the tac-net screen. The Sienna Madira was forced on a suicide run and there were only a couple of minutes left to get the main gun up to save it.

It was possible that one of the systems would cool down enough for a shot or two in two to five minutes but Joe didn't think that was likely. They were screwed.

Hull Tech Buckley had worked in the bowels of the flagship of the U.S. Navy fleet for seven years and knew every nook and cranny of the coolant flow systems and there was just nothing left to do. The liquid metal flowing around the ship to cool any of the large heat generating systems such as the engines, the catapults, the SIF generators, and the main DEGs was all overheated—all of it. There wasn't a flow system left that wasn't overheated. It had been rerouted and rerouted and rerouted again in order to keep the SIFs up or the DEGs firing. Joe had never seen the flagship in such a tight spot.

"Well, Fireman's Apprentice King, I guess this is going to be a typical Navy day!" Buckley told his subordinate. The sarcasm wasn't lost on the Fireman's Apprentice.

"Goddamn it, HT. This is a bunch of shit! I don't want to fuckin' die!" The new guy in the "shit hole" had just picked the wrong week to join up and that is all there was to it. Some guys do life in the military and never see any action, not one fucking iota. But then some poor dumb unlucky bastard draws the short end of the stick and has to rush Normandy on his first combat mission, or has to guard the embassy during the Tet offensive, or has to raid the Seppy farms on the first day of the Desert Campaigns, or, in Fireman's Apprentice James King's case, work in the bowels of the shit flow pipes for the flagship of the United States Navy during the mass Exodus of the entire Separatist population in the system.

"That's right, Jimmy, this is just a bunch of shit. Seppy

motherfuckers!" Hull Tech Buckley shouted at the top of his lungs and banged his fist against the bulkhead. They only needed a small flow loop. Just enough to give them a few seconds of the main gun! One little flow loop of coolant. Hell, they didn't even need anything exotic for just a few seconds. Just one little goddamned flow loop that wasn't already overheated.

Jimmy's right, Mija. This is a sock full of shit! Buckley thought to his AIC. *It was nice knowing ya.*

You too, Joe. Somebody has to take the shit and I guess there's nobody better trained for it than us, Mija replied almost light heartedly. *Sorry Joe.*

Shit . . . shit . . . Joe shook his head and then a thought struck him, almost.

Joe? Are you all right?

Shit . . . Hull Technician Petty Officer Third Class Joe Buckley was in the makings of a moment of genius. Not Nobel Prize winning genius but perhaps ass saving genius.

Hull Technician Joe Buckley? His AIC grew worried. She had never seen Buckley react this way.

"Shit!" Joe screamed at the top of his lungs again. "Shit, shit, shit and more shit! That's what we have plenty of down here in the shit hole! Shit!" Buckley paused for just a second and smiled like a mad man on a mission and hell bent for something.

"Uh, HT? You OK?" Jimmy asked.

"Fireman's Apprentice, grab that BFW on the console over there and get over here! I want you to beat the flying fuck out of this empty flow pipe at this juncture." Joe pointed Jimmy to the big fucking wrench and a joint where the DEG liquid metal coolant could be routed to flow through.

Mija, lock off this part of the pipe and flush it, then turn off the SIF on this joint for a moment. He thought to his AIC.

Pipe is empty and SIF is off, HT3 Buckley, Mija responded. There was a faint swooshing sound through the pipe for a split second.

Great.

"Jimmy, start banging!" Joe pointed at the juncture on the pipe.

"If you say so, HT3." Jimmy grabbed the BFW and started pounding away at the flow conduit juncture. *Clang, clang, clang. Clang, clang, clang.*

"Mija, I'm going voice so Jimmy can hear this too. Turn the SIF back on in that pipe." Joe brought up the heat pipe flows in his virtual DTM and highlighted the flow loop on the two forward DEG batteries. "We've got two sewer plants and one water reservoir on this ship. Mija, how much of that would it take once flushed into the system to cool off and allow us to fire the forward DEGs for a few seconds?"

"Quick and dirty calculations show all of the water and one full sewer plant." Mija announced over the deck intercom speakers. "We would need the water in there to keep the sludge from solidifying."

"Ok. I figured we'd need the water. We have to purge the hot liquid metal out of the pipes now! There is no place to do that quickly but here," Joe said as he pointed to the pipe that Jimmy had been beating with the big fucking wrench.

"Joe, that will kill us," Fireman's Apprentice King said in a panic.

"Like we weren't dead already . . . but maybe not if I'm in the shit hole." Joe said. "Jimmy, get the hell out of here now, that is an order."

"Joe, we can't fit in there. The biggest openings are only thirty centimeter pipes into the topside of it. And the topside is four stories up," Mija corrected him.

"I know that, Mija Kitty. Once Jimmy is out you will close off this room including all electronic hatches and exhaust ports. This is gonna be some shit." Hull Technician Joe Buckley took the big fucking wrench from King and stood in front of the main pressure drain valve on the bottom of the sewage bladder and started banging the living shit out of it. "Jimmy, I thought I told you to get the fuck out of here."

"Sorry, HT. Guess I'm just hard headed." Jimmy picked up a second BFW. "You're gonna need some help to bust that one. It's too big."

"Suit yourself. But once it goes you get as high as you can on the aft wall. Mija, the instant this deck is filling with shit you purge the heat pipes for the forward DEGs into this room and then flow the water and the shit through the DEG coolant pipes. Got it?"

Joe raised the giant pipe wrench and brought it down against the valve stem at the boot of sewage tank. *Clang.* Then Jimmy hit it with his giant crescent wrench, *clang,* then Joe, *clang. Clang, clang, clang* went the BFWs against the shitter's release valve.

"Goddamnit, let go!" *Clang.* Buckley hit the valve stem one last time and then *ka-thunk* went the valve head as it was blown across the room into the far bulkhead from the pressurized sewer bladder. Joe and Jimmy dropped their makeshift hammers and looked for a spot with higher ground. Jimmy made it to the top of some tool shelving on the aft wall of the shit hole, but the high pressure flow coming out of the sewage release valve had him cut off from anything other than standing on the deck.

The SIF fields around the bladder squeezed it inward and forced it empty, throwing a fire hydrant force flow of human waste across the room. The pressure of the flow ricocheted across the room and quickly washed Buckley off his feet, covering him from head-to-toe with shit. The pressure burst the nasty brown liquid into his nostrils, ears, eyes, and mouth, choking him.

Joe Buckley swam through the lake of shit as it filled the room with the mixed methane smells of decomposing waste from thirty thousand human beings and he was beginning to lose the fight against the high pressure current and the horrendous stench.

Now, Mija! Joe thought as his head slipped under he took one last nauseating breathe of the methane filled air and fought harder to keep his head up.

The structural technician AIC triggered the software per Buckley's orders and a string of valves were released in order to allow the flow of the DEG liquid metal coolant to flow through the damaged heat pipe conduit. The extreme pressures in the flow loop didn't take long to overcome the weakened metal in the pipe. Mija released the structural integrity field around the pipe at that location and the eight hundred degree Celsius liquid sodium-potassium alloy flowed out of the pipe in a high velocity jet with nearly explosive force. A small rupture in the pipe vented the liquid metal like a rocket nozzle or a water jet cutter that passed through both of Buckley's legs, cutting them off instantly and cauterizing them almost as quickly.

The heat pipe forced more and more of the liquid metals into the raw sewage that at the same time was converted quickly to steam. The heavy liquid metals began to settle into the bottom of the pool of sewage and was forming dense methane gas clouds just above the surface of the brown sludge. Buckley had had a good idea from a mechanical and industrial flow point of view, but his lack of chemistry knowledge was going to be his undoing.

The chemical reaction of sodium and potassium metal and water created sodium hydroxide, potassium hydroxide, heat which was already in abundance, and hydrogen gas which was highly explosive and had a very low flashpoint to boot. Plus there was a cloud of methane vapor rapidly forming just below the cloud of hydrogen that was rapidly percolating to the top of the room. The natural buoyancy of the two gasses forced the heavy methane to pool on the surface of the sludge and the lighter hydrogen to pool at the top of the room. The sewage continued to drain into the compartment and was just as rapidly vaporized by the influx of molten liquid sodium-potassium allow that was now covering the deck of the engineering room and beginning to eat away at the deck coverings.

Fireman's Apprentice James King had held on firmly to the aft bulkhead as Hull Technician Joe Buckley had ordered him to do. The sight of the young sailor was one of the last things Joe would ever see as he struggled to keep his head above the surface. As if the searing pain from his amputated legs, the noxious gas fumes that were burning at his lungs, and the sodium and potassium hydroxide eating away at his skin weren't enough, finally the heat from the searing liquid metal exploded out of another failing part of the conduit spraying his face with a mist of the molten vapors melting his face and eyes to beyond flesh all the way to the bone.

Mija . . .

Rest, Joe. I'm here.

Did it work . . . ?

Rest Joe. I'm here. Mija uploaded the control code to Uncle Timmy with priority status since she knew that she would not last long enough to execute the final commands of the flow system that Buckley had engineered. The AIC had figured out the chemistry a little too late herself to warn her counterpart, but she had figured it out in time that they wouldn't die in vain.

Finally the hydrogen gas cloud reached critical density for the heat in the room, the heat from the liquid metal, and the exothermic reaction. The overpressured clouds of gasses in the room and lack of oxygen had kept the room from igniting initially, but the heat of reaction and molten metal had finally reached the flashpoint for the volatile mixture which then ignited with explosive force. In turn, the compressed hydrogen gas cloud explosion ignited the methane fog with the force of several tons of explosives that blew a hole forty meters in diameter and out the three decks below and out into space and upward six decks, killing hundreds of unsuspecting sailors. The explosion did blow out the fires created by the failing heat flow systems in the engineering decks but in the process it covered hundreds of sailors with septic human waste products on several decks. Several members of the crew were lost from explosive decompression and others just simply suffocated before they could make it to oxygen bottles. The remains of the sewage and the liquid metal quickly vented into the vacuum of space and the remains of Hull Technician Petty Officer Third Class Joe Buckley and Fireman's Apprentice James King would never be found.

Chapter 20

"Prepare to fire the gluonium tipped torpedoes, XO," Captain Jefferson ordered the suicide command. There was no way that the *Madira* could survive a close range terraton explosion. But the Separatist hauler was on a collision course for the Tharsis Mons region of the planet below and that would kill millions. Maybe as many as ten or twenty million. It had to be done.

"Aye sir!" the XO said begrudgingly then at almost the same instant the ship vibrated with a myriad of notes that sounded almost like a bosun's pipe combined with the jarring of the tracks on a garbage conveyor. The ship lurched forward and that was followed by a secondary explosion. Warning klaxons sounded throughout the ship for fire and damage control teams.

"Shit!" The helmsman was thrown face first into his control console, busting his forehead open. Bright red blood streamed down his face, getting into his eyes, and he frantically rubbed at it trying to regain his composure and right the attitude of the ship.

Uncle Timmy detected the explosion only milliseconds after the upload from Petty Officer Third Class Mike India Juliet Alpha Kilo One Tango Edgar and realized what was happening. Mija Kitty's last heroic effort was to upload the instructions to the flagship's AIC on how to bring the main guns online. Timmy quickly flushed the DEG flow systems with dry air and then ran the water reservoir and forward sewage into the pipes while shunting off the bleeding end of the flow loop on the aft and below decks of the ship where the explosion had just occurred. What was left of the molten liquid metal coolants flowed out into the vacuum of space where the below deck aft engineering room had been. Timmy also made record of the heroic activities of her counterpart's last moment of life that the AIC had uploaded. If they survived this situation Petty Officer Third Class Joe Buckley would posthumously be promoted to Petty Officer Second Class and Fireman's Apprentice James King would become a Fireman. Of course the *Madira* would have to survive first.

"What the hell just hit us?" the CO exclaimed.

"Goddamnit!" The COB's coffee cup was jarred loose from his hand and cracked on the deck. "That ain't a good sign."

"I don't know, CO, but the forward DEGs are coming online!" the XO replied with extreme enthusiasm. "I've got several targeting solutions on the kamikaze."

"Take out its propulsion and attitude control first. Then go for its structural integrity," Captain Jefferson ordered.

"Aye sir! We've got those solutions locked in and ready to fire, sir!" the XO replied.

"Fire!"

The main DEG batteries of the Sienna Madira opened full bore with blue-green bolts of directed energy that targeted exactly onto the propulsion power plant of the Seppy hauler. The DEGs burned through the hull plating into interior bulkheads, vaporizing the carbon-metal alloys into plasmas that jetted into space explosively.

"Fire all torpedo bays onto lead Seppy target!"

"Aye sir!"

"Keep pouring everything we have onto that enemy boat!" The CO watched the BDA numbers continuously changing in his virtual sphere and screens. But the simple fact was that the DEGs were not putting enough energy onto the large vehicle to make it structurally unstable. The energy weapons could take out parts of the hull and major components of the ship but it would take many direct hits to cause catastrophic structural integrity failure.

"CO! DEGs have about five, four, three, two . . . that's that! The main guns are gone sir!" the XO looked up from his console to the captain. "The DEGs took out the propulsion of that thing, sir. It bought us at least three minutes before it is too close to the planet to go full nuke on it. We could concentrate all of our fighters there, sir! Damage the forward hull plating enough so it will burn up on reentry!"

"Roger that, XO! Air Boss . . . "

"On it, CO! All fleet vehicles, all fleet vehicles, all fighters, all fighters, pull off present attacks and converge all weapons on kamikaze hauler on coordinates being trans-ferred to AICs! If they detonate their gluonium bomb on us, it's better they do it here than on the surface. But keep that damned ship from reaching the surface!" The Air Boss ordered and told his AIC to take care of the coordinate calculations for all the fleet vehicles and fighters.

The Seppy hauler had lost all of its propulsion drive system and was beginning to take on an uncontrolled roll, but it still fell on a collision trajectory for the large city below. The hauler was more than two kilometers long, a half kilometer wide, and more than a quarter kilometer thick. The ship was filled with power plants and ordinance, but worst of all there was the major likelihood it was carrying a subnuclear gluonium force fission fusion fission bomb. To trigger the device alone required a several hundred megaton hydrogen bomb. The trigger alone would wipe out the city. The added effect of the gluonium would take out the entire Tharsis region; only the cities at the very tops of the mountains and at the bottoms of the gorges might have some chance of survival. The body count would be . . . unacceptable.

Plasma and oxygen fires vented into space from the enemy hauler as the Martian gravity well pulled it closer and closer to the thin Martian atmosphere. If the fleet vehicles could just give it a yaw or a pitch and force it to tumble rather than just roll on its axis, the friction with the Martian atmosphere might break the vehicle up and protect the city. But the vehicle still maintained its attitude control. And the remaining Seppy fleet understood what the Americans were doing and bringing all their forces to protect the kamikaze behemoth.

"You heard the Boss, Saviors! Let's go take hell to that enemy hauler!" Marine Captain Janice "Bigguns"

Cameron ordered her Marine FM-12 Strike Mecha squadron.

"Oorah!" Offspring replied over the tac-net. "I'm breakin' off my present attack vectors now and hunting for the big fish!"

"Oorah! Bigguns, I'm on your three-nine line going maximum velocity with maximum ferocity!" Goat replied.

"Roger that! Watch your wingmen, Saviors, those Seppy Gomer bastards are pursuing hard on our six! Oorah!" Bigguns flipped the fighter mode toggle on the HOTAS and the bot mode mecha leaped upward from the deck of the *Madira* and rotated through the transfiguration into the fighter mode. The main DEG that had been in the bot's left hand was now under the nose of the sleek canard forward stealth winged dual tailed plane. The dual cannons were now separated by the fuselage aft of the cockpit and forward landing system one on top and the other on the bottom. Bigguns led the remains of the Marine mecha squadron—a mere fifteen planes—converting to fighter mode to burn at maximum velocity toward the falling Seppy hauler. In a few seconds they would revert back to bot and go to maximum ferocity!

As she pulled away from the deck of the *Sienna Madira* near the main DEG batteries she did so cautiously. The Seppy Stingers and Gnats didn't care that she was no longer after them and continued to press in on her. Bigguns pushed the HOTAS to full acceleration and put the upper and lower cannons on full automatic anti-aircraft fire. She and the remaining Utopian Saviors screamed at maximum velocity from the engagement on a death defying hurl towards the kamikaze hauler.

"Boss, these Gomer bastards are gonna follow us in!" Lieutenant Junior Grade Connie "Skinny" Munk exclaimed. She was one of the newer Saviors but was a good pilot and could take care of her own. She had gotten her callsign for being busted as a cadet for skinny dipping with some of the senior cadets. She had a permanent reprimand in her file for being "out of uniform on duty". But she had made such high grades as a cadet and her flight school proficiency was so near to perfect that a fighter squadron was the only place for her. Anything else would have been a waste and the Navy understood that.

"Well, Skinny, if they didn't come along we wouldn't have any Gomers to shoot back at!" Ensign David "Beanhead" Winchester—from Boston, hence the Beanhead—replied.

"Well, how about that big fuckin' ship looming toward us?" Goat asked.

"Damned right, Goat! Saviors, lets open up the DEGs full on the forward deck and see if we can't make us an entry hole! Oorah!" Bigguns replied to her squad.

"All right, Dawgs, we can't let them glory hogging gyrene leatherneck bastards get all the medals!" Lieutenant Armando "Rabies" Chavez announced over the tac-net to the Demon Dawgs. His Ares fighter squadron had originally been doing quite well until the ghost squadrons of the Seppies came out of nowhere and then chewed them up like meat in a fucking grinder. But the CO realized what was happening and pulled them out of the engagement zone, so they missed a lot of the action in the middle. Then sensors came back online. And the

Dawgs enthusiastically rocketed back into the grinder for some fucking payback that was due to those Seppy Gomer motherfuckers. The Dawgs had taken heavy casualties and were down to only a dozen good, or at least lucky, pilots.

"Maximum accel to the hauler and it's time to vomit!" Rabies ordered the Dawgs.

"Roger that, Rabies!" JavaBean rolled his Ares fighter over nose first toward the Seppy hauler and initiated a vector correction that would push him at max velocity and minimum transit time to the enemy hauler. At the same time his acceleration line pushed him toward the hauler he pivoted the little snub-nosed fighter about its center point, scanning and firing on targets, giving his wingmen cover. The maneuver was often referred to as a "pukin' deathblossom" because the wild spin put constantly changing g-loading on the pilot and his inner ear would pretty much go ape shit while at the same time the ship was a spinning menace spewing death from cannons and DEGs in all directions of the sphere around it. The spinning was usually more than the pilots could take and would force them to vomit retchingly from the inner ear confusion. But most good Ares pilots could take a little vomit in their e-suit helmet and the inner recycle layer of the suits usually absorbed the vomit in seconds. The suits had been designed for just such emergencies. It was the retching followed by the pressure suit squeezes and the high g-loading that took real presence of mind to overcome. It would take them a few seconds on the other side of the maneuver to be worth a damn. But there was usually very little in the way of targets left following the eighteen second maneuver.

"I'm with you, boss!" BreakNeck replied, following suit and throwing his Ares at max acceleration past the cover of JavaBean's pukin deathblossom and then initiated his own spherical cyclone of puking mad destruction.

"Roger that," came the reply from a dozen more fighters from the Demon Dawgs all rolling into the wild deadly spin maneuver.

"Huuuuhhhhhhh . . . uuuuuuunnnnhhhhh . . . .aaaar-rarggghhhh!" JavaBean screamed over the net as his ship lurched from the deathblossom into a normal flight approach toward the hauler.

"Wooooaaaaaaaa . . . hhhhhhhuuuuuuuuuuugggggghhh," Rabies vomited and wretched violently as his ship righted itself from the mad spin. The world around him went from a pounding rush of blood to his head and stars streaking madly around him—both real ones and ones that weren't there—to an abrupt jerk into normal flight mode.

"Uuuunnnnnnhhhh, goddamn I love flying these things!" he puked into his facemask again. Now that the sensors were working, the eyeball obfuscation—puke on his visor—was no problem as Rabies kept a full world view through his DTM virtual sphere display.

"Rabies, Rabies! This is Bigguns, copy?" Bigguns had led the remaining Marine FM-12s of the Saviors in a mad sprint, with DEGs blasting away the blue-green energy bolts at the forward hull of the kamikaze Seppy hauler with hopes of getting on deck and maybe inside the thing to do some real damage to it.

"Roger that, Bigguns! Go!"

"Rabies, you think your Dawgs could give us some fuckin' cover, while I'm takin' my Saviors for a stroll on the deck?" Bigguns asked. Rabies understood what she meant. Her intention was to take her mecha squadron down on the surface of the enemy vessel and maybe even inside it to create havoc and maybe destroy some important systems.

"You goddamned right we can, Saviors!" Rabies replied. "Dawgs, Dawgs, converge on me and spread cover fire for the gyrenes. Do whatever you can to keep those Seppy Stingers and Gnats off their backs!"

"Gracias, Rabies!" The Marine fighting mecha squadron had gone to bot mode and spread over the forward section of the ship like a small swarm of angry bees on an elephant looking for a soft place to bite. And bite is just what they planned to do.

"Denada, Bigguns! Good hunting. We'll keep these motherfuckers off your ass. You just stop that fucking thing!" Rabies replied.

"We will!"

"Goddamned Seppy Gomer bastard . . . uunnnnhhh!" Bigguns jumped upwards into a forward rolling flip and twisted in mid arch to go to guns to take out a Stinger in bot mode that had made it through the Demon Dawgs perimeter. "Guns, guns, guns!" she yelled.

The cannon fire from the Marine's bot mode mechastrafed across the deck of the enemy hauler, throwing plasma jets and sparks as it tracked the enemy mecha across its zigging and zagging path behind bulkhead extensions and exterior hull cannon turrets.

"On your six, Bigguns!" Goat warned her. "Fox three!"

The missile left Goat's mecha, leaving behind a smoky purple and blue ion trail as it twisted and turned across the deck of the ship. The enemy mecha ran with three giant steps and vaulted itself upward and rolled over into fighter mode while the whole time its upper cannon fired away at the missile. The little mecha-to-mecha missile zipped in and out of the cannon fire with precise sensor driven motion as the enemy mecha continued to fire on it. The enemy fighter mode plane accelerated upward and away from the deck and then turned into a steep dive at the hull at full velocity.

As the mecha rapidly approached the deck it rolled into eagle mode, bringing its DEG to bear on the missile. The DEG detonated the missile before it could hit the enemy fighter but the force from the explosion tossed the mecha over onto its back like a turtle. The right hand of the eagle mode mecha pounded to its side into the deck until it found enough of the loosened hull plating to grab and then it righted itself quick and went to missiles.

Two missiles streaked from under the wings of the vehicle into the cannon turret that Bigguns and Beanhead were taking cover behind. The two of them dove their bot mode mecha to the deck face down for cover. Then Goat, Skinny, and Deuce ran across the exterior catapult deck to a cover position behind a large spherical radome. The enemy mecha continued to spread cannon fire, DEG blasts, and missiles.

"Shit, Bigguns! This Gomer bastard is good!" Goat said. The enemy eagle mode mecha weaved in and out of the surface obstructions on the deck of the Seppy hauler faster than the bot mode FM-12s could.

"Goin' eagle mode!" Bigguns toggled the switch on the HOTAS transfiguring the standing mechanical robot beast into a bird of prey.

Charlie, where is he? she asked her AIC. *Come on Charlie, lock me on.*

Searching, Bigguns . . . searching, the AIC replied.

The view in the DTM virtual sphere of Bigguns' mind showed the dots of her squad and multiple red and blue dots overhead, but the Seppy mecha that was causing them problems on the deck of the ship was skittering in and out of detection. It was using the radar multi-path clutter to ghost itself from her sensors.

Trying multi-path algorithms, Bigguns. The brilliance of putting the AIC in with the pilots wasn't just their addition to the reaction and control times of the mecha but also their abilities to react on the fly to new problems and apply innovations to each new situation. The AIC took the analysis code from the low range multi-path radar and applied it across the board of all the wireless sensors. The algorithm cleaned away the ghosts and then the lock tone went off and a red dot appeared in Biggun's DTM view.

Got him now!

"Fox three!" Bigguns fired a missile and then went full throttle toward the red dot with the DEG a blazing. The enemy mecha was distracted by the impending missile long enough to give Bigguns an edge on it. The DEGs of the enemy mecha detonated the missile just as the blue-green energy blast from Bigguns' mecha tore through the cockpit of the enemy bird of prey. The enemy mecha exploded in a bright red and white-orange fireball almost at the same instant that her missile had detonated. The two near simultaneous explosions blew out a hole in the hull plating where a bulkhead exterior door had been.

"Great flying, boss!" Skinny said over the net. "Looks like we got ourselves a doorway to boot!"

"Roger that! Into the hole, Saviors!" Bigguns ordered.

Chapter 21

The Saviors ripped through bulkhead after bulkhead until they pushed into the side of a large engineering room. There had been almost zero resistance and only the occasional e-suited soldier firing HVAR rounds at them. The ship must have undoubtedly been flying on a skeleton crew with the kamikaze mission part of its original plan. There were no mecha left on the ship and there was little any poorly armored Seppy groundpounders or squids could do to hold up a bunch of Marines in FM-12s. The Marines had plowed through the ship pretty much unabated by anything other than their own size, being much larger than hallways and doorways of a spaceship. Several times they had to go to guns to blast a path for them to travel through, because the bulkheads and decks were too close together for the FM-12 mecha to fit through. But that was ok, as the FM-12s were loaded with ordinance and Marines loved to use it.

The Marines kept to hangar decks and below deck

engineering sections as best they could, because these
were bigger decks designed for moving cargo and mecha
around in. Several cargo rooms were large enough to
accommodate them, but they weren't there for comfort.
They had a bomb to find and/or a ship to stop before it
reached the planet below. They needed to hurry.

The engineering room they had just burst into was part
of the power generation plant that had been hammered by
the DEG of the *Madira*. The room had been blown inward
by the DEG bolts and then it looked as if it had blown
outward from secondary explosions. The structural integrity
fields were the only thing keeping the bulkheads from
collapsing under the weight of the ship's gravity field.

The large room was filled with spewing busted flow-
lines and sparking broken wiring harnesses. Liquid metal
coolant lines poured molten sodium alloys out into the
corner of the ship. There was a pocket of the coolant
building up that was trapped in a force field. The force
field was sapping power from somewhere and as soon as
that went the deck would be flooded with molten liquids.
Bigguns thought it would be best to get out of this room
quickly. It looked like the whole damned thing was gonna
cave in on them.

There were flames rolling in several corners of the
gymnasium sized compartment of the large ship. Smoke
filled the dimly lit section the Saviors had entered, but
that was of little hindrance to the Marines, who were
using QM, IR, visible, radar, and lidar sensors anyway.
Bigguns scanned the room, looking for the right path to
take.

Captain.

Yes, Charlie? Bigguns thought.

Here. A corner of the room opposite the side where the liquid metal coolants were pooling was highlighted in her virtual mind view. *That is the attitude control power plant and just aft of that is the torpedo room.*

Can we spoof the attitude control and just give this thing a yaw from here?

Probably not in the minute or two we have. I'd suggest mayhem at this point, ma'am. And then push through to the torpedo room.

Where is the gluonium bomb?

I'm still narrowing it down but it is in the torpedo room just aft of the far bulkhead of this room. It's a straight shot.

Roger that, Charlie. Transfer the coordinate system to the team.

Roger.

"Ok, Marines. Let's tear this fucking rust bucket apart starting with the far section of the room! The nuke is on the other side of that wall. Let's move fast!" Bigguns said. "Guns, guns, guns!" She set her DEG and cannons blasting at the highlighted target. The other FM-12s did the same.

Secondary explosions filled the compartment and a gaping hole into a larger room on the other side of the bulkhead was blown out. The Marines rushed inward, covering each other in case there was enemy fire, but there was none.

The torpedo room was about twice the size of the gymnasium sized engineering deck and was lined from wall-to-wall with empty tubes. The ceiling of the room

contained four different torpedo racks and each of them
was loaded with missiles.

It has to be one of those, Bigguns! The missile racks
thirty meters above her head were highlighted in her
mind view, and then a red x crossed over the nose of one
of the missiles. *There it is! There!*

"Skinny, cover me. The rest of you gold brickers
knock us a whole in one of those torpedo tubes so we
can get the fuck out of here!" Bigguns pointed with the
giant robot hand of her mecha toward the port torpedo
tube and then fired her jump boosters to the top of the
room. Skinny followed suit, scanning her DEG left and
right and up and down in case of any resistance from the
Seppies—there was none.

Bigguns quickly studied the missile rack and decided
on a plan. She grabbed the nose of the missile where the
warhead was and then looked down the missile tube for a
vulnerable point in the casing.

You sure this won't detonate this thing?

*Not unless it is boobytrapped. Besides, my sensors are
showing the computer is active and is set to detonate in
ninety-seven seconds! The dumb computer in the missile
doesn't realize that the ship's propulsion has been taken
out. It will detonate early,* Charlie warned her.

Well, that is great for Mars, shitty for us!

Yes, ma'am, her AIC agreed.

Bigguns karate chopped the shiny slender missile
casing with her left mecha hand, tearing the thin aluminum and composite materials clean with a shrieking
sound like fingernails on a chalkboard. She yanked the
nosecone of the missile several times until it broke free.

The force of the missile nosecone letting loose caused her to slip backwards almost into a tumble before she regained hover control of the bot mode mecha.

"Where's my fucking hole, Marines?!"

"Right fucking here, ma'am!" her squad replied as they burned the torpedo tube bulkhead away with DEGs and cannon fire. The torpedo tube splattered plasma and liquid metal sparks as it weakened until internal atmospheric pressure was more than the weakened torpedo tube cover could take and it blew outward.

"Fox!" she squawked to her Marines, letting them know that she had just released a live missile set to detonate on impact. The missile hit the failing torpedo tube and added to the decompression explosion. The hull bulged outward and blew bulkhead into space, leaving a hole larger than two FM-12s standing side by side.

"Oorah!" the Marines rallied.

"Skinny, on me! The rest of you Saviors get out there and make a nuisance of yourselves!" Bigguns dove head first through the hole in the Seppy hauler and rolled over into eagle mode, the Seppy subnuclear force warhead gripped in her right hand and her DEG in her left.

"Ahhhhhh . . . shiiit!" Bigguns cried as she burst through the hole in the enemy ship only to fly right through a hail of cannon fire from an Ares fighter that was on the tail of a Seppy Gnat. She yanked at the HOTAS to dodge the friendly fire and the Ares fighter.

"Holy shit! Watch out Marine!" one of the Dawgs called over the net.

"Fuck!" Bigguns was thrown into her seat as the automated evasive maneuvers increased the g-load on her to the point that she thought she felt something pop in her gut.

"Warning, airseal breeched. Warning, airseal breached." The mecha's "Bitching Betty" told her.

"Yeah," she grunted. "Well hopefully I won't be needing this bird much longer anyway."

She pushed the eagle mode mecha to maximum acceleration on a vector as far out to space as she could manage and away from the engagement zone. The g-load put more pressure on her than she had expected. It almost *hurt*. Skinny followed right behind her in fighter mode, firing her DEG and rear cannons as needed.

Captain, I'm reading a drop in your blood pressure.

I'm fine.

Also showing extreme heart rate and temperature drops. You're hit, Captain.

I said I'm fine, goddamnit!

"*Madira! Madira!* This is Bigguns, copy!" she grunted.

"Go, Bigguns!"

"*Madira*, I've got the big bomb in my lap and taking it out to space. The hauler is just falling garbage! The bomb is on a timer and is set to detonate in thirty-two seconds," Bigguns said as the maximum acceleration of the mecha pushed her back into her seat at over seven gravities.

"Roger, that, Bigguns! Great work!" the Air Boss replied over the net.

"Skinny, I'm punching out and you grab me! Got it!"

"Roger that!" Skinny toggled the mode control and her fighter mode mecha slammed over and then back up into eagle mode. "Unnnhhhh!" she grunted from the g-load.

Charlie, lock the controls of the fighter on this trajectory!
Done!

"Eject, eject, eject!" Bigguns pulled the ejection lever and the canopy slid away as the ejection field threw her clear of the fighter. The g-load on her felt like a ton of bricks hitting her in the gut and face all at once, and then the dampening field of the ejection seat took over, reducing the effect to more tolerable levels. Her fighter sped off in a straight trajectory into space.

Skinny tracked the ejection chair's trajectory and adjusted hers to catch it. Her eagle mode mecha easily overtook the now drifting ejection seat. She grabbed it and did an immediate rollover and thrust reversal. That bomb was going off any second and she wanted to get as much distance between it and them as she could. Had they been on a planet with atmosphere the shock wave would spread out for fifty kilometers or more and there would be no way to outrun it. But in space that wouldn't be as big of a problem. The big problem was going to be radiation dose.

"Detonation in five, four, three, two . . . " Bigguns's AIC announced over audio so Skinny could hear. Of course her AIC had the countdown timing as well.

The FM-12s could reach a top speed of about two thousand kilometers per hour in space. Once Skinny had picked up Bigguns and reversed direction, the relative velocity between the abandoned fighter stuck on full throttle with the bomb in it and Skinny's fighter was four thousand kilometers per hour. In the twenty some odd seconds before the bomb detonated they had managed to put nearly twenty-three kilometers between themselves and the bomb. The massive warhead exploded with the force of a thousand hydrogen bombs, filling the space above the battle with bright white light expanding in a perfect sphere outward from a singularity point. Imperfections in the tamper shielding of the bomb caused secondary jets of light to expand in different directions as expanding circles of plasma.

Just as a gluonium bomb detonated, more than ninety-nine percent of the energy of the explosion was released as high energy gamma rays. The gamma rays seared through Bigguns and Skinny, knocking free nucleons in their bodies, causing radiation products to form. The result would be extreme radiation exposure. They would need treatment in less than thirty minutes or they would have serious life threatening problems. Not that that was anything that the Marines didn't have on a day-to-day basis.

"Awesome, Captain!" Skinny shouted. "We better get to sick bay and take some rad meds pretty soon. My radiation meter is going off the fucking scale."

Bigguns didn't respond.

"Captain? Bigguns!" Skinny called out and looked at the pilot she was holding in her mecha's right hand. The pilot wasn't moving.

"Captain, do you copy?"

Zoom the blue force tracker, Alan. Skinny told her AIC to zoom the blue force tracker display so she could see any live soldiers in the range of her sensors in her DTM virtual mind view.

You got it, Skinny.

The blue dots filled the sky until Skinny zoomed in

tightly around the fighter. Bigguns' blue dot was there on Skinny's fighter with her; she could tell as the zoom came in. Then . . . the blue dot faded out.

"Fuck!" Skinny cried as her commander and friend died literally in her mecha's arms.

Chapter 22

"Look at that!" Joanie Hasad pointed up at the brilliant flash in the sky. Even in the afternoon sunlight the flash was more than brilliant. She hadn't seen that type of fireworks even during the Triton Raids and this one was the second such flash that had taken place in the past ten minutes or so. "There goes another one."

"Keep your head down, Joanie." Senator Moore leaned back against the foxhole wall and stared up at the sky. There was a serious battle taking place up there. He could discern flashes and glints here and there from the opposing fleets. And there had indeed been several large scale explosions that had been more than just fascinating in the late afternoon sky.

Moore had only noticed the last couple of minutes, though, as before that he had been fighting ferociously and fearlessly against the encroaching Separatists' forces. In a mad rush into the enemy troops he had fought until he was out of ammunition and could do nothing but cover and hide. He had made his way back to their original foxhole—the one they had dug after leaving the mechanical spider. The foxhole was the closest to the escarpment at the edge of the Olympus Mons volcano of all the cover locations he had managed to find. It was just behind a small outcropping of lava stones only thirty meters or so from the edge of the cliff.

They had ended up there after what any sane person would describe as his suicidal run. But Senator Moore would call it an effort to draw fire away from his beloved wife's and daughter's escape over the side of the drop off. At the time he was certain it would be the last thing he would ever do. But to Senator Moore, who absolutely adored his little girl and loved his wife with all his heart, giving his life to make sure his wife and daughter could live would have been an easy trade to make. On the up side and fortunately for him, the Cardiff's Killers, a Marine FM-12 Strike Mech squadron, crested the escarpment's edge and zoomed hell bent for destruction into the encroaching Seppy tank lines just as he and the AEMs with him were running out of ammo and just as the Army Tank Squadron Warboys' Warlords were being forced to retreat.

The Marine survivors of the crashed *U.S.S. Winston Churchill* had risen from the Martian gorge like harbingers of death. The two dozen survivors from the sabotaged supercarrier brought the full bore of their revenge on the Separatist Orcus drop tanks in pursuit of the Warlords M3A17 Transfigurable Tank Mecha Squad. The high tech Marine FM-12 Strike Mecha made light work of the over-whelming numbers of inferior enemy mecha, especially once the senator's AIC had told them how to fix their sensors to stop the enemy cloaking software.

Stingers and Gnats had buzzed into the mix as well but there were squads of Ares fighters there, and only moments before the big flash in the sky more M3A17 tanks and FM-12 mecha dropped in from orbit right into the mix. The Seppy line had been pushed way back up the mountainside toward the city. The battle still raged in the distance, but for now the senator from Mississippi and the refugee from Triton along with a reporter, a cameraman, and three armored e-suit Marines sat in the foxhole licking their wounds and relaxing for the moment. It had been a long morning.

"Senator Moore," Mars News Network correspondent Gail Fehrer turned to the senator. "Could you give us a statement at this point? What you did here today was more than heroic, and we have the footage to prove it."

Moore raised an eyebrow at the reporter. He had never liked the press all the way back to his Heisman Trophy days. His distaste for reporters was probably why he went into the Marines instead of the NFL. Several years in a POW torture camp in the Martian desert had cured him of his intolerance of most things. Moore gave his POW camp days credit for his patience as a parent with his overzealous six year old daughter. So Moore had to admit and allow for the damned reporters. And after all, for a politician they were a necessary evil. Sometimes he wished he'd just stayed a Marine. He could only bite his tongue for the moment and speak minimally as the cameraman thrust the videosensor in his face. He would think of better videobites later. Right now he was still worried about his daughter, and the anger and adrenaline of hard combat still coursed through him. He relaxed and let out a slow breath before he responded.

"I just did what any father and husband would do. I did everything within my power to make sure they were safe," he said and closed his eyes for a brief moment. He had seen Reyez, who was carrying his daughter Deanna, and his wife, Sehera, bounce over the edge just as the FM-12s attacked. But he had been so caught up with the fighting that he had lost contact with them. He had called to them a few times over the QM and optical comms but had gotten no answer. He hoped it was just a range and line of sight issue.

"Sehera? Are you there?" he said over the QM. But there was no response. "Sehera! Reyez? Dee?" Nothing. He checked the transceiver on his e-suit helmet and smacked the side of it with his hand. The visor display didn't even flicker. "Commercial piece of garbage."

"Allow me, sir," an odd male voice said over the QM net.

"BIL?"

"Yes, sir. Those cheap radios in your suits will not connect over the edge to the bottom, which is almost a kilometer away. They are very shortwave and don't bend over or around edges and out here there is very little multi-path bounce. Since there are no repeaters out here for your AIC to hop on you can't reach very far. But I can," the mechanical spider-like garbage hauler AI said. When Senator Moore had told it to find a hiding place it did, a very simple one.

"Well, where the hell are you?" Moore asked.

"I'm hanging on to the rocks just over the edge of the escarpment just about two hundred meters from you, sir. That is why I can still receive your transmissions. If you will wait I'll reroute your AIC through the infrastructure uplink through the big ship in orbit and back down to the appropriate ships. I certainly hope little Deanna is all right, although I do see two vehicles at the bottom of the ravine with my optical sensors. If you leaned over the edge you could probably contact them. But please be careful, sir."

"Thanks, BIL." Moore waited impatiently for what seemed like forever and wasn't sure he wanted to decide it was safe to get up yet, especially since they were out of ammo. All of them were out of ammo.

On the other hand, he *was* getting more and more worried about his daughter and his wife. *Had they made it to the bottom safely? Had they been evacuated out?*

I'm sure they made it, sir, Abigail said. *BIL is connecting me now. I'll let you know in a few seconds.*

"Sergeant Clay!"

"Yes sir, second lieutenant?"

"As we are completely out of ammo and for all intents and purposes out of this fight, why don't we see about finding those evac ships and see if we can find any surviving wounded out there," Second Lieutenant Thomas Washington said. Moore approved of the young lieutenant and thought to himself that he would watch him closely and maybe even see what he could do to help the young Marine's career.

The second lieutenant stood and ran a quick sensor

sweep over the battlefield and could see no immediate threats. Since they had reset their software Moore suspected that the Marine would trust his suit's sensors. Washington whistled in amazement and horror as he looked across the battle field at the dead mecha and soldiers and pockmarked and bloodstained Martian landscape. Moore decided to give it a few seconds to see if the Marine was shot down, and when he wasn't, joined him.

Moore rose to his feet cautiously beside the second lieutenant. The sun was beyond the overhead point and was beginning on its way into evening. The evening sun glinted off the hundreds of fragments and torn asunder mecha and armor suits. Moore whistled at the sight.

"Hell of a fight, hey, lieutenant?" Private First Class Vineat "Kootie" Kudaf said.

Abigail? the senator asked his AIC.

I'm communicating with them now, senator. The evac ships set down at the bottom of the escarpment. They have your wife and daughter and Reyez Jones safe and sound, sir. Apparently Deanna would like to jump off the cliff again as she thought it was a lot of fun.

That's my girl.

Yes, sir. Acorn didn't fall far, did it?

Humph.

But, the battle still rages in orbit and the pilots of the evac ships tell us that they have no place to return to, so they are staying put for the moment.

What about the Naval base to the south? Can't we go there?

For right now, sir, they say their instructions are to stay put out of harm's way.

Then tell them that we are clear up here and could use help with wounded.

Yes, senator.

Timmy! Captain Jefferson wanted to avoid a suicide run with the *Madira* if at all possible but things weren't looking good at the moment. The DEGs had bought them critical minutes that the fighter squadrons could put to good use and in a heroic last effort one of his Marines had ripped the weapon of mass destruction from the bowels of the Seppy hauler and rocketed it out into space to detonate harmlessly in space. But that goddamned hauler was still falling on a collision course toward Mons City and would hit in minutes if they couldn't break it up. Or at least push it out of the way.

Aye, sir?

Get the vulnerable attitude control point of that hauler transmitted to the squadron AICs! Get all the firepower available focused on that spot to push the hauler off course.

Aye, sir! Uncle Timmy had already analyzed the Seppy haulers and decided the best places to concentrate fire in order to make its attitude go unstable or at least push its trajectory an arcsecond to the West so it would miss Mons City—or at least the main dome. Since the Marine FM-12 pilots had gone onboard the enemy ship and taken out the guidance and control powerplant stabilizers it was now a matter of just pushing the ship hard enough to make it tumble. If they couldn't make it tumble and burn up on reentry then they'd push it over some. But it was a big ship with lots of forward momentum.Worse, just as the

Marines were entering the ship the Seppies had put a roll on it so that it was spinning about its axis of travel, giving it gyroscopic stability. Therefore the concentrated firepower at the nose of the ship was causing it to precess about its axis just like a tilted planet does about its poles or a top does before it falls to the ground. It would be hard to push it over. It would be hard to move. And if they didn't, millions in Mons City were about to have a very bad day. A. Very. Bad. Day.

"CO *Madira*! CO *Thatcher*!" squawked over the command net.

"Go, *Thatcher*."

"Wally, we've got propulsion and that's about it! Life support is failing rapidly and I'm ordering all hands to abandon ship. I don't think the *Thatcher* is salvageable after this. She's been a good boat," the CO of the *Margaret Thatcher* informed the fleet commander. "I've got an idea."

"What do you need, Sharon!" The CO was now down to three supercariers and most of them only had missiles and cannons and were limping along at half normal space propulsion. The DEGs had overheated and fused on all of them and they were all venting life support into space. The Separatists' attack on the fleet had been brilliantly orchestrated and had completely crippled the U.S. Navy fleet and whittled it away to only three out of eighteen supercariers remaining in any form of useful operation. The U.S. military had been taken totally unaware and beaten to a pulp, a bloody messy pulp. General Ahmi had executed the battle nearly flawlessly, much more flawlessly than a simple terrorist cell could. This had been a brilliantly developed and executed plan with multiple waves and levels of attack ranging from global ground force movement, to electronic and cyber warfare, to air and space combat. It had been a brilliant command of an army that nobody even suspected existed.

The plan was so well thought out that there were multiple failsafes. Even after the Marines had taken the WMD threat from the disabled falling ship, it was still a massive enough ship that it would cause tremendous damage to the city on the planet below if it crashed on a valid target. Its trajectory had been planned well. From the second that ship entered normal space from the hyperspace conduit, even while it was deploying its hundreds of fighters and mecha, even after its propulsion plant had been destroyed, and even after it had been defanged of its weapon of mass destruction it was still a serious threat that took all the attention of the surviving fleet, which was still having to fight for its life against the surviving Separatist fleet ships. The death toll would be considerably more than the tens of millions if the entire Tharsis region had gone up in a super nuclear fireball, but still with just the crashing ship it would be pushing the millions.

"Well, sir," squawked the net. "If you would kindly run blocker for us, I was thinking about running one right up the gut just like we did back in the Army-Navy game our senior year," Captain Sharon "Fullback" Walker a former aviator turned command crew said. Fullback had been her callsign because in her Navy Academy days she had played fullback for the Navy, which was not a position that many females played. It was especially not a position that many females played with the expertise and drive that Sharon had. Sharon was built more like a stack of bricks, a big stack of bricks, rather than a brick shithouse, and had a face that her mother might say was "handsome." On the other hand she could have been a champion body builder, but she was more ambitious and way smarter. And on top of that could run a four point one second forty yard dash and do it over and over for four quarters while being hit hard by mean Army linebackers. She was definitely Navy Fleet Officer material. Captain Wallace Jefferson had played lineman a couple of the years that Sharon played and they had been teammates for a very long time. He was used to making holes for her to run through!

"Roger that, Sharon! I-formation through the two-hole on the snap!" The CO of the *Sienna Madira* didn't have time to reflect on the fact that he had just authorized his friend and teammate and fellow officer to carry out a suicide mission. Perhaps she had an escape plan. After all, Sharon was smart. But it didn't matter, because Sharon was a soldier and she would do her job whatever it took. It was fourth and one and they by God needed a first down.

Timmy, spread the word to the fleet to block for the Thatcher!

Aye sir!

"All Fleet vessels, all fighters, all mecha, form blocking formation and protect the *Margaret Thatcher* and make sure that she makes it to the enemy kamikaze!"

"XO Burley," Fullback called to her second officer. The *Thatcher* had been a good tough ship and she had enjoyed her command onboard her for the last four years, *but all good things must come to end,* she thought. Her ship had taken a beating and she was going to give it a send off that was honorable!

"Aye, sir!"

"Are the troops away?" She scanned her crew manifest briefly in her mind but was more concerned with moving SIFs around to weak points in the hull and rerouting power as needed. Since the majority of the engineering crew had abandoned ship most of those functions were rerouted to the bridge. There were a few crewmen who couldn't see it in their hearts to leave the ship and those brave stupid souls had stayed behind to work diligently at their tasks to keep the ship functioning as it was being torn apart around them by enemy fire and soon by one mother of a collision.

"All escape pods are launched captain."

"Helmsman, you have con discretion to give us the shortest path for a collision with that damned hauler!" Fullback ordered her young helmsman.

"Aye, sir!"

"Burley, get me every ounce of structural integrity field you can put on my forward hull!"

"Aye sir!" the XO replied.

"Helmsman Lee, get us moving at full out balls-to-the-wall maximum acceleration!" the CO ordered.

"Aye, sir! Helm at max accel," the ship's pilot replied.

"Time and trajectory to impact, Navigator?" She turned her head and looked through her virtual sphere of the ship and the battle around it at the young lieutenant junior grade who had volunteered to stay at his post.

"Trajectory is plotted now, ma'am. Forty-two seconds to impact!" Lieutenant JG Joey Gugino replied.

"Understood." Fullback nodded.

The *Thatcher* rocked hard to starboard, vibrated and shuddered harshly and then damped out as the inertial dampening system compensated. At least it was still working, even though it did seem to be a bit sluggish and erratic. Warning klaxons would have blasted the bridge had the captain not had them turned off a long time prior. The helmsman managed to hold her balance but sprained her wrist doing so. The XO was flung forward into the front window and bumped his head against it so hard he was knocked unconscious or worse. From the looks of it the inertial dampening field wasn't working uniformly within the bridge and the health status monitors showed that that was the case throughout the ship.

Her AIC informed her that the XO's AIC had alerted it that Burley's neck was broken but he was still breathing. It didn't matter. They were all going to be dead in a few tens of seconds anyway, just as long as they took that damned Seppy hauler with them.

"Captain, we're taking heavy missile fire on aft sections," the Navigator said as he looked up from the CDC interface screens. The CDC had been evacuated and rerouted sensors to the bridge. The Navigator was the CDC now.

"We won't be needing those sections in a few more seconds anyway." Fullback replied. "Helmsman, stay on course! Full acceleration!" She continued juggling power around the ships SIFs, attitude control systems, and propulsion systems.

"She's driving like a goddamned beached whale, ma'am, but she's moving where I point her!" Helmsman Lee shouted over the ringing and pounding from the hull being blasted to hell.

Chapter 23

"Rabies, Rabies! Got a Seppy bot motherfucker sneakin' across the bridge hull, Got it?" BreakNeck alerted his boss. Rabies was closest to that part of the *Thatcher* and he could get there quickest. "Guns, guns, guns." BreakNeck trailed off after a Seppy Gnat that just passed him head-to-head at several hundred kilometers per hour relative.

"Roger that, BreakNeck! Uuuuuuuuggggggggg . . . ummmmmmffffff!" Rabies pulled back on the HOTAS into a full reversal of his acceleration path and rolled over going full throttle into a dive at the bridge of the supercarrier.

"Warning, maximum g-loading. Warning, pilot blackout probable," the "Bitching Betty" sounded in Rabies' cockpit.

"Uhhnnnnn . . . no . . . . .fuuuuckkiinnn . . . .uuuuuhhhhh . . . kidding!" he screamed and squeezed his abs and bit the hell out of his TMJ mouthpiece. Pure oxygen flushed his face, helping keep him alert. Rabies shook his head and normalized his flight path to something more humanly tolerable.

It would have been a damned sight more tolerable of a flight path if it weren't for all the enemy fire and debris and shit in his way. Debris was venting upward explosively from every bulkhead and deck vent of the once pristine supercarrier, but it looked like hell hung over, nicotine deprived, and on a bad hair day to boot at the moment.

"Shit, Rabies, on your six, too! Moooove, Rabies! Move!" BreakNeck shouted as he took on fire himself. "Goddamnit, Fox three!"

"Got it! Guns, guns, guns!" Rabies went to guns to track in on the Stinger pounding across the bridge of the ship and yawed hard left one hundred and eighty degrees to get a firing solution on the Gnat that was taking station on his six. "Uuuuuhhhggg. Fox three!" he yelled and probably would have vomited if he hadn't already puked up everything in his stomach during the deathblossom moments before. The mecha-to-mecha missile burned from beneath the wing of the snub-nosed fighter on a short and abrupt path through the tail of the Seppy fighter plane. The purple ion trail the missile left behind tracked right up to the orange-white exploding fireball that was once an enemy fighter plane.

Pull out, Rabies! his AIC warned him as the deck of the supercarrier rushed up at him.

"Aaaaaaarrrrrrrrgggggggg . . . ooooooooommmmmmmffff- fuuuuuucccckkkkinnn cocccckkkkksssucccccckkkkeerrrrrrr!" he yawed and rolled the fighter back to normal nose forward into the dive and then yanked back on the HOTAS with his left hand and pushed left and forward with his right hand just as he passed through the expanding fireball of the exploding Stinger mecha. Debris and plasma whirled and clanged against the fighter and a large chunk of the exploding mecha's empennage slammed into the nose of the fighter, pounding the armor plating loose at the laserweld joints. He passed by the bridge windows so closely that he could see the faces of the crew inside and could have sworn he saw one of them hit the deck. As the deck of the supercarrier rushed by underneath his cockpit he pulled the ship up and away from it.

"Warning, enemy radar lock on! Warning, structural integrity at minimum safe levels! Warning, enemy missile launched."

"Goddamnnniiiiittt! Guns, guns, guns!" Rabies went to guns to track the incoming missile but there was no time and flying though that fireball did major damage to his plane. It was reacting sluggishly to his control commands and the HOTAS was erratic.

"Warning, impact imminent!"

Eject Rabies! Eject!

"Eject, eject, eject!" he screamed and pulled the red lever and was flung hard away from the ship almost immediately. The Seppy missile impacted the fighter less than a second later. The debris from the explosion slammed hard against his ejection seat, sending him spinning and careening uncontrollably through space into a hornet's nest of friendly and enemy mecha, cannon fire, DEG bolts, and exploding debris fields all around him. A shit storm of bad news zinged past him in every direction at hundreds of kilometers per hour or more.

"Oh, fuck!" Rabies yelled at the top of his lungs as a hot

slag of debris whipped through his right arm, taking it off just below the elbow. A tiny spurt of red blood had time to escape before his e-suit resealed itself. But Rabies never saw it because he was spinning wildly out of control. The ejection seat dampening thrusters tried to compensate, but the spin was too much angular momentum for the thrusters to overcome. The impact of the debris made the wild random spin of his ejection seat even worse than it had been before and Rabies' day just kept getting worse.

A problem with debris fields in space is that if there is one piece of debris there are probably more—lots more. Almost as soon as the searing pain from his severed arm registered in his mind more debris cut through his body, ripping gashes in his abdomen and back and severing his left leg almost at the hip, and several smaller millimeter diameter pieces passed through him like HVAR rounds. The last thing Lieutenant Armando "Rabies" Chavez heard was his own terrified blood curdling screams as one of the pieces of the exploded debris slammed through his helmet faceplate, killing him instantly as it passed out the back side of his head.

"All hands, this is the captain. If you are still with us, you have fought well and it has been my honor. Brace for impact! Shit . . . " the CO of the *Margaret Thatcher* hit the deck reflexively as a Seppy Stinger exploded just outside the bridge window, splattering the armored transparent material with debris from the fireball. Just as the fireball began to dissipate milliseconds later a Navy Ares fighter punched through it with its cannons firing full auto. The fireball formed a collapsing plasma ring from the effects of the fighter passing through it at high speeds. Almost as soon as the fighter pulled away from the ship it was hit by a Seppy missile and blown asunder into a streaming red plasma debris field. The pilot had been able to eject but was consumed by the fireball debris of his exploding ship almost immediately.

"Thanks and Godspeed, pilot." Fullback whispered under her breath.

The ship began to list hard to starboard again, but this time not as violently. The captain watched the health monitors in her head. Entire rear port sections had been blown out. Atmosphere, fluids, and debris jetted from the destroyed section, pushing the supercarrier slightly off course and giving it a yaw.

"Helmsman can you compensate the yaw?"

"Ma'am! We're crabbin' it in, but they can't hit us hard enough to stop us now!"

"Good! Stay on it Lee!" Fullback looked at the incoming missile tracks in her DTM virtual view and did some numbers in her head. The CO keyed the 1MC. "This is gonna be a rough ride! Everybody strap in for impact now!"

"Ma'am, we just lost propulsion!" the young ensign at the helm shouted.

"Just hang on, Ensign Lee!"

The Seppy hauler could no longer be seen from end to end as it rushed upward toward the listing supercarrier at several hundred kilometers per hour. The window and the viewscreens were filled with the collision view as the nose of the supercarrier dug into the hull plating of the enemy hauler. The nose of the hauler gave way to the momentum of the supercarrier's forward decks, and the impact flung the entire crew of the ship against their restraints so hard that the Navigator was killed instantly from the impact of his brain slamming against the inside of his own skull. The inertial dampening field caught up a microsecond too late for him.

But for the captain and Helmsman Lee it might have saved their lives. The force of the impact was muted by the dampening field just quick enough that Helmsman Lee's left arm was crushed against her console and both clavicles were snapped through and through. Splinters of her right clavicle pierced the top of her lungs. The swishing of her internal organs against her restraints ruptured her spleen and bruised her kidneys and bladder.

"Oh, God!" Helmsman Lee screamed in agony and fear, until the Navigator's console tore loose and slammed into the side of her head, knocking her unconscious.

"Get some!" Fullback held on, screaming a guttural battlecry at the top of her lungs as several of her bulging muscles ruptured from the strain. Her left leg was broken from behind as a chair mooring tore from the deck and cut into her calf muscle, bruising it and snapping the bone. The bone forced through the front of her shin squirting bright red blood with each heartbeat. Fullback screamed in pain only briefly and pounded her right fist into the captain's chair madly to distract her from the pain and sheer terror.

Metal on metal screeching and breaking and clanging sounds vibrated and rang out through the ship at deafening levels. The inertial dampening field was keeping up but it was still a very rough ride as the supercarrier continued to tear forward into the giant Seppy hauler. It tore and ground and screeched its way until the forward decks actually poked through to the other side, and then it stopped any forward motion and continued on the fall with the hauler. The angular precession of the hauler was brought almost to a stop by the added unbalanced mass but the collision was not enough momentum exchange to cause the now combined mass of the two ships to tumble.

Secondary explosions erupted in a rainbow of plasma colors and sparks across the decks and throughout both of the decimated behemoth ships as they approached the Martian atmosphere. Captain Walker looked out the window and could see hull debris and torn metal bunched up against and around the deck of the supercarrier where it impaled the Seppy hauler a few hundred meters in front of the bridge tower. There was also blood on the window in places from the where the XO's body slammed into it on impact. Debris that had been thrown free of the ships was already glowing red and ablating due to reentry heat. And large shards of metal hull plating that hung loosely from the wreckage flailed and flopped wildly from the heating and aerodynamics of reentry. Fullback could see several very large chunks of hull from each ship peel away and fly off behind them.

The friction from reentry heated the armored windowscreens, but the structural integrity fields of the strong ship held. The bridge environment systems flushed the room with cold air to adjust for the rapid heating. Fullback gritted her teeth from the pain and tried to put it out of her mind. She had to make certain her mission had been accomplished and then see if there was a way to survive this mess.

Marley! Give me all the SIF power on the bridge that you can! If there are other rooms that have been plussed up don't rob them. There might be survivors in there. Can you check? the CO called the ship's head AIC and her friend.

I'm checking it, Captain. Sensors are failing every-where but I show forty-seven crewmen still on board in various locations.

What about our trajectory? Did we push the hauler out from over the city? Obviously, the goddamned thing didn't blow up.

Sorry, captain, all external sensors are down. We do have QM comms.

You're our only hope now, Marley. Keep us alive if you can. We'll need extreme inertial dampening when we hit the ground!

I understand, ma'am.

Open a channel to the Madira.

Aye sir.

"CO *Madira*! CO *Thatcher*!"

"Holy shit, Fullback! You're still alive!" Captain Jefferson squawked back.

"Probably not for much longer, captain. Propulsion is down and we're stuck to the Seppy rust bucket." Fullback grimaced at the pain in her leg. "Did it work? External sensors are down over here, Wally. Did we push the hauler out of the way?"

"Is there any way you can get out of there, Sharon!"

"Negative, Wally. All the escape pods are down and I

probably couldn't make it to one anyway. Besides, I couldn't leave Helmsman Lee behind. Did we save the city, Wally?"

Chapter 24

"What was that?" Rod heard a sound almost like an insect buzz overhead. *Spitap, spitap*, went the sound again. "Did you hear that?" He turned to the pregnant lady, Carla, on the park bench beside him and then shrugged at Vincent.

"I heard something. I thought it was just my damn ears ringing from my nicotine withdrawals." Vincent replied. Then a wave of people rushed toward them, forcing them to push the people around them off the young lady. "Get the fuck off me!" he yelled and turned to the man pushing at his back and punched him square in the face.

"What the fuck is wrong with you?" Carla screamed as Rod and Vincent did their level best to protect her.

"Let's stay ahead of this rushing crowd instead of fighting it." Vincent grabbed Carla by the hand and pulled her with him. "Rod. Get behind her, bud!" Vincent had been in enough adrenaline-hyped gliderchute afterparties when people started moshing in the pit to know that you can't fight a crowd.

The three of them pushed their way along with the wave of the crowd as they passed through the park, being pushed toward the central elevator of the Open Court near the giant JumboHoloTron. Mons City Central Park had been designed to hold eighty thousand but there were more than a hundred thousand or maybe twice that being held in it with Seppy force fields. There was little more than standing room only, and with the wave of the crowd moving there had to be hundreds or maybe thousands of people being trampled to death.

Vincent jumped up as high as he could in an attempt to see over the crowd. It didn't help much. All he could see was wave after wave of people behind him and the force field closing in on them from the far side of the park.

"The motherfucking Seppy motherfuckers are squeezing the forcefield on us. They're gonna squish us all!" Vincent said in a panic. He really wished he and Rod had gone with that senator fellow earlier when they had had the chance.

"Why are they doing that?" Carla screamed.

"I don't know!" Vincent continued along with the wave of the crowd jumping up as often as space would allow between him and the next guy. He was very careful not to lose his footing, though. Falling down could be the end of them.

"We gotta think of something fast, Vince!" Rod jumped and looked over the crowd ahead of them and could see a wave in the sea of people headed back towards them. The forcefields were closing in from all around. "Vince, we can't keep going with the crowd. We have to get to the center of the park and stay there as long as we can hold out."

Zip, zip, zip.

Separatist railgun rifle rounds tore through the crowds of people, splattering the corralled citizens like the old expression "shooting fish in a barrel". The automatic railgun fire was coming from above the crowd on the third floor near the elevator and from other upper floor locations around the periphery of the park.

"Goddamned cowards!" A man behind them held his fist in the air and shook it defiantly at the Seppy snipers. "Come down here and fight like men!"

Rod, Vincent, and Carla struggled to push toward the center of the crowd and prayed that the luck of large numbers would fall their way. There were thousands more people in the park than there were snipers and it would take them a while to kill them all considering the ranges they were shooting from and size of the park itself. The force fields continued pressing inward, occasionally knocking over trees and park benches and play sets and monkey bars and other park constructions.

Several people realized what Vince, Rod, and Carla's strategy was and they also noticed Carla's condition and began forming a pocket around her. They kept a hand on each other's shoulders to hold the pocket together. A zipping sound passed by Vince's left ear and he felt something wet splatter his face. He turned to see the man beside him and saw clean through a dark gray and red outlined hole in the man's head and through the chest of the woman behind him. The two victims were pressed together by the crowd and couldn't fall over at first, and then were eventually trampled under thousands of stampeding human feet.

Vincent and crew continued to protect Carla as best they could. There were pockets forming in the crowd where the Seppy HVAR rounds had cleared them out.

"This way!" Vincent pushed back toward one of the growing pockets of dead.

"Are you fuckin' nuts," Carla screamed. "That is toward the gunfire!"

"Watch those little vapor trails streaking across the park. They fire for a few seconds and then they stop. And then they do it again." Vincent pushed them toward the nearest wave of people rushing away from the gunfire.

"They're reloading?" Rod asked. "Yeah so! Then we'll be standing in the open and easier to shoot."

"Not if we play dead." Vincent said. "When I say drop. Drop. Rod, we'll cover Carla as best we can." Vincent hated running into gunfire and laying around playing dead. But it was the only plan he had and at least it was a plan. Before they had just been running scared and aimlessly.

"Now!" Vincent screamed once he could see only about ten rows of people between him and the oncoming hail of railgun vapor trails. The trails tracked through the rows of people and then stopped for a second. Vince, Rod, Carla, several others fell to the ground and tried to cover each other from being trampled. Several wounded and scared people tripped and kicked at them. One of them landed a knee right into Vincent's back so hard that Vince was afraid he'd be pissing blood, but then the wave of people pushed away from the blood soaked pile of bodies as the railgun fire started back up.

A few rounds hit just a few centimeters to Vincent's left

but they missed them and they were safe for now. Several of the wounded were screaming in pain around them and some of them even rose and tried to get back to their feet, but the Separatist snipers seemed to care little about them.

"Oh my God, oh my God!" Carla almost screamed, but managed to keep her voice subdued by biting her hand.

"Hold it together, honey," a woman lying still next to them said calmly. "They can't hear you that far away and over all these poor wounded bastards a-screaming. You need to calm yourself or you could force yourself into premature labor." Rod put his arm over her and hugged her, not sure if that would help or not.

"Are you a doctor?" Carla asked the woman.

"Naw, honey, I've just had a few kids in my day."

"Ok, Vince. They're not shooting at us right now. But what do we do when the force fields start to close in on us?" Rod asked. His hands were trembling wildly. He was scared to death.

"I'm working on it, bud." Vincent said. "Holy shit, will you look at that!"

"What now?!" Rod asked, the panic in his voice never so obvious.

"Look up through the dome. Now there is something you don't see everyday," Vince said. "What the hell is that?"

Above them fell a bright glowing red fireball that showered and glittered with thousands of smaller fireballs spraying off it and around it falling along behind in its path. Initially, Vincent thought it was a meteorite but it was moving too slowly and way too big for that. A meteor that size and that shape would break up or destroy the planet. Something was holding it together. From the looks of it the giant fireball was the shape of a cross and had to be at least a kilometer or two wide and maybe twice as long. It was glowing brighter and brighter and looming closer and closer.

The goddamned Seppy bastards never even let up to look at the falling fireball. The HVAR rounds just kept zipping through the crowds of people as fast as they could fire and reload the things.. Fortunately, for the people trapped in the force fields the Seppy rifles didn't hold the large magazines that American HVARs did and they were forced to reload more often.

"Maybe that thing'll fall on us and kill those sorry motherfuckers," Vince said. "Goddamn, I wish I had a cigarette."

Chapter 25

"Look at that, Daddy!" Deanna pointed up at the sky at the falling fireball while she sat comfortably in her father's lap. She was so tired of her e-suit and wanted out of it horribly bad, but at least she was with her daddy. Alexander was tired, too, and had to rest for a few moments. The work of finding wounded was slow and tedious. Moore decided to take a few minutes for himself and his family and then he would rejoin the AEMs and Joanie Hasad in their relief efforts. But to this point, they had only found two survivors and those two were so severely wounded they might not live if they didn't get real medical attention soon.

"What the hell?" Flight Gunner Third Class Sammy Jo Tapscott was startled by the scene when she looked up from inflating the environment dome. "Vulcan, you want me to check squawk?"

"My AIC is on it, gunner. You and Yo-yo and Pac just keep working on that shelter," Lieutenant Junior Grade

373

Seri "Vulcan" Cobbs, Angel One, of the Search and Rescue squad replied. They couldn't evac to anywhere right now so she decided to assemble a staging area with two inflatable environment chambers. "Sounds like it's a Seppy rust bucket and the *U.S.S. Margaret Thatcher*," she said.

I'm getting the same information, senator. The link through BIL is working fine still.

Thanks Abigail. Senator Moore looked over at the big metal beast that was sitting beside the two boxy shaped SH-102 Starhawks near the edge of the Olympus Mons base escarpment.

Any idea when long range comms will be back up? Even though they had managed to override the Seppy software spoof on sensors and local comms, the long range jam had not been stopped yet. Long range communications still depended on line of sight, internet, or QM router-to-router connections.

I think the battle is still taking precedence right now, senator.

Just keep us posted.

Of course, sir.

"Well, it looks like it is going to come down right on top of the Main Dome. My God, all those people," Reyez Jones said. He had put up tents before on overnight safaris across the inhospitable planet and was pretty useful in that regard. He was helping the SARs team with the staging area shelter. One dome was already inflated and the airseam in place. They needed to move the wounded into it soon.

"Tell me you're getting this, Calvin," the MNN reporter Gail Fehrer asked her cameraman. For her and her cameraman this day had just been getting better and better. She had to get this footage on air as soon as she could. She could just smell Pulitzer.

"You're getting this, Calvin." Calvin replied.

"Nobody likes a smartass, Calvin." Gail punched his arm. "Can you zoom in and get a better look at it? And let us see it."

"Hold on." Calvin had his AIC negotiate with the e-suit visors displays and then had the data QM wirelessed to them. "Look on channel three."

"All hands, this is the captain. If you are still with us, you have fought well and it has been my honor. Brace for impact! Shit . . . " Squawked over the Engine Room 1MC intercom of the *U.S.S. Margaret Thatcher* where Engine Technician Command Master Chief Petty Officer William H. Edwards was feverishly rerouting coolant flow loops from all over the ship to keep the engines. Bill had actually been the Chief of the Boat for more than a year now and was the senior CMC on board the *Thatcher*. But when the CO gave the abandon ship order he knew that someone had to stay in the Engine Room and keep the ship flying to the last second. He wasn't about to let any of his junior enlisted men and women do that. After all, CMC Edwards had started the Navy in the Engine Room. Learning the ins and outs of the propulsion system of the supercarrier had been the only thing that kept him from committing suicide when his wife of twenty-one years had died of rejuvenation cancer, and it was fitting that since he started his career in an engine room that that is where he would end it, instead of up on the bridge with the officers. He had always been uneasy up there anyway, not because of the officers. The CO and the XO and the other command crew were the best, absolute best, but it was too damned clean up there. Bill liked the dirty hard work of keeping the boat running and the orange heavy coveralls with grip pads in the knees and elbows and grimy smudges across his face fit him much more than the clean and pressed uniforms of the bridge crew. Down below is where he belonged.

CMC Edwards really did know the supercarrier engine room like the backs of his hands. He had spent his first tour as a Fireman's Apprentice on the *Mandela*, a deployment as an HT2 on the *Washington*, and then there was that horrible time on land while he was in school, but at least he had been studying about the propellant drive system for the Navy supercarriers. He left the tech school as Engine Tech First Class, ET1, and then went back to the supercarriers, where he stayed. He had done a stint on the *Washington* and for two weeks he had been a visitor on the *Churchill*, learning about some engine upgrades the newest boat in the fleet had implemented.

His last boat assignment change had been more than seven years ago and it stuck. Bill was transferred to the *Thatcher*, where he had continued to stay on, learning every thing he could about the Engine Room and what made the giant spaceship function and, more specifically, what was unique about this spaceship. All the spaceships, supercarriers, had little nuances about them that were different and Bill knew all of the *Thatcher's*. Even after he had been sent up above to the command crews, he kept up with his teams down below.

Then his wife got sick and he took all the leave he could until she died. He considered the Reserve so he could stay with his wife longer, but she was strong willed and wouldn't allow him to do that. They had had twenty-two wonderful years together and they were both happy for that time. Then she lost the fight against the one cancer that resists the rejuvenation treatments that could defeat every other terminal or chronic illness known to man. Bill had thought several times of ending things then but never could take the final step, because there was always the nagging thought in the back of his mind that there was something on the *Thatcher* that wasn't battened down just right or that some punk Fireman's Apprentice was about to royally fuck up his beloved boat. So he stuck with the Engine Room, his only other true love. It had taken the CO and the previous COB months to convince him to take the CMC Program, but finally, reluctantly, he did, and then his Engine Room was down below and out of reach. Oh, he could wander through it and inspect it and visit it anytime he wanted, but he couldn't get down there and get "intimate" with it.

Well, now he could. He was there with his true love and was absolutely going to keep her running until his last breath. The flow loops for the coolant were leaking like a sieve since major chunks of the ship had been completely destroyed by the enemy missiles. Liquid metal and other fluids on the port and aft sides of the ship were spewing vital coolant out into space. CMC Edwards had a DTM virtual sphere around him that displayed the entire boat coolants and electronics that were connected in any form or fashion to the propulsion plant. He had locked down leak after leak and rerouted the flow loops through systems that were still intact or at least partially intact to the point that the flow could be routed around the leaks or missing sections of conduit.

Bill ran from panel to panel throwing breakers that the software couldn't trip because of a malfunction or a missing circuit. A couple of times he even had to use a crow bar or a BFW to close a gap across high voltage power couplings.

Mimi, how long to impact? he asked his AIC

Twenty seconds, Bill! You need to strap in, she replied.

I've got to keep the propulsion systems on line!

Bill, strap in, please!

Remind me at five!

A missile impact or secondary explosion or whatever the fuck it was caused a short within one of the power generators. That in turn caused a voltage source to have a path of zero impedance for current to flow through. Since Ohm's law means that the current through a wire is equal to the voltage of the source across that wire divided by the resistive impedance of that wire and the voltage source was a large finite value and the impedance of the short circuit within the power generator was approaching zero there was a *problem*. A finite voltage divided by zero resistance is equal to infinite current. So all the sudden the power coupling conduit through that part of the Engine Room from that power generator had a spike of infinite current through it for a millisecond. A millisecond is how long it had taken for the power cables to melt, explosively. It also threw the oversized breaker and blew it into a million pieces. He would have to close that open switch somehow, probably with a crowbar or BFW, once he got the cables replaced.

"This is gonna be a rough ride! Everybody strap in for impact now!" squawked over the 1MC. The CO sounded nervous. But she could see what was about to happen and Bill couldn't. It was about that time that the propulsion system went offline, lost power, and was overheated to boot. Then shit got really bad.

Five seconds, Bill! his AIC screamed in his mind.

"Shit!" Bill made a mad dash for the nearest station and pulled the chair restraints over his shoulders. Just as the safety belt harness went click he was slammed forward hard into the restraints. He kept his arms crossed and held the restraint straps with both hands and cursed with every breath. Even though Bill was being shaken like a rag doll in his chair he managed to pay at least some attention to the DTM virtual sphere ship health monitor. Red highlights started appearing all over the virtual image of the ship in his mind, most of them on the forward decks of the ship. Sounds rang out with horrendous screeches of metal against metal and odd natural frequencies vibrated throughout the Engineering Room. The safety chair Bill was strapped into had reached a natural vibration and was singing like a crystal wine glass. For what seemed like an eternity, the Engine Technician Command Master Chief was shaken and rattled and vibrated until his teeth hummed, but otherwise the Engine Room inertial dampening fields had done their jobs and protected him. Finally, the ship came to a stop and normal gravity returned to the room. The jolts and the jarring were gone. So were the main propulsion units.

Bill quickly unstrapped himself and checked back on the power generator that he was about to fix. There was a blown superconducting inductance coil bank that was used to store the power from the vacuum fluctuation energy collectors. Without the storage coils there wouldn't be enough power storage to bring up the main propulsion plant. Bill raced potential solutions in his mind. He needed to replace that coil, but the goddamned thing weighed more than four hundred kilograms.

I can't replace the goddamned coil, Mimi. It's too fucking heavy. Any suggestions?

Yes. Don't move it if it is too heavy.

That might work but I'd need a shit load of high power rated conduit. Where is there enough for that? Bill flipped through manifests of materials and parts in the stores but didn't see what he needed.

You're right. The only cable rated for that type of transfer is in the DEGs and it would take too long to get to them and scrounge it.

That's it! Fucking Christ! That's it. The DEGs. We'll use them.

I just said that we don't have the cable to get from there to here. The nearest junction to the DEG power cables are two bulkheads port and one deck up.

Then we won't use the damned cables. Get the DEG with the closest junction up and running and storing power and map for me the best way to get to it given the present damage to the ship.

Roger that, COB.

Bill grabbed the nearest adjustable powered BFW and went to work pulling the bolts out on the panel to the power unit for the propulsion plant. He took the bottom four holts out first and then the top two. The metal cover for the power generation unit was more than two centimeters thick and it didn't fall off on its on. The metal was so thick that it stood in place and was too heavy for Bill to push loose with his hands. Bill looked around for that crowbar that he had been considering to use on the blown power coupling switch across the room and found where it had ended up after the collision with the Seppy rust bucket.

"Come on, you son-of-mother!" CMC Edwards pried the bar in a good leverage spot and pulled at it with all his might. The plate finally broke free from the box where some dumbass had applied the wrong lubricating sealant around the edges where the cover was attached. The lubricant had reacted with the metal, rusting it together. If he survived the crash he'd have to tear some Fireman's Apprentice a new asshole for letting that thing rust together like that. The plate made a sucking sound from the rest of the box and then fell heavy to the deck with a loud metal to metal *clang*. Bill jumped out of the way to keep from getting his toes cut off.

DEG unit is stored full and functioning normal, CMC! Right.

Bill looked were the power conduit entered into the back outside of the power unit and then followed that to find where the coupler lock nuts of the two five centimeter diameter cables were on the inside side of the box. He grabbed a spanner and spun the lock ring nuts off. The giant nuts fell to the deck of the box with a heavy *kathunk*.

Bill made his way over the cables and grid work to the other side of the box and pulled the two cables loose. One of them was red and one was black. He tugged and threaded them through nooks and crannies, underneath equipment racks, through knock out holes in some of the Power Room metal Faraday Cage grid work, and finally over the main tool box where the two wires went into the wall leading into the propellantless propulsion system.

He dragged the cables just a few meters more to two flow conduits. Bill double checked the drawings in his mind to be sure that they were the right two conduits. One was marked as an outflow coolant pipe and the one beside it was a return coolant pipe, both of which went off behind him to the liquid metal reservoir cooling system in the aft end of the Engine Room. The pipes went the other direction to the port side DEG cooling loop. Bill suspected that the captain had no desire to fire the dead DEGs so they wouldn't be needing their coolant pipes. He took the red cable and wrapped it around the outflow as many times as he could bend the giant flex cable and then tucked the cable under the last two wraps. Then he followed suit by wrapping the black cable around the inflow pipe.

"Shit . . . where is that damned . . . ah, there it is." He grabbed the directed energy hand welder and the goggles from one of the tool box cabinets and rushed back to spark the cables hard welded to the pipes. He had to cut a notch out of the the two centimeter ceramic insulation with the handheld metal saw first before he could weld the cables to the conduit in both cases. "That's got this end!"

I understand what you are doing now, CMC! I think it might work. We need to flush the pipes into space first so they don't explode on us. And, Bill, we have to hurry!

Good, hadn't thought of that. Do it.

Engine Tech Command Master Chief William H. Edwards grabbed the spot welder, a metal saw, a torch cutter, a crowbar, and a BFW just in case. You never knew when you might to beat something with a big fucking wrench. Then he fumbled with the tools, trying not to drop them as he ran out the door and up the ladder. He rushed as best he could without dropping the tools up the deck and over two bulkheads. The ship was deserted and from deep within it there was little damage other than an occasional spewing liquid from a bust flow pipe or sparks flying from the end of a broken electrical cable. But the deck he was on was in pretty good shape. It had taken Bill at least thirty seconds to get there and he was huffing and puffing every breath.

Shit, I've got to get more PT.

Here it is, CMC! Mimi told him.

Got it. Bill pulled the engineer's access panel from the bulkhead with the crow bar and stepped through the hatch, tracing two five centimeter diameter red and black cables into the wall from the DEG power generator.

Hey, you got this thing open circuited, right? I don't want to get fried before I get a chance to crash into the surface of Mars at thousands of kilometers per hour.

The switch between the DEG and the DEG power source is open, yes CMC, Mimi acknowledged.

Bill grabbed the little metal saw and spun up the blade at the same time he slipped on safety glasses. The metal saw blade sliced effortlessly through the two high voltage power cables.

"That is much fucking quicker than a goddamned spanner!" he muttered to himself.

Then Bill dragged the heavy cables to the edge of the engineer's hatch where the coolant conduits ran through the room about ten centimeters off the deck. He had had to step over them to get into the room. He wrapped the two pipes with the cables in the appropriate configuration—red cable to outflow, black to inflow. He sure as shit didn't want to cross the power couplings now. He ran the metal saw across the insulation on the pipes a couple of times and then he switched goggles and fired up the torch, quickly welding the cables in place.

He stepped back through the engineer's hatch into the hallway and went quickly through his process and the steps he had taken to get the dirty repair job done. He hadn't forgotten anything, he didn't think.

Throw the switch to the DEG power unit, Mimi.

Got it CMC, she replied to him. There was a clicking sound he could hear through the wall but nothing else happened. He looked at the DTM virtual information and could tell that no power was getting to the propulsion systems.

"Fuck! That should have goddamned fucking worked!" Bill kicked the bulkhead three times and then regained his composure. And he and Mimi remembered the problem at the same time.

The open switch back in the Engine Room! they thought simultaneously.

Bill dropped everything but the crowbar and the BFW and ran as fast as he could back by two bulkheads and down a deck to the Engine Room. He was completely exhausted and out of time and his one armed paper hanger act was in severe need of an understudy, especially if there

was going to be an encore. He finally got to the point
where he was standing in front of the blown out high voltage breaker.

The switch had originally been about ten centimeters
long and several wide and thick, but when the power spike
had hit it the switch was completely vaporized, leaving a
hole in the switch panel with two large cables with charred
frayed ends protruding from spanner lock rings on each
side of the box. Bill held the crowbar and the BFW
together in both hands. If he used one of them they might
melt. If he used both as conductors to bridge the gap then
the two should be able to withstand the current flow. Hell,
Bill had used just a crowbar before but why take chances
if you didn't have to.

Here goes nothing, he thought to Mimi, and with an
underhand pitch tossed the two metal tools into the box
between the broken cable ends.

The BFW and the crowbar made a slow arc into the
cable box, and as soon as the BFW got to within four
centimeters or so of the cable ends a high voltage arc
jumped out across the air to it and immediately and
explosively welded the BFW to the cables, completing the
circuit. The explosive weld flashed the room with a bright
white hot burst of light and Bill quickly and reflexively
shielded his eyes. The crowbar on the other hand . . .

The crowbar was fractions of a second behind the
BFW and the explosive force of the BFW being grabbed
and welded to the circuit vaporized parts of the metal box
and air around it explosively and never allowed the
crowbar to make an electrical connection. Instead, the
explosive gasses ejected the crowbar out of the box pointed

end first right through the Engine Technician Command Master Chief's left shoulder, knocking him off balance. The crowbar impaled him just below the collar bone and came out his back.

Bill pulled himself up to his feet and looked down at the metal bar protruding out the orange coveralls and from his body. There was a lot less blood and even pain than he would have expected. Then he started to pull it out. One slight tug at the bar gave him other ideas about that.

"Oh fuckin' Jesus goddamned fuckin' Christ!" he screamed in pain.

Leave it there, Bill. Pulling at it will make you bleed worse.

Fuck that. Bill grabbed at the crowbar and gave it a yank. He promptly passed out and fell out on the floor. The bloody crowbar clanged to the deck beside him.

Chapter 26

The two conjoined spaceships had fallen from near a Mars-synchronous altitude where half of the battle had taken place and dropped through space, slamming into the Martian upper atmosphere at over sixteen kilometers per second. The initial heating and impact with the atmosphere caused anything on the pile of wreckage that was the least bit loose to let go. The battle had taken place in non-Keplerian orbits ranging from Mars-synchronous altitudes of over thirty thousand kilometers to near-space at thirty kilometers above the surface of the planet. As the ship fell it didn't fall as a typical deorbiting spacecraft would since it was not in a typical orbit: The hauler had the same type of gravity modifying proppellantless drive that enabled such orbits. Although the hauler had lost its main propulsion capability, it still had attitude control to some degree and managed to put itself in a spiraling non-standard trajectory that would lead into the large Martian city below.

Atmospheric drag chewed away at the two wrecked ships, their exterior hull plating ablating away as the friction ionized it layer at a time. The carbon nanotube, titanium, and composite fiber reinforced metals held up to a lot of stress, but the force of reentry impact was beyond the limits of many of the joints and connections of a healthy ship, much less two ships that had been battered to hell and gone and then stuck together by the sheer force of collision.

The structural integrity fields of the *Thatcher* continued to hold while the Seppy hauler rust bucket began to strip away like one onion layer at a time from the aerodynamic forces. At one hundred kilometers from the surface of the planet the ship was still screaming through the upper atmosphere at sixteen kilometers per second. The ships continued to deorbit into the atmosphere on a trajectory leading them for the Mons City domes. At fifty kilometers altitude the aerodynamic friction had broken off most of the pieces that were going to break off and the falling ships had shed more than three fourths of their energy, reducing velocity by a factor of sixteen times. By the time the vessels reached twenty-five kilometers altitude the conjoined ships were traveling at about eight hundred kilometers per hour and were beginning to shake loose from each other.

"Captain, propulsion just came back online!" Helmsman Ensign Lee had regained consciousness and was attempting to help with her job, but her left arm was broken in several places, her right wrist was sprained, and both collar bones were broken. Her head pounded from a light concussion and there was a bit of blood that trickled from her mouth if she coughed—and she felt like she need to cough often. She suspected that she had a broken bone that had punctured a lung.

"Transferring helm control to the captain!" Captain Sharon "Fullback" Walker announced. Her muscles were sore and there were several of them torn and she had a compound fracture in her left leg, but other than that she was functional. She was in extreme pain, but she was still functional.

"Captain has the helm!" Ensign Lee replied.

Outside the windows of the bridge all that could be seen was the glowing fires and streaming plasmas and shockwaves from any structures and edges across the two ships. The CO wasn't exactly sure which direction she should go, but adding some horizontal component to their fall couldn't hurt and it might push them past the city below.

"Full forward," Fullback said, engaging the engines. The ship began pushing forward further into the Seppy rust bucket that was now about to break into several larger pieces. She kept the throttle at max, driving the ship deeper and deeper into the hauler. The ship sang with ringing, banging, clanking, and metal on metal screeching.

"Captain, Sensor Engineer Lieutenant JG Morgen Kirby has repaired the power to the main sensor array. I've got forward sensors and navigation!"

"Give me a continuous feed on our trajectory," Fullback ordered. Her crew was nothing more than brilliant heroic gods and she loved every last one of them like the children she never had.

"Aye, sir!" The injured ensign moved her right hand

about her console as best she could and what she couldn't do that way accomplished through her AIC.

The trajectory of the falling ships went online in the CO's DTM virtual mindview. Their present trajectory had them crashing just across the top of the Main Dome at Mons City and into the Southeast where the *Churchill* had gone down. Fullback added ten percent upward force to the propulsion to see how the ship would react. The hauler began to collapse upward along the outer decks and metal buckled like a flimsy empty beer can. Fullback added more z direction acceleration, upping it to twenty-five percent. Secondary explosions and superheated plasma vented from failing systems on the hauler's outer decks. The trajectory calculations showed that they might just miss the southeastern dome by a slim margin if they could maintain the propulsion. The ships continued to screech and tear each other apart, but the supercarrier was faring far better than the Seppy rust bucket. The structural integrity fields were doing their jobs and holding the American warship together.

"Going to full z accel!" Fullback said and put all the propulsion power into the upward direction. The Separatist hauler finally collapsed under the strain and buckled completely. A seam formed along a large buckling ripple in the center of the vehicle and then it tore itself apart. The larger aft half tumbled loose and the lower one simply peeled itself apart like a disintegrating onion. Debris from the hauler's breakup smacked into the bridge windows and across the deck and exterior hull and in some cases pieces actually penetrated the hull and stuck there. But the *U.S.S Margaret Thatcher* broke free of the hauler and began to rise away from the broken up Seppy rust bucket.

"Great flying, ma'am!" Ensign Lee yelled triumphantly.

"We ain't out of the woods yet, Ensign!" The CO continued pouring all of the ship's normal space acceleration power into the upward axis, buying them more time before they impacted the surface. The probable trajectories in her head now were showing that the *Thatcher* would miss the domes, but pieces of the hauler were going to scatter very close to the Southeast dome. The Southeast dome had been compromised anyway so if it had more damage it wouldn't be as devastating. Besides that, the *Thatcher* had done all she could to protect the Martian city. It was time to think about herself and her crew for once. The Iron Lady of the fleet had done her job.

Captain, I've gone through all the possibilities. There is no way to pull the ship out of the fall and maintain flight. The best option is a controlled crash, her AIC informed her.

I figured as much.

Any suggestions?

Yes, crash down the mountain.

Of course! Good idea. Give me a trajectory?

It would be easier for me to take the helm.

Right. Captain's AIC, take the helm.

Aye sir! AIC has the helm!

"All hands brace for impact!" the captain announced over the intercom.

"Holy . . . " Alexander Moore began but fell speechless from the sight. The glowing fireball split into several

pieces that had fallen just south of the dome nearest them
and threw dust plumes into the air. The fire falling from
the sky scattered the retreating Separatist soldiers who
were still trying to put up a fight. But this was the final
straw that weakened them to the point where there was
no longer any cohesive attack grouping of them. The Seppies
were down to single or handfuls of snipers scattered
about, with maybe a handful of tanks and mecha left. The
air had been cleared out by the Killers, the Gods of War,
and by the last few contingents of mecha that dropped in.
The ground battle on this side of the city was over and the
majority of the American fighters and mecha had moved
on to the Main Dome. But what amazed Senator Moore
the most was the sight of a flaming United States Navy
supercarrier bursting out of the midst of the plummeting
fireball.

The supercarrier's path was stabilizing and stretching
as far up the mountainside as it could. If it hit near them
at that speed the secondary fall of debris would kill them
all.

"Is it going to hit us, Alexander?" Sehera reached out
to her husband's hand and held it for a second. Her
daughter was inside one of the inflatable domes with her
helmet off. She had needed a little break from the suit.
"Should I grab Dee?"

"Naw. Look at it. I think it is going to try and sled down
the mountain over there." He pointed at the giant flaming
ship. He could ask the Marine second lieutenant or one of
the SARs pilots, but they were busy dragging wounded
around. The reporters kept their camera on the crash and
had moved to a slightly better vantage point atop BIL the

garbage hauler, but Moore didn't want to talk with them right now either. "Let's just watch. I'm tired of acting right now."

"You did well, Alexander. Even the great President Sienna Madira wasn't as heroic," his wife said to him.

"You're biased, in more ways than one." Alexander smiled at his wife.

"Yes, of course I am." Sehera smiled for a moment. A brief moment is all the remaining grim tasks would allow. They would soon need to get back to helping with the wounded and their break from this horrible messy day would be over. "Do you think there are people still on that thing?"

"There must be. That is a controlled crash and a damned smart one," Moore said.

The supercarrier impacted at about three fourths of the way up the Eastern most side of the mountain that was unpopulated. Debris and dust and smoke plumed into the sky, creating reds and oranges in the early evening sunlight. It was breathtaking against the giant Martian mountain. The tough behemoth warship tore a gouge in the mountainscape as it sledded its way through rocks and soil as it turned westward around the mountain. There were flashes of secondary explosions and occasional glints of sunlight from flying chunks of metal, but after a long arduous ride of more than a hundred kilometers down the mountain the ship came to a stop less than twenty kilometers away.

"Somebody should get into touch with them and see if they need help," Sehera thought out loud. Then they were quiet. The two of them stood there in silence, holding hands, looking out across the devastation, dust storms, and the giant crashed supercarrier up the mountain.

"CO *Madira*! CO *Thatcher*!"

"Goddamn, it's good to hear your voice, Fullback!" Captain Jefferson replied.

"Aye sir. We've got some serious damage and there are three dozen wounded on board that need attention. But we survived, sir. And, we steered the hauler away from the city." Fullback's voice was clear but she sounded gruff, much more gruff than usual.

"Goddamned if you won't make admiral before I will," the CO said. "Are you in any shape to take on crew and wounded? We've got a lot of troops on the ground that could use some help."

"I'll put out a recall to the escape pods to return to duty, sir. We can't go anywhere right now, but we most certainly can take on wounded and act as a staging ground," Fullback replied.

"Great work, Sharon. *Madira* out!"

"CO, the *Washington* has DEGs back online and the *Kolmogorov* and *Blair* have propulsion and missile batteries back up. They are going full bore on the remaining Seppy ships," the XO said. "The squadrons have pulled back to cover for the remaining fleet and are beginning to overwhelm the Seppy bastards, sir!"

"Roger that, XO." The CO had the battlescape continuously updating in his DTM virtual mindview and knew that the fleet ships were coming back online from the fact that they were starting to reengage the enemy. But he hadn't been watching the DEG and missile battery readiness readouts of those ships at the time. It was quite a pleasant surprise to see the brilliant blue-green bolts of directed energy blasting away at the two remaining Seppy rust buckets.

"Looks like they're on the run, captain. Just like that time at Triton last year," the COB added. "Army Starlifters are loaded and ready to go to ground, sir. And Colonel Warboys is reporting that he thinks it's clear for SARs to drop."

"Deploy them and have them stage back to the *Thatcher's* location."

"Aye sir." The COB nodded at the Air Boss. The Air Boss took the information from the Army squads as the COB passed it along via the AICs and issued deployment orders to the squads.

The Fleet Angels were already in space and immediately started dropping the SH-102 Starhawks in for search and rescue operations. The Army Starlifter squads would drop in on the Army M3A17 Tank squads and either resample or load and transport them to the staging grounds, depending on the needs of the ground commanders. Typically, once the Starlifters were deployed the battles were well in hand. Captain Jefferson was glad that this battle was finally coming to a close.

"Senator. Mrs. Moore." Vulcan stretched her arms and legs as she stepped up behind them. Alexander hadn't heard the SARs pilot come up behind him and it startled him some. His nerves were shaky as hell from the events of the day.

"Shit, Lieutenant don't sneak up on me like that." He smiled at her.

"Sorry, sir. Thought you would like to know that we've got full up comms open again. The Naval base up the mountain has been retaken and most of the Seppy forces on the ground are dead. What is left of the 34th Marine Mecha division that had originally been deployed in the northwest domes have regrouped with several Army squads and are taking the main dome back as we speak," the Starhawk pilot told him.

"What about up there?" Moore nodded toward the sky.

"The tides have turned there too. But they are still fighting."

"Lieutenant, shouldn't somebody help them out?" Sehera pointed to the crashed supercarrier.

"Unbelievably, ma'am, they are in pretty good shape. In fact, what I came to tell you is that we are about to move this staging area to there. That ship has a full hospital facility in it. There are no doctors there, but they are on the way." Vulcan pointed to the east at the swarm of escape pods that were descending on the crashed super-carrier and about the same time several Starhawks screamed overhead, flying westward toward the dead mecha littered battlefield.

"Then we should go with you to help," Sehera told the young rescue pilot.

"Thanks, ma'am. Don't take it the wrong way, but there are trained professionals landing there now that can work more efficiently without you," Vulcan said. Sehera looked as if she were about to let the young pilot have it so Alexander stepped in.

"You're right, Lieutenant. But we might help with morale and keeping the press at bay. Although, now that the long range is back up, that will soon get to be a full-time effort. We should go with you," Senator Moore said with southern politician's charm.

"Yes, sir."

Chapter 27

"Don't move a muscle," Vincent warned his friends. The railgun fire into the sea of Mons City residents that had been corralled into City Park was continuous and relentless. The screams of victims were getting worse and worse as more and more wounded piled up. The force fields continued to push inward on the remaining survivors and had collapsed to an area smaller than a football field. Vince, Rod, and the pregnant lady Carla and several others lay helpless but unharmed for the moment at the center of the mess, playing dead. At first people had scattered from the gunfire and left the pockets of dead and wounded lying about the park, but unfortunately the collapsing forcefield was pushing them toward the center where Vincent had led them to play dead. Soon they would be overwhelmed by terrified and panic-stricken people trampling over them. Vince and Rod could probably handle that, but Carla's unborn baby most certainly could not.

"They're getting closer, Vince. Think of something!" Rod panicked.

"Bud, I'm fresh out of ideas now. It's out of our hands," he replied. A wave of terror stricken people pushed its way over the bodies toward them and the railgun fire splattered all around them. One of the rounds passed through Vincent's right thigh and then on into the ground beneath him. Vincent screamed at the burning sensation and grabbed his leg. Blood poured profusely out both sides of the wound. He sat up screaming in pain, and wrapped both hands around his' leg as the red blood squirted around his fingers. The railgun fire continued to track in on the herding people and he could see Rod doing all he could do to cover the pregnant girl with his body.

I'm proud of you, bud, he thought as he started feeling lightheaded. And then several people kicked and trampled over him and somebody fell on top of him. Vincent's leg continued to burn with pain but the weight of the body and the trampling herd of terrified people on top of him kept him from being able to do much about it. He could hear Carla weeping close to him. The wounded's cries all around him was one of the most horrible things he had ever heard in his life and he couldn't help them. He couldn't help himself. All he could do was to wait until one of the railgun rounds had his name on it or he bled to death. All he could do was lie there and wait to die. "Fuckin' Seppy cowards."

The herd moved further to their left and behind them and Vincent could feel the weight on him move. He pushed at it and it rolled off him. Rod was pushing at the body from the top side.

"Don't move, Vince. We gotta stop that bleeding some-how." Rod looked around not sure what to do.

"Bandage it with something," Carla told him.

"Right. Bandage it." Rod crawled around on his hands and knees trying to find something to use for a bandage and for the moment didn't think about the possibility of being shot down. A blue ion trail streaked across the park overhead and tore into the third floor balcony where the concentration of sniper fire was coming from. Then the balcony exploded in a bright orange flash and an echoing thunderous sound. Following that explosion came several more and then a continuous *spitap, spitap, spitap* and *zip, zip, zip* of massive amounts of railgun fire from all around. The ground began pounding rapidly with the sound of large chunks of metal stamping the sidewalks and pavement in the distance.

"Missiles!" Vince exclaimed and raised his head just enough to see where the fire had come from. There were more than twenty armored transfigurable tanks standing like giant metal gladiators running and firing weapons in different directions. Vince could see armored soldiers with jumpboots jumping across the park and from building to building, street to street, tree to tree, and anywhere else he looked.

"The military is here!" Rod yelled. Carla squeezed Vincent's hand and her whimpers began to turn from sobbing to cheers of joy. "About fucking time," Rod said and started to stand up, but his friend stopped him.

"Don't make yourself any more of a target than you already are, bud. Let the soldiers do what they came to do before we start running about all happy and shit." Vince paused and let himself enjoy the possibility that he just might live after all. "Pull that dead guy's shirt off and wrap it around my leg."

"That's right, sir, we've got tens of thousands of wounded here in Central Park and many more than that dead. The goddamn Seppy cowards were just killing them mass murder style. Women and children. Hell, they're was even a couple of dead dogs we found. It is just fucking awful, sir," armored E-suit Marine Gunnery Sergeant Tamara McCandless told her commanding officer, who had taken a group of AEMs to the shelter on the north side. The gunnery sergeant had the assignment of supporting the Army tank squadron in retaking Central Park.

"Yeah, gunny, it's the same pile of shit over here. There has to be fifty thousand dead and as many wounded in the shelter. We're getting word that it is the same all over the city." Captain Roberts responded over the quantum membrane net. The QMs' range had picked up once the jamming had been stopped and full tac-net comms were available. They would be needed just in the mop-up of this horrendous mass murder. Marines, Army, Navy, and Martian Air Force were dropping whatever support they could to help. It was the worst disaster in more than a century.

"What should we do, sir?" Tamara asked her CO.

"Shit, gunny, that is way above my pay grade. But if you've got the area secured then start helping whoever you can help however you can," Captain Roberts said. "We are trying to do the same here, but it's a goddamn cluster fuck."

"Yes sir, copy on the cluster fuck. We'll do what we can." Tamara couldn't believe that something like this could happen to America. But it had and she had to make certain that the Marines did what they could to help.

"Excuse me, Marine." One of the civilians with a bloody t-shirt wrapped around his leg approached him.

"Corpsman!" Tamara called a few feet over to the Navy Corpsman tending to another wounded civilian. That one was more critical.

"I'm busy right now, gunny!" The corpsman worked diligently in an open chest wound of the victim trying to stop the bleeding.

"Are you still bleeding, sir? Here," Tamara pulled the instaseal bandage from her own pack. "Let me see your leg."

"Uh, no ma'am. I'm fine. Save that bandage for somebody else. We just wanted to know how best we could help." The wounded civilian pointed a thumb over his shoulder at a handful of other civilians including a very young looking pregnant lady. "And . . . "

"And?"

"You wouldn't happen to have a cigarette on you, would you? I'm dying for a freakin' smoke."

"I don't smoke, sir. Hold on." The gunnery sergeant smiled at the man. "PFC Young!"

"Yes, Gunnery Sergeant?" one of the AEMs called from a few meters behind them.

"Give this man a cigarette and show his friends how they can help out."

"Right away Gunnery Sergeant!"

"Fish, behind you!" Lieutenant Commander Jack

Boland warned his wingman but didn't give her time to respond. "Guns, guns, guns!" he grunted after yawing his fighter one hundred and eighty degrees and then going to his DEG. The Seppy Gnat burst into four pieces and flew apart.

"Goddamn, where did that fucking Gnat come from?" Fish said over the net.

"I told you to keep an eye out. Just because the Seppy bastards are beaten don't mean there ain't some hiding out in the wreckage with their power off," Boland reminded his young wingman. He would have thought of her as inexperienced, but after the day they had just been through she had seen more experience than a lot of pilots would in a lifetime. But Jack feared that wasn't going to remain true either. With the Seppies gone to who knows where he feared that the real war was just beginning.

"Demonchild, you've been quiet on that side of the ship for a while. You got anything over there?" Boland looked through the virtual mindview of the wreckage for potential bogies down at the *Madira* for a brief second. *What a fuckin' day.*

You got that right, sir, Candis replied.

"We got nothing over here, sir. Must be an hour now that we haven't seen a fuckin' thing," Demonchild said over the tac-net.

"Well, keep your eyes open. We just got one over here." Boland yawed his Ares fighter back over to get a closer look at his wingman. Her little fighter was pockmarked and scarred to hell. It would need a new paint job and probably a shitload of maintenance. They had taken on Gnats and the new Stingers from space to Mars and now back out into space for the mopping up. He could see repair crews in suits and mecha already scurrying over the *Madira* like worker ants putting it back together.

"Roger that, DeathRay. Hey, you think after today we might get a few days leave?" Demonchild laughed.

"I was thinking of sleeping on a beach somewhere for a few days." Fish added.

It sounded good to Jack. Hell, he had been up since way before daylight taking care of a high risk mission and barely had time to eat before being thrust into an even bigger shit storm. As CAG he had a lot of letters to write. It was going to be hard to write the ones for Bigguns and Rabies. They were good pilots, good friends. Hell, it would be hard to write all of them.

Shit, this has been one long fuckin day.

Yes, sir.

"Gyrene, that is one mean son of a bitch hot shit metal machine you got there, but the damned pilot is the ugliest sorry sock full of shit I ever seen!" Army M3A17 Transfigurable Tank Mecha Commander Lieutenant Colonel Mason Warboys shook his long time friend's hand, bumped his shoulders, and patted his back.

"Well, you Army puke, that tank mecha ain't so bad either, but goddamn if you ain't rough on the eyes." Marine FM-12 Strike Mecha Commander of Cardiff's Killers Lieutenant Colonel John "Burner" Masterson laughed. "How bad are your boys?"

"Lost a bunch of good tank drivers, John. And you?"

"As far as we know we lost our entire supercarrier. The Killers, well, we lost a lot of good Marines, Mase." Burner looked at the Starlifters dropping in behind their mecha. As soon as they were reloaded they were going to help out with the clean up of the domes. Normally, other soldiers would step in, but they had lost so many that they were the only seasoned soldiers available. More were on the way from Luna and Earth, but they were reserve units still mustering in North Carolina. It would be hours before they got there and some of the Seppy stragglers could get away by the time reinforcements showed up.

"Your boys ok for more work?"

"We're tired and down, but we can hang with you jarheads. Damn, I'm glad you made it, Burner. When I heard about your boat . . . "

"Yeah, thanks, Mase."

"Warlord One! Lieutenant Colonel Warboys," one of the Starlifter crews was calling him. "Sir?"

"Duty calls, Burner."

"See ya soon. Watch your six!"

"Roger that. You, too."

"Chief of the Boat Command Master Chief William Edwards!" Captain Sharon "Fullback" Walker called across the hospital room at her COB. The corpsman working on her leg was finishing up with the instacast. Once the young Hospital Corpsman First Class had shot her full of pain meds and immunoboost, she placed the instacast around her leg and pulled the string. The cast expanded antibiotic gel into the compound fracture wound and then expanded until it forced the bone back into place. Then the gel material hardened enough to support her leg but still give with muscle tissue movement.

"Captain Walker, ma'am!" Bill snapped a salute with his right hand. He had a gelbandage on his left shoulder and his back. Something had impaled him, it appeared. "You've looked better, ma'am, if you don't mind my saying."

"You don't look so hot yourself, Command Master Chief." Fullback smiled at her COB. He single-handedly had saved the Martian City by getting the propulsion back online. "Good work Bill. Hell, Excellent work. I don't know how you did it, but I'm putting you in for the medal."

"Captain, I was just doing my job."

"A brilliant leader once said, 'Look at a day when you are supremely satisfied at the end. It's not a day when you lounge around doing nothing; it's when you've had everything to do and you've done it,'" Fullback said. "I think that sums up what you did today, Bill."

"I think it fits us all, the entire crew, ma'am. Who said that?"

"Former British Prime Minister Margaret Thatcher." The captain smiled at her COB as he nodded in agreement. "Now, shouldn't you be tending to my crew?"

"Aye, sir!"

"Sergeant Clay, PFC Kudaf, Second Lieutenant Washington," Alexander shook the AEMs' hands. Of the squad that was deployed to bring him, his wife, and daughter to safety they were the only three that had survived. "Thank you for what you did for us today. Semper Fi."

"Semper Fi!" they nodded to the senator.

"If any of you men ever need anything . . . seriously

. . . if y'all need anything all you have to do is have your AICs tag mine and you will get to me directly. Any time." Moore told the Marines.

"We were just doing our jobs, senator. You take care of yourself." The second lieutenant paused and then saluted him. "Major!"

Moore returned the salute, nodded, closed up the hatch of the Starlifter, and then banged on the door three times with his fist. The AEMs were being transported into various domes of the city to help with mop-up and search and rescue. Moore turned and walked back toward the elevator of the hangar of the giant supercarrier as the Starlifter lifted quietly off the battered flight deck of the ship. The large transport ship along with several other vehicles passed through the airseal forcefield at the open end of the hangar. A flurry of rescue and resupply vehicles continued in and out of the hangar deck. Medical crews had set up emergency triage units along the bulkheads and wounded were being attended to there. The walking wounded were unloaded from the rescue vehicles and then directed to other decks.

"That was a very touching moment, senator. The networks have been running our footage of you fighting to protect your family and the details of your story. They would love to go live in an interview with you." Gail Fehrer stood in front of him at the elevator shaft.

"Can I change clothes first?" Moore looked down at the blood splattered and dusty e-suit. He had tossed the helmet aside an hour earlier but hadn't had time to change, as he was making rounds to see soldiers and civilians and was shaking hands every chance he could. He even had helped carry some gurneys for a while. He was tired and he let out a long sigh.

"It might be more authentic if you didn't." Gail cocked her head sideways and raised her left eyebrow in thought. "Whatever you prefer is fine by me. But they would like to go live as soon as you are ready."

"Gail . . . uh," Moore paused for a second and reached over to the cameraman pushing the camera down. "Turn that off for a minute."

"What?!" Calvin gasped.

"Go ahead Calvin. Seriously." Gail knew when to turn the cameras on and when not to. And sometimes it was that trick that got you the real story.

"Calvin, stay here a minute." Moore held up a finger at the cameraman. Then he grabbed the reporter by the wrist and led her a few meters to a tool room with a big window in it overlooking the hangar. He pulled her through the doorway to it and then closed the door behind them.

"What's this about, senator?"

"Gail. There is a story here, a story that could make both of us if we played it right. Oh, sure you are a big correspondent now, but I'm thinking much bigger than that." Moore paused to see if there was any reaction, but the reporter had a good poker face.

"What is this story?"

"Hell, just look out the window at all of that! Look how many wounded are pouring in here and to the hospitals across the city and at the Navy base. It will last for days. Then they will have to start moving the dead. That will take even longer!" Moore thought about how to say what needed to be said.

"Yeah, it is horrible. I get it."

"Oh, you get the fact that this is a horrible thing that happened, but the bigger story is HOW did this happen? How did America allow this to happen? How did President Alberts allow this to happen? How did the democratically controlled Congress allow this to happen?" He paused again and pointed at the streams of wounded that continued to pour into the hangar deck. A smile started to grow across Fehrer's face. Moore knew she would get it. A reporter isn't a good reporter if they can't find somebody to make a hero and if they can't think of somebody or many somebodies to crucify.

"I see . . ."

"Think about it. Why didn't we know that the Seppies had that big an Army and Navy? Where did they get all that mecha and the carriers and the haulers? Somebody in the government either was asleep at the wheel, which is unforgivable. Or they were in on it, which is even more unforgivable. And by God I'm gonna find out who." Moore had her now. "WE, are gonna find out who and fuckin' draw and quarter them, metaphorically speaking of course, on systemwide television."

"And . . . there is always an and or a but. You need something more from me than just me doing my job." Gail was sharp. Moore knew that she would be the right person for the job.

"I never thought of this until now, believe me or not I don't care, but all day long I've only thought of one thing, and that was keeping my family safe. But now that I've reflected on this for a few moments I want to make certain that this will not happen again in this country, or at least it will not happen to us with our pants down and so unsuspecting."

"Mmmhmmm. How will you do that, senator?"

"That's the key you just said. Senator Alexander Moore from Mississippi can't do a diddly thing about it. But President Alexander Moore could." Moore stopped and stood looking Gail in the eye. "Make me President of the United States and I'll not let this happen again. And you can be an anchor, a White House Spokesman, or whatever you want. The right ally in the press could do this. You can do this!"

The press, if they played it right, had the power to sway most anything they wanted. Moore was a good candidate. He had given years as a Marine and showed how powerful and selfless and caring he was on this horrible day, on camera. Gail and Calvin had caught it all and America was about to see it. With the right spin he could take the White House in November by a landslide. The GOP would have no choice but to choose him as their candidate. He continued to stare Gail in the eye and didn't make another sound.

"Deal." Gail held up her hand and Moore shook it with a smile. "Now come with me and let's get started on your campaign." Gail opened the tool room office door and led the senator back out to the cameraman, who was standing around perplexed at the shots he was missing by having his camera off.

"So what was that about?" he muttered to his boss.

"Calvin, get the live feed ready. We're about to interview the senator," she replied.

What a day, hey, Abigail? Moore said to his AIC.

She's a good ally, sir.

I know.

Yes sir. What a day. It has been a long one.

Sir? Your wife and daughter want to go home.

So do I, Abigail. So do I.

Chapter 28

" . . . with this exclusive interview to go along with the footage you have just seen from the brave senator's exploits today on Mars, MNN correspondent Gail Fehrer has the senator live from the hangar deck of the crashed supercarrier the U.S.S. Margaret Thatcher, where a staging area has been set up to treat the hundreds of thousands of wounded. We go now live to the supercarrier. Gail?"

Elle pulled off her ski mask and threw it across her bed. She stood staring out the window as Mars got further and further away as she pulled her uniform off and slipped on a comfortable cotton non-designer dress—she never got to wear normal clothes anymore. Maybe some of that would change now that she would be out of the system and away from the deathly reach of the American CIA assassins. Maybe for a while she could rest and think. There was still much work to be done, but she wasn't going to think about that just now. Instead, she was going to walk around in her bare feet for a few minutes, pour herself a stiff drink, and put her feet up and think about how she was going to burn forever in Hell for what she had done. But burning in Hell would be a small price to pay for what she had accomplished today.

Elle listened to the MNN interview with her old acquaintance and was proud of the Marine turned politician for what he had done with the situation he had been thrust into. He had been caught up in the revolution, but then again she hoped all of America would be. But Major Moore, of course, that was now Senator Moore had not taken the day lying in a hole and sniveling like a typical politician. Moore fought. He fought to protect his family and the things that were dear to him. Ahmi had always liked those qualities in the Marine when she had kept him in her camp. And he was smart, too. Now he was using the momentum of this day to change his status from a political nobody to an American hero. Everybody liked a hero. Moore might just be useful someday after all. Elle was happy about that.

"All hands, this is the captain. Prepare for hyperspace in thirty seconds." The bosun's pipe and the intercom startled and annoyed her a bit as it cut into the interview. She would have to get a replay of all of it once they dropped out of hyperspace in a month.

Elle stretched her body left and right and twisted her chin from shoulder to shoulder listening to the creaking and popping in her neck and back as she looked at Mars, where she had been born, where she had grown up, where she had raised her first kitty, where she had fallen in and out of love for the first time, where she had gone to

college and become a software developer, where she had
started her software company that had become a multi-
billion dollar corporation, where she had had children,
where she had run for mayor of Little Tharsis for the first
time, and where she had learned to kill. Mars was a part
of her very being lost and now it would be gone to her for
a long time.

"Meeeoooowww."

"Ah, Socks. Now come here." Elle called to her AIK. The
artificial cat nuzzled up to her shins and purred. Unless it
was analyzed with QM sensors or it was torn apart and
examined it was indiscernible from a real kitty cat. Elle
picked up the AIK and gently stroked the robotic pet's fur.

The planet jumped way off into space and vanished as
a single point as the whirlpool of converging purples and
blues opened up around the ship. The ship jumped
through the hyperspace opening into the conduit and
normal space was behind them. In a month when they
dropped out of hyperspace a light year away in the Oort
cloud would be the next time they saw normal space.
Then a few minutes after that she would lead the ships
through the Quantum Membrane Teleportation portal
there, and the Free People of America would see their
new home on the largest moon of the gas giant fourth
planet from the star Tau Ceti. Had her spies within
America not discovered the QMT above top secret
research program and brought the details to her the day
would not have been possible. There was no way that that
many of the Free People could escape the system at once
and to go beyond the reach of the Americans. To her
knowledge the American scientists had not figured out

how to use the technology yet. Hers had. With hyperspace Tau Ceti was a year's travel from Sol, but with QMT it was a few seconds. This allowed her people a year at least to prepare for any retaliation.

"Raaaaoooooowwww." Socks looked up at her.

"It's good to see you too, kitty. Your brothers and sisters did very well for mommy today." Elle caressed her pet and then set it down. Her kittens were perfect unsuspecting electronic warfare transceivers that nobody ever suspected were wandering through the cities of the United States of America collecting computer signatures and jamming and downloading viruses—sleeper viruses—across the Sol System. "Good kitties." She allowed herself to grin only for a short time. As successful as the Exodus had been it was still horrendous and terrible and made her question it all. But her resolve couldn't waiver now.

Elle poured herself a drink and sat back in her recliner, putting her feet up. She spun the recliner around to face the window. The General's quarters were the largest on the ship and furnished with a small living area and a four-poster king-sized bed looking out the full transparent exterior wall of the room. Elle could close the blinds and curtains if she needed to, but she never did. She liked keeping the lighting low in her quarters so she could see the wonders of the universe outside her. She loved the beautiful swirling blues and violets and flashes of dim white light created by the hyperspace conduit. The beauty took her mind off the horrible things that she had done to humanity. She was almost drifting off to sleep when her door buzzer sounded.

"I said I didn't want to be disturbed."

"It's your old friend," the male voice replied through the door intercom.

Copernicus, is he safe? She had her AIC run scanners on the man outside her cabin.

He's alone, unbugged, and unarmed.

Very well. Let him in.

"How are you madam . . . " the man paused until the soundproof door was closed and then finished, " . . . President?"

"Oh, stow it, Scotty, and have a drink." Elle rubbed at her eyes.

"Don't mind if I do." Scotty poured himself a drink and then sat on the loveseat next to the recliner. "I have something for you." He handed her a gift wrapped in birthday paper.

"You remembered my birthday?" Elle smiled at her long time friend and cohort.

"Hell, millions of people remember your birthday, ma'am," he said.

"Scotty, stop with the ma'am shit. We're alone in here," she said as she unwrapped the gift. Elle tore at the red and white paper and ribbon like a kid.

"Old habits . . . new habits, I just can't help it sometimes." He took a long draw from the scotch he'd just poured himself. "Damn, I needed that."

"How about that?" Elle held up the gift so that the light from the hyperspace tube would reflect on it better giving her a better view of it.

"Two of the most idealistic and naive fools to ever shit between two shoes wouldn't you say?" Scotty grinned, sighed, and took another drink.

Elle examined the picture closer. It was in a nice Mars cherry tree wood frame and covered with an anti-glare pane of glass. The picture was of the newly elected democrat President Sienna Madira shaking the hands of freshly congressionally approved Supreme Court Chief Justice Scotty P Mueller. The Chief Justice had just sworn in the new President and they were shaking hands. There was handwriting on the picture that amused Elle to no end. She laughed at it.

"The best minds are not in government, if they were business would hire them away. Thanks, Sienna Madira President of the United States of America."

"You know I stole that from Reagan?" she said, and laughed again.

"Of course I did. I'm the Republican, remember." The former Chief Justice of the Supreme Court of the United States of America laughed. "Jesus, were we naive. I must say, though, I like your hair a lot better now."

Elle looked at the picture and at her reflection in the big window. Her hair was longer and the gray streaks had long been removed and she had been rejuved a couple of times since then. She actually looked younger, but she felt so old.

"Think of all the lives that had to be lost. What a sacrifice. I'm going to Hell, Scotty."

"Madam President, you did what had to be done to achieve the freedom that our forefathers fought so hard to protect. We simulated this thousands of times. Without the mass carnage humanity just wouldn't have paid attention and the new Free People wouldn't understand just how hard it is to acquire and hold on to true freedom. A bigger war is coming, but for today we did what we had to. It was necessary, and I think God would understand." Scotty swirled the ice in his tumbler.

"Maybe. I have some thoughts on how to prevent a full-scale system on system war. But that can wait. Perhaps God will understand, if he exists. He sure did his share of murder in the *Bible*. I know I've sold myself on that one. It helps me sleep at night," Elle said and took a long drink from her glass.

"Elle, I haven't known you to sleep since we first thought of this so many years ago." Scotty almost smiled at his long time friend and leader.

"We've been planning this a long time haven't we, Scotty?" Elle yawned.

"Yes, we have, madam President. And it took all those years of planning and plotting and scheming and faking our deaths and hiding and running, but America, a true America, is going to go on. Thanks to you. Thanks to your brilliant plan, your sacrifice, and your resolve. It has been a long time coming, but we finally had our day. Our last day in our home star system. We are leaving the old world to attain a new one."

"A long wait for a long day. But it is more than that, Scotty. One day we will return and right the Sol System and return America to its original greatness there as well. One day on Mars the true voice of freedom will be heard again. One day on Mars liberty and the pursuit of happiness will prevail again!"

"Yes ma'am. One day."

"Here's to it." Elle held up her glass and tapped it to her friend's. "Here's to a new America, to the Free People, to the lives lost and the suffering souls, and to those that fought today, this long day, for that *one* day on Mars!"

The following is an excerpt from:

ONE GOOD SOLDIER

TRAVIS S. TAYLOR

Available from Baen Books
December 2009
hardcover

PROLOGUE

October 31, 2388 AD
Earthspace, 100,000 kilometers above Orlando
Monday, 7:40 AM, Earth Eastern Standard Time
The Separatist Terrorist Attack on Luna City

"Goddamn, what was that?" General Elle Ahmi was tired of asking that question. The Separatist battle cruiser *Phlegra* rang with secondary explosions, and warning Klaxons sounded throughout the ship.

"I think we were hit by the moon's mass driver," Captain Sterling Maximillian answered. The mass driver of the Oort Cloud facility's moon had fired on them just before they had entered the quantum membrane transport to Earthspace.

"Damage report?" Elle said impatiently. Still, Sterling was a competent captain and the terrorist general had every confidence that he would get them to their target.

"I'm still checking. The teleport is operating as planned." The buzzing and popping from the Quantum Membrane Technology (QMT) projection stopped, and the Moon filled the view of the bridge. Luna City twinkled brightly beneath them as the shining metropolis that it was. Glints from Earth and Sol glared off the Luna City domes, through the portals, and onto the viewscreens. The tens of millions of inhabitants of the domes had no idea what disaster was about to rain down on them from space.

"Well, shut those damned alarms off. We're here." Elle sat back at the empty station behind the captain's seat. She drummed her fingers against the console, waiting for Maximillian's report.

"Sublight engines are down. We're venting like mad from every seal."

"Tell me some good news."

"Uh, yes, General. The auxiliary drive is unharmed, and we can reroute to that one. I'm working it. Propulsion will be up in five, four, three, two . . . there." Maximillian smiled triumphantly.

"Good. If Aux is all that is left, she'll be going there. All security personnel are to report to that section of the ship and stop that bitch." Elle slammed her fist into the screen of her console, cracking the cover. The CIA agent who had managed to infiltrate the *Phlegra* had been captured and tied up down in sickbay, but somehow she had managed to escape and was causing all sorts of problems for the terrorist's plans. She had already managed to knock out several key power systems somehow. "Stop her! Is that understood?"

"Yes, ma'am."

"Full forward to Luna City. Ramming vector!" Elle ordered. The plan was to slam the ship into Luna City, killing millions of American citizens with one attack. Elle Ahmi's sole purpose for the attack was to kill off a voting district and thereby sway an election—an election for president of the United States of America.

✧   ✧   ✧

"Damnit, Jack, I'm cut off. I don't think I can get around to you. That last blast closed off several sections between us," Nancy Penzington warned Commander Jack "DeathRay" Boland. He and his mecha wingman had followed the *Phlegra* through the QMT transport from the Oort Cloud combat in an attempt to stop the ship and rescue the CIA agent. The hallway Nancy had been going down was completely destroyed, and air was beginning to vent out of it. She had been lucky that whatever had just hit them hadn't crushed her in the process. So instead of being killed instantly, she was probably going to die slowly of hypothermia or from lack of oxygen.

"Roger that, Penzington. Can you get out of the ship?" Jack pushed his bot-mode Ares-T Navy mecha back up to its feet and looked out of the gaping tear in the ship's hull above him. The Moon loomed overhead, maybe a hundred thousand kilometers or so away. They were running out of time, and Jack had no real, good idea of how to stop the battle cruiser.

"I don't think so. I think I'm trapped in here." Nancy looked in every direction but could see nothing but crunched metal. The hull of the ship had collapsed all around her, and it would take hours to cut her out with a laser cutter. There was no way that one mecha was going to dig her out in a few seconds.

"Hold on, we're coming to you. I'll blast you out if I have to."

"Don't, Boland. I'm too deep in the ship. I did my job. I got some good info on the Separatists' plan. I'm downloading it to you now. I haven't even had the chance to read all of it. You read it and then figure out what to do with it. And don't share this with anyone that you don't trust completely, and be wary even of them. I mean it." Nancy sat down in the corridor, listening to the air hissing through the cracks in the wreckage. She had done her job.

"That's defeatist talk," Jack said. "Now get your ass up and find a way out of there."

"Sorry, Jack. I'm stuck here, and my air is running out." She paused for a brief moment in thought. "If you can't stop this ship, you have to get out with the data I just gave you. Now, go. That data is more important than I am."

"Come on, Jack." Fish pulled her mecha through the gash in the ship to the exterior hull. The Moon continued to loom closer. At their present rate of acceleration, they would hit Luna City in less than a minute. Fish rolled her bot over into fighter mode and throttled toward Earth. Then her blue-force system dinged at her. There were two supercarriers not far from their location. "Jack, I've got two supercarriers Earthward.

"I see." Jack thrusted his mecha up through the ship and outward into open space, where he toggled his bot back to fighter mode. He paused during the maneuver, only briefly but long enough to look back at the *Phlegra* solemnly. "Godspeed, Penzington, or whoever you are."

Jack? DeathRay's artificial intelligence counterpart (AIC) spoke into his mindvoice. The implant in his brain translated the computer's communication direct-to-mind, or DTM, through a quantum neural interface between the AIC and the user.

Yes, Candis.

Blue-force tracker identifies the nearest ship as the USS John Tyler. Perhaps it can stop the battle cruiser. Right.

"Captain! We've got a major electromagnetic disturbance Moonward, and a Seppy battle cruiser just appeared out of nowhere!" the CDC officer of the *Tyler* warned the captain over the command net.

"What the hell?" Captain Westerfeld looked confused.

"Sir, we're being hailed by the CAG of the *Sienna Madira*."

"Can't be. Wally's ship is way out in the Oort somewhere."

"Well, sir, his security codes validate."

"Patch him through."

"CO *Tyler*, this is Commander Jack Boland of the USS *Sienna Madira*."

"Commander, this is Captain Westerfeld. What can I do for you?"

"Sir, this battle cruiser is on a ramming vector for Luna City, and we can't seem to stop it! I thought you might be able to help us out."

"Captain," Alexander Moore interrupted. "I have an idea." He shoved the *Sienna Madira* robot onto the teleport pad. The corrupted AI inside the robot likeness of the great president from Disney World had been under the Separatists' control. But for now it was being jammed by President Moore's AIC temporarily, but that would only hold a few more seconds. When the robot AI broke through the jamming signal, it would most certainly detonate the multiple megaton gluonium bomb hidden within it. Gluonium bombs used the actual quantum mechanical force that held quarks together and were the most powerful weapons developed by man.

"Agreed." Westerfeld nodded. "Commander Boland. I recommend that you get out of there as quickly as you can. We'll take care of it."

"Trick or treat, bitch!" Moore said to the AI-driven Sienna Madira robot look-alike.

"General, the propulsion system is locked on. Even if it was knocked out, at this point our trajectory will still take us to Luna City," Maximillian said, nodding toward the bright silver and blue dome of the great metropolis in the Sea of Tranquility. The captain of the *Phlegra* tapped a few keys on his chairarm and moved several virtual icons around in his DTM mindview. Then he turned to Ahmi and said, "We should go now, ma'am."

"Alright. Very good. Activate the QMT projector snap-back routine," Elle ordered.

"Yes, ma'am. Recalling all personnel to original Tau Ceti QMT projection in three, two, one . . ."

Nancy Penzington, or Kira Shavi, or . . . well, her real first name had been Nancy, at least . . . sat with her back against the collapsed bulkhead of the *Phlegra*, hugging her knees and waiting for the end. The air hissed by her, and it was getting very cold in the corridor, and she was shivering uncontrollably. None of that really mattered at this point since the ship she was trapped in was about to crash and explode in seconds. She didn't want to die, but she was making her peace with it.

Nancy, we did our job, her AIC consoled her.

Yes, we did. And hopefully it will save some lives or do some good.

It will. Boland will figure out what to do with it. Allison had had the time to read the data when she had finally decrypted it. There was some very interesting information in there, and some contacts that went all the way up to the White House. The data was more important than Nancy or Allison themselves. *The data was worth the sacrifice.*

I hope it isn't too big for him.

He'll figure it out.

Nancy?

Yes, Allison?

I've really enjoyed being your friend.

Me, too, Allison.

The ship started popping and crackling around her, and then white light filled her vision. Through the light, she caught faint glimpses of the ship exploding all around her. She braced herself for the pain of the exploding hot ionizing plasma rushing toward her. And she braced for death. . . .

But death didn't come. A distinct sound of hissing and popping like frying bacon filled her ears, and the exploding ship seemed to freeze in place. Nancy's mind raced with her life's story as she knew that these would be her last seconds to reflect on her thoughts.

Nancy! I'm receiving an All Hands AIC ping!

So?

It is for a recall to Tau Ceti!

Can you hack it!

It didn't require a hack. It was an open handshaking call to all AICs on the ship, but you need to be prepared for escape and evade.

Damn right!

The exploding ship on the other side of the bright light filling Nancy's vision vanished from her field of view as bluish flashes of stars popped in and out of her sight. The high-energy cosmic rays from the QMT transport passed through her body mostly without any interaction, but occasionally one of them would affect the electrodynamic properties of the atoms in the aqueous-humor liquid of her eyeballs at speeds faster than the speed of light in the liquid and therefore generating Cerenkov radiation. The characteristic flashes of blue light then impinged on her retina, with the outcome being as if she were "seeing stars."

Then, as quickly as the exploding Separatist battle cruiser had vanished, it was instantly replaced by the inside of the QMT transport facility in orbit around Tau Ceti just inward of the orbit of the planet Ares. The electromagnetic whirlwind around her subsided abruptly, leaving Nancy sitting and hugging her knees on a large pad with over sixty Separatist battle cruiser crew members including the captain of the ship, a dead doctor, and several dead, mangled, and injured crew members. Near the center was Elle Ahmi in her trademark stars and stripes ski mask. The sight of the evil Separatist general refreshed the fear of the torture Nancy had gone through less than a half hour before. The remembered feel of those cold black leather gloves caressing her naked body and then slamming into her face made her shiver with spite and hatred for the woman. The residual pain and memories of the torture drugs they had used on her fueled a rage deep insider her. Oh, yes, Nancy was going to get that bitch one day. One. Day.

The crew quickly started scurrying about and dispersing, and Nancy stood and rushed purposefully off the pad amidst several soldiers who had materialized near her on the QMT pad. Two men just to her left were battered and bloody, and one was applying an organogel patch over the other's missing arm. There were several cries of pain across the pad. The massdriver round that had struck the ship, the two mecha pilots, and Nancy herself had inflicted some damage to the battle cruiser before it was evacuated, and clearly there had been casualties. The teleport pad was in chaos, and that worked to her advantage. Nancy still hadn't figured out how they had teleported all the way back to Tau Ceti without bringing the ship. But there were more urgent thoughts on her mind—like getting the hell out of there and staying alive.

"Hey, you!" A bloody man in orange coveralls lying on the deck pleaded for her attention.

"What?" Nancy turned to see more clearly that the man was holding his stomach, which was ripped completely open. Blood trickled from his mouth.

"Help me," he said faintly. "Oh God, help me."

She paused for a moment and scanned around her. Someone would help him eventually. *Shit*, she thought. *That might be too late for him.* Some other time she might have to put a bullet between the guy's eyes, but right now wasn't that time. The right thing to do was to help. *Shit!*

"Medic!" Nancy yelled and then tore the bottom half of her shirt off and stretched it out in her hands to see if it would be long enough for a bandage.

Allison, what do you suggest? Her AIC used the visual information from Nancy's eyes as recorded through her brain from a DTM link and analyzed the damage to the man. His large intestines were clearly loosened and falling out. There was a bloodied red and dark gray jagged metal shard penetrating through his left side and out his back.

Other than getting the hell out of here, Allison started, *don't touch the metal object in him. Let a doctor remove that. Carefully put his body parts back in and bandage it off.*

Hell, I knew that. Got anything more?

Not much you can do without the proper equipment and supplies.

Okay.

"Hold still." Nancy undoubled the torn piece of shirt and slid it underneath the man's back. The slight movement made him scream in agony and fear. "Focus. Try to relax your breathing. You're gonna be okay. I'm Nancy. What's your name?"

"Alan," the man said faintly. Blood gurgled from his lips each time he tried to speak.

"Nice to meet you." Nancy reached into his abdomen and began placing his intestines back in gently. At one point she had to actually push hard to arrange them in place. Alan screamed again. "Listen, you have to help me here. Hold your hands here until I can tie this off!"

Alan did what she told him, but he had lost so much blood that he was almost too weak to apply any pressure. He was bleeding out pretty fast, and if he didn't get the right attention in a matter of seconds he wasn't going to make it. Nancy pulled at the jagged tear in the man's skin and then placed the makeshift bandage over his entrails. She tied it as tightly as she could and then pressed down with the palms of her hands. Blood oozed out through the bandage and between her already blood-red fingers.

"Where's that goddamned medic? Medic!"

"Here." Nancy felt a tap on her shoulder as a Seppy soldier with a red armband knelt beside her. He instantly slid an injection into the side of the man's neck and then popped open a large pack of organogel. "Good job, soldier. Now, don't move your hands until I tell you to."

"Roger that." Nancy held fast to Alan's abdomen as the medic squirted the organogel over her fingers and the large jagged gash. Then he applied more of the gel to the metal shard protruding through Alan's side. The injection must have been immunoboost and stims, because Nancy could tell that the coloring in Alan's face was already better. The medic pulled another small pouch from his bag and tore a seal-tab on it. The clear pouch expanded and turned a deep blood red.

"Sir, I'm giving you some instaplasma that should help alleviate the stress of so much blood loss. You're gonna make it, so just hang in there." The medic taped the pouch down to the wounded man's arm and jabbed the sharp tube into a vein at the wrist. The tube hissed and made a completely hermetically sealed connection between the plasma container and Alan's circulatory system.

"He needs a gurney," the medic stated. He whispered quietly to Nancy, "He's not out of the woods yet." He reached in his bag again and this time pulled out a roll of dull green material about three quarters of a meter wide and then rolled it out beside Alan. The material was a good two meters long once it was rolled out. The medic then pressed a membrane button on the top of it, and the material hardened and formed handles on each end. "We're gonna move him right up on the gurney. On three!"

"Got it." Nancy nodded that she understood him and adjusted her position in order to help move the injured man onto the gurney.

"One, two, three!" They both carefully dragged Alan onto the gurney. Nancy couldn't really do a lot as her hands were solidifying to Alan's midsection. The clear organogel was turning an opalescent pale pink, almost skin color.

"Okay, slowly, very slowly, pull your hands out. Don't worry about the bandage. The immunoboost and organogel will eventually eat it."

"Right." Nancy slowly retracted her hands with a sickening *squish* and *pop* as they escaped the viscous bloody goo. Her hands looked and felt as if she had been soaking them in a vat of petroleum jelly, and she was covered in blood up to her elbows. Her face was still swollen and battered, and several times during her first aid on the wounded man blood had squirted her in the face and on her clothes. She was a mess.

"Grab that end." The medic pointed and got a grip on the other end. Nancy did as she was told, but began thinking about an exit strategy.

Any suggestions? Nancy thought to her AIC.

Go about your business, Nancy, Allison warned her. *As far as they know, the CIA agent died with the* Phlegra.

Got it.

Nancy heaved her end of the gurney and continued on with it for several meters, letting the medic lead.

They were several very long meters, to a passageway on the edge of the teleport pad. The pad was in a cavernous room the size of a professional basketball coliseum. It had clearly been designed to transport many troops and a lot of heavy equipment in a single teleport. Nancy also knew that the facility could teleport ships hovering over it as well. The Seppies had a serious technological advantage with this facility, and somehow the U.S. needed to be prepared for the types of attacks it would enable. But Nancy didn't have time to really focus on strategy at the moment. Survival tactics were about all she could manage. She had to get away from here to the planet below, where she could disappear into the population.

"Thank you, Nancy." Alan looked up at her and managed as much of a smile as he could. He was looking a lot better than he had just seconds before, but he still looked like leftover Hell twice warmed over.

"Just hang in there," she replied.

How did they develop all this? Allison thought to her, referring to the teleport facility.

Worry about it later. Let's get the fuck out of here and get lost somewhere a long damned way from Elle Ahmi. Nancy's first thoughts were survival. She couldn't believe she'd let herself get wrapped up helping the wounded. But it might work out for the best.

Agreed.

"Ma'am, are you alright?" the medic asked her.

"Sure. I'm fine. Superficial stuff—nothing to worry about." Nancy had already taken mental steps to put out of her mind the torture that she had endured just minutes before. While she realized that it must be still apparent on her face and body that she had recently been through physical torture, the simple fact of the multiple wounded around her was cover enough for it. She could feel the immunoboost working, the one she had been given by the man—Scotty, she recalled—who had helped her escape. It had removed some of the swelling and had started to close the various abrasions. She was wearing what was left of the commandeered clothing, which was way too big for her, and she had no shoes. Her battered look fit in with the surviving battered Seppy troops, but her clothes, well, didn't. She stood out. But hopefully, the other sixty soldiers scurrying about with their own frantic agendas wouldn't notice. Her bloody nose and mouth and Alan's blood covering most of her upper torso and arms actually worked to her advantage as a disguise. The first chance she got, she planned on commandeering herself a better one.

I'm picking up a hangar bay around the corner. I'm trying to handshake with some of the transport-manifest AICs. Maybe we can stow away to Ares, Allison said.

Right. Good plan.

CHAPTER 1

July 1, 2394 AD
Earthspace, Sea of Waves, the Moon
Friday, 7:40 AM, Earth Eastern Standard Time

"Watch the Gomer on your three-nine line, Dee! He's gonna lock you up!" Deanna Moore heard blasting in her ears on the tac-net. Her wingman, Jay Stavros, held as close on her ass as he could and continued to nag her about the crossfire, but it didn't faze her. She had to be cool in order to close the energy gap on the enemy mecha Stinger in front of her.

"You just cover my ass, Jay! I'm staying with this Gomer in front of us." Deanna stomped on her left pedal and pulled back on the stick with her right hand, all the while trimming the throttle with her left hand to maintain a steady energy relationship between herself and the enemy fighter. "Come on, goddamnit, make a mistake!"

She pulled into as tight a turn as the Marine mecha could withstand, and when she did the g-suit constricted on her legs and abdomen like a giant anaconda squishing its prey. Deanna grunted and cursed against the extreme gravity loading but held her course on the tail of the enemy Stinger.

Bree, give me some alternatives here! she screamed in her mind at her AIC.

Roger that, Dee, the AIC responded and placed several red lines and blue lines in her DTM mindview. The lines were alternative aircraft trajectories of her and the enemy's fighters spiraling around each other in a corkscrewing sinewy ballet of angular momentum and propellantless propulsion energy application. *Too close for missiles—gotta go to guns!*

The yellow targeting X blinked and jumped around in Deanna's mindview but couldn't quite lock on to the Stinger. The X blinked red then yellow and then hopped off the enemy fighter again. No matter what type of juke or jink she tried, the damned enemy mecha managed to squirm, bob, or roll its way out of her targeting solution.

"Shit! Come on you bastard. Hold . . . fucking . . . still." She grunted against the overwhelming and crushing load on her chest. The g-suit squished her breasts flat as pancakes and her abdominal muscles were squeezed so tight that she wasn't sure she'd ever be able to unsqueeze them.

Then the enemy mecha did something. Dee wasn't sure if it was brilliant or stupid. The mecha, in fighter mode, flipped over forward and began to transfigure to bot mode. The transfiguration took only a fraction of a second and left the mecha standing upside down on its head and facing Dee and her wingman with both arms pointing forty-millimeter cannons in their general direction.

"Warning—enemy targeting lock established.

Warning—enemy targeting lock established," the Bitchin' Betty of Dee's mecha chimed. Times like this the mecha's automatic warning system was more distracting than helpful.

Tracers tracked out of the right-arm cannon of the enemy fighter across her nose and into the empennage of her wingman's plane. Dee could see Jay jinking and juking his fighter around inside the firing solution of the enemy weapons, but there was little he could do at the time. The rounds continued to rip through his mecha, throwing bits of armor plating off into space with an orange and white spray of plasma.

"Pull out, Jay! Pull out!" Deanna, with her hands-on-throttle-and-stick (HOTAS), slammed the throttle full forward and the stick all the way forward against the stop, rocketing her fighter-mode mecha into a horrendous dive toward the deck.

"Shit, Dee, I'm hit! Eject, eject, eject!" Jay shouted.

Just as her mecha nosed down, her wingman's mecha exploded behind and to the right of her, and brilliant orange tracer rounds zipped by her canopy, only centimeters away. She didn't have time to see if an ejection couch cleared the fireball or not. The Gomer off her three-nine line to the right was closing in and firing. Then several rounds from the bot-mode mecha that she had been tailing zipped through her tail section but only caused minor damage. While Jay had been with her it was two against two and she had an enemy in her sights. Things had been looking up. Suddenly, in less time than it takes to blink an eye, the situation had switched in favor of the enemy. It was now two against one, and both of them were targeting her. Dee continued down at alarmingly increasing acceleration until it was clear that the mecha behind her and to her right were going to follow.

They're on you now, Dee! Bree warned her.

Roger that!

Dee toggled the transfigure button on the HOTAS and stomped the right, lower foot pedal all the way down to give her more slip as the Marine FM-12 transfigurable strike mecha rolled and flipped over and then transformed from a fighter plane into a giant armed and armored robot.

Let's see if what is good for the goose is good for the gander! she thought.

Dee, watch your altitude! Bree warned her. The landscape of the small moon they were fighting over filled her entire field of view and was rapidly approaching. It looked a lot like Pluto's moon, Charon.

She gripped the throttle and pulled it full-force backward with her left hand while controlling the flight path with the stick in her right. The standard HOTAS controls mimicked most fighter-control systems that had been developed for centuries with the innovation, of course, of the DTM-control links between the plane and the pilot and the AIC. There had been experiments where mecha had been piloted by AICs alone, and those mecha could make maneuvers that human bodies couldn't withstand. But there was a certain art to combat flying that only humans in the cockpit could bring. The experiments always showed the same results. Human and AICs together in the cockpit always came out on top when flying against a plane with just one or the other in it. The DTM connections between pilot, AIC, and mecha enabled modern fighter mecha to do things that no others in history could have done, and Dee was pushing the combination to the limit.

The bot-mode mecha now stood on its head, which was upside down in relation to the other fighters, and backward, facing the pursuing mecha. The g-loading of the full-force reversal caused Dee to vomit dryly into her helmet, and her vision began to tunnel in around her. But she fought through it and held on to the HOTAS.

"Aaarrhhggg, woo!" She grunted and flexed her abdominal muscles again, trying to hold off blacking out long enough to lock up her pursuers. Two yellow Xs filled her mind, bouncing around the fighter-mode Stinger to her right and the bot-mode mecha on her tail. The quantum-membrane sensors locked up on the fighter-mode plane, and a lock tone sounded in her mind. "Fox three!" she shouted as she loosed a mecha-to-mecha missile. The missile spiraled out toward the enemy fighter, leaving a very faint blue ion trail through the almost nonexistent atmosphere of the small moon.

"Warning, surface collision imminent. Warning, surface collision imminent," her mecha's Bitchin' Betty announced.

"One more . . . second . . ." Dee grunted as the yellow targeting X turned red. "Guns, guns, guns!" she shouted as she triggered the cannons on both arms. Tracers tracked out and blew the enemy mecha into a fireball of orange and white debris.

Pull out, Dee! Pull out!

"Warning, surface collision imminent. Warning—"

Dee tried to pull the mecha over into a horizontal run with the ground but didn't make it. Her mecha slammed into the surface just as she began to black out.

✧　　✧　　✧

"Apple didn't fall far from the tree, if you don't mind my saying so, sir," Thomas Washington commented to President Moore as they watched the president's eighteen-year-old daughter, Deanna, on the large viewscreen at the Mecha Combat Training Simulations Center located at the south end of the Sea of Waves near the limb of the Moon.

"I was never a mecha jock, Thomas." Moore smiled back at his bodyguard, only briefly taking his eyes off the simulation displays. Three other Secret Service agents stood behind them and didn't flinch or make a sound. The president's daughter was in a large metal box suspended on repulsor fields. The box whirled and bounced and twisted madly in place, simulating a combat scenario. Inside the box was a replica of a U.S. Marine FM-12 transfigurable strike mecha fighter cockpit.

Deanna had logged thousands of hours in the sim over the last five years and had reached a point where her proficiency was approaching that of a seasoned Marine mecha pilot. Of course she hadn't gone through all of the basic Marine training, as it was against the law to enlist before the age of twenty-one. Deanna was only eighteen, and for more than a century, as life expectancies had increased, the age to enter active duty as soldiers, firemen, policemen, and a few other dangerous professions had been set to the legal adult age. So Dee would just have to wait a few years, but Moore could tell by watching how she handled the simulations that she had the skills to be a good mecha pilot. She just needed the benefit of age and training. And train she had. Since she had been thirteen,

Dee had studied and trained and competed in any and all mecha jock activities she could. She had been accepted into the most prestigious military academy in the Sol System. And while there were plenty of skeptics out there, Alexander had never once needed to use their family's political pull to help her. Moore hated that Dee had been living in a dorm at the Sea of Waves Powered Armor and Mecha Academy for the past four years instead of at the White House with him and Sehera.

But Dee had put in the work and Alexander was proud of her. Fortunately, Air Force One often made trips to the Moon. He wished that Dee would have taken up lion wrestling, or football, or shark baiting, or chainsaw juggling, or anything less dangerous instead. But she hadn't. For the past six years, since that incident in Orlando, she had thought of nothing but being a goddamned U.S. Marine mecha pilot. When she saw those marines tromping around Disney World in bot-mode mecha, bringing all kinds of hell to the robot AIs that were trying to capture the First Family, her life changed. U.S. Marine Major Alexander Moore wanted to say "Oorah!" President of the United States of America Alexander Moore wanted to say, "Good work, and your country would be proud to have you serve!" But for just plain old Alexander Moore, hick from Mississippi, daddy to a little girl, it was *his* little girl, his princess. He didn't ever want to see her in harm's way.

But Alexander knew that Dee was gonna be Dee, and the best he could do was support her and try to make her as damned good a marine as he could manage. That might just keep her alive in the future.

He still had three years to talk her out of it. He wasn't giving that much of a chance—snowballs and Hell came to mind.

"Goddamned gutsy, if stupid," USMC retired Colonel Walter "Rat Bastard" Fink III stood at ease behind the president, with his hands behind his back.

"I agree." Moore turned to the mecha pilot instructor and frowned at the former marine. Of course, Moore knew well and good himself that there was no such thing as a former marine. "She is no good to anybody dead. And she can't move on to the final rounds of the competition, either."

"Permission to speak freely, Mr. President?" Colonel Fink asked.

"Go ahead, Rat."

"She isn't thinking of life and death at all, only about killing her opponent to win a competition. She still thinks of this as a game, sir. A game with a reset button. Oh, she is damned good at it, and with her and her wingman there we'll probably snag the trophy at Ross 128 next week. But I'm here to train marines, sir, not just simulation-competition winners. And like you said, she's no good to anybody dead, sir," Fink said without moving a muscle or changing the expression on his face.

"I think somebody should make her . . . aware . . . of her problem, Colonel Fink. Don't you?" Moore smiled at the instructor.

"Yes, sir," Fink replied as a large toothy grin covered his face. "And I think I know just the person, sir."

The "box," as it was affectionately referred to by mecha trainees, or "nuggets," drifted to a resting spot on the floor of the sim center, and the side opened up by folding over into steps. Two instructor techs rushed into the box to help Dee out of the pilot's couch. The box for her wingman a few meters to the left of hers had already been opened. Moore could see the young man's face was pale, and when he stood his legs were shaky.

Deanna managed to walk upright down the ramp but only with the support of the instructor techs under each arm. Once she made it to the bottom of the ramp she motioned that she could support herself and then twisted off her helmet. Alexander could tell by the look on her face that she was physically exhausted but proud of herself for having killed her pursuers. Fink was right. She still didn't understand the life and death of the predicament that she was considering getting herself into—the predicament of being a United States Marine.

"Cadet Moore!" Rat shouted with a rough, gravelly tone at the "First Nugget," as Dee was known.

"Sir!" Dee snapped-to tightly, her exhaustion showing through her expressionless face. She and her flight gear were soaked in sweat from her shortly cropped Martian-dark hair to her toes, which were a long, athletic, and curvy one hundred seventy-six centimeters down.

"How do you think you performed on that mission, Nugget?"

"I killed the enemy, sir." Dee didn't move or flinch or even blink.

"Your wingman is dead!"

"Yes, sir."

"You are dead!"

"Yes, sir."

"The entire nation is going on a week of mourning because the First Nugget has died uselessly, if heroically, in combat! Sorry, Cadet Stavros, but only your family will be mourning for you, as you are dead as hell as well!"

"Yes, sir," Dee and Jay answered simultaneously.

"You think this is a goddamned game, nuggets?" Fink stood looming over Dee, his nose only inches from her face. Then he glanced and glared at her wingman.

Again, simultaneously, Dee and Jay responded. "No, sir."

"Then what the hell was that! Your mission was to go in and support the recon unit infiltrating that facility, and you ended up getting yourself and your wingman killed. Now, what if those heart-breaking, goddamned life-taking, and God-fearing AEMs down there needed some more air support? Huh? Just what in the flying fuck were you thinking? Those marines had a mission, and now, because you were too busy up there goddamned hotdogging it out like some goddamned virtual world goddamned gamer, this mission has a larger probability of failure. That is failure with a capital fuckin' F! Do you understand me, Nugget? Failure!"

"Sir!"

"And fucking failure, with a capital fuckin' F, is one thing that I WILL NOT accept from my nuggets! Do you two hotshots under-fucking-stand me?"

"Yes, sir!" Dee made the mistake of letting her eyes glance at her father standing in the background, but only for a fraction of a second. But that was a fraction of a second too long.

"Cadet Moore! Do you think just because your daddy is Alexander Moore, one of the most decorated marines in the history of the universe, and also happens to have gotten himself elected president of these here United States of America three times in a row, that you are gonna get some sort of preferential treatment? Huh?"

"No, sir!" Dee's eyes fixed, and glowered, at Fink. Alexander watched his daughter's body stiffen, and he could tell that Fink had hit her main nerve. He seemed to be enjoying himself a little too much. But Moore wouldn't do anything. If Dee wanted to be a real marine, she would have to make it on her own from here on out with no preferential treatment. He absolutely hated his little girl having to go through this. But, God, he was proud of her.

"Then why don't you turn around and crawl your asses back into those simulator boxes, and let's do this mission goddamned right this . . ." Fink continued to yell at the two nuggets for a few minutes as they were loaded back into the simulators by the techs standing by. The two pilot trainees were physically exhausted, but that was all part of the job. A good marine marches when told and trains harder than everybody else no matter how tired he or she is.

"Well." Alexander turned to his bodyguards. "This is gonna take some time, so why don't we go find the First Lady and grab some breakfast and shake some hands and kiss some babies."

"Yes, sir." Thomas nodded at the president and then to the other agents. He sent a DTM order to Dee's bodyguard that they would see them at the departure platform in a couple of hours.

❖   ❖   ❖

"No, I didn't really get to talk to her at all." Alexander smiled across the table at his wife. It amazed him how much Dee looked like her mother and frightened him how much Sehera looked like her mother. The three women could be confused as triplets if Dee let her hair grow back out and if Sehera and her mother timed rejuves appropriately with a family photo. But one thing that both Alexander and Sehera knew for sure was that they never wanted their daughter close enough to Sehera's mother to ever have such a photo take place. After all, Sehera's mother, the famous one hundred eleventh president, Sienna Madira, a.k.a. Separatist terrorist General Elle Ahmi, was, in their minds, the craziest and most evil human being in the history of mankind, though Ahmi would argue that she had done what she had with the future of mankind and the United States of America at the heart of it all. But the Moores thought differently.

"Alexander, what is it?" Sehera asked. Moore had given up trying to hold out on his wife years prior. He must've been giving something away with his expression.

"Nothing really, I just . . . hate thinking of her in a fighter in some horrific space battle somewhere. It . . . kills . . . me."

"Ha. The big tough Marine," Sehera said.. Alexander had stared enemy mecha down practically with his bare hands and beaten them, and once he had killed over ninety of the meanest Separatist thugs all by himself, but his one weak spot was Dee. "She's your daughter alright."

"You're kidding. She's more and more like you every

day." Moore fiddled with the blood red steak tips on his plate and pushed at the scrambled eggs with his knife and fork. He took a brief moment to glance out across the moonscape from the window at the Armored E-suit Marine training grounds and staging area in the distance. He knew that place all too well. The reflection of the holoview in the window also caught his attention. Earth News Network ticker tape at the bottom of the reflection was about his tariff plans for the colonies and how the Governor of Ross 128 was complaining of unfair taxation. The window of the restaurant held views to the things that had engulfed his life for a very long time. Moore tried to ignore the view and focus on his wife. She was a much more breathtaking vision anyway.

"Well then, she should be fine shouldn't she?" Sehera goaded him again as she reorganized a strand of her long black straight hair out of her face and tucked it back behind her ear where it belonged. "What time is her flight again?"

"We've got time. It's in an hour. She jaunts from here to the QMT facility at Mars orbit, from there she rides the *Sienna Madira* to the Oort gate, and then she'll teleport to the Ross 128 system on a passenger transport. The competition isn't until next Tuesday. We should be able to make it with no problem. I need to spend some face time with the Governor there anyway."

"That all sounds fine. I'm sure she'll enjoy her ride on the supercarrier."

"Oh yes, she'll be fine. Several of ships of the fleet are engaged in wargames there and she'll get to see them loading up the mecha afterwards before jaunting out to the Oort. Nothing to worry about. Besides, Clay will be with her all the way. And she's in good hands with Colonel Fink."

"You're right," she said. Sehera sipped at her coffee slowly and then had an afterthought. "You do recall that you have a meeting with the ambassador from Ross 128 over lunch in the Rose Garden, right?"

How could I forget, he thought. But, Moore was amazed at how his wife kept up with him and without an internal AIC to boot. She had an AIC in an earring but wouldn't allow an implant or DTM connection with the AIC. Her earring used a subaudible signal projected to her eardrum to transfer information. It was slow but safe. Alexander knew that Sehera had a built-in fear of internal AICs and DTMs after watching her mother use them to terrorize the minds of her captors during the Martian Desert Campaigns. Perhaps she would get over it someday. In fact, Sehera had told him that she would get over it when she had to. And to date, she hadn't had to.

Abigail? he asked his AIC.

Yes, sir. Air Force One is standing by and we have everything going according to schedule for today.

Right then, he thought.

"Don't worry, Abigail will keep me on track. The ambassador will be QMTing from Ross 128 to the Oort and then from there to Mars. The *John Tyler* will bring him in from there and QMT him directly to the White House." He pushed his plate away from him. He didn't want the eggs anyway. "If you're finished we've got just enough time to walk around the city a bit."

"Suits me."

❖   ❖.   ❖

"Approval ratings for President Alexander Moore today are the lowest they have been in the history of his three terms as President of the United States," stated Walt Mortimer, one of the so-called expert panel members for the Round Table of News and lead White House columnist for the *Washington Post*, almost too enthusiastically. But then again, the media icon had made his editorial political position quite clear over the course of his illustrious career and the news of the latest polling data from the nation's capitol pundits fit right in with his agenda. Mortimer had long been considered one of the "graybeards" of reporters on Washington D.C. and systemwide politics helping the populace, but it was quite clear that he was just another of the Beltway Bandits making a living by feeding shit to the American public. But it was a good living. Or at least it had been until Moore came along.

"His campaign promises following the attack on Mons City and the Martian Separatist Exodus led him to a whirlwind landslide election and his policies following the attack on Disney World and Luna City led to approval from pollsters systemwide which led him to re-election," Mortimer continued. "Defense against potential terrorist attack from outside the solar system at the expense of systemwide economic growth and a strong defense against inter-system competition of market goods and commerce due to cheaper products from the Colonies seems to have turned the American voters lukewarm on the President." Mortimer leaned back in his chair and scribbled some notes on a pad in front of him. He maintained a smug look of triumph on his face.

"The latest polls do suggest that to be how the American people feel about it anyway," Britt Howard, the show's host and anchor for the Earth News Network (ENN) at the New York City anchor desk, replied. "It would appear that the 'defend the system at all costs' policy is beginning to wear thin. Especially, since the manufacturing base has yet to fully recover since the Separatist Exodus almost twelve years ago. It turns out that the 'Buy American' policy of the previous Democrat Administration of President Alberts has been adopted by this Republican Administration but for a different reason. Indeed the President has lobbied extremely hard to increase the tariffs on all imports from the four extra-solar colonies, same as his predecessor. However, where President Alberts used Sol System economic stimulus as the reason, President Moore is using the cost of defending the three heritage colonies and the two new start-ups from the rogue Tau Ceti Separatist system as his reasoning. This policy once seemed to be broadly accepted by the American public, but the latest polls show that the public is overwhelmingly for reducing the burden on the extra-solar colonies in order to increase the number of colony manufactured goods available within the Sol System. Prices have gone up and availability has gone down." Britt Howard summarized, and then nodded across the round table at the only female on the panel.

Alice St. John of the *System Review,* the more radical voice on the panel, replied, "Well, I have to say that I think this will cause the wedge to be driven even deeper between the actual states here in Sol's System and the colonists at Proxima Centauri,

Ross 128, Lalande 21185, and the start-ups at Gliese 581c and Gliese 876d." Alice never minded showing any restraint when calling one of the "elder reporters" on something that she thought was utter bullshit and she particularly agreed with President Moore on most things. Originally, and fortunately, for Alice, she was smart and pretty and therefore what little bit of radical viewership the Earth News Network had liked her and so she was able to keep her job secure. That was until Moore was elected and the Republican viewership of ENN more than quadrupled over night. Between her and the primetime anchor Gail Fehrer, who were both bent toward Moore, ENN had found a new niche to cater news to and thus improve their ratings.

"The Colonies have shown little interest in getting involved with the military buildup that President Moore has called for. The White House policies since, on the surface at least appear to be purely Sol System defense oriented according to the Governor of Ross 128," She continued.

"I agree Alice," Britt replied. "That does seem to be the present view of the colonists as well as the Dems in both houses of Congress. The colonists' argument is that they are of no threat and therefore no interest to the Separatists and therefore are being taxed, without representation, unduly. An ambassador from Ross 128 is coming here today to speak to the President and to Congress about waiving the tariff on them as it is pushing them into a recession."

"In fact, Britt, the President is talking out of both sides of his mouth on this issue. Though he will not waive the tariff on the Colonies he is asking Congress to approve an economic stimulus package for them.

I'm not certain I can see the logic in that." Walt interjected with a raised eyebrow.

"That sounds like an oxymoron at first glance." Britt laughed.

"Well, it isn't though," Alice replied. "The President's economic advisors all seem to agree that the downturn in the Colonial economies is a temporary effect of the increased tariffs that should be well overcompensated for in the future once they pick up the manufacturing pace and fill the void left by the Exodus and the secession of Tau Ceti. The stimulus should enable them to play catch-up."

"Ha, ha. Alice, sounds good on paper. But I wouldn't hold my breath waiting on Congress to approve his package. All of the scuttlebutt on the Hill is that President Moore's stimulus package is dead on arrival and there are not enough loyal Republican seats in the House to sway that." Mortimer nodded his head approvingly as he responded.

"Well, be that as it may," Britt interjected himself into the debate with an attempt to maintain an even tone. "The main issue for today is that the Separatist took away a major manufacturing source for the country. The citizens in the remaining colonies do seem to have little desire to support this Administration or its policies. In fact the governors of all three of the remaining original colonies have issued statements that their Executive Branch and Judicial Branch lawyers believe that President Alberts' and then President Moore's tariff packages to the Congress were and are in violation of the Inter-System Free Trade Agreement and that they have been seeking appeals of the policies through the Supreme Court."

"Well, I think that is the right course of action, or perhaps, the only real course of action that could be taken from a colonial standpoint," Walt Mortimer replied.

"And one would hope that the remaining colonists don't take a play from the Separatist's playbook here," Alice added. "After all, they are just territories without representation in the House or Senate."

"Oh, come now, Alice. You really think in worst case scenarios don't you?" Mortimer replied.

"I'm just saying that I hope the colonists don't feel the same way the original Thirteen Colonies felt when King George upped the tariffs on them to protect them from France. You know what happened then . . ."

—end excerpt—

from *One Good Soldier*
available in hardcover,
December 2009, from Baen Books